DEADLY TREASURE

Bring It Up Series
Deadly Treasure
Deadly Rivers
Deadly Currents
Deadly Storms
Deadly Darkness
Deadly Cold
Deadly Enemies
Deadly Discoveries

DEADLY TREASURE

FIRST ASSIGNMENT · ENEMIES WITHIN

WILLIAM W. BENNETT

AUCTOREM
HOUSE

Auctorem House
276 5th Ave, Ste 704-2591
New York, NY 10001
www.auctoremhouse.com
Phone: 1 888-332-7718

Published by Auctorem House: 10/15/2024

ISBN: 978-1-965687-06-2(sc)
ISBN: 978-1-965687-07-9(e)

Library of Congress Control Number: 2024919239

Because of the dynamic nature of the Internet, any web addresses or links contained in this book may have changed since publication and may no longer be valid. The views expressed in this work are solely those of the author and do not necessarily reflect the views of the publisher, and the publisher hereby disclaims any responsibility for them.

CONTENTS

To my beloved children and grandchildren

Special thanks to my lovely wife, Cathy.

[13]The conclusion, when all has been heard, is: fear God and keep His commandments, because this applies to every person. [14]For God will bring every act to judgment, everything which is hidden, whether it is good or evil.
–Ecc. 12:13-14 *NASB*

CHAPTER 1

Legend

All thoughts of work ceased, as Lieutenant Junior Grade Tom Wilson looked out his window at the white Ford Crown Victoria drawing up outside the office of Admiral Runion. Watching the tall powerfully built Captain step from the car to the curb with clinical interest and a gift for details, he sighed. James Robert Shepherd was a living legend, and Tom Wilson had been looking forward to meeting the man for three days, ever since he first learned of the appointment with the Admiral. Tom Wilson was Admiral Runion's "rookie" secretary.

Working for Admiral Runion was a step up in any man's career, and Tom Wilson was as ambitious as the next Naval officer. If he did well here, his next assignment would be on a ship or submarine as a Lieutenant. Thus far, working for the Admiral had been interesting, challenging, and less stressful than he thought it might be. But then, Admiral Runion was old school. He wasn't interested in politics like many of the new Admirals. The Navy was his life.

Captain Shepherd was wearing his dress blues. The four twin gold braids of rope on his sleeve and epaulets with the gold star signified his rank. Silver eagles on his shirt collar gleamed in the morning sunlight. Rows of ribbons and medals decorated his coat over his heart including a purple heart with clusters. Wilson identified the medal of honor ribbon, silver star, bronze star, meritorious cross, and distinguished service ribbon as well, all clustered in rows of service ribbons that denoted his illustrious career in the Navy. Tom remembered watching President Royce award this amazing Captain that Medal of Honor, recognizing the respect of all present at that particular ceremony. It had been a great day for the U.S. Navy.

Noting all that almost instantly, Wilson also noticed that there was something about the Captain that set him apart from other soldiers. By the time Captain Shepherd reached the door Wilson decided it was the way the man walked. There was a fluid motion to his movements, much like that of a stalking tiger, powerful and purposeful, full of danger and menace. He'd seen it in SEALs, Delta Force, and Special Ops servicemen, but never as pronounced and obvious as it was with Captain James R. Shepherd. That the Armed Forces of the United States produced such men was common knowledge, but it was always thrilling to be in the presence of one of these legendary soldiers.

Once inside the door Jim Shepherd looked at Tom Wilson, standing at attention, giving him a smart salute. Smiling a little he tossed his dress hat on the hat stand and instead of returning the salute reached out a well-tanned hand. Tom stared into green eyes that were, at the moment sparkling with some inner light, perhaps of humor.

"No need to salute, Lieutenant," Jim said quietly, grasping Tom's hand with a firm handshake. "I'm Jim Shepherd and I have an appointment with Admiral Runion," he added.

"Yes sir, Captain," Tom said and was interrupted as Jim raised a hand.

"Just Jim will do LT," he said with a grin.

Wilson felt a flow of pride at the designation. Most officers of superior rank felt the need to remind him that he was a Lieutenant Junior Grade, and most of them simply called him Mr. Wilson, as opposed to recognizing his rank. Jim had treated him as if he were a full lieutenant and, more than that, an equal. Both pleased and surprised he did not forget proper procedure.

"I'll let the Admiral know you're here, Sir, er . . . Jim." For a moment he felt awkward leaving off the proper designation. Captain Shepherd seemed to notice.

"It takes getting used to," he said with a grin and a wink.

A gravely voice interrupted his thoughts. "Don't start teaching my Administrative Assistant bad habits!" Admiral Runion barked that sentence from his doorway, standing there in his dress white uniform without his coat. He was smiling to Tom's relief. Jim winked at Tom as he passed his desk and entered the Admiral's office.

Admiral Runion closed the door behind them and looked Jim up and down for a moment before the smile disappeared. He gave Jim a quick bear hug before stepping back and motioning him to a seat. That was a sign that the admiral was excited about something. When he exhibited this kind of excitement it meant something was going to happen that would give the rest of the Admiralty apoplectic fits, if any of them ever found out. None ever did. Noting the signs Jim prepared himself for what he knew must follow, though truth be told, he'd expected a very different greeting.

He'd come, at the Admiral's request, sure that this was the end of his illustrious career. Still conflicted about that he'd come with a chip on his shoulder, willing to leave it all behind, knowing he would miss the military life very much. The report he'd written, again at the Admiral's request, was a scathing commentary on a military hierarchy that was driven by politics, not patriotism. Admirals, generals, and other high-ranking officials did not like having their dirty laundry exposed by a lower-ranking officer, and Jim had done that and more. Stung by what happened to his brother and his Recon unit he'd responded to the request with the anger still brewing inside. After a full investigation, despite attempts to thwart his efforts, he knew the whole truth, every ugly detail. This was not to say he regretted the report. Honesty was a trademark of his he cherished. Still, one did not prove that the military leadership of one's country was corrupt and vile and expect a commendation!

Jim grinned as he sat easily in a well-kept comfortable leather chair that had to be a left over from the Korean War. Admiral Runion moved behind his ancient wooden desk and sat in a comfortable new desk chair, the only new piece of furniture in the entire office. Nothing in the office suggested that the Admiral thought highly of himself. This, Jim knew, was not true of the opulent offices of other Admirals Jim met in his service in the Navy. Captain Shepherd's eyes swept the files on the Admiral's desk, sealed and therefore top secret. Whatever he was about to learn could be revealed to no one. Again, because he thought his career was over, the presence of those files came as a surprise.

At least that was Jim's thought. Nothing in all his years of service and training prepared him for what he was about to read, or the course that his life would take. At twenty-six years of age he'd put in eight years of service in the Marines and Navy and was the quintessential poster model for the perfect Intelligence Operative. As an experienced operative he knew the value of that particular accolade. It might have surprised him to learn that Admiral Runion, new Secretary of the Navy and still Director of Operations for Navy Intelligence, thought James Shepherd the best trained operative the Navy had ever produced.

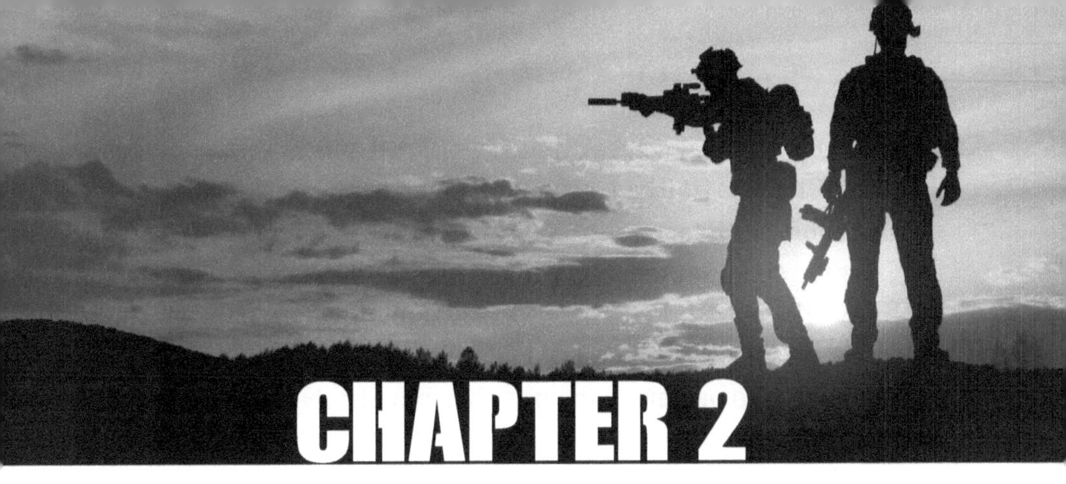

CHAPTER 2

A Dangerous Paradigm

"Your eyes only," Admiral Runion said unnecessarily, picking up a file folder and tossing it across the desk. "You already know most of it," Runion was grim in that statement. Jim took the folder, thumbed the paper seal apart, and opened the file. One eyebrow raised as he read the title of the report and he quickly glanced down the list of contributors. For a few minutes he sat quietly and read through the papers in the folder, looking carefully at each one, committing to memory every detail. Admiral Runion sat back, lifted a cup of coffee to his lips, and prepared to wait. His pale blue eyes watched the Captain closely as the man read carefully through the report. Occasionally he would sip some coffee, but for the most part he sat quietly, giving Captain Shepherd ample time to read the salient points of the report.

Jim's eyebrows drew together, furrowing his forehead with wrinkles as he concentrated on the papers, and occasionally he narrowed his eyes, or raised one eyebrow as he read. Reading quickly, knowing what to look for, his eyes devoured every page. No other signs did he give in reaction to the information within the report, but then, the Admiral had expected no less. Captain Shepherd rarely showed any emotion at all unless he was excited about a sporting event or in a personal contest. Furthermore, Admiral Runion knew that when Jim was finished, he would remember every salient detail in that report necessary for carrying out his assignment.

Over the course of the last year Jim Shepherd had proved himself the finest and most skilled officer in Naval Intelligence, on or off the field. He was the best the Navy ever produced. Covert operatives were supposed to be among the best, but Jim Shepherd was perhaps nearest perfection of any of the men who served in that capacity. To the Admiral it seemed that he was driven by some deep need to prove himself the very best. However, he had almost always been that way, right from the beginning. And now he was, in the Admiral's estimation, the best in the service.

That was the new training methods, of course, coupled with experience and natural ability. Covert ops soldiers were chosen from the top two percent of the field and subjected to training that would break most men. Jim Shepherd was far from average. He was, in the Admiral's opinion, a multi-million-dollar weapon worth every penny of expenditure. Admiral Runion doubted there was an operative that could best Jim Shepherd at anything.

In twenty missions as a SEAL Team Captain, Jim Shepherd brought every one of his men back. Some, including him, had been wounded. None had been killed. Twenty successful missions, every one among the most-deadly assignments, gave Jim Shepherd a reputation. His skills as a strategist were uncanny to say the least. When it came to adapting, especially to dangerous situations, there wasn't anyone faster, or better, at making the right decisions than this seasoned officer. Somehow, he seemed to have a special intuitive spark that he used often when it looked as if the whole mission would fail.

When it came to fighting skills, the man had an edge that only two in every hundred thousand trainees developed. His motile actions were off the charts, giving him extra speed and strength that set him apart from all other operatives. Oddly enough, his brother John, a Marine, was another soldier the Admiral knew with that special edge.

Twenty-one minutes of silence passed before Jim slowly closed the file and slid it back to the Admiral. His green eyes were hard now. A cold rage burned behind those eyes, but it was controlled. Admiral Runion took the file and set it aside without comment. He passed the next file to Jim, waited ten minutes, and give him the final file, watching Jim commit all the details to memory without saying a word. Closing the final file Jim tossed it on the desk on top of the other two.

"Assessment!" Admiral Runion grunted as the file landed.

"It goes that high," Captain Shepherd said softly. It was not a question. Admiral Runion was sure Jim already guessed. Now he knew.

"Political ambitions have become the bane of my profession," Admiral Runion complained with heat, slamming the heel of his fist on his desk. "Every one of these boneheads wants to get on the guaranteed retirement band wagon and has the idea that he'll make millions to boot!"

"And treason is now a way to advance a political career in America. If anyone knows you gathered this report, your life isn't worth a wooden nickel! Everyone will suspect that you shared this report with me and so my life is also on the chopping block," Jim mused all too blandly.

"You know me better than that!" Admiral Runion smirked. "But if we can get proof, we can hobble these traitors!"

"This terrorist thread shows that some of our enemies are using their seemingly limitless funds to weave their own future plans around those very political ambitions," Jim mused, steepling his hands under his chin, his eyes boring into those of the Admiral. "Surely that threat is one that needs some careful thought. They seem to be stepping into the twenty-first century political scene with a strong hand, almost as the Russians did in the fifties and sixties. We both know how deadly that threat was!"

"We are not equipped to fight the terrorist ideal any more than we are equipped to fight the war against drugs in our country!" Admiral

Runion grunted with some heat. Purposely he had phrased that statement to nudge the Captain into a response he knew would come.

"I beg to differ, sir!" Jim snapped, sitting up suddenly. "We could end the drug problem within a year with a military solution. My recommended new military solution could be applied to the terrorist ideal as well!"

"*If*, and it's an impossible *if*, we could elect a congress with the balls to sanction your military solution to either one!" Runion sneered. "The Gulf War, the War in Afghanistan, the War in Iraq, Israel's war with Palestine, all began as military solutions until the bloodshed started making lawmakers squeamish. The only real military solution is total annihilation! I don't think we'll ever see an America again that can sanction that, or sanction what you proposed. Our politicians are too busy protecting their soft office-chair molded rear ends to even consider such a decision. They are afraid of what the rest of the world will think or say about them," he stated the last with utter derision in his voice.

"All too true," Jim agreed, but he didn't back down. "We did have some solutions, even within this system, with which to deal with such threats. I did that in the past year, with considerable success! However, I had you looking after my back, and you would never withhold vital information and sit by at your desk and watch American soldiers die. If justice can't deal with this man, then I will!" Jim delivered that last line as he sat back in a quiet but firm voice. A moment of poignant silence followed that promise, and Admiral Runion knew it was a promise! He'd hoped Jim would express it, because he wanted Captain Shepherd to be thinking that way.

"That's exactly why you are here today," Admiral Runion said. Resting his elbows on his desk he looked at Jim for a moment. "Current military solutions don't always provide the finish we need. Your ideas on a paramilitary unit have been reviewed at the highest level. Today we are going to break with tradition, and we are going to try a new solution, your solution! Not one of our allies or enemies believes we would ever even consider such a move," his grin was triumphant as he said the last.

"Sir, with all due respect, my recommendation was presented as a metaphorical twisting of the knife in the wound of our current leadership paradigm. Hell would freeze over before any self-respecting high-ranking officer would even consider that solution! You know as well as I that the current leaders need to have control. My idea would take control out of their hands. It's political suicide!" Jim replied, his head tilted, his lips twisted in a wry grin.

"You are quite correct, my boy!" Admiral Runion nodded; his eyes now alight with an inner fire. "Several Admirals and a General or two have been clamoring for your head! If I wasn't SecNav they would have it by now! But I decided to take your ideas to a very select group of men who represent the highest level of intelligence in the civilized world! I've been asked to invite you to a meeting with six of the most powerful intelligence leaders in the world. These are men to whom politics is still a dirty word, and they want to talk to you in person. They are all like me, and don't care if this is political suicide. Politics be damned! Our country's future is at stake here, and that is a threat I take very seriously. The future of other countries is at stake as well, and patriotic men like you and I are ready to do the only thing that makes sense! We will not sit idly by and watch terrorists destroy it all."

Jim sat forward, his shoulders tensed, ready for battle, his entire demeanor suddenly transformed. Admiral Runion thought, not for the first time, that Jim Shepherd was like a cobra, ready to strike, when he was like this. It took a great deal of courage to remain still, even though he knew the man meant no harm to him.

"I'll talk to anyone who listens to reason, but whomever I speak to had better be absolutely serious about this, sir! This is throwing the paradigm out the window and starting over from scratch. These men better be ready to go the distance, or I'm not going to listen to one word! It will be me and my men in harms way, and I will not put lives in the hands of men who are not committed!" Jim's jaw was thrust forward and his eyes were as hard as stone, as full of danger as an oncoming hurricane of epic strength. Admiral Runion shivered inwardly and wondered if it showed on the outside.

"I think you will find that these men meet your criteria. Will you come?" he requested after clearing his throat.

"Only because I trust *you*, sir. You understand that I mean *only* you. My brother learned the hard way that some Admiral's do not merit such trust," Jim replied. His eyes were still hard, but his body relaxed, if a watchful cobra could be said to be relaxed. For a moment the two men sat staring at one another, saying nothing, and then Admiral Runion nodded and smiled.

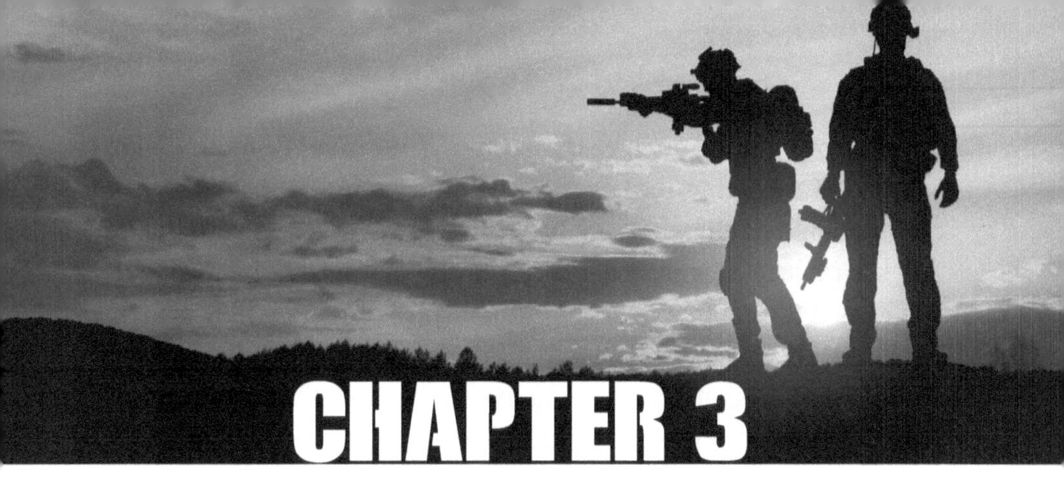

CHAPTER 3

The Construct

"First, I'm going to trust you with a secret that no one but myself knows about. Follow me," Admiral Runion stood up and walked to his inner office. In all the years Jim served under the Admiral he had never been invited into the inner sanctum, as the men referred to that inaccessible chamber. Not even the cleaning crew had ever entered through that door!

Curiously looking around Jim followed the Admiral, taking in quick glances the whole picture. The room was bigger than the Admiral's office, with a cot along one wall, a reading table and lamp standing next to it, with books piled as one does when reading in bed. There were file cabinets, and a complete communications center along another wall with links to everything including Air Force One. This was a high-tech side of the Admiral Jim had never seen, but suspected. No wonder he never allowed anyone in this room! It gave away an unexpected advantage for anyone else to know about it.

To Jim's surprise, the Admiral led him into a tiny bathroom, motioning him to step in ahead of him, and then following and closing the door. Jim found himself standing between the tiny shower and the toilet while Admiral Runion opened the medicine cabinet above the pedestal sink. There were various medications in there, the usual type for men getting on in years. Grinning, Admiral Runion opened a bottle of medicine for constipation, and drew out a small black cylinder with a red button on the top. He depressed the button, and quickly replaced the cylinder in the bottle, put it back on the shelf, and closed the cabinet door.

Suddenly, without a sound, the floor began to sink. The tiles on the floor hid the platform, leaving the shower, toilet, and sink above. Admiral Runion smiled at Jim and nodded.

"Slick, eh?" he asked, obviously proud of his little deception.

"Very!" Jim replied, duly impressed.

Four minutes later the elevator platform came to a stop in a dark arched concrete tunnel. Lights flickered on immediately, lighting about twenty feet of the tunnel in front of them. An electric golf cart stood facing away from them, plugged into a charger unit. Admiral Runion unplugged the charger, slid behind the steering wheel, pulled the cart away from the wall, and waited while Jim stepped in beside him. Climbing on the padded seat Jim looked ahead with interest, curious now to see where this long corridor ended.

Once the cart began to move the LED lighting began to flicker on in front of them. Jim turned back to note that the lights behind were already off and the elevator platform on its way back up to the bathroom. During the thirty-minute drive along the unchanging arched tunnel Admiral Runion filled Jim in on the history of this labyrinth, making the minutes slide by quickly.

President Grant built the original labyrinth, and other presidents through the history of America used it until Teddy Roosevelt made improvements on the old mine shafts, cutting out actual tunnels and lining them with concrete. John F. Kennedy made some dramatic changes to the whole plan during the cold war but never got to see his dream finished. Some presidents were never told about the secret of these labyrinths or their clandestine purpose.

Jim gleaned from the history that only presidents that were strong supporters of the politically untainted military leaders and heeded their advice ever knew about this secret. That didn't surprise him in the least. Military leaders had always protected that inner circle of men who loved patriotism above all else, who served God and Country and supported the Constitution of the United States of America with unswerving loyalty. He listened in silence for the thirty-eight-minute trip to the end of the tunnel, and his respect for Admiral L. Charles Runion, Secretary of the Navy grew by every mile they traveled.

Massive armored steel, with one inset hydraulic door met them at the end of their drive. Admiral Runion turned the golf cart around after asking Jim to step out, plugged in the charger to top off the batteries, and then walked to the identification module to the left of the door. He placed his eyes into a scanner, his right hand on a glass plate that scanned his palm, fingerprints, and blood vessel signature. Once his identification was confirmed he punched in a number code and the door hissed open. Those were impressive security measures!

Looking around with appreciation Jim saw that they were in a rotunda, approximately two hundred feet in diameter with a domed ceiling that towered at least sixty feet above the floor. At one section of the rotunda Jim could see a host of equipment that reminded him of NORAD and other military installations. At the moment there were no personnel at those stations. Scattered around the huge tiled floor were comfortable arrangements of furniture, set for meetings and conferences.

Admiral Runion led Jim to one near the center occupied by five men, with two men serving drinks. There was no mistaking a Secret Service Operative, and both the servers were obviously just that. Not surprised, Jim saw President Jack Royce seated comfortably between Sir Edward Marsh, Director of Operations, MI6, and Ira Lehman, Director of Operations, Mossad. When they entered the conclave, Jim recognized both of the other men: Petros Kladas, Director of Operations, Greek Intelligence and General James March who currently directed the SAS forces in Australia. Every one of these men had distinguished military records and Jim understood immediately. The only real surprise was Jack Royce, who appeared to be the only politically connected member of this elite group.

It was obvious to Jim that they were relieved to see that he was accompanying Admiral Runion, and Jim, a bit bemused, allowed himself to be introduced by his superior and seated in a chair where all six men could look at him. He accepted a diet Coke with lime and a glass of ice and sat back, sipping his drink slowly, looking from face to face. It was President Royce, predictably, who took the floor after a moment of quiet.

"We don't stand on decorum here, Jim," President Royce said with a genuine smile. "We're a group of friends, having a friendly discussion about the problems all of us are wrestling with. We call each other by our first names and trust each other to keep what is said here secret." President Royce settled back into his couch seat with genuine pleasure and sipped a root beer float with obvious enjoyment.

Ira and Sir Edward drank tea, General Marsh was drinking a glass of Scotch, and Petros sipping from a glass of wine. Admiral Runion accepted a cup of coffee with a smile of thanks. President Royce waited a moment before continuing.

"There are some very influential people demanding your resignation from military service, Jim. It seems you've ruffled some feathers and stirred up a hornet's nest! I hope you'll forgive us for setting you up for this, but that is exactly why I asked Charles to have you complete that particular assignment.

"Admiral Runion came to me with your recommendations, and Ira happened to be here. Ira approved immediately and suggested your recommendations be taken seriously when Sir Edward joined us. He too, it seems, likes the idea. Your exploits have impressed some very serious allies. You need to know that this group of people represents a very exclusive and private gathering of minds, much like a thinktank, and that we operate in a heretofore unknown alliance. We intend to be the last word in defense against terrorism in our world. All of us face an end to our careers if we are discovered.

"General March was very interested, and Petros decided to follow along. He at least knew about you," Royce continued. "As you can see, we are a very select group, and this is all of us," he waved his hand to include them all.

"You are so right, my friend, to suggest that we change our paradigm when it comes to terrorism. Military precision and training are necessary, but a paramilitary unit is brilliant! A ghost unit that does not exist anywhere on paper is even more brilliant. And the solutions you recommended are necessary to target and destroy the support for these terrorists! Find where the funding is coming from and remove it, and then isolate the terrorists and deal with them! This makes sense!" Ira spoke with passion, picking up the conversation, his arms waving in his usual fashion when excited.

Jim sat forward. "You gentlemen do realize that a paramilitary unit operates outside of normal controls. It is a separate entity. Using one this way is like sending a group of trained killers in a black-on-black operation off the reservation!" Looking around at the six men he weighed their reaction to the word 'killers' he'd used purposely. "Oversight by the usual military organizations is non-existent."

"Every one of our military units has proved that conventional oversight is a recipe for disaster," James March said quickly, almost defensively. "Even the new anti-terrorist units are hampered by the conventional military, and especially political, oversight element. Our paradigm for conventional warfare evolves somewhat, but not enough and certainly not fast enough to effectively deal with this threat."

"What we're proposing is to let you form your paramilitary unit and work your brand of magic on our enemies for a few years. If it works, and I believe it will, we can develop the program further, with you at the helm," President Royce added. "There will always be a team, like this one, to support you and join with you," he added.

"You do understand that at times a team of this nature will kill enemies and destroy enemy supplies, businesses, homes, or operations? That is, occasionally, the only military solution that presents itself and often includes collateral damage," Jim queried, scanning each face carefully as he talked. He needed to know they'd thought it through properly, because it was political suicide if word ever got out. Perhaps, in a group this tight, the secret would remain safe.

"You want to know if we have thought this through," Ira said with a smile. "As long as you complete these missions in such a way that no one knows who was actually responsible, and there is no evidence to indicate your guilt, you are safe. And we know that you can do that, Jim. To this day a certain dictator in an African country, is still trying to discover who killed his death squad, and who released me from their clutches!" Ira smiled at Jim. "You could easily have taken credit for that, and you deserved it! Yet you knew if he did not know, you had a stronger hand!"

"But *you* will know," Jim insisted quietly. "I am no fool. Some of the things my team will be forced to do will sadden, even sicken you. Hell, they sadden and sicken me! Are you certain you can stand beside your decision to give me a completely free hand?"

"Jim, I have studied your operations. There were three separate occasions in the past year where killing individuals or opposing forces was an option you could have taken without fear of reprimand. Yet in each situation you chose a different answer, one that was probably even more effective than killing them. I've filled these men in on those operations and we all agree that you can be trusted. And I mean only you!" For a moment Admiral Runion's eyes were hard. "Yes, you've had to kill, and probably will again. You're a soldier, and the best we have at the moment, in my opinion. As an intelligence operative you've consistently proved that you can be trusted. When you had to kill, you did so. We understand that," Admiral Runion insisted quietly while the other men nodded.

"You're not a butcher, and not out to establish yourself as a minor military dictator," Ira said with a smile. "Even when you have to kill, you hate it! That, I have seen first-hand," Ira nodded sadly.

"Jim realized at that moment that these six men were serious, and he was both honored and terrified by the trust they placed in him. That was the problem with being the kind of soldier he was. He loved being a soldier, but he feared and occasionally even hated the responsibilities that sometimes came with the job. Most of the time they didn't, but occasionally, like now, the burden became heavy. He sighed inwardly and wondered if he had what it took to carry this assignment to success.

"NATO is inept, as we know, in dealing with too many modern threats," Sir Edward shook his head with that statement. "A unit such as yours, working for more than one government agency, yet one that cannot be traced back to any of those agencies, will work."

"Every one of our agencies will help you, covertly, of course. Even our governments and the agencies that we run will not know that your group exists. Only the men in this room will ever know the full truth about you," President Royce continued after a pause. "Governments want too many answers, too many guarantees. We're stepping out on a limb here, not as far as you and your team will be, but far enough to end our political and military careers if we are ever discovered. We do not do this lightly, and what you've said is true. We too will be a part of making the final decision to carry out those less than savory assignments that lead to death. It saddens all of us that this is necessary, but we accept the responsibility.

"You are looking at the foundation of *Omega*, the last word on terrorism!" President Royce smiled at Petros as he said that, and the rest of the men nodded. "Like you, and your team, we don't exist on paper anywhere."

"Starting this is going to cost a lot of money. Money is easily traced. How do we keep that covert? Many have tried and failed!" Jim warned evenly.

Ira smiled and sat forward, his right finger stabbing the air at Jim. "You already have the money!" he exclaimed, his eyes suddenly dancing with laughter. "Do you remember that boatload of arms shipped from Iran to Palestine that you and your SEAL team captured for us?" Jim nodded, wondering where this was going. It had been his last mission. "In the hold we found everything you said would be there. Guns, ammunition, missiles, launchers, explosives, the works!" Ira ticked each one off on a finger. "Hamas was being equipped for a major offensive against Israel, and something else was going on as well!

"Our Muslim fanatics were also financing something! There were two containers that were full of money. One was full of American currency, and the other full of gold ingots! I was able to keep those two containers off any lists and away from any curious eyes!" Ira laughed and nodded to Admiral Runion to continue.

"We have arranged for you to win the Maryland Lottery. You will receive, after taxes, a check for seven hundred and fifty million dollars! We were able to flood the lottery with funds and keep any winning numbers from coming up!" Admiral Runion chuckled appreciatively as he spoke. "We've divided the rest of the money amongst our representative agencies to fund other such ventures, should yours prove successful."

"Just how much money was on that ship?" Jim asked. His mind was momentarily diverted.

"One hundred and sixty billion dollars," Ira announced with a smile.

The amount rocked Jim. It also told him why they were considering using his plan. No one knew what that money was going to fund, and it was far too much for something small. It also explained the fanatical response of Iran to the seizure of that ship.

"Do we know where the money came from?" Jim asked softly.

"Some of it came from Iran, but most of it came from China," Ira replied. "It will take some time to track down where it all originated, and you'll be the first to know when we have that INTEL, Jim. We need you on this one!" All the men nodded.

"I think it's time I started putting my team together, establishing my cover, and getting to work," Jim announced after a long moment of silence. Covertly he watched all six men respond; even grow more excited. They were truly serious about this! "I'll work on finding out who was behind those funds and what they wanted as well," he was surprised when all six men suddenly stood, looking thrilled.

"Right!" Sir Edward took control. "Charles has all the communications arrangements and will brief you on those. You can tap us for information and help when you need it. Godspeed, Captain. We are giving you the proverbial license to kill. Don't get yourself killed, old chap," he added as the men in the group nodded agreement.

President Royce shook hands with Jim, and the other men followed suit. Jim stood at attention, facing them, and saluted the men together, and then saluted the President. Jack Royce smiled at the gesture, returning the salute, and the other men nodded their heads in understanding. Jim was letting them all know that he was first an American soldier. He noted the acceptance of that gesture. It was enough. They stood quietly and watched as he moved away with Admiral Runion at his side.

"It is begun," President Royce sighed quietly.

"Yes!" Ira said. "Let us hope we are in time, my friends."

"I rather pity the psycho blokes who end up in that lad's sights," General March said, a grin on his face. "Not much, of course. It's nice to know that none of them will expect it, because they know we would never do anything like this!" he laughed softly.

"I have seen him in action!" Ira stated, looking at each man. "If anyone can take down this new threat, he can!"

"Will he go where we point him?" Petros Kladas asked.

"We will not need to point him!" Ira replied. "They will make themselves known to him, and when they do, he will destroy them." The others knew Ira's reputation and the absolute certainty in his statement gave them hope.

Jim was quiet as they left the rotunda, and for most of the trip back to the elevator that would return him to Admiral Runion's office. Watching him out of the corner of his eye Charles kept silent with a grim smile on his lips. He could see that Jim's mind was actively working through his initial ideas and formulating a plan. At the other end of the tunnel the Admiral plugged in the charger just as the elevator platform came to a stop.

Captain Shepherd began talking as soon as he stepped onto the platform, and as Admiral Runion listened, his eyes brightened with anticipation. They entered the outer office and took their places again. Charles behind his desk, and Jim seated in the chair across from him. The Admiral glanced at the clock on his wall as Jim

Shepherd continued outlining his plan. When he finished Runion glanced at the clock again.

"We have about eleven minutes left. I'm giving you your usual quarters to work in. Today is Monday. Let's say we get back together again on Friday morning for our final briefing. Eat breakfast with me each morning to keep me updated," he ordered.

"I'm going to take some of your best men away," Jim stated, his face suddenly twisted into an evil grin the Admiral knew very well.

"And won't their superiors hate it!" Charles laughed. "You're going to make yourself very unpopular around here!"

"Even more than usual?" Jim asked.

"That paper of yours really stirred up trouble!" Admiral Runion nodded. "Two Admiral's are calling for your resignation, which means they just went to the top of our suspect list. One we already knew about. The other one will probably replace me when Royce is out of office."

"Hogg?" Jim asked, an eyebrow raised.

"You go to the head of the class," Runion nodded.

"If the two of you meet face-to-face be careful. He's a crafty manipulator," Charles warned.

"I'll try not to disappoint you, sir," Jim said with a laugh.

"Get going, you pirate!" Admiral Runion said, standing up and walking Jim to his door.

"Give Captain Shepherd the keys to the officer's apartment, Mr. Wilson, if you please," he said to his secretary as he opened the door. "He will be doing some work for me over the next few days."

"Yes sir," Tom Wilson replied. He picked the key up from the desktop to show that he had anticipated the need.

"Thanks Tom," Jim said, taking the key and shaking hands.

"I'll see you in my office on Friday at eight hundred hours, Captain." Admiral Runion ordered as Jim was shaking hands with Wilson. Sighing he looked over his shoulder and nodded to the Admiral, and then Jim winked at the lieutenant.

"Four days to do three weeks of work, as usual!" he whispered and winked again. Tom grinned, and watched the Captain walk out the door. The sound of the Admiral's door closing brought him back to his duties.

The same white Crown Victoria waited for him. Its driver, another Lieutenant Junior Grade, Owen Mitchell by name, enjoyed this passenger much more than any he had so far chauffeured. Captain Shepherd treated him like an equal, something none of the other officers he'd driven thus far had done. Jim waved him to stay seated behind the wheel and climbed into the front seat next to him, also unusual. Usually the officers waited for him to come around the car, salute, and open the door for them, seating them in the back. Jim Shepherd would have none of that.

"Hope it wasn't too boring waiting two hours for me," Jim greeted as he settled himself and snapped his seatbelt in place.

"No sir. I washed the car and shot a few games of nine ball with another driver," Owen answered.

"Please don't call me sir, Owen. Did you win?" Jim responded.

"Broke even, er, Jim," Owen said somewhat sheepishly.

"See, it isn't so hard, now is it?" Jim grinned. "Breaking even means your skills and those of your opponent were about equal, which isn't a bad situation in billiards. It sucks in battle, but in games of sport it only sweetens the victories! Before we go to the apartment, I want to stop by a grocery store, but not the PX!" Jim added, putting his head back. "Onward!"

Owen grinned and drove out of the U.S. Naval Station along Robbins Road, exiting onto Firth Sterling, making a right on Summer, and another on Martin Luther King Drive. Pulling into a Food Lion grocery store parking lot Mitchell slid into a parking spot close to the door. Jim was out of the car before he'd turned off the ignition, so he settled back to wait. Twenty minutes later the Captain returned with a shopping cart holding six paper bags, two gallons of fat free milk, and two twenty-four pack cartons of Diet Coke with Lime and Coke Cherry Zero. Owen pushed the button to open the trunk and Jim put the bags and drinks in, slammed the trunk, and after returning his cart to the proper place jumped back into the front seat.

"Now I can cram three weeks work into four days (the Navy's usual workload) without having to worry about starving to death. I would like a ride to the B.O.C. (Base Officer's Club) for breakfast each morning at 06:30 hours, and a ride back when we've finished breakfast," Jim added. "Breakfast is my treat. Least I can do for a man who has to pull such ridiculous duty. I could easily check out a car, and drive it myself, but will the Navy allow that? Heavens no! Such mockery of tradition would have me burning in hell." Owen joined him in laughing.

Jim's apartment was on the Anacostia Naval Annex, overlooking the U.S. Botanic Gardens and the D.C. Tree Nursery. North facing windows looked out over the Anacostia River to the Washington Navy Yard. Owen helped Jim carry up the groceries, for which Jim seemed grateful and offered no tip, as other officers might have. He just shook hands and sent Mitchell on his way, accepting the service as though they were friends. Owen felt a wave of satisfaction as he planned to drive the Captain to the B.O.C. over the next few days.

One thing military life drilled into Jim Shepherd was discipline. Once he was unpacked, and his clothing neatly folded in the dresser drawers or hung in the tiny closet, he changed out of his dress uniform into comfortable black Carhart jeans, a crisp clean T-shirt, and comfortable running shoes. In the kitchen he carefully put everything in its proper place before moving to the tiny office.

Setting up his PowerBook he connected it to the Epson Stylus printer provided by the Admiral, and then connected with the high-speed modem. Maritime books and other resources were already provided, and Jim stood for a moment, looking around, satisfied that he was ready to dig in. Taking an early lunch of a simple tossed salad he cleaned the counter, dishes, and sink, and poured a glass of Snapple Peach Tea over ice, which he set on a coaster on his worktable. It was time to create the construct of a new organization and make a dream come true.

CHAPTER 4

Bona fides

Jim and John Shepherd grew up on Boston, actually a block from the harbor, sons of a local tugboat and fishing boat captain. Robert James Shepherd was a hardworking seaman, and he brought both of his sons up to the same discipline. One dream the three shared was to one day own a deep-sea salvage and rescue operation. A Sicilian uncle, Andrea Orvieto was part of that plan, for he and Robert were fast friends, even though they lived on different continents. Twice each year Andrea flew to Boston to be with his sister's family.

Robert Shepherd never saw his dream. He and a hired deck hand disappeared at sea when the boys were in their senior year of high school. The Coast Guard discovered the boat adrift, but both hands were missing. It was a stormy night, and the consensus was that one hand went overboard, and the other, trying to rescue him, also went into the unforgiving icy Atlantic waters. Jim and John were never sure, because their father had been a powerful swimmer, and a resourceful man.

Their father's death changed many things for both young men. Decisions, very difficult and emotionally devastating decisions had to be made. Honoring their father's wishes and memory carried them through that difficult time, and both young men came away from that experience suddenly much more mature. Yet the mystery of his death never allowed full closure.

Both sons had plans to join the Marine Corps after graduation, because they knew this was something their father wanted. He too had been a Marine, and he knew the corps had equipped him for his role as a businessman, husband, and father. The boys also shared a best friend in Wade Adams, who also decided to join the Marines.

Life insurance and the sale of the fishing boats and tugboats provided for Gwyneth Orvieto Shepherd, Robert's widow. In honor of their father's memory both boys and young Wade joined the Marines and in the armed services distinguished themselves.

Now, through a strange twist of fate, Jim Shepherd was going to fulfill a lifelong dream. He was going to establish a deep-sea salvage and rescue operation and it would provide the perfect bona fide cover for a clandestine paramilitary unit. Hours passed as he jotted notes, entered the outline of his business plan in the computer, and researched other successful companies that operated the same type of business. Meticulously, patiently, and wisely he drew out his skeleton plans and then began a regimen of serious study.

Each morning at four o'clock Jim rose from his bed, slipped into his running outfit, and ran five miles. At the conclusion of his run he showered, dressed in his casual white uniform, and met Owen for the short drive to the BOC for breakfast. Good to his word Jim bought Owen breakfast each day, though Owen didn't join the Admiral and Jim at their table. There were always friends there for him to join, so he didn't mind. The Admiral made it quite clear he wanted Jim to himself for those breakfast meetings, and Owen was a great believer in pleasing Admirals.

Admiral Runion was astonished at the amount of work Jim was able to accomplish over that week and looked forward to their Friday meeting with the kind of anticipation a great coach might exhibit in looking forward to watching his star player execute his skills. Jim Shepherd was, to the Admiral, the finest example of the new intelligence officer of the Navy.

Runion chose Tom Wilson for two reasons. Wilson had a great many friends and acquaintances, and he was known to gossip. He never crossed the line and talked about anything he was instructed to keep secret, but he did love to tell stories, and was good at it. For that reason, he was popular at the club after work with other secretaries and aides. Admiral Runion wanted news of what was going to happen in just three days time to spread quickly.

The second reason Tom Wilson served the Admiral was because he had potential, and the Admiral intended to direct this young man into areas of service to which he was particularly talented. On that fateful Friday morning he greeted both men with a smile and nod and waved Jim into his office. Wilson followed with a cup of coffee for the Admiral, then left, quietly closing the soundproof door behind him.

An hour passed as Jim described his plan, in detail, and with passion. As the Admiral listened, he leafed through the thick files Jim provided. When Jim was finished with his briefing the Admiral set aside the files and sat looking at him for a few moments, his intense blue eyes staring into those stormy green eyes.

"How soon can you actually begin operations in the Mediterranean?" Admiral Runion finally asked, after carefully sifting through all he'd heard.

"It will take three months to outfit the ship and train my team," Jim admitted. "It may take that long, or even longer, to accomplish our first salvage operation. With the crew I have in mind, and the equipment I can provide them with, I think that's a fair estimate. To appear as a bona fide salvage and rescue operation we will need a second salvage operation immediately following our first. My team will be training that entire time, and we should be able to begin to operate safely in nine months. Much of that depends on how successful we are on those first two salvage jobs. I intend to be very successful," Jim added after a moment of thought.

"That makes sense. We need you to be invisible, and by then everyone who is the least bit suspicious will accept your cover. Moreover, because of the nature of what you will be doing, you will have an excuse to move anywhere in the world we might need you, provided of course there's an ocean or sea in which to work," the Admiral mused.

"River, lake, and land searches are not uncommon for treasure hunters!" Jim interrupted with a smile. "I researched two outfits that have operated in very unusual places in search of lost treasure, including the Amazon region and up the River Nile. Both of them are successful, and well known, and their exploits are often written in publications other treasure hunters read. I've studied what they do very carefully," Jim admitted with a smile. "I do want to be successful at both my jobs or my cover will no longer be bona fide. Besides, if I am successful, I can fund my operation totally better than *Omega* ever could!"

"You're that sure!" Admiral Runion sat back and stared at Jim, and the Admiral decided that he was. He began to rub his hands in anticipation.

"I see you've chosen your first ship," Admiral Runion said, looking down at an open file. Suddenly he laughed. "The *USNS Sioux* is going to be retired for a new vessel. She'll be the perfect vessel for your outfit, and easy to purchase. We're going to auction her off in a closed bid auction. Your bid will be exactly one hundred and eighty dollars higher than the highest bid that comes in. No one will question it. What do you plan to do with her, once you've purchased her?"

"Him, sir!" Jim grinned. "This ship is going to be definitely masculine! He'll be outfitted in Portsmouth, England." Jim said quietly. "Sir Edward assures me that he has a special team working there who will do what is needed without ever talking about it," he informed the Admiral. Runion nodded.

"What exactly made you choose a *Powhatan* class fleet ocean tug?" Admiral Runion asked with real interest.

"According to Military Sealift Command he can slug it out with whatever Mother Nature throws at him and still tow a 54-ton crippled tanker. I believe this particular ship did just that, towing that tanker through a force five hurricane. He has room for all the equipment

I want too, including that special feature in his hold," Jim replied. "He can sail with a crew of twenty. Anything bigger would require a bigger team, and I'm not ready for that yet," he added, the latter an honest estimation.

Nodding Admiral Runion opened the top drawer of his desk, took out a box of cigars, still individually wrapped, and lifting several out of the way he pulled a slip of paper from the bottom of the box.

"These are the numbers you will play this very afternoon!" Admiral Runion said with a grin. "You're actually going to drive to Mt. Airey, Maryland, drop in at a convenience store, and purchase a ticket with this ATM card," he handed the card and numbers over. "Zeke Kline is 99.7% sure no other ticket sold will have this number," he added, pointing to the winning number on the paper in Jim's hand. "If someone does, the amount won will double and you'll split it with them. Zeke is certain no one will, though I don't know how he can tell that. You're going to take him away with you, aren't you?" the Admiral grunted.

"Tomorrow you'll drive into Baltimore to claim your prize. Ken Worthington will meet you there. He's a retired attorney who has the Midas touch. He's barely forty, and he's fast becoming one of the richest men in America through his own investing. I'm meeting with him today, because we both sit on a board of directors of a local bank he's rescuing. As a favor I'm asking him to look after you. Whatever he tells you to do, do it!" Admiral Runion was smiling when he made this last comment. "He'll turn your fortune into something serious, if you let him," he added, shaking his head. "I trust him implicitly." Jim nodded as the Admiral made the last statement, accepting his assessment of the man without question.

"On Monday you'll come back here and announce that you won this lottery, and that you're resigning your commission and starting your own salvage and rescue operation. It will come as a complete shock to me, and I, of course, will be livid, yell and scream at you so that young Wilson hears it all because my door will be out for repair, and following that send you packing with your tail between your legs!" Admiral Runion was practically laughing as he said the last.

"So . . . it's to be business as usual, then," Jim said flatly.

Both men broke into laughter at that. Admiral Runion had indeed vented his wrath on Captain Shepherd on occasion.

"You leave here with a little vacation time planning to return on Monday to continue working on whatever it is we're supposed to be planning in here," Admiral Runion reached into a drawer and pulled out a small bound book, entitled *Operating Your Digital Camera*. "Inside this book you will find all the codes, phone numbers, and computer links to your support personnel, including the President's private line. That alone should tell you how serious Jack Royce is in this endeavor. Memorize it and then destroy the book. No one writes this information anywhere or stores it in a computer," the Admiral added unnecessarily.

"Clever!" Jim said with appreciation. The first few pages actually were about operating the camera. The codes and numbers he needed were tucked into the middle eight pages. "I'll leave most of my stuff in the apartment until Monday then," he said rising.

"This is going to be fun!" the Admiral said, rubbing his hands again, his eyes alight.

"This is the modern Navy, sir. Fun is not allowed," Jim joked.

"Get out of here, you pirate!" Admiral Runion laughed. "Come back alive."

Jim smiled. Admiral Runion always said that when he sent Jim on a mission. They shook hands and Jim left with a spring in his step. He paused to wish Wilson a good weekend, expressing his desire to rent a car and tour the area for a couple of days while enjoying his leave. Tom, pleased that Captain Shepherd paused to speak with him, wished him a relaxing weekend as the Captain headed out the door.

Owen Mitchell was glad to drive the Captain to a nearby Enterprise car rental agency. Jim had already reserved a Chevy Trailblazer, and in less than half an hour he was driving back to the apartment to pack for a light weekend trip. He liked the feel of the vehicle as he drove and wondered if he could indeed find a Jeep trail to do a little four-wheeling, one of his favorite hobbies. With a grin he thought he might just be able to do that.

With his uniform hung behind him, and a small duffel bag for the trip, he was packed and ready to go in less than ten minutes. Smiling with anticipation he studied his map, chose a route that would keep him away from freeways and toll roads, and left Washington, D.C., just one more escaping weekender off for a lark. The usual snarled traffic of Washington didn't even bother him. His mind was too busy going over his plans.

Being the soldier he was, his mind wandered down pathways related to his new mission and venture, focused and trained to sort and remember every thought he had. Jim Shepherd was a realist. Battle taught him that. There are no super soldiers and every human being is vulnerable. The unexpected is normal. Captain Shepherd had no delusions of his own prowess or abilities. That is why he spent most of his time thinking about the proper training his team would need.

One trained, kept an edge, and hoped that edge was sharp enough. There was a job to do, and there was training to do the job, and then the job itself. If you failed, someone else would take your place. Work never stopped, and the job or mission had to be accomplished.

A particular edge Jim possessed was his ability in the area of strategy. Both he and his brother John excelled in that area. Part of that came from their father who began teaching them strategy using a chess game when they were very young. Chess taught one that every move included thousands of variables, which meant one lost as many as one won. It was an important lesson to remember. Increasingly they learned to strategize escapes and counters until one day they realized that almost every game they played ended in a draw. Robert Shepherd nodded when they mentioned it, and Jim never forgot his words.

"We know each other well enough to anticipate every move. When you are in a battle, knowing your enemy that well will give you the edge you need to win. But he must never know that you are studying him! Remember what I taught you about reading people when you're playing poker? Never let them know you are reading them, never talk about it, and never give anything away. One day you boys will thank me for the training."

Well, Dad, I do thank you for the training. Jim thought gratefully. *The problem with terrorists is that most of them are damn idealists and many of them are cowards, hiding somewhere behind their money men and ideals, sometimes so well hidden you don't even know they're there until it's too late. So, I'm going to have to study the brains behind these idealist cowards, follow the money trails, and eventually take all that security away from them. They'll run then, because they are fundamentally cowards and bullies, and when they run my unit will be waiting.*

Eventually, enjoying the scenery along Route 27, Captain Shepherd found the convenience store in Mount Airy. He filled the gas tank, bought his lottery ticket at the counter, and used the numbers he'd memorized. His trip to Baltimore was a bit more mundane because he had to take Route 70. Still, according to plan he arrived at the inner harbor and checked into the finest hotel, if one believed the travel brochures, as directed.

Luxury wasn't something Jim was used to, and the opulence of the hotel was almost overwhelming. Ken Worthington met him for dinner at the agreed time in the restaurant in the lobby of the hotel. Jim wore his tan work uniform so that Mr. Worthington would have no difficulty picking him out.

He liked Ken right from the start. Worthington wore a simple gray suit that probably cost in the vicinity of two thousand dollars, a silk shirt, and a conservative tie, also silk. His hands were typical of one who spent most of his time in an office under fluorescent lighting, but his grip was firm.

Sparkling brown eyes studied Captain Shepherd as they clasped hands. Then they were being seated. Jim listened as Ken shared how he had come to his expertise, which was an interesting story and took up most of the main course. Worthington had a wife and daughter, a little girl named Emma upon whom he doted. One thing was clear to Jim as the man drew is own story to a close. Ken Worthington was the right man.

During dessert Jim discussed his plans to launch a deep-sea salvage, search and rescue company. Admiral Runion informed Jim that Ken Worthington had helped set up the entire plan, so he was cleared for basic information. Jim was no fool, knowing whom he could trust was life and death for him. Worthington could be trusted. Jim told him what he needed to know to make good decisions for the company and Worthington recognized the trust. Jim could tell he hadn't expected it this early in the game, and also tell that it pleased him to be trusted. By the end of the meal the two men were developing a friendship as well as a mutually beneficial business relationship.

On Saturday Ken accompanied Jim to the lottery claim center where Jim's ticket was validated. Zeke had been correct. He was the only one with the winning numbers. This particular lottery did not pay out over a period of years, but paid the whole winnings in one lump sum, after taxes of course were taken out. It was a very popular lottery for that reason. For Maryland this was the largest pot ever won in one payment. News vans rushed to the scene when it was learned that a decorated officer of the United States Navy won the prize. Jim had his picture taken holding a giant check by just about every news agency in town before finally being allowed to slip away.

Worthington had prepared everything beforehand, and he personally handled the transfer of funds to the various banking institutions chosen as best for the business. His knowledge of banks, both domestic and foreign was formidable and Jim trusted his judgment on which banks would best serve the company's needs. More than that, he would move the money around as needed to get the very best percentages on the principle sums in the bank. Worthington was now a full partner in the business and he and Jim parted as trusted friends.

At the hotel Jim was moved to a suite at the top accessed only with a proper key card in the proper elevator. Grinning at that fact he stood for a few moments and stared in wonder at the opulence surrounding him. With a sigh he put down his few belongings and familiarized himself with his new digs.

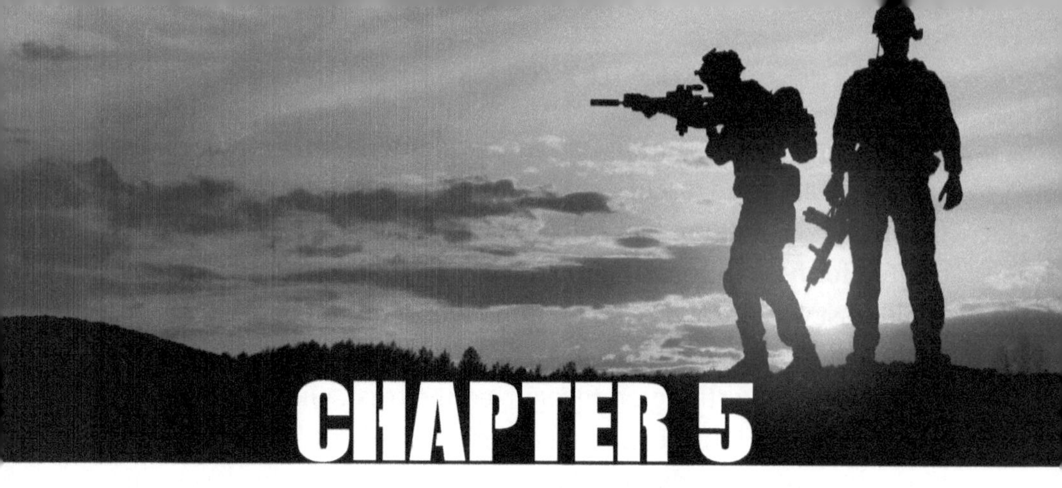

CHAPTER 5

Unexpected Direction

Admiral L. Charles Runion watched the repair team remove his door, replacing it temporarily with a wooden door complete with a glass panel. Jim arrived soon after the door was installed, and the Admiral did not disappoint Jim. The "L" in his name was for Lyndon, but he'd grown tired of being nicknamed Lyn, which he thought a sissy name in school, and taken to using his middle name. Jim had never dared to call him Lyn or Chuck, but in the middle of the tirade he almost grinned as he thought about it. The decibel level was definitely climbing.

In top form the Admiral yelled at the top of his lungs, slammed a book of coastal charts on his desk, and pounded his wood desk and steel file cabinets with the heel of his fists. He called Jim inconsiderate and unpatriotic (both of them knew this was just a charade) but Jim actually blanched at a few of the phrases the Admiral used. As far as the Admiral was concerned, it was a very successful act, carefully rehearsed all weekend. Twice he winked at Jim, just to remind him this was all a charade.

When they appeared in the outer office Tom Wilson was studiously working at his desk, his head down, face white. He never looked up as the Admiral followed Jim to the door, continuing his outburst in a blaze of temper, shouting at Jim until the officer escaped through the door and ran to his car. The Admirals' rage did not abate. Raising his hands in mute fury he turned back to a very frightened Lieutenant Junior Grade.

"Cancel all of my appointments for today and get out of this building! I don't want to see anyone! Do you understand? Lock the doors when you leave!"

Admiral Runion slammed his door shut with such aggression that the glass shattered and grinned as a very frightened secretary hastened to obey his every command. Tom would spread the word quickly. It wasn't secret and it wasn't meant to be. The Admiral gave himself a pat on the back for an Oscar performance and sat at his desk still acting, looking like he was trying to accomplish something, but still too angry to do anything. Wilson took a hasty look at him before bolting from the office.

He picked up his phone and made a call to the base commander at Pendleton regarding John Shepherd and Wade Adams, still sounding very angry. When he was done, he went into his inner sanctum and allowed himself to laugh and relax. It was begun.

Later that evening, out of uniform and wearing his usual casual Carhart jeans, and a Carhart western shirt Jim sat in his room. Ken Worthington had just left to return to his family in Langley. Lounging in the comfortable chair he tapped his pen on the table beside him, thinking carefully. On the bed were five credit cards, two checkbooks, and several legal documents. It felt good to see the company name on them.

With a lazy smile Jim stretched out, picked up the phone, and called a number in Camp Pendleton, near Oceanside, California. John picked up his phone on the second ring. Jim smiled to himself as the phone conversation began exactly as he had anticipated.

"Captain Shepherd," John identified himself briskly.

"Yes, this is he. How may I help you?" Jim said lightly.

"Jim! How in the world are you? Where in the world are you?" John exclaimed, excited to hear from his brother. It had been three months since their last contact.

"I'm in Baltimore at the moment. Are you busy?" the question was innocent, too innocent. John and Wade were probably doing nothing more than daily training because of their last mission failure. An Admiral withheld vital intelligence from John, and all but four of his RECON unit died. In the Marines that was a disaster, and even though it wasn't John's fault, it would be months before he would be asked to command a unit again.

"Spare me," John sighed.

"Do you suppose you could both get about a month off, and come to Washington, D.C.?" Jim asked quickly. "I think I can get a certain Admiral to release the two of you for thirty days of deskwork. That's how he'll describe it. Something to keep you both out of the public eye for a while, or something else is my guess. I don't know how he does it but can you?" Jim asked again.

"I don't know," John answered, his voice suddenly changing timbre. Jim smiled, knowing he was going to enjoy whatever his brother said next. John could always find something funny and clever to say. He didn't disappoint.

"There's a band of red-necked fozzlebutts wearing chartreuse wimples threatening our position even as I speak. We may not be able to escape. Worse yet, they are waving UK47 hair dryers at us. My unit had a bean feast last night and the hot air coming at us was disastrous. Half my men in the back lines are casualties of friendly fire!" His grin could be heard all the way across the country and Jim burst out laughing. His brother could always come up with a quip or a joke to lighten the atmosphere.

When he finally gained some control over his mirth Jim spoke again. "Write out that request. The Admiral will expedite things for you. There's a house for rent in Kitty Hawk. I'll pick you up at Baltimore airport tomorrow night. You'll be flying out of San Diego. I already purchased your tickets. Pack for the beach."

"Will we be on leave? Are we taking a vacation?" John asked, the curiosity in his voice coming through clearly.

"Let's just say our careers are moving in an unexpected direction," Jim replied with a laugh. "You're never going to believe this!" Jim laughed again.

"Tomorrow, then!" John said. They talked a little further into the night before hanging up, but Jim never gave a clue as to what was going on. When he hung up the phone he stared at the ceiling for a few minutes and just laughed. Then he made his call to Admiral Runion.

"Admiral! Those two Marines we talked about are flying in tomorrow."

"My orders for that leave are already on the Base Commander's desk!" Admiral Runion laughed. "He thinks I'm going to be boring them out of the service with desk jobs, I suppose. What will you be doing, and where?"

"I've rented a house in Kitty Hawk. They'll be helping me put together the team, the crew, and our equipment list," Jim replied.

"Sounds like a desk job to me!" Admiral Runion grunted. "Don't let those Jarheads corrupt your sterling career! And give me the address of that house. I'll drop in for a visit in, oh let's say two weekends from now. You know how I love driving a desk," the Admiral added. "I've got to drive my desk for the President starting on Tuesday next for about eight days."

Jim laughed. He knew Admiral Runion hated the political scene more than anyone could guess and being appointed Secretary of the Navy put him right in the middle of that ugly mix. That meant he would be in his official office for a few weeks. He would be meeting with the President in the mornings to discuss events of the world. "Okay, Admiral," he replied, giving the address and directions. As he pushed the end button his phone began ringing again.

It was John. "Is this some kind of joke?" John said in a dangerous tone. "How do you get this kind of pull, bud? Our request was never made because some Admiral, whom we shall leave unnamed at present, has ordered us to fly into Baltimore where we'll be met, the orders don't say by whom."

"I'll be meeting you as you come off the plane," Jim replied evenly.

"It was you!" John retorted. "The Colonel seems to think our careers have been flushed down the toilet," he replied with some relief.

"Just a shift in current," Jim replied evasively. "I'll see you tomorrow."

"Two Marines against one SEAL isn't fair odds, you know," John said banteringly.

"I know," Jim replied with a deadpan expression. "I'll try to take it easy on you." They both grinned and hit the end call button at the same time. John loved the Marines, but Jim missed the sea. After his first tour of duty with Force Recon Jim transferred to the Navy, with the hopes of getting back on the sea. The Navy, however, seeing his amazing potential had other ideas and put him into SEAL training immediately and though he sailed from port to port on a mission, he spent most of his time on land.

It made Jim grin, thinking of taking on John and Wade. Wade Adams grew up with the two boys. Since John and Jim were only ten months apart, their parents wisely decided to wait until both were able to start school together. Wade Adams became their good friend in Junior High when they entered the world of sports, and the three became inseparable. Their friendship grew over the years, and now it appeared it would continue on into the future.

Hard work on the fishing and tugboats owned by Robert Shepherd made them strong. Of course, their father taught them about weightlifting, jumping rope, and running and encouraged them in those pursuits. Wade took an interest that at first delighted his father.

Calvin Adams was a veteran police officer, presently serving as a homicide detective in Boston. He and his wife Claire were Bostonians to the core and could trace their ancestry back to Boston's first settlers with great pride. What Calvin wanted was for his son to follow his footsteps and become a police officer. The physical training he was getting, working for Robert Shepherd, seemed to be a good thing.

Wade was the tallest of the three boys, topping out at six feet five and a half inches in height. After his Marine training he weighed an amazing two hundred and forty-five pounds, every ounce of it the kind of muscle a Marine needed. He was, in many ways, the ultimate soldier physically. John stopped growing at six feet three inches and weighed in at two hundred and twenty-five pounds, another example of the ultimate Marine. Jim, at six feet two inches, weighed two hundred and twelve pounds. Though the shortest of the three he was the quickest.

Their entry into the Marine Corps did not dismay Calvin Adams. He thought the Marines would turn his son into exactly the kind of police officer Boston needed. All through Wade's High School years though, Calvin came to hate that Wade worked for Robert Shepherd on the sea. He never understood his son's love of the sea, or his desire to become part of a deep-sea salvage and rescue operation. Wade had the skills, but not the training, to become an aquatic engineer. In the Marine Corps he was able to learn about engineering with hands-on experience, take courses, and study engineering with an almost insatiable appetite to learn more.

All three men were ably equipped for the task they were about to undertake, thanks to their military training and experience. Jim couldn't think of two men he would rather share command with than John and Wade. Not only were they close friends, they trusted and knew each other. They knew how the other thought and could act together in unison almost without communication.

And over the years their friendship had grown into something serious. That, and the camaraderie that came with being soldiers together, helped that relationship mature and grow into something that made them even closer than brothers.

Formation

Early the following afternoon, Jim stood at the exit door of John and Wade's flight, having talked his way past the security check points with the help of his credentials and security clearance. John and Wade came off third and fourth in line, because Jim's tickets had been first class, a surprise to both of them. They both watched him for their cue.

As Jim expected, both wore their dress blues and could easily have passed the most stringent inspection. To honor them, Jim wore his own uniform, perhaps the last time he would wear it, stood to attention and saluted the pair of them with a smart salute. They jerked to attention and returned the salute.

"If you gentlemen will follow me," Jim said, turning on his heel and smart marching down the corridor. John and Wade grinned at each other and fell in line beside him, side by side, marching in step. People looked at their uniforms, the rows of ribbons and medals on their chests, some of the more noteworthy showing clusters, their rank, their presence, and either smiled and nodded at them, or quickly looked away. People either appreciated the military, or hated it, depending on their politics. It was obvious to anyone with any knowledge of the military that these were dedicated and decorated soldiers, the kind of men other solders held in highest regard. Other soldiers who saw the ribbons and recognized them for what they were stood at attention and saluted the three as they marched past.

Once their luggage was retrieved, one duffle bag each, the men followed Jim out to his Trail Blazer rental, stowed their bags in the back with Jim's and jumped into the vehicle. John sat in front with his brother, and Wade sat in the back seat, behind John. Wade was somewhat surprised at the room he had for his long legs in the vehicle, and John was busy checking out the dashboard and controls.

"This drive is going to take about five or six hours," Jim warned as he backed out of his parking space.

Once they were on the road and out of Baltimore the questions began.

"Okay, Jim. What's this all about?" John asked, his face seriously.

"Partly it's about settling a score," Jim began, glancing at John. He looked in his rearview mirror at Wade too. "Thirty Marines were given bad intelligence and as a result twenty-six of them died. We're going to take care of that," both men heard the iron in his voice.

He was not surprised to see tears in the eyes of both men as they thought of men they had known and come to love and trust. A soldier forms a bond with his fellow soldier that goes as deep as a marriage bond, or a family bond. There was also rage behind those tears, rage for the withheld intelligence that could have saved those lives, and rage for the unfairness of war. Somehow, they survived. Survivor's guilt was a curse they would live with for the rest of their natural lives, something that never fully went away.

After a pause he continued. "The other part is more complex. The Admiral who withheld the intelligence from your unit is part of something new, within our own military forces. No one knows how deep it goes. Our job is to find out, and then deal with it. We're also dealing with some very dangerous terrorists whose agenda is not yet clear," Jim continued after a moment of quiet.

"When you say, 'deal with it,' what exactly do you mean?" Wade asked, his eyes hard, his face fierce.

"We're going to form a paramilitary unit that will not exist on paper anywhere. This unit will begin with twelve men, the best in their various fields of expertise. We won't exist because we will be part of a deep-sea salvage, search and rescue operation that is one hundred percent legitimate. This is not a covert operation, or a black op. This is an invisible black on black operation," Jim announced quietly. He managed to slip around some slower traffic with ease as he spoke, driving with skill.

"It won't work!" John interrupted. "There will be a money trail. There always is. You know that!"

"Yes," Jim replied with a huge grin. "But the money trail begins and ends with me!"

"What? You win the lottery or something?" John scoffed.

With his eyes sparkling Jim handed the Sunday edition to John, turned to page three, where his picture receiving the check was on the top right corner. John's eyes bulged as he read the report, and then he handed the paper back to Wade without saying anything. Wade's comment summed up their thoughts.

"Jesus, Mary mother of God!" Wade had an extensive Catholic background, much like his two friends. They tended to avoid bad language, and this was not a curse, but a quietly breathed prayer.

For several minutes there was complete silence in the Trail Blazer. Jim watched the road and traffic and John and Wade wrestled with their thoughts. Suddenly John burst out laughing. He banged his fists on the dashboard, pounded the roof of the vehicle, and stamped his feet while Wade clapped Jim and John on the shoulders. All three gave a rebel yell of joy that was deafening in the confines of the truck cabin, yet they were celebrating and did not care.

"What intelligence assets do we have?" John asked, when he had gained some control over his excitement.

"Our Commander and Chief, President Jack Royce, and his SecNav, Admiral L. Charles Runion. Sir Edward Marsh, D.O. (Director of Operations) MI6, Ira Lehman, D.O. Mossad, Petros Kladas, D.O. Greek Intelligence, and General James March from SAS down under," Jim replied. "We also have a special financial asset in a man named Ken Worthington, an attorney with the Midas touch. By the time we're ready to purchase our ship, he claims he will be able to increase our wealth by half again as much!" He added. "I believe him!"

"What about oversight?" Wade asked as soon as Jim finished.

"None," Jim replied with a nod and a look at both men that said volumes. "Any oversight would give us away. We plan and execute every operation. Admiral Runion trusts us, and so does Ira. The others will come to trust us more in time."

John leaned back in his seat, put his hands behind his head and grinned at Jim. "And here I was thinking I'd be on the shelf for a year or so."

"In a way, we will be. We have to have a bona fide cover, and to produce that, we need two or three major treasure salvage jobs that put our names on the books and put our enemy's minds to rest. It won't be boring though. Treasure hunting on the ocean floor is never boring!" Jim finished. He believed that but would soon discover that he was very wrong.

"Saba's barge?" Wade asked, his eyes wide.

"Saba's barge first," Jim nodded. "Uncle Andrea is going to be part of the crew."

"So, we go to the Outer Banks, sit in a fancy house for a month, living life large in our newfound wealth, and put together a team and a crew for our venture!" John said with anticipation.

"In order for us to succeed they will have to be the very best in their respective fields," Wade added, nodding in agreement.

Jim reached into his shirt pocket and pulled out two credit cards, one with John's name on it, and one with Wade's name on it. Tears came to John's eyes when he saw the name of the company. *Bring It Up SAR (Deep Sea Salvage, Search, and Rescue)*. Once, when they were much younger, their father and Andrea picked that name for their dream company.

"Man, Dad will love this!" John said, his voice husky with emotion.

"Our credit line is $50,000.00 on each of these cards. A Merchant Bank in England issued those cards, and the money behind each card is our own. What we use the card for we pay off before the end of the month. Because we are working mainly through the bank, our APR is only 2.4% for as long as we're in business. That money goes to the bank, not to us, for this service," Jim explained.

"Are these activated?" John asked. He looked with pleasure at the Ekatrin Maritime Gold Visa card with his name stamped on it below the company name.

"They are," Jim replied. "Now, let's get down to some business," He handed them both a folder with schematic drawings and plans for their Powhatan class ocean tug. "Wade, you've always wanted to be an engineer. Well, now you are one! I want you to design a hidden chamber in the hold of this ship that will be a weapons and equipment storage room large enough for a team of thirty-six. You have to design it so that customs agents will never notice it, and no one but us will ever know it is there," he turned to John.

"I want you to start thinking about the salvage equipment we want, including diving equipment. I'll work on some of the legal stuff, the business plan, and then we'll work together on selecting our team and the crew," reaching into the bag at his side he pulled out two Apple iPads, handing one to John, and one to Wade.

As they drove through the highways, often following the inner coastal water ways, they excitedly discussed and analyzed the company, sharing ideas, making digitally recorded notes when they all agreed the ideas were good ones, so that the trip to Kitty Hawk seemed to fly by. It was with some surprise that Jim saw the bridge crossing the Currituck Sound to the Outer Banks.

CHAPTER 7

Birth of a Legacy

All three were impressed with the house in Kitty Hawk. It was a four-story building with eight bedrooms and seven bathrooms. They took the three bedrooms on the third floor, spending most of their time on the top floor where the kitchen and family room were located. A spectacular view of the Atlantic Ocean and parts of the beach were visible from the windows facing east and north.

Before appearing at the Real Estate office for the keys to the rental they stopped at a nearby grocery store and stocked up for their four-week stay. Soldiers like good meals, and they had plans for some of their favorites, and spent the money for the best cuts of meat and fish, fresh vegetables, lots of fruit, eggs and other staples. Each of them knew the importance of eating the right kinds of foods to maintain their strength and endurance.

Although they were now independently wealthy, old habits would be hard to break, and many of them they planned to keep. They didn't think about eating out more than once each week, though they could easily afford it. Instead they continued as they always had, sharing the cooking and cleaning chores and working together. Nor did they grow tired of their fare, for all three were good cooks, learning how while working on the sea as youngsters.

Seeing this four-weeks as a working vacation, they paid careful attention to their physical, mental, and emotional fitness. Allowing themselves a little extra sleep time, they rose at six in the morning, drank down a glass of milk with three raw eggs in it, and then ran five miles along the beach. After strenuous calisthenics, made all the more so by their fierce competitive natures, they showered and ate breakfast.

Eggs, often scrambled, bacon, fruit and oatmeal were consumed in large portions along with about a gallon and a half of milk. John and Wade usually drank a cup of coffee after breakfast. All three drank at least eight ounces of fruit juice, and Jim usually drank iced tea with lemon. He kept a bowl of limes and lemons on the counter to squeeze into his tea and Coke Zero. After breakfast they worked hard to clean the kitchen and put their laundry through the wash cycle.

Getting down to business by seven-thirty in the morning wasn't a chore. Excitement and anticipation drove them to eat a little quicker, clean a little faster, and tidy up earlier than usual. Bill and Zeke Kline arrived the following day with all their computer equipment, set it up and had it running, including the plotter Wade ordered to draw the plans for refitting the ship. Each officer now worked on the latest Macintosh laptop with high-speed wireless cable connection and Epson Stylus printers. A local Apple dealer helped them with all their equipment, excited to have the business. Having been given leave for only two days the Kline twins returned to active duty, awaiting the order to muster out of the Navy when it was time. Both of them were on the list of recruits for the new company.

There were those who would argue that a lesser PC would have been a better choice. Zeke, one of the men they chose for their team on the ride to the Outer Banks, was a computer specialist, considered by many to be the most innovative and savvy computer genius of his time. Affectionately known by his friends as "Uncle Zeke" because he often said: "Uncle Zeke is watching you!" the FBI and other government entities were constantly making offers to try to lure him away from the Navy.

Bring It Up Deep Sea Salvage, Search and Rescue Company was going to succeed where all others failed. Although Zeke could manipulate any computer in the world, he exclusively chose to use Macintosh computers. Jim, having worked for four years with Zeke, picked up on the reasons why this computer expert would use nothing else, and chose to follow that example. It was Jim's respect for Zeke's expertise, and the promise that he would be able to build his dream computer unit with carte blanche that would bring him on board.

John and Wade were also familiar with the Macintosh and its operating system because the Marine Crops discovered that there were far fewer problems with that computer system, especially when more than one person used it. Wade would have chosen the Macintosh, because most military engineers designed from CAD programs written specifically for Macintosh. John didn't really care but bowed to Uncle Zeke's knowledge without demure and with utmost respect. When the experts active in their field told you what to do, every soldier knew he was getting the best advice possible. If their lives depended upon the reliability of the equipment it was indeed the best.

From Jim's SEAL teams seven men would be chosen for the paramilitary unit. Like him, they began their military career in the Marine Corps, served in Force Recon, and received both Delta and SEAL training in counter terrorism and modern warfare. They knew and respected each other. John and Wade chose the other two survivors from their last mission to round out the team to twelve good men. Eventually, Jim hoped to expand his unit to forty-eight men, four teams of twelve. First, however, he needed to prove that a paramilitary unit paradigm was trustworthy and more efficient than current conventional military units.

By the end of day three, the twelve-man unit was complete, and every one of them accepted the call to duty to serve with Jim and John Shepherd. Both of those men were honored to be given such trust, and without saying anything aloud, committed to being the kind of leaders such men deserved. Looking into each other's eyes they read the resolve there and nodded in agreement.

From the Navy, again, Jim recruited Charles Lincoln, a very talented cook. For some reason, which Jim had never fathomed, Lincoln had been given the nickname of Abe. He didn't look anything like Abraham Lincoln. Charles Lincoln was a Senior Chief Petty Officer, and besides cooking he loved free weightlifting. Standing six feet one inches in his stocking feet Abe weighed an amazing two hundred and ninety pounds, every ounce sculptured muscle. His awesome physique would not make him the kind of soldier Jim and John were seeking, but then Abe was the cook, not one of the soldiers. That didn't mean he couldn't fight. His prowess and skill with a pistol was legend, and when it came to hand-to-hand fighting, he was more a wrestler than a boxer, and usually overpowered his opponents.

Abe always worked with Thomas Sturdevant, his closest friend. Tom Sturdevant towered at six feet eleven inches in height and weighed three hundred and twenty-five pounds. Sharing Abe's love for weightlifting he was also massively muscled, though not as bulky as his shorter partner. Everyone called him Sturdy, and though he was too tall to make a good solider, he was an excellent second to Abe in the kitchen, had a steady hand with a rifle or pistol, and was a fierce fighter. Both men knew their bulk slowed them, but it gave them other advantages too.

Once recruited Jim gave them permission to hire two other crewmembers to work in the kitchen. These two men were not military men, and neither had ever set foot on a ship. According to Abe, whose judgment Jim trusted, they would be green recruits, but would become loyal crewmembers and excel in time. Jim's only concern about the two men was that both were recovering addicts, one to alcohol, one to drugs and alcohol. However, if Abe vouched for them, they were now clean, and on the way to staying that way. Not particularly worried about either man he knew Abe and Sturdy would run a tight department. Both of those worthy men were glad to be going back to sea. As for their recruits, they accepted their new jobs with humility and a little fear.

Andrea Orvieto, the Shepherd's uncle, spent his entire life on the sea. He would be an excellent addition to the crew because he knew the Mediterranean area, and he knew the sea. Serving as an outside machinist and doubling as a helmsman he would bring years of experience and wisdom to the company. At sixty-one years of age he was still hale and hardy. He wasn't in top physical condition, but then most men at that age would not be.

Admiral Runion supplied three names for Jim to consider in order to complete his crew of twenty. They needed a surgeon and nurse who were experienced with the type of injuries common to SEAL teams. It never ceased to amaze Jim that most injuries occurred during training. An aircraft carrier that was recently retired produced the perfect pair for the medical team. Charles Lyle Wozniac and his wife Millie René Wozniac were both sixty-one years of age. When they lost their positions on the aircraft carrier the Navy decided it was time for them to retire. Neither wished to retire, yet.

Some years past both of their sons were murdered while coming to the aid of an eleven-year-old boy who was unfortunate enough to get caught in the crossfire of two rival gangs. The boys were twins, in their senior year in high school, and lived mostly with their aunt and uncle in Oxnard, California. They were honor students, well liked by their classmates, and mourned by all. With nothing to go home to, Charles and Millie wanted to finish their careers at sea. Jim both understood and respected that decision.

One thing the Navy excelled at was keeping its medical personnel up to par in the latest techniques and surgical breakthroughs. Navy doctors were encouraged to continue their education and attend at least two conferences each year. Both Dr. and Mrs. Wozniac were not content, as other doctors, to remain at the status quo. Both of them attended two extra conferences a year, paid out of their own pockets. Jim knew that if Charles and Millie met Admiral Runion's standards, they were perfect for his needs. Both would be trusted with designing and supplying the sick bay area of the ship, and Jim wanted the best.

The other crewmember was one James Paul Warner, a Master Chief Petty Officer, and according to Admiral Runion, the best diesel engineer and mechanic the Navy ever produced. James Warner retired from the Navy at age sixty, to attend to his wife in her last months of battling pancreatic cancer. Within six months of his retirement she died, and now he wanted to come back to the sea. His age was against him, but Jim knew that men like James Warner were worth their weight in gold. Experience was important, and Master Chief Warner had more experience than anyone else on the list. He might be a few years older than Jim liked, but that hardly mattered because what was important was that knowledge and understanding of ships at sea.

It fell to him to interview the three and he made plans to meet with them during the third week of their working vacation. His plan was to fly to Chicago, and rent a car, driving to Hebron, Indiana to meet with James Warner first. Then he would catch a late afternoon flight to Bob Hope Airport in Los Angeles, rent another car, and drive up to Oxnard. He would spend the night there, meeting with the Wozniac couple in the late afternoon. If everything went according to plan, he would return that next afternoon to Raleigh, and take a single engine Cessna flight to Kitty Hawk.

Admiral Runion arrived, as promised, on the weekend. Choosing to fly down in his own PBY he landed without mishap in the Currituck Sound. Jim, John, and Wade did know how to work some relaxation into their schedule. Determined to show the Admiral a good time they treated him to a fine seafood dinner at one of the better Outer Banks restaurants. That evening they did little more than sit on the fourth-floor deck and enjoy the evening breeze coming off the Atlantic. A few dolphins even showed up to entertain them, swimming back and forth along the beach for almost an hour as the light faded into night. Dancing across the waves, breaking the surface in spectacular dives, they gave a great show to the watching people on shore.

Most of Saturday he spent looking over their plans, and equipment lists. Sitting in the family room, on comfortable vinyl couches and chairs, enjoying the air-conditioning, the four of them worked through the day. The few times they moved included trips to the kitchen for more drink, or trips to the bathroom. They ate lunch at a Chinese restaurant for a break in the routine of the day. That evening Jim and John grilled shrimp and scallops, Wade prepared salads and a rice pilaf to accompany the meat, and the Admiral sat at the counter and watched.

On Sunday morning the Admiral left, making sure the men knew he was very pleased with their progress and planning. As his PBY roared into the sky, shedding water from the pontoons like two red clouds bursting, the three watched with mixed emotions. John and Wade had never had the experience of working directly with the Admiral, but they knew good officers when they met them. In just one evening and a day they came to realize what Jim had been expressing over the past four years. Admiral Runion was one of the few great men in the top ranks.

"He's a rare breed, that one," John said softly as the plane lifted into the sky. "I wish we could have worked with him!"

"In a way, we will be working with him," Jim replied, resting his hand on his brother's strong shoulder for a moment. "Just remember, there are a lot of good men up there. Most of them work behind the scenes because they aren't interested in playing politics. It's the ones who love politics that get the promotions. Only during wartime do we promote the officers who deserve the posts. The rest of the time it's the bootlickers and butt-kissers who rise to the top."

"It's getting harder and harder to see the good guys rising, even during wartime," Wade interjected.

"That has to change eventually. Too many people think American's are stupid, self-centered, only interested in narcissism. I admit, when the President who would be King was elected, I thought we'd about hit bottom!" John said as he turned and headed back to the rented Trail Blazer. Jim and Wade walked alongside him listening. "And when I look at the narcissistic mental pigmies in congress, I almost want to believe that Americans have indeed lost all their desire to keep this nation great. But that's changing, even now. I guess what I'm saying is most of the people in this country deserve better than what their government offers at the moment. I know twenty-six Marines, twenty-two widows and thirty-eight children who deserved better than they got. They're the ones who matter!" Hot tears stung John's eyes as he said the last, and Jim put his arm around his brother's broad shoulders, saying nothing. John was right. There were people who still made this country great. Whatever sacrifices were required, he knew he and his team would always stand for those who mattered, and despite what the government leaders of the day said, they would always uphold the America of the Constitution.

CHAPTER 8

Meetings and Surprises

Hebron proved to be a mid-west small town, with a special character that said this was a place for good people to live, even if it did look a little shabby in spots. Most of the houses boasted well-trimmed yards, very green, and old houses with wood siding, most well kept, even if the roofs of some sagged in the middle like a swayback horse. Jim liked the town after his travel through Chicago, and he found the address he was seeking without difficulty.

Master Chief Petty Officer James Paul Warner was almost average in height, perhaps five feet six or seven inches tall, and weighed about a hundred and forty-five pounds. Although he was sixty-one, he was still in pretty good physical condition, his bare forearms corded with muscle as he moved an old push-mower over his lawn. The lawn looked like it was cut at least three times each week, and it was bare of leaves of any color, even though several trees grew in the yard itself. James paused to stare at the tall young man stepping out of the rented GMC Yukon.

Jim Shepherd chose to wear gray dress slacks, a lighter shade gray dress shirt with a raised mandarin collar. On his feet he wore his favorite shoes, a pair of well-polished black cowboy boots. Warner watched the way the man walked across the yard and decided that

Admiral Runion had not exaggerated in describing Captain Jim Shepherd. Jim stepped up and held out his hand in a friendly gesture for a handshake. James Warner wiped his sweaty hand on his pants first, then shook hands with a firm grip.

"I'm Jim Shepherd. By Admiral Runion's description I recognized you right away. To make things easier for both of us, I'm going to refer to you as James or Master Chief, since we share the same first name. That alright with you, Master Chief?" Jim asked.

"Come on in the house, Captain, and we'll get acquainted properly," Warner replied, leaving the lawnmower where it stopped. He led them into the house, which had a new coat of ivory paint on the outside, with a neat brown trim. Inside the house looked as old as it was, and it seemed somewhat empty. Without knowing why Jim understood that it was because Warner's wife no longer lived here. She had been the life force in the house, and now that she was gone, it was just an empty shell.

"I was away mostly at sea," James said quietly, somehow connecting with Shepherd's thoughts. "This was really Brenda's house. Now that she's gone it's just not the same. It feels empty now, at least to me," there was a catch in Warner's voice as his eyes traveled to the photograph of the two of them, taken some time in the not to distant past.

Jim walked over to the photograph and studied it. He looked across the room at James Warner. "You may have been gone much of the time, but she loved you, and you loved her. That can be seen in this picture. Losing her must have just about torn your world apart."

Without answering Warner went into the kitchen, pulled a pitcher of lemonade out of the refrigerator, and pulled two clean glasses out of the cupboard above the counter next to that appliance. Opening the top door freezer, he shoved some ice cubes into the glasses, poured the liquid over the ice, and handed a glass to Jim, who had quietly entered the room.

"Didn't expect you to understand," Warner said, by way of an apology for his display of emotion. He wiped a few stray tears off his weathered cheeks.

"My father died when we were still in high school," Jim replied. "Neither of us has ever forgotten, and his shadow seems to loom large on our lives from time to time. People one loves tend to do that, I guess."

Warner nodded, leading them back to the tidy living room. He chose his favorite chair, a rocking recliner of the fifties vintage, avocado green, worn thin by years of use. Across the reading table with a reading lamp, also from the fifty's era, another rocking recliner sat, equally worn. Jim took a confortable wide reading chair that faced the two.

"Admiral Runion told me a little about what you're going to do," Warner said, sipping his drink and keeping it in his hands. "Was he telling the truth about the partnership part?"

"Yes. We are actually going to run a business as a cover. We are purchasing a Powhatan class ocean-going tug, and will operate a deep-sea salvage, search and rescue business. Every crewmember shares equally in the profits," Jim answered.

"Ah!" Master Chief Warner said with a nod. "Powered by two GM EMD 20-645F7B diesels. She's a powerful ship, and Mother Nature can dish out whatever she wants against her to no avail. 5.73 MW sustained; 2 shafts; Kort nozzles; cp props; and a 300-horsepower bow thruster. Length two hundred twenty-six feet, beam forty-two feet, displacing 2,260 tons fully loaded. She's a beauty, and no doubt."

"I'm impressed!" Jim said with a laugh.

"And you need a chief mechanic who doubles as an outside machinist. Wouldn't do to sign on a ship I didn't know about, now, would it?" James Warner admitted, his brown eyes bright now. "I've always admired those craft."

"You'll sign on at your former rank, of course," Jim said quietly.

"Who else knows about the ghost unit?" Warner asked, leaning forward in his chair, the springs beneath venting their age with a squeal that made him wince.

"Every crewmember knows," Jim replied. "Our team will need all the help we can get."

That, Master Chief Warner knew, was a break from tradition. Admiral Runion had been right about this Captain. For him, his crew was part of the team, an integral part of everything that happened. At that moment there was a momentary interruption as a school bus appeared outside the house and three children disembarked with all the excitement of children coming home from school. There were two boys who appeared to be about seven and nine or ten years old, and a girl about twelve.

"My grandchildren," James announced with a grin. "Sarah Marie is the oldest, she's twelve goin' on sixteen. Mark is the serious ten-year-old, and Jimmy is the little tornado."

The little tornado was first through the door with all the energy of a twister and moving in erratic patterns across the floor, dumping school stuff on the polished wood as he made for his grandfather.

"Hi grandpa!" He chirped, hugging James, and then looking shyly at Captain Shepherd.

"This is my new boss," James said to his grandchildren as they came to a halt in front of the stranger in their grandparent's living room.

"Does that mean we have to go to grandma Jean's after school then?" Little Jimmy said sadly. His little lip stuck out in a cute pout.

"Until I come back," Warner said, putting the boy down and patting him gently on the back. "Now you three go out and get some snacks in you before you fade away completely," the latter he said with a grin as the three rushed into the kitchen.

"So, you'll sign on?" Jim said. "Great. I've got all the necessary papers. Fax them to the number listed or email copies, but you keep the originals until you get to Portsmouth. Can you get to Portsmouth, England sometime next week? In the papers is a credit card with your name on it. You travel first class if you fly, everyone on the crew does. When you get there and find the ship, which is named *Bring It Up Coral* in Beardsley's shipyard, you're in charge of modifications to the engines and machinery. My brother John, and Wade Adams will meet you at the airport and explain everything to you."

"You don't beat around the bush, do you, Captain?" Warner commented with a grin. "I can be there on Wednesday next."

"Welcome to our crew, James," Jim replied with real warmth. Shaking hands once again. "I'll just go get those papers for you to fill out and fax. Then I've got to head back to the city to catch a flight to Los Angeles."

Jim suited his words with action as he walked out to the Yukon and retrieved the envelope with Master Chief Warner's papers. When he returned it was to find that Sarah had taken his empty glass away and was now seated at the dining room table with her books out. Warner was tussling with the boys but stopped when Jim returned.

Taking the papers, he opened the envelope and looked at the contents for a few moments and then grinned. "I have one question, before you go, Captain," he mentioned. When Jim nodded, he continued.

"Just what did you mean when you said I was in charge of modifications to the engines and machinery?" he asked.

"I'm quite sure you know that ship and its power plant well enough to have some ideas how you can make it more efficient, more powerful, and more capable for our missions. You'll discover that in our company you are the expert, and therefore have carte blanche when it comes to modifications and machinery. Whatever tools you think you need, purchase. Whatever machinery you think you need, purchase!" Jim said easily.

"You're serious!" Warner said, his eyes suddenly filled with purpose. "I've been wanting to get back to the sea!" His brown eyes were no longer heavy with loss but now filled with anticipation.

"Nice meeting you kids," Jim said with a wave as he shook hands with Warner one last time.

Oxnard was very different from Hebron, Indiana. Jim always liked the California coast, and Ventura and Oxnard offered many different vistas. One passed from farm country right into the city as though the two were jammed against each other on purpose. Charles and Millie Wozniac lived in a small bungalow inland, in the city proper. It was a neat little house with no yard, several fruit trees growing out of a brick patio, and a neatly tiled roof.

Charles was an inch shorter than Jim in height, looking more like a sports coach than a doctor. Millie was around five feet four and carried a little extra weight, looking very much like a sweet grandmother type with her white hair and sparkling eyes. Jim liked them both immediately, and he felt the same from them.

"Admiral Runion's told us so much about you!" Millie said as she busily began setting out cold drinks on the redwood table.

"If it was complimentary, then I admit that it's all true," Jim replied jokingly. His deadpan face and blank expression told her he was making a joke and she saw a mischievous gleam in his green eyes.

"I think the word pirate came up more than anything else!" Millie said with a little laugh.

"So, you need a doctor and nurse?" Charles said as they sat down on the back porch, shaded and comfortable around a redwood table with an umbrella above it and four padded chairs neatly spaced.

"I asked the Admiral to give us the best he could," Jim said nodding as he studied the doctor's serious eyes. "You were at the top of his list. I've read your dossier, and I must admit that I think the Admiral did us proud," Jim replied with honesty. "Your experience alone tells me that," he added.

"And your ghost unit will be much like a SEAL or Recon team?" the doctor asked. Millie set aside the tray with the pitcher of mint tea, filled with ice and amber liquid, listening carefully.

"Yes. That's our expertise. We'll really be more of a hybrid version, a mixture of the newest techniques. The crew and team will also operate a legitimate business that has all the potential of making us very wealthy," Jim added, sipping the delicious tea with pleasure.

"Admiral Runion said you drank iced tea almost exclusively," Millie said, noting his pleasure.

"Did the Admiral tell you why he was suggesting us?" Charles asked.

"You had no intentions of being sidelined before your time," Jim nodded his green eyes suddenly hard. "Some of our Navy bureaucrats forget that they're dealing with people, and especially people of skill. The Navy losing you is a real boon to my company, doctor."

"When do we start, Captain?" Millie asked with an answering gleam in her eyes.

"Immediately," Jim replied, putting his glass down.

He drew out the envelope with their papers prepared inside. "You'll find two company credit cards with your names on both inside. Book a first-class flight to London next week, as early as you can. When you fax these papers to the number listed, include your travel plans. I'll meet you at the airport and give you a tour of our ship and then turn you loose," Jim stated quietly.

"Turn us loose?" Doctor Wozniac said, his eyebrows climbing his forehead.

"You get to design and stock the medical unit on the ship. I'll give you a company checkbook for your purchases," Jim replied with a grin.

"Just like that? Carte blanche?" Doctor Wozniac's eyebrows were now as far up as they would go.

"No limits," Jim almost laughed. "Money is not an object this time, and I want a medical unit that can handle anything we might bring to you in the way of injuries, wounds, or illnesses," Jim's eyes were suddenly a stormy green and a little sad.

"Wow!" Charles said quietly, rubbing his hand across his forehead as though smoothing his eyebrows back into place.

"To whom do we answer when it comes to these purchases?" Charles asked after a moment of thought.

"You answer to yourself, Doctor. None of us know a thing about medicine. You're the expert. You determine what's needed," Jim replied.

"That could cost millions!" Charles said, his face suddenly lit up.

"I would expect nothing less," Jim replied. "The well being of my crew is first and foremost in my mind. This isn't the Navy, sir.

It's good business. We will be visiting many places in this world and only someone with your experience knows all that entails."

"Young man! I believe you are quite serious!" Charles said, as if he was having difficulty with the concept.

"That I am, sir," Jim replied evenly. "It is your medical unit, you run it, not me."

"We're in!" Charles said suddenly hugging his wife, both of them laughing. "We can be ready to leave by the end of the weekend!"

When Jim told Charles and his wife he planned to go back to LA, they extended an invitation to sleep in their spare bedroom. Jim accepted and was glad he did. They spent the rest of the afternoon and evening discussing their plans.

Returning to Los Angeles the following morning Jim flew back to Raleigh, then rented a plane and pilot to take him to Kitty Hawk. John and Wade met him and were very interested to hear his report on his meetings with the three unknowns on their list.

At the end of the week, their initial plans complete, they packed everything, flew to Raleigh, and then to Boston to visit with their families before flying to London to begin their new venture.

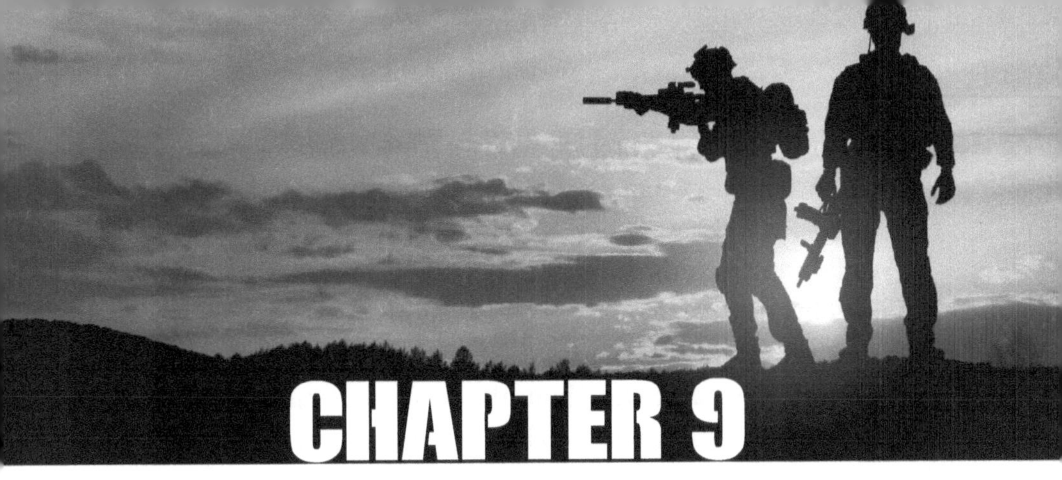

CHAPTER 9

Illicit Treasure

Three times in Boston Jim Shepherd felt that all too familiar rising of the hairs on the back of his neck. That's what it felt like, and it was always a sign that something was very wrong, and that danger was near. Jim wasn't superstitious, nor was he a mystic, but he knew the feeling and had learned to trust his instincts. More-or-less, that was how he viewed these strange alerts to impending danger. Nor was he alone in developing this sense of danger. Both John and Wade commented on the same feelings, though in very different ways. Perhaps it was because they had all been in situations where developing that sense was paramount to survival, and maybe years of training added layers to the ability.

Whatever it was all three felt it the first time while walking through the corridors of Logan International Airport. Passing one of the sports bars Jim happened to catch a swarthy individual of Middle Eastern descent staring at him. John elbowed him inconspicuously almost at the same moment he first noticed the man, and Wade cleared his throat, letting his eyes drift to the left to show the direction of the danger he sensed. Jim nodded to both to let them know he understood, his nod barely perceptible, and watched the man retreat into a protective posture of mock nonchalance. It was a good performance, which was precisely why it triggered the same response from all three observers. They were watching a professional in the field, a man who knew about surveillance.

Wade adjusted his sunglasses, which housed a switch that activated his tiny camera on the button of his sport coat sleeve. He shot four frames of the man as they passed. None of them could have identified what it was about the man that first warned them, but they were careful to research his identity as soon as they reached the Shepherd home and had a moment to themselves. His actions made that a necessity. Knowing he wasn't there because of them didn't change their determination to find out everything they could about him.

Fezik al'Loudi proved to be a trouble-shooter for an export firm in Marrakech. Jim, John, and Wade all agreed that their paths would probably cross again, though none could explain why. Most interesting, Al'Loudi's past history was a blank. Interpol had a question mark after his name and indicated that ongoing research was being done, which meant he had somehow managed to capture the attention of that worthy agency and they didn't like the way he looked either. To them, the real question was simple. What had Al'Loudi done before he worked for the export firm in Marrakech? All three knew that only two kinds of people hid their past. Covert operatives and people with some crime in the past from which they were hiding.

Spending most of Saturday with their respective families they met at the Catholic Church in the morning and at noon went for dinner at one of their favorite restaurants. Usually, Del Frisco's Steak House required waiting around for about forty minutes before the beeper indicated that their table was ready. Today, because Wade knew the owner well, they were whisked past surprised people who had already waited some time for a table. After a sumptuous meal they decided to walk to the Shepherd home, passing, as was their ritual from days past through the cemetery where the marker lay for Robert Shepherd.

Entering through the wrought iron gates they made their way to the familiar marker, pausing a few moments to pay their respects and reflect on the life of a man who so poignantly influenced their lives. The mystery surrounding his demise left an empty place in their lives, for there was no closure, no answers to the nagging questions surrounding the accident at sea. It was while standing there that the second warning of danger came.

This time Jim felt it first, looking up and around, seeing only a large family at a funeral some distance away. His keen eyes searched through the crowd and finally came to rest on a woman of South American descent, perhaps Brazilian, mixed with European ancestors as well. She was too tall to be anything else. Her dark eyes were fixed on Jim and his two companions, but her body language did not say anything about a threat or hatred. Still, without quite knowing how, he knew it was she who had triggered his sense of impending danger. He guessed the man standing beside her, white hair blowing gently in the breeze, his blue eyes distracted, was her father. He was definitely of Eastern European or German stock, but it was the way she acted toward him that suggested the family relationship.

John and Wade both looked at him, eyebrows raised. He nodded to them briefly and then the three turned and walked away. Behind them Marta Hess continued to watch them. Immediately she was reminded of soldiers, just by the way they moved together, or perhaps lawmen. Were they there to identify her father? She knew that some were still searching for war criminals from the Nazi regime, and her father, though not famous, certainly belonged in that group. She made a mental note to check the marker they visited and to make some inquires. For her, protecting her father and his ultimate goal was all that mattered, and Marta was ruthless in that pursuit.

"I felt true evil from that woman!" John commented as they exited the cemetery.

Jim nodded slowly, and Wade voiced his agreement. All three sighed.

Wise soldiers knew that truly evil people never apprehend the illicit treasure they ultimately seek. Blinded by self-centered desires they become enslaved to their own lusts, and spend their lives in malice and envy, filled with seething hatred, vainly reaching for that which is ultimately unobtainable.

With purpose they sow the seeds of anarchy, foolishly expecting others to obey their demands, thus all to often ruling despotically. Nor are they able to understand their own enslavement and eventual doom. History is littered with the ugly scars and rotting remains of evil men and women. Each one sowed into his or her own life the seeds of his or her own destruction, and each was never able to comprehend the enormity of that folly.

For those who are upright, who believe in the highest moral standards, and who understand man's need for law and order, and man's inability to govern himself apart from these values, truly evil people have nothing but contempt. Considering such people weak and easy prey they disparagingly rebuff, ignore, and scorn those who will ultimately rise up and defeat them. The forces of darkness have ever been blind to the threat of the mighty power held by those who walk in the light. Mocking that which gives man his ultimate value they think of other humans as less than themselves and thus invariably bring upon themselves their deserved humiliation.

So blinded by their own wickedness, even when they are soundly defeated by the forces of good, they refuse to see the error of their ways. Since the fall of man these two forces have clashed, and the result has always been war and death. Until the end of the age of evil, heroic warriors will be needed to rise up against the despotic slime of humanity. Unfortunately, truly evil people do not believe anything can stand in their way, or anyone can stop them.

No one knew this better than the three young men who walked in step, passing through the wrought iron gates once again, and moving along the sidewalk with purpose. Once more Jim felt that sensation, the internal warning of danger, somehow focused on the three of them. They were passing a popular coffee house and three women sat beneath an umbrella at a curbside table. They were obviously from Middle Eastern countries but had adopted some western dress and mannerisms.

Perhaps it was in the way that the three glowered at him, but Jim thought it went deeper. He saw Wade once again taking photos with his tiny camera. Little did he know that when they put those photos up for identification that they would connect with Fezik Al'Loudi. They owned the export business named Mercury. *What illicit treasure did they seek, and was there a connection between them and the woman in the cemetery?*

Jim knew that occasionally threads of destiny connected people. Whenever evil people plotted against humanity, somehow some higher entity seemed to take a hand in making sure that the right people were aimed at them, so that they ultimately failed in their attempts to destroy innocent lives. Innocent lives were often lost, but rarely did the perpetrator escape his or her due punishment. For a moment Jim considered the possibility that his destiny was woven together with those four women. He hoped not.

CHAPTER 10

Bring It Up Coral!

In these troubled times intelligence officers that had permission to carry firearms in flight on all commercial airlines were welcome, even by nervous pilots who feared incidents involving firearms in the air. British Airways offered truly first-class service, regardless of the fact that they were flying from John F. Kennedy Airport in New York to Heathrow Airport west of London on the redeye. The attendant crew aboard the aircraft recognized that these men were not the usual type passengers, and they were pleasantly surprised by polite and cooperative attitudes.

Good soldiers always knew that getting sleep was important, and they grabbed every opportunity to do so. One never knew when a mission would require hours, even days without sleep. All three were adept at falling asleep, even when people were moving around the plane. Because they were also careful, only two of them slept at a time. One kept watch, and they switched off every two hours. As a result, they arrived in the morning, refreshed, and ready for work.

Ken Worthington met them that morning at the Savoy. He needed signatures for some investments, and he was pleased to show them that healthy profits had already been made in his early investment endeavors. Ken was making a profit from these investments, a silent partner in the corporation. The company also paid his travel expenses, and he had been instructed to travel first class whenever he flew, for which he was truly thankful. In all, it was a mutually beneficial arrangement and he was excited to be part of something historic, and proud as well. Thrilled to show them how successful he'd been he welcomed the meeting.

After that meeting, still staggering from the sums the company had already pulled in, they traveled to Portsmouth by train, arriving in the late afternoon. There they met Calvin Beardsley, the foreman of the crew that was making the modifications of their ship. Beardsley was short, almost as wide as he was tall, burned brown by the sun and wrinkled prematurely from constant exposure to the sea. His hands were scarred and as hard as granite. Behind him his men stood, similar images, exuding competence and purpose. Never having worked with Yanks before, Beardsley wasn't sure what to expect, but measured these three men carefully and decided they were exactly as Sir Edward described.

Bring It Up Coral was already dry-docked in an enclosed boathouse and the crew had been cleaning the hull. Beardsley walked them through the building, introducing the men who worked for him, and then took them into his tiny office where one set of plans covered the tiny desk. Through that office they entered a conference room big enough to accommodate a large crew.

Counters were built along three walls, and a huge table sat at one end of the room. Jim estimated that the room itself was ninety feet long by sixty feet wide. There were windows, but Calvin informed them that anyone outside could not see in, though they could see out without difficulty. The windows were thick, and the walls insulated to protect from eavesdropping. No industrial secrets would be easily stolen from this room! Jim knew, from experience, that they could still be stolen.

On Tuesday Wade met Jim Warner at Heathrow and brought him out to the ship. Master Chief Warner hit it off with Calvin Beardsley immediately, and from the moment they met they were inseparable until the work was finished. Jim Warner was indeed everything

Admiral Runion claimed, and everyone sought after his input in the modifications of the ship.

Wednesday also saw the arrival of the team. Dorf Bernard led them into the conference room, ducking through the doorway, and turning sideways to fit between the doorposts. Dorf was six feet nine inches tall and weighed in at two hundred and forty-eight pounds; every ounce well defined Marine muscle. Like every member of the team, he started out in the Marine Corps, but later transferred to SEAL training, and then to a team.

Dorf was born Waldorf Samuel Bernard, the son of Marcus and Martha Elizabeth Bernard. Marcus, at present, is a Captain in the Boston Police Department with aspirations of becoming chief and then perhaps mayor of Boston. A social climber and astute politician, he pushed Dorf toward the same vocation, especially political.

Martha was behind changing Mark's name to Marcus, and her own Elizabeth Rae to Martha Elizabeth. Her total attention was focused on helping Marcus rise politically, and she is, fortunately, connected and motivated to pave the way. As a result, her attention is wholly on her husband, and Dorf, to his relief, was largely ignored.

Although Dorf went into the Marines with the idea of becoming an electrician, his fighting abilities kept him from following that career. He was a helicopter pilot, and he could fly fixed wing propeller driven aircraft and even some commercial jets as well. A competent Marine pilot, a certified expert diver, and expert deepwater diver made him an asset to the team. Dorf would lead the crew behind Jim, John, and Wade, seeing to the day-to-day details that were always required at sea.

Rank, the men had already decided, was not going to be as important in this venture, and for the most part, the men rarely paid attention to rank, other than the top man who led the team. Jim would serve as Captain on the ship. John would hold the rank of Commander, and Wade that of Lieutenant Commander. Dorf was given the rank of Lieutenant. Jim already knew that his Lieutenant would be the best man for the job, having worked extensively with him in the field.

Behind him came his second, Lieutenant Junior Grade Mark Aaron Drumheiser. They were inseparable friends. Mark stood only five feet four inches in height and weighed one hundred and forty-five pounds. Before joining the Marines, Mark mastered seven martial arts, and by the time he joined this venture, he had mastered eleven. He was, perhaps, the most skilled martial artist on the team, and everyone knew it, and respected his fighting abilities and accepted him as one of their chief trainers. Like Dorf he was a helicopter pilot, fixed wing propeller driven aircraft pilot, marine pilot, and an expert diver certified in every diving technique.

Bill and Zeke Kline were behind Mark. They were identical twins, and though they looked so much alike, like most twins of that nature, they were very different from each other when it came to personality. Both stood six feet one inches in height and weighed perhaps one hundred and seventy-five pounds. Bill Kline had been dubbed "Sparks" because he was a certified electrician. He was also a demolitions expert with uncanny skill. As a SEAL he had become an expert diver and was certified for all depths.

Zeke was light-hearted, where Bill was reserved. In all of the military there wasn't anyone who could match Zeke's skills on a computer. The F.B.I. and other organizations had been trying to lure him away from the sea for several years because of that ability. He was often heard to quip "Uncle Zeke is watching you." As a result, almost everyone who knew him well called him that. Like his brother he was a trained SEAL, a soldier through-and-through, certified diver and expert marksman. His true love was computers and his learning curve was impressive in that field. Any new technology having to do with computers he devoured.

Because of their special skills, and the work they would do for the company, both of them were given the rank of Ensign. One other Ensign was assigned in the crew, John Smith, who was inevitably nicknamed "Smitty." He followed the Kline brothers through the door and was carrying on with Zeke. Smitty was average in height, five feet nine inches, and weighed one hundred and seventy-five pounds, though he looked lighter.

A navigator with special giftedness, Smitty's two hobbies were interesting in their diversity. He loved treasure hunting, but his real gift was in weather, especially storms. Twice the Navy passed him over for promotion because he was outspoken about its inability to change paradigms.

The Navy relied too heavily on the global positioning system (GPS), which occasionally was inaccurate because of sunspots and other phenomenon. The Air Force adopted the E6B Computer, which establishes a position by celestial navigation based on the position of the navigational stars in relation to the different locations on the earth's surface. He had never been able to convince the Navy that their ships would benefit from the same technology. That hadn't prevented him from pointing out those failures, especially when lives were at stake. Higher-ranking officers often did not like being reminded that a subordinate had been correct in his evaluation.

Serving under Jim, Smitty learned that there were officers that appreciated expertise, and when Jim invited him to join *Bring It Up Coral* he leaped at the opportunity. When it came to designing the ship's navigation systems, he had been promised a free hand, and some of his ideas were so innovative they would soon be patented. Perhaps then, the Navy would listen, and improve its ability to pinpoint with accuracy global positioning.

Chief Petty Officer Frank Miller was next through the door. A stocky five-foot ten-inch one hundred and ninety-pounder, Miller was another demolitions expert and certified to operate just about any submersible he could get his hands on. He was also a certified mechanic, a job he'd picked up while shorebound before he entered the Marines, and then was transferred to a SEAL team training project, and finally assigned to Jim's team. Frank Miller had a very special personality that endeared him to just about everyone, laid-back, easy-going, fun-loving, and gentle, constantly keeping everyone involved and often bringing down the house with laughter.

Close behind him came the crew's other submersible operator, Jack Boswell. Jack was average in height; about five-foot eight inches, and he weighed one hundred and sixty-five pounds. His uniform insignia identified him as a Petty Officer, First Class. He too was a certified diver. With Jim's SEAL Team Jack showed a special knack for marksmanship with a silenced pistol and knew how to use a knife to kill silently when necessary.

Clancy Franklin and Vince Hall followed at the rear. Clancy was a six-footer, with whipcord motions, and his friend Vince two inches taller, and about five pounds heavier. They served with John and Wade and were two of the four members of the last unit that returned alive. Both bore the rank of Seaman. Close friends they were both savvy in the use of explosives and demolitions, crack shots, and very good in hand-to-hand combat techniques. Both men exuded that Marine toughness that all of Jim's team possessed.

Once the fighting team was assembled Jim spent some time describing their status and operations. He introduced them to Doc and Millie, and then to Jim Warner. Master Chief Warner looked the men over for a few minutes in silence, his brown eyes taking in the physique, attitude, and some hidden qualities as well. In his own mind he decided that these twelve men were among the most-deadly soldiers he had ever laid eyes on in his long and illustrious career.

Doc Wozniac had worked with SEAL teams in the past. He knew that these men underwent the most stringent training, and that only a small percentage of them made it through and qualified. Taking them in as a group, and then individually, he decided he was looking at men that probably were top of their graduating class. That made them very dangerous indeed!

Smitty and Uncle Zeke were in charge of overseeing the refitting of the compass deck and the communications and computer center, usually referred to as the CIC or Command Information Center. Upon receiving their budget both men's eyebrows climbed their foreheads, and then both grabbed pen and paper and began to make a list of the equipment they meant to purchase. Jim watched them with a smile in his eyes. One thing the Navy did well was keep up with modern technology. However, both men had often been turned down in requests for expansion equipment, and he knew that for the first time in their careers there were no limits. Excited to see the end result he left them to it.

Sparks, Master Chief Warner, and Wade joined forces to work out the logistics and materials for the special bulkhead wall that would hide their weapons and equipment room. Wade already had the design, having created it earlier, but he was soon upgrading his design with the help of Sparks and Master Chief. Jim Warner helped him design a much more advanced hydraulic system to operate the doors, and by the time the finished plans were completed it was a masterpiece.

Deep inside the ship's hold two bulkhead walls had to be built, shortening two holds by ten feet each. Customs officials who inspected the ship would never be able to detect that the holds were smaller unless they actually measured them and looked up the original blueprints. One of those bulkhead walls was designed with a set of doors, operated by electronics and hydraulics, set in tracks inside the hidden storage compartment to pivot inward and iris open. Closed, the doors fitted behind what appeared to be a solid grommeted joint seal.

Inside that room all their weapons, explosives, and special protective military gear would be stored. No expense had been spared in equipping his team with the best and most modern weapons of choice. Communications equipment, demolition equipment, handheld weapons, special rifles, sniper rifles, shotguns, assault rifles, missile launchers, and even tranquilizer guns had been purchased. At the moment they were stored in boxes awaiting the completion of the weapons chamber.

Those that had never seen a ship under construction marveled at the amount of work undertaken, the constant activity, the air of purpose, as men went about creating the vessel that would serve them at sea. Doc and Millie watched with amazement as the medical section of the ship took shape. Some of the designs for the storage of medicines and surgical tools demonstrated the true shipbuilder's art of creating adequate storage in small spaces. Though the necessary changes seemed daunting, steadily, day-by-day, the ship began to take shape. It was all extremely exciting.

Jack drove Dorf and Mark to Estleigh Airport to pick up the CH-53D Sea Stallion the company purchased. Like the ship, the helicopter had been refitted, and its engines rebuilt. Jim, John, and Wade chose the CH-53D because it was designed for the transportation of equipment, supplies, and personnel during amphibious operations. It was capable of carrying 55 passengers or 14,000 pounds of supplies. Theirs had been modified to carry no more than thirty-nine passengers with supplies.

At the airport Jack watched Dorf and Mark walk around the newly painted and completely fitted chopper. Like the ship it was painted a two-toned pattern with a third color stripe. Most of the chopper was painted in a high gloss pearl white, but the bottom was a stunning turquoise. Between the pearl and turquoise was a bright burgundy line about six inches wide. The line began where the fuselage joined the tail boom and ran down past the rear-loading ramp to run beneath the pontoons to the front, stopping just before the antenna rigging that jutted out from the nose of the craft. Her designation numbers were painted in the same vibrant color on the left side portion just above the rear-loading hatch. Standing there on the tarmac the craft looked distinctive and stood out because of the vibrant colors.

The rear fin was painted turquoise, and the horizontal stabilizer at the top pearl white. Both pontoons were painted in the pearl color with the bottoms in turquoise. As the men inspected the craft, they noted that the 3xGET64-GE-416/416A engine looked brand new instead of rebuilt. Whoever had done the work took great pride in presenting his product. After a pre-flight check the two men fired up the engine and checked that the anti-torque tail rotor and top rotor were running properly. The rotor span on this chopper was seventy-nine feet, but it could be folded for transport on board the ship. That was another reason this particular aircraft had been chosen, because space on a ship was always of utmost importance.

Upon arriving at the shipyard there was some difficulty in finding a place to land, because a large flatbed truck had arrived with their Kockums Salvage Bathyscaph and NEWT Suit. Hovering over the yard they watched while the bathyscaph and NEWT Suit were carefully placed on the deck of the ship. The submersible was placed on a cradle and strapped down with cargo straps designed to hold it in the worst possible weather.

Once the NEWT Suit was finally stored in its deck locker Frank Miller took up a position to guide them down to the deck. Dorf brought the craft down smoothly, setting the wheels down gently, and watched as men rolled underneath to attach the chain ratchets designed to hold the craft in place. Slowly the blades stopped spinning and only then were the men able to release the pin and fold them back. Dorf, on a special ladder with wheels, clamped them together in two places to insure they were not damaged. Half an hour later the aircraft was stowed properly and the ship back inside the boathouse.

Some of the men used part of their lunch break to look over the Correct Craft High Speed Boat (HSB), painted the same colors as the ship. Correct Craft made the boat especially for the Navy, a prototype that the SEALs used and approved. She was powered by two turbo 350 cubic inch Chevy engines and boasted almost a thousand horsepower. A special sling was fashioned at the rear of the ship, holding the HSB above the bollard pull and cable winch. A vinyl cover was buckled over the open areas for protection.

A Rigid Raider, which is a fast assault boat, also stood proudly in its specially designed cradle near the stern. Powered by a 290-horsepower engine, this beauty was designed for high speeds and to carry twelve fully armed men. She was twenty-one feet in length and weighed 3,633 pounds. With full fuel tanks she could range 230 miles at speeds up to 36 knots.

Three weeks later *Bring It Up Coral* was fully refitted and seaworthy. In the week prior to finishing the ship the two crewmembers from the kitchen arrived with Abe and Sturdy. Since the freezer and refrigerators were operating at full capacity food was quickly transferred on board and stored by the four men. Abe and

Sturdy brought the two new crewmembers on board. One had once been a successful attorney, though bad choices, difficult times, and severe alcoholism had nearly wrecked his life. He was bright and talkative and soon earned the nickname "Windy."

When not at sea, Abe and Sturdy worked at a mission in Boston trying to help men who had wrecked their lives put them back together. With Windy they seemed to have succeeded. The other crewmember bore all the earmarks of being trouble. He was morose and reclusive, rarely talked, and almost never made eye contact. Because of his apparent attitude the men of the kitchen crew nicknamed him "Stinky." When the rest of the crew picked it up, he didn't seem to mind. His real name was Robert Stankus. Wendall March was the one-time attorney.

Jim didn't really worry much about the kitchen crew. They were Abe's concern and he would deal with them as he saw fit. He trusted Abe to run a tight ship. Once he inspected the kitchen, he decided that Abe did indeed run a tight ship. Everything was in place. Admiral Runion found great pleasure in stealing Abe away from a certain Rear Admiral (lower half) who seemed to think the Navy's best were destined to serve under him alone. Jim grinned, thinking about Abe's defection to civilian life.

None of the officers that lost their best men knew that all of them had joined forces. Word would get out, but once they established their cover the reason why would be quite clear to all concerned. Jim wasn't worried about that, or about ruffled feathers. By the time he was working with them again much of it would be forgotten. Those who harbored such grudges weren't worth their salt and he knew his time with such men would be limited.

More and more equipment arrived daily, and everyone on the crew kept very busy putting his or her ship together. For regular workdays the men wore bright orange waterproof jump suits if the weather indicated that they might get wet working on deck. Otherwise they wore simple tan uniforms, short sleeves for the summer and long sleeves for the winter. None bore any insignia of rank. Calvin Beardsley's crew noted that the Captain of this crew worked as hard as any other man. No task seemed beneath him, which made him one of the good ones in their eyes. Men followed such leaders with intense loyalty.

Hard work pays good dividends and soon *Bring It Up Coral* was completed and declared seaworthy. It was an unusual morning for that time of year in the south of Great Britain. The sun appeared in an almost cloudless sky and the breeze was gentle and warm. Calvin and his crew of thirty-nine were invited to the christening ceremonies, where he would receive a bonus check for completing the work ahead of schedule. Seventeen men and one woman joined them; their dress whites resplendent in the morning sun.

Jim, John, and Wade stood facing the other sixteen crewmembers, and Dorf, towering over everyone but Sturdy, a full step ahead of the others. He saluted the three higher-ranking officers smartly.

"All present and accounted for, Captain," he announced clearly. Jim looked down the ranks and noted that Bob Stankus and Wendall March wore their uniforms with as much pride as the rest of the men. Someone had helped them figure out how everything worked, and they looked perfectly turned out. He was neither surprised nor disappointed, nodding his head in appreciation. The Captain returned Dorf's salute.

Dorf stepped back in line. Calvin Beardsley, not to be outdone, stepped forward with a wicked grin, and gave Jim Shepherd a proper British salute.

"Aye, Captain. Beardsley's forty thieves all present and accounted for, sir!" he bragged jovially.

Jim threw his head back and laughed. "Judging from the size of this bonus check, you've earned your reputation, gentlemen," handing the check to Beardsley he firmly shook his hand. Somehow over the months they had become great friends, sharing a mutual respect that comes from professionals working together. Beardsley held the check above his head and his crew clapped and carried on with real pleasure. Every man shared in the bonus, and after this job they all had two weeks paid vacation. Needless to say, each man was filled with pride and satisfaction at a job well done.

And well done it was. *Bring It Up Coral* gleamed in the sun. Her bottom, right up to the maximum draft water line was painted burgundy. The stabilizer fins were also burgundy, as was the rudder. From the water line up the hull was turquoise. From the main deck to the observation tower her color was creamy pearl white, and all the railings were painted in turquoise. On the stern, in burgundy with the cream shadowing, was painted *Bring It Up Coral* in a bold Boulder font. Below the name of the ship were the words Boston, Massachusetts. Just behind the Stockless anchors, on either side of the bow the company logo had been painted, again using the burgundy with cream shadowing.

Jim thought the logo impressive. It was a brown Peregrine Falcon with a white head, fiery red eyes, and extended exaggerated talons coming in for the kill. Beneath it the company's logo was written. Every insignia for the men on the ship had that logo.

Both her funnels were painted turquoise two thirds of the way up, followed by a wide cream stripe, and then the ventilators topped with burgundy. Her radar and communications mast stood proudly between the funnels. Forward on the bow was the telecommunication mast with its impressive array of antenna, satellite dishes, and weather sensing equipment.

"It's been an honor working with you and your crew, Captain," Beardsley said as Jim's eyes returned to him. "I've not seen or worked with a finer crew. Any time you need our services, we're available," he shook hands again and Jim smiled.

"Thanks, Calvin. I believe my crew feels the same about yours," Jim replied.

Zeke stepped forward, raised a digital video camera, and began recording the christening Ceremony. The ship's three commanding officers climbed to a platform just in front of the bow. Wade lifted a bottle of Champagne from a bucket of ice and handed it solemnly to John. John turned to the bow and Jim faced the crew.

"Today marks the maiden voyage of this fine ship. I christen him, *Bring It Up Coral!*" he declared in a voice loud enough to carry to his men.

Bring It Up!" rang from the lips of every crewmember on the dock as John struck the bow with the bottle, shattering it, while Calvin Beardsley pushed the brake release to allow the ship to slide backwards into the ocean. A length of cable prevented the ship from floating out too far and it settled in the water and stood waiting. Men from Beardsley's crew used grappling hooks to grasp the ropes on the bow and stern and make the ship fast to the dock before that cable was released.

As the cheering followed, and the ship was made fast to the dock, Jim and John looked at each other for a moment, both filled with pride. Thinking of their father, remembering that this was part of his dream too even though he was not there to share it with them, brought a smile to their faces. Wade put a hand on each shoulder and quietly spoke.

"I'm sure your dad knows, and he is watching with pride," he said. "Now, let's get on board and see what this mighty fellow can do on the water!"

CHAPTER 11

At Sea

*B*ring It Up Coral gleamed in the early morning light, breaking through the light cloud cover as they made their way into the channel, on a westerly heading, making for the Atlantic. Every crewmember wore his tan work uniform, waterproof boots with special soles designed for tight grip on slippery wet decks, and a tan hat with their business logo on the front. No one wore any insignia of rank and everyone pitched in with intensity at any job that needed to be done.

Millie happened to be passing by one of the upper deck lavatories when Jim came out, cleaning bucket and supplies in hand. Sweat stains showed under his arms and beneath his powerful neck. He nodded once to her and hurried up the steps to the next deck. The smell of bleach suggested the good Captain had been cleaning something.

Out of curiosity she peeked inside the lavatory and found it spotless. Stainless steel sinks and toilets sparkled under the fluorescent lights. Following her nose, she found a spot in one corner that obviously caught the Captain's eye, for it had been scrubbed into conformity with the rest of the room. Shaking her head, she walked out to find her husband grinning at her antics in the hallway.

"I just knew you couldn't resist inspecting the good Captain's work!" Charles said, putting his arm around her shoulder and walking beside her.

"He got on his hands and knees and scrubbed a dirty corner of the floor, if you must know," she declared, smiling up at her handsome husband with real warmth. "This is a very unusual Captain. I like him a great deal, but there is something inside of him that makes me ache."

"He's a soldier, a former SEAL Captain, and he has seen the very worst of combat and the worst scum that walks this planet," Charles said, his eyes focused inward as he thought about the man they now served.

"It's different," Millie said pensively. "I can't put my finger on it, but there is a great sadness in his heart. I'm sure this adventure will bring it to the surface."

"If not, Aunt Millie can work her usual magic," her husband replied, giving her shoulder a gentle squeeze.

Jim lived by the motto that a leader should never ask his men to do something he is not willing to do himself. Nor did he call attention to the work he did. He knew that his example was enough, and that the respect and loyalty of his crew depended on his leadership. More than ever he faced the overwhelming responsibility of leadership, a fact that did not surprise him in the least. In the military he took orders, he followed them, and those who gave them were ultimately responsible for any screw-ups. Now he was the one giving the orders, and the responsibility of that weighed upon his heart and mind.

Some of the men noticed what he was doing and on the following day he was not surprised to find that the lavatory corners had all been scrubbed to perfection. His crew was like that. They learned quickly, excelling like no other team under his charge. Other cleaning was accomplished with a little more panache than the day before. Making sure the men knew he noticed, and was pleased, he patted shoulders, said a word of thanks, all the little things that let the men know he appreciated the efforts they made. Such attention would only motivate them toward the perfection they all ultimately sought.

On the bridge, Jim listened to the chatter from his crew. Each man wore communication headgear, so that he or she could speak to one another no matter where he or she was on the ship. Already the nicknames, by which they were best known, or the new ones given, were the conversation openers.

Jim Warner's voice sounded over the radio earpieces. "Command, this is the engine room."

"Roger TRT, we copy on the bridge," Wade responded.

"TRT?" Jim had not heard that one.

Wade grinned at him. "You remember that huge plaque the Master Chief has hanging above the hatch to the engine room?"

Jim did. It was a wooden plaque with a huge sixteen-pound sledgehammer, and crossing it, the scarred and burned tube and handle to an acetylene torch. Below the tools were the words: "Delicate adjustments made here." Jim nodded his head and chuckled.

"Well, he calls that oxyacetylene rig of his a thermal removal tool. Hence the acronym TRT," John added, laughing at the picture. Several times during the modifications of the ship Master Chief Warner had called for his thermal removal tool.

"Well that's a new one!" Jim said, laughing himself. "Somehow the moniker fits our Master Chief," he added.

"When you two are finished discussing my obviously superior skills in the engine room, I'd like to continue," the voice of the Master Chief said sardonically.

"Roger that, TRT. Go ahead," Wade replied with a straight face.

"Let's nail the throttles to their stops for about twenty minutes. I'd like to see how these engines hold up under full pressure," TRT ordered.

John, who was at the helm, reached forward and slowly pushed the throttles to their stops. They had been running at about twelve knots for an hour. Now the full roar of the engines pushed the ship even faster through the water. Smitty in his Plexiglas enclosed compass bridge watched their progress carefully while Zeke read out the numbers as they climbed.

"Forbes Log now reads fourteen knots," his voice said over the communication gear.

"Isn't that the top speed for this hull?" Smitty asked, noting that the boat seemed to be picking up speed.

"It was," Master Chief Warner replied cryptically. "I made a few modifications."

"Forbes Log now reads fifteen knots!" there was a note of excitement in Zeke's voice as he watched the needle to continue to rise. He called out the speed in increments of one tenth of a knot. At last his final report sounded over the radio. "Forbes Log now reads a steady nineteen point eight knots! E6B and GPS confirm!"

"Bring It Up!" echoed in every earpiece as the crew shouted the name with excitement. Anytime a crew can get more out their ship than expected was a moment for celebration and pride.

"E6B Computer, VOR, and GPS show us on course, Commander," Smitty spoke into his mouthpiece.

"Roger that, Smitty," John responded.

"How are we doing down in the engine room, Master Chief?" Jim asked.

"Captain, I always thought I was a good mechanic, but this guy is pure magic!" that was the voice of Frank Miller, whom everyone called FM. "I never heard any pair of engines purr like these two, synchronized perfectly! Man, can these babies put out the power too, Shep! You should be down here to see this!"

"On my way, FM," Jim said, walking out the door and down the steps, heading for the bowels of the ship.

"Sorry, Shep. I got carried away," FM apologized.

"Not at all, FM. I want to see it from your viewpoint. See you in three."

When Jim entered the engine room, he grabbed his earplugs and blocked out most of the noise. Master Chief Warner sat in a swivel chair bolted to the deck, watching the gauges and indicators, his eyes constantly searching them from right to left and back again. Frank Miller was standing between the huge engines, and one reason for the noise was that the cam covers were both raised at the moment.

He was checking that the overhead cams were turning properly, and oil was being distributed, as it should be. As soon as the Captain entered the engine room, he hastily pulled the covers closed and wiped his oily hands on a blue shop rag. The noise level lessened considerably.

"Wow!" Jim said, listening to the roar of the diesel plants. "You can feel the power here!" he admitted with a grin.

"Look at the torque TRT can get out of these engines!" FM said loudly above the noise, pointing to a meter that showed the foot-pounds of torque.

"Isn't that almost elven foot-pounds above the factory specs?" Shep asked.

Master Chief Warner heard him and looked up from his gauges for a moment, surprised. "You know your engine specs well, Captain!" he said. "And yes, it is. Diesel engines are easy to adjust and improve. We're getting that extra speed because of those extra foot-pounds of torque. Man! These engines are definitely state of the art!" the Master Chief breathed his statement with deep respect.

"No need for those delicate adjustments just yet, eh Chief?" Jim grinned.

"Not for a good while, yet!" TRT replied with a smile.

"You guys did us proud! Well done!" Jim waved to both men and told them to keep up the great work, and he turned and headed up to the bridge. FM and TRT looked at each other for a few moments after the Captain left.

"Is he always like that?" Master Chief Warner asked.

"Mostly. I've never seen a man who could get the best out of his team like Shep. You know he's rootin' for ya, right from the start. It's just natural to do your best for a guy like that," FM said after a moment of thought. "I've done things I never thought I could accomplish serving under him. And I pity the man who pits himself against our Shep!" FM added quietly. "That man is death walking, and I don't mean maybe!"

Master Chief Warner looked at FM quizzically. Frank Miller stood five feet ten inches tall and weighed a good one hundred and ninety pounds, every ounce on his stocky body was hardened muscle, the kind that didn't slow a man down. Warner knew soldiers, and he knew this one was among the deadliest of them. The respect he showed for the Captain's prowess surprised and impressed him even further. Watching all the men work these past months told him much about this team, and he didn't doubt FM's word about the Captain. Only such a man could lead men like this. Deep inside he felt the swelling of pride to work with such men, to be accepted by them as one of the team. This crew did not treat noncombatants as "second class" citizens, as did many fighting units.

CHAPTER 12

Sudden Change

No one ever knows how a day will shape up, and what changes may come. Such a day came when ten days later they passed through the Straight of Gibraltar without mishap and passed through what many called the Alboran Sea, which was really the western tip of the Mediterranean. When they drew level with the Balears Islands, even though they could not see them, John called Andrea Orvieto to alert him that they were only a week's journey from joining him at his home on the island of Corsica. Andrea owned and operated a small fishing business out of Solenzara. Assuring them that he had already arranged for the sale of his boat and business so that all was in readiness, Andrea bade them a safe journey.

Dinner was usually almost a formal affair. By dinnertime four days later, the day seemed much like any other. Tablecloths were used only at dinner. Linen napkins were provided at each place setting. Abe's crew was creative, and dinner often surprised the crew. Lighthearted conversation filled the room as the crew enjoyed five-star meals. Planning a menu that was not static was something Abe and Sturdy loved, and the crew never knew what to expect for meals. Abe and Sturdy meant for each meal to be something to which the men looked forward, and they succeed masterfully.

Jim sat at a table with Doc, Millie, and Master Chief Warner. Wade and John would also be joining them. Every night Jim sat at a different table with different people, but on Sunday evenings he liked to sit with these five friends. Wade came into the dining room, filling the doorway for a moment with his broad shoulders, and sauntered over to the table. Zeke came in behind him, walking directly to the Captain's table and silently handed Jim a note.

Glancing at Zeke's face Jim knew instantly that something was amiss, and he read the note quickly. He looked up at Zeke. "Please ask John to step into the conference room, Zeke. Wade?" Jim looked at him and he rose to follow immediately.

Zeke nodded quietly, leaving quickly to relay the message to John. Wade made no comment, simply wiped his mouth with his napkin and stood up to follow Jim to the conference room. The other men remained silent knowing that Jim would brief them when he was ready. All of them knew that something was up, and the attitude in the room changed instantly.

Wendall, a master at reading a room full of people, noted the change and stopped eating to look around. He couldn't put his finger on it, but he knew the atmosphere had changed, and that the room was suddenly charged with a kind of intense energy. All of the men were eating, but they were eating a little more quickly, as if they might need to finish sooner than intended. Something in their body language said that these men had suddenly become watchful, and somehow that made them seem even more deadly.

His first storm at sea seemed deadly, as storms at sea often are, but this was a very different storm building, and somehow Wendall knew that once unleashed, this storm would be the deadliest. He couldn't have told how he knew it, but he did, and a shiver went down his spine.

"Captain Rob has the ship," John announced, entering the conference room quietly. "Dorf came up to keep an eye on things for me," he added, sitting down next to Jim.

Without comment Jim handed the note to John. *Andrea Orvieto seized by Antonio Scalini thirteen hundred hours today. Imminent danger. Scalini psycho, connected to Arvis Caineli (enforcer) and father Walter Scalini (family heavyweight). Agent in place Arturo Veniti, owns local fishing fleet, will meet you in hotel bar. Buy some fish.*

"How do you read it?" Jim asked his two friends quietly.

"Andrea sold his fishing boat and business. Scalini wants in on the profit," John said quickly.

"My read too," Wade agreed, nodding his head slowly. "But why now?"

"Selling the boat and business meant he was going to leave. Scalini has an old score to settle, and he figures this is his last chance," Jim replied after a moment of thought.

"And our response?" Wade asked, a slow grin forming on his face.

"We go in and get him back!" Jim replied tersely. "Nobody messes with one of our crew! Nobody!"

"Let's get the team in," John said, tossing the paper on the table.

Wade reached for the phone at his station and was immediately connected to Zeke. "Let's get the team assembled in the conference room," he commanded.

"Hot damn!" Zeke crowed. "Action!"

"Enthusiast!" Wade grinned as he hung up the extension. For a moment the three looked at each other. There was anticipation in all three sets of eyes, not excitement exactly, but the beginning zeal for the upcoming battle.

Less than two minutes passed before all twelve men on the team were seated around the conference table. Curious about the gathering, Charles and Millie Wozniac wandered in, wondering if they would be welcome. When no one seemed to mind their presence, they took seats at the conference table, which was designed to seat thirty-six people, receiving nods and smiles from those around them. Wendall asked Abe if he could also see what was going on, and Abe grinned and nodded his permission. Wendall slipped in to sit beside the doctor and his wife, also surprised to receive nods and smiles of welcome from the members of the team.

"Andrea was seized by an Antonio Scalini. He's being held prisoner with, we think, the view of extorting money from him. We don't have much intelligence yet, but it looks like we're going to have to go in and rescue him," Jim said when everyone was seated. "We make a point here, gentlemen. Nobody messes with one of our crew, ever!"

"Do we have any intel on the enemy force?" Sparks asked, looking at his brother first. Zeke shook his head in the negative.

"Scalini is small time, an embarrassment to his father who is big time in Sicily. But he may have a large retinue of enforcers. We just don't know at this point," Jim answered calmly. "We're going to pull out all stops to get to Corsica as quickly as possible. There is an agent in place who can give us more Intel, once we arrive. After that we'll decide on a plan of action. Everyone knows what to do," he added.

"Four-man teams?" John asked in the silence that followed.

"Yes. Team one, JR in command. Dorf, Mark, and Sparks are yours," Jim stated. The four men nodded and stood to leave. "Team two, Wade in command. Wade, you have Jack, C.G. and Vince." Wade nodded and stood to leave, the other three standing with him.

"Stick me with three Jar-heads!" Jack said in mock dismay.

"Quit flappin' your whiskers SEAL. Maybe we'll be nice and let you juggle three grenades on your nose or something!" Wade said with a grin. "At least I only have one of you to worry about."

"Zeke, Frank and Smitty, you guys are with me," Jim said. "Zeke, let's make contact with our friend in MI6. I want full background on the Scalini operation on Corsica. Try to get some air surveillance and topographical maps of the island around and under the house. Smitty, you work with him and see if you can shave a few hours off our trip," he added.

Nodding the two men sprang up and headed out the door. Jim turned to Frank. "Take Master Chief Warner with you and get the boats ready, including the submersible, in case we decide to go in under water," Frank nodded and headed out the door, Master Chief

Warner at his heels. Millie came over and put a tiny hand on Jim's shoulder.

"We'll be praying for your uncle, Jim," she commented.

"I think you'd better pray for the guys who took him!" Wendall said under his breath. Millie heard and nodded her head as Jim left the room.

"Yes. They have no idea what they've bitten off," she said quietly.

For a few minutes Wendall stood in the conference room. He noted the high-tech design of the table, each of the thirty-six places supplied with a laptop computer, the latest in the PowerBook line from Macintosh. Wendall knew that Zeke was a real computer genius, and he wondered why Zeke would choose Macintosh over an IBM or clone. He decided he would ask, after the men returned from their mission.

Once again, he went through his impressions of the last hour. He could feel the storm building, and he knew instinctively that this storm was far more deadly than anything nature might throw at them. Deep inside he wondered what he could possibly offer to help a team of this nature. That he would try was all he needed to know at the moment. Shivering again he moved to the door, his mind on the way the men moved. *I'm glad they're on my side!*

One by one the team gathered in the weapons room, behind the cleverly designed bulkhead wall that effectively hid its presence on the ship. Each man had a locker that contained his personal body armor suit, bulletproof vest, and other items that made this suit perfect for storming an enemy stronghold. Since this would be a night insertion, they pulled out their shadow gear, as they called it, designed to be almost invisible at night. Hues of grays, blacks, greens and browns were digitally arranged on the fabric, making it blend into almost anything except a white building.

Darkness was the time they operated at their best. The night was their playground, their most effective cover, and through the night they could move like shadows, undetected, unnoticed, indistinguishable from anything else in the vicinity. Technology of the latest version enhanced night vision and allowed them to move with freedom.

Batteries were checked and then loaded into the night vision goggles each man would carry. Fresh batteries with a full green reading went into their packs. Communication gear was carefully checked to be sure the batteries were at full charge and the units were working properly. More static than was usual made the equipment useless, and it was immediately turned in for repair and another unit checked out. In the field communication was most important.

Light banter between the men went on through the exercise. Jim knew this was part of the pre-operation jitters every man experienced. Some needed to joke, to talk, and others, like him, needed silence. The men knew which was which and respected each man's unique disposition to the phenomenon.

As the banter went on each man concentrated on what he was doing. A prepared soldier who was well trained had the best chance of coming back. The men knew that any one of them could die, even during training. It was not that they accepted death, but that they understood the risks and accepted them. If death came, it would find them concentrating on what they had to do, not thinking about or fearing what might happen. One kept one's edge, prepared as best as one might, and then did his duty.

Jim put his Motorola AN/PRC-112 unit on the shelf, the batteries standing next to it, ready for when they would be needed. He tested his Trimble Scout M-GPS unit, and took the batteries out before putting both on the shelf next to his Motorola. After checking everything in his locker he went to his weapons box. Each tem member had his own weapons box and his own key.

Unlocking the box Jim opened the top and front, folding them back to rest against the bulkhead wall, exposing drawers and an open storage space at the top. He pulled out a thick vinyl case and opened it. Inside rested two of each of six different knives. For this mission he chose a Mini Tac to go in a sheath that hung just behind his neck in the small of his back, under his entire outfit. Bypassing the Camillus boot knife, he reached for his Cold Steel Recon Tanto knife, the seven-inch blade black coated carbon V steel. It had a nice feel to it, and he pushed it into a sheath on his equipment vest. The Al Mar SF-SOG Special Ops knife remained in the case, with the KA-BAR knife. He pulled out the Ontario Navy knife with a six-inch black finished stainless-steel blade, checked the edge, and slid it home in his utility belt sheath.

Another thick vinyl case came out, this one revealing several foam-filled drawers with cutouts for his six pistols. His Beretta M92F went into his holster, and his H&K MP-10SD went into the holster that would be strapped around his right ankle. Both weapons were 9-mm and already tested for accuracy. In time he would have to replace the barrels to keep the accuracy levels at peak performance, but for now they were perfect.

Inside the case was an FN Five-SeveN, not as light as the H&K P-10 by about three tenths of a pound. It was a 5.7-mm gun. A Glock 17 also rested in the case, and below it an H&K Mark 23 .45 caliber. Lovingly he checked each weapon before sliding the drawer closed. His ability with these guns was legendary, even with his present team.

He was not surprised to see each man working the safety of an H&KMP5SD or MP-10SD rifle. Each one was silenced and fired 800 9-mm or .45 caliber rounds per minute on full auto. Most of his men kept the setting on a three-round burst, and some preferred the single round. Laser sights made these weapons triple threat firepower in the hands of an expert, and every man on his team was an expert. Jim checked the spare magazines in his utility vest, and the magazine that would go in the rifle.

C.G. Franklin was working the bolt action of his Accuracy International L96A1 sniper rifle. During his four years as a member of John's team he had eighteen confirmed kills, none at under a thousand yards, and three in high wind situations at over twelve hundred yards. In his box was a Barrett M82A1 for real long-distance shots, and the new Barrett M99, a lighter and more compact gun than the M82A1.

One man from each four-man unit would carry a Mossberg 590 Tactical shotgun, or a Franchi PA3/345. There were assault rifles in the box, but no one would be needing that kind of firepower for this mission. The ever-popular Colt M16A2 and the new H&K SA80 were in every man's box, ready for heavy firepower situations.

From each four-man unit one man would also carry a CO-2 tranquilizer pistol with a box of tranquilizers, some for animals, some for people. The pistols were almost silent in operation and accurate up to thirty feet. Most of the time his men could move silently enough to get within six feet of a dog without being detected. Soon the team was finished checking their gear and preparing for the mission. They left in pairs or threes, until Wade, Jim, and John turned out the lights and closed the bulkhead doors, making the bulkhead wall once again look innocent.

CHAPTER 13

First Test

It was nearly three in the morning when *Bring It Up Coral* sped through the Straight of Bonifacio, the narrow body of water that separated French Corsica from Italy's Island of Sardegna. John was at the wheel, and Jim stood on the observation deck above the bridge. He could hear the pounding of the surf against the rocks of both islands, magnified as it was in that particular place. Beneath his feet the engines roared at full capacity, pushing the boat along at twenty knots, thanks to some adjustments made by Master Chief Warner.

John turned the wheel to a heading of 33.75 degrees northeast by north, watching the Gyro-Turn Indicator and the Rate-of-Turn Indicator. Zeke was looking at the French Geodetic Survey chart for the navigable costal waters. When the time came Smitty ordered another turn to 1.25 degrees north. Jim listened to the chatter on his headset and watched the lights of Porto Vecchio off the port bow coming into view. Sainte Lucia came next, and finally Solenzará. Slowly the ship settled her bow into the water, coming to a full stop to drop anchor in the bay.

Dawn was approaching, the first silver line of daylight pushing back the blanket of night. On the after deck five men prepared to launch the HSB. Correct Craft manufactured the forty-foot beauty for the Shepherd company, a one-of-a-kind boat. This one had a pair of Chevrolet engines that could propel her 13,500 pounds through the water at a steady seventy knots. The HSB was painted to match the company colors and bore a commercial registration out of Boston. She was designed to mount a British 50 caliber automatic Gatling gun on either gunnel. Working spotlights at the moment covered those mounts.

Dorf operated the crane mechanism that lifted the boat over the side and lowered her into the water. Mark stood by, directing the operation with hand signals. Jim, John, and Jack wore their dress uniforms. Jack would drive the boat, chauffeuring the two senior officers to and from the ship. All three climbed aboard the boat and Jack started the blowers, waiting a full three minutes before firing the engines. They roared to life. Casting off the lines, he moved behind the wheel again, and thrust the throttles forward.

In the sheltered bay area Jack expertly pulled the boat to a pier and Jim negotiated with the dock master to rent a slip for their boat, speaking in perfect idiomatic French, much to the surprise of the night master. Jim paid for the slip, using the company credit card, and thanked the dock master for his help.

"You speak French very well," the dock master commended with a smile.

"That is high praise, and I thank you," Jim replied formally. He bowed his head and left a bemused dock master who had expected typical Americans who insisted that everything be done their way. These men were obviously different, and extremely courteous. He looked out to sea at the ship and recognized it as a deep-sea tug, wondering what business brought them to his part of the world. It was a small town and he would soon know. Yawning he returned to his comfortable office chair to await the changing of staff in the morning.

Jim and John made their way up the cobblestone street, carefully committing everything they saw to memory. Some of the houses and shops needed paint, the sea air eating away at them relentlessly, making them look old and shabby. Other buildings were freshly painted, bright colors in many cases, leaving the visitors with the impression of an ancient village trying to make it into modern times, on the verge of becoming a town.

At the hotel they found the only restaurant open at that time of the morning, offering the usual French breakfast items. Jack left them at the hotel, continuing to walk through the village. He had a digital camera hanging around his neck and he often paused to take a picture of the village, the images going directly to one of Zeke's computers. Jim and John went inside to order some breakfast and wait for their contact to arrive.

Arturo Veniti proved to be a small, thin, weather-beaten Italian with sparkling dark eyes, thick eyebrows, mustache, and beard, all salt and pepper. The amount of hair growing out of his nose and ears told the Shepherd's that Arturo was not fastidious in his appearance, as did the state of his wrinkled and well-worn clothing that gave off the pungent odor of fish and the sea. His smile was genuine and showed yellowed teeth. Beaming at them he extended his arms and welcomed them to his village with the traditional hug and touching each cheek.

"Ah! My American customers!" he said expansively, rubbing his hand in anticipation. "I am delighted to meet you!" he certainly sounded delighted. Jim and John stood, towering over Mr. Veniti, and bowed correctly. Jim spoke Italian like a native from somewhere north of Rome. He returned the greeting. Arturo's smile brightened.

"It is a pleasure to meet you, Senior Veniti. You once sold fish to a friend of ours, a chef named Charles Lincoln from the American Navy. Perhaps you remember him?" Jim knew that this was true, a once-in-a-lifetime chance meeting between the two. Abe mentioned it when he heard who Jim planned to meet. Arturo thought for a moment and then smiled.

"Ah, yes! A giant of a man with great muscles! I remember him!" he replied, gesturing expressively with his hands.

"He is the cook on our vessel, and he insisted we contact you," Jim added.

"At that time, he was cooking for an Admiral, if I remember correctly. Are you an Admiral?" Arturo asked.

"No. I am simply the ship's Captain. We have a crew of twenty, and Abe wishes to serve us some of your excellent fresh fish," Jim replied.

"Twenty! This is good, no? You have eaten, I see. Good! Let us go to my boat and I will show you what we have fresh from last night! This will please our Mr. Lincoln, no?" Arturo led them from the restaurant with a spring in his step, and those watching knew he was earning some money today.

"Indeed!" Jim replied to his question about pleasing Abe. Jim knew that Scalini would know that a ship had dropped anchor, and that the Captain had appeared in the hotel and met Arturo, and then purchased fish. It wasn't the best cover, but it would do!

As they walked back to the wharf Arturo kept up a running dialogue about the village, pointing out places of interest to men shopping for their crew. He led them to a dock where five fishing boats were docked, presently unloading their night's catch. Ignoring the hustle and bustle around them he led them up the gangplank of his own vessel and into his galley.

"Here we can talk freely," he assured them, sitting down after pouring himself a cup of coffee. John did likewise, but Jim declined.

"Andrea was taken two days ago, right off the main street. Antonio's men pulled up in their black Mercedes, leaped out, grappled him to the ground, and after binding him hand and foot they stuffed him in the back seat between two of them and drove off. All of this happened in broad daylight!" Arturo repeated with feeling, shaking his head in the negative as if he still had trouble believing.

"What do you know about the house?" John asked quietly, sipping his coffee carefully.

"One of the daily cleaning women is married to one of my men," Arturo said, winking at them outrageously. "She has been wearing a miniature camera pin on her dress for the past three months. As a result, I can give you detailed drawings of the house and furniture, and I can tell you where everybody sleeps. A plane will take pictures of the property again today, and one took pictures last night. The film will be dropped off in the shipment of fish I deliver to your boat. You will know everything I can tell you!"

"How many men does Scalini have at the house, and what kind of armament do they carry?" Jim asked.

"There are fifteen men at the house. One, his personal bodyguard, is the only one you really need to worry about. Antonio does not go anywhere without Leo. Leo is deadly, psychotic, and proud of it. He likes killing and everyone is afraid of him, including our chief of police. There is not much that frightens our chief of police! The others carry various pistols, mostly automatics, mostly nine-millimeter, and one or two carry an FN FNC, two carry the FAMAS. They are not military trained, just thugs with guns. Leo is everything they are not," Arturo warned, watching the two men for their reaction.

"Do you have a decent picture of the men, and especially of Leo?" John asked.

Arturo grinned and reached into his pocket. He pulled out a small envelope of photographs, all black and white. Printed at the bottom of each photo was the name of the subject. Jim looked at the picture of Leo.

"Leonardo Caineli," he mused quietly. There was in his eyes something that told Arturo that Leonardo Caineli was known, and more, that he was despised.

"You know him?" Arturo and John inquired together.

"Yes. He was recruited from the Foreign Legion to GIGN ten years ago. After all their training he became one of their ninety full-time members, until an incident at Loos-les-Lille, a French prison. He was summarily dismissed, and he went to work almost immediately for the Scalini family operations in Djibouti. My team took his operation down two years ago, but he had already been assigned to Antonio. Antonio was just getting out of prison. This is a very evil man," Jim informed them soberly, tapping the picture on the table.

For a moment Arturo studied this strange new young American. He noted the broad shoulders, saw the tightly formed sternocleidomastoid and trapezius muscles that suggested both great physical strength and speed, seeing clearly now a well-trained soldier, a coiled spring, ready for action. Leo might be a powerful man, but his strength was animal strength, not the carefully trained power of the true soldier. Arturo smiled and nodded. His friend Andrea had been correct. These men would handle the situation professionally, and he hoped, quite permanently.

"We will go to the deck now, and the people watching me will see you shake my hand, and everyone will know that I have begun my day with a good sale, no? I allow them to think that I do not know they watch me, and I know each one by name," he winked outrageously once more, putting his finger beside his nose. "But we will not speak of that until later!" Arturo said.

"Everyone will have shore leave from my ship, and my men will be gathering intelligence most of the day. I'll wait until your shipment of fresh fish is delivered," Jim agreed, rising with the other two men. As suggested, they paused on the deck in full view of anyone keeping an eye on them, shaking hands. Arturo was expansive in his thanks, as was his custom, especially when he made a bit of money. Jim and John left Arturo and walked back to the docks where Jack waited patiently.

Although Jim and John never asked for it, the crew treated them with utmost respect when in public. Jack, true to nature, snapped a sharp salute, and Jim and John returned it.

"Back to the boat sir?" Jack asked respectfully.

"Thanks, ensign," Jim replied with a nod and smile.

Operating the boat expertly Jack came along side *Bring It Up Coral*, settling the boat perfectly inside the arms of the sling. Frank Miller operated the lift, bringing the boat up and over the side, and setting it on its cradle so gently no one felt the bottom contact the rubber padding over the steel cradle. Jim, John, and Jack stepped out of the boat and climbed down a ladder to the deck, with deck hands already busy beginning the process of washing away the salt and seawater from the hull.

Half an hour later an old wooden boat, weathered and chugging under the power of a three-cylinder diesel engine, pulled along side. Two large tubs of fresh fish on ice were lifted to the deck with the crane. Abe was on deck to inspect the fish, and when he nodded, Jim handed the check over to Arturo. Sturdy and Abe lifted crates of fish easily and went below with them. In the walk-in freezer they carefully removed the items hidden beneath the fish, and packed the fish carefully in the appointed storage, before returning topside with the empty crates. Half an hour later Arturo and his boat left.

Shortly after lunch several of the crewmembers climbed onto the HSB and were shuttled to the dock by Jack. All of the men and Millie wore their dress uniforms. They appeared to be American crewmembers, coming to shore to visit this quaint village by the sea. In groups of three or four they wandered around, taking pictures of each other, in the background the object of their interest. No one suspected they were anything other than what they appeared.

Hunched over his keyboard, studying the pictures on the monitors before him, Zeke made occasional notes. Several satellite photos enhanced so that the house and cliff on which it was built were clearly visible also appeared on monitors for his scrutiny. At the base of the cliff was a cave, and after careful searching Zeke discovered that the cave was the reason for the location of the house.

In the library Jim and John unearthed some history behind the cave and its many uses over the years, especially during the Second World War. All of that information went to Zeke for his study as well. It was evening by the time he had everything ready for the crew. Nodding to himself he pulled the memory stick from his system, and he connected it to his laptop.

"Uncle Zeke sees everything," he quoted softly to himself as he pushed his chair back and rose to go down for a quick supper.

In the dining room Windy was picking up on subtle changes. It seemed to him that there was an air of expectancy, and again the men were different somehow, though it took him some time to put his finger on what he was feeling. Looking around he suddenly shivered. Several of the men reminded him of a coiled rattlesnake, or a cobra, poised and ready to strike! There was, in the room, an almost tangible aura of death. He walked up to Sturdy and expressed what he was feeling.

"What do you think?" he questioned the giant who had become his mentor and friend. Sturdy looked around the room slowly and then down at Windy.

"They're getting ready for a night insertion into enemy territory." Sturdy said, drying the plate in his hand as he continued to look at the men. "They know that they are mortal, that death could take them tonight. They also know that they might be called upon to kill. None of them like that, but they'll do what's necessary to succeed, and to protect each other. Captain Shepherd has never returned from a mission without all of his men, even though some were wounded. These men are the best I've ever seen. I doubt if any will even get a scratch tonight. Yet they will not allow that thought to take form in their minds. Discipline rules the moment."

"Do you think I would be allowed to watch how everything unfolds?" Windy asked. Sturdy heard the question and knew what lay behind it. He smiled at his friend.

"It would be good for you if you did," Sturdy said, stopping his work of drying dishes long enough to look down at Windy once more. "The men accept you as one of the crew. They won't mind you learning everything you can about how they operate," he added. "See if you can get Stinky to go with you."

Bob Stankus was the crewman with the nickname, Stinky. His attitude left much to be desired because it was usually bad. However, the men knew his background, and so they waited patiently, trusting Abe and Sturdy, and especially Windy, to help him fit into society, or at least their peculiar society. Windy nodded and immediately began talking to his friend, Bob.

After the meal the men moved quietly into the conference room. Windy and Stinky followed them in, along with Doc and Millie, and

Jim Warner. They sat at empty places at the conference table and watched, listened, and learned.

Each position on the table had its own laptop computer open and hooked into Zeke's laptop. Zeke manipulated the computer while Jim talked them through the plan. John and Wade sat quietly, knowing the plan already, because they had worked with Jim to design it. Planning was the key to success in any mission. Jim was a master at military strategy, and John and Wade were not far behind him in skill. Yet all three felt the deep abiding sense of the need to move quickly. It chaffed them that they had to wait an entire day.

When Jim was sure the men knew the plan, and the contingency plans should anything go wrong, he led them down to the weapons chamber. This was a master design, a portion taken from two holds, with retractable bulkhead walls. When closed the doors were undetectable, and only someone with the exact measurements of the holds and design of the ship, and a tape measure, could tell that secret room was there.

Windy was amazed at the amount of equipment the men carried. Each one dressed first in what looked like a wetsuit but was actually a Kevlar body suit. Over this they put on their fatigues, digitally designed shades of gray and black, with some greens and browns thrown in, almost invisible in the darkness. Over these went their vests with pockets for storage, also made of Kevlar, lined with Gortex. A utility belt went on around their waist with more storage, canteen, and other important survival equipment. Oddly enough, each man had twenty-four-inch plastic restraint ties, black, twelve on each side tucked into that belt.

They wore the cabbage patch helmets, Kevlar lined, designed to disguise the human head to unfriendly eyes. Each man also had a Motorola AN/PRC-112 radio for communication. A Trimble Scout M+GPS accompanied their radio equipment. Windy watched as the men checked their weapons. Most of them carried the H&K MP-10SD, silenced, with a laser sight. Jim let his men choose their pistols, and some carried the Beretta M92F, some the H&K Mark 23, and some the Army Colt.

Each team leader carried a tranquilizer pistol in case they encountered the guard dogs obvious from the photos of the day. Frank Miller carried the semtex and plastic explosives.

Fully assembled the men stood in line while Jim checked their packs and vests. This wasn't technically necessary, but he did it before every insertion to make sure nothing was amiss. The men expected and appreciated it. For Jim this was serious business, because this was their very first test as a team in combat.

"Light's out!" Jim commanded into his radio.

On the bridge, Master Chief Warner hit the switch, killing the deck lights. Like shadows the men climbed out of the hold and made their way to the stern where the Rigid Raider sat ready. John and Sparks took the bow, they would be first to set foot on land. Dorf and Mark were right behind them. John's team knew what they had to do, and they were ready. In the middle Jim sat with his team, Zeke, Frank, and Smitty. Astern Wade sat with Jack, C.G., and Vince. Windy and Stinky watched them as the Rigid Raider moved silently away from the ship. Once they were beyond the reach of the deck lights Jim Warner turned them back on.

Phantom Force

Reaching the shore fifty yards from the cave entrance, JR and Sparks leaped out, weapons ready, moving about five paces up and crouching, their heads turning from side to side slowly. Dorf and Mark dragged the raider up on the beach, and after the other teams were out, covered the boat with a camouflage net.

Climbing the cliff was done in silence, every motion carefully orchestrated to avoid dislodging small stones, or cracking any branches. This was the type of activity that took time and care, and when the men were anxious to arrive, they had to exercise great discipline to move slowly and deliberately. All of them hated it, but understood the need, and so discipline carried the moment.

Jim, now in the lead, marveled at the skill of his men. They were as silent as the grave. Twenty minutes later everyone was up and over the ledge of the cliff, huddled in the shadow below the ten-foot wall that surrounded the Scalini house. Dorf cupped his huge hands and Mark stepped into them and was lifted easily to peek over the wall. After about forty-five seconds he lifted his right arm away from his body and held up two fingers, then dipped them, signifying there were two guards on the second-floor balcony of the house, and two patrolling the grounds.

"No dogs outside that I can see," he whispered, once he was on the ground again. "The two guards on the balcony are looking our way, but they are smoking and talking. The two on the ground are walking the perimeter. Judging their pace and the distances I think it would be best to go over another portion of the wall. If we go over the east wall, I think we can take the guards without raising any alarms."

Jim nodded and led the men to the east wall, about halfway from the main gates. Dorf lifted him up so he could look over the wall. He waited for a moment until he could see all four guards through his night vision goggles. Silently he lifted himself up and dropped over the other side, bending his knees, landing on his toes, making no sound. Wade dropped beside him, then John, then C.G. and Vince almost together. Mark came last, and Jim smiled. At only four feet distance he barely heard their feet touch the ground. Not one of the guards was aware an enemy force had invaded his territory.

C.G. and Vince raced to the side of the house silently, then leaped up and carefully climbed onto the second-floor balcony. Jim was poised to shoot if either of the guards turned their way, but they didn't. Mark and Wade took the two walking around the perimeter. One of the men was relieving himself in the bushes. He heard a muffled thud, turning just in time to see a shadow rise up and strike. On the balcony the guards went down with equal speed. Restraint ties were employed, binding the men and then gags were inserted in their mouths and duct tape applied to keep them in place.

Jim signaled that the coast was clear for the rest of the men to come over the fence with two clicks of his microphone. He watched them come over, Dorf last, lifting his huge body easily over the wall and dropping silently to the other side. He led the men to the second-floor balcony where Mark picked one of the outer sliding glass door locks. Dorf sprayed the runners at the top and bottom with WD40 lubricant before they silently slid the door open. This room was an exercise room, and empty at that hour of the night. They were in undetected.

Mark pulled a round object from one of his vest pockets. It looked very much like a hockey puck. Silently he moved out into the hall and to the door of a room where six guards slept. He carefully opened the door wide enough to slide the object into the center of the room, and once he rotated the top of the object, he slid it in and closed the door just as carefully. Moving to the next room he repeated the operation, and twelve of the guards were rendered unconscious. The gas was quick acting and long lasting. None of the men would awaken for about eighteen hours. When they did, all of them would have terrible headaches and most of them would vomit.

There were women and children in the other rooms upstairs, so the men silently moved to the steps and made their way down. Two Mastiff's rose to their feet, only to sink to the floor with soft whines as John and Jim fired their tranquilizer pistols together. Hugging the walls as they traveled down the steps, they came to the first floor. There was one guard posted on this floor, and he was in the living room, by the front door, the flickering light of a television reflecting on his face. Wade used his tranquilizer pistol. That guard raised his hand halfway to his neck before slumping forward unconscious. Wade carefully glided across the floor, removed the dart, and arranged the guard so he looked like he'd fallen asleep. When he was satisfied the guard was postured correctly, he moved away. Jim watched him work and grinned as his friend returned to the group. He gave Wade a thumbs up and a nod before turning to lead the men further into the house.

Jim led the way to the kitchen, where a door opened to the basement. Zeke stepped to the door and visually checked it for alarms, then ran a sensor along the door jam. He nodded to Dorf to spray the hinges, then to Jim to open the door. Like passing shadows they ghosted through the door and made their way cautiously into the cellar. It was here they knew they would find a hidden entrance to the cave structure beneath the house.

Wade stepped forward as Jim halted everyone else, knowing it was his observation Jim needed most. His interest in engineering and consequent studies would now be put to the test. Standing in the center of the room he turned three hundred and sixty degrees. Slowly he walked around the room, looking closely at each wall. None of them knew how to access those tunnels, but Jim and John had faith that Wade would figure it out. Finally, he stopped in front of the wine rack, which covered an entire wall. Smiling back at the men he stepped forward suddenly and put his hand on one of the bottles. Pushing it, getting it right the first time, activated the hidden spring and part of the wine rack swung open.

"Under two minutes!" John whispered in his ear. "Show-off!"

"Signal here, Shep!" Sparks warned, pointing to two wires at one corner juncture of the secret door.

"We'll expect company. Leo and his boss, I imagine," Jim whispered back.

Once through the secret entrance Wade pushed a button on the wall and the door closed behind them. The tunnel that had been excavated to the caves below was similar in construction to a mine, and lights were hung every eight feet, single bulbs, shining dully in the subterranean darkness. In that tunnel noise was amplified, so the men moved carefully, making sure none of their metallic gear made contact or noise.

A shriek of pain, cut off by hoarse coughing, followed by a groan stopped the men in their tracks. They could clearly hear two men cruelly laughing. Quickly now they made their way to a steel door, thirty yards from the basement entrance. There was a small window with three bars in it. Jim looked in and saw two men standing over a third, who was shackled to the wall, his naked body covered with blood and bruises. It was Andrea. There was still life in the old man, for he suddenly lashed out with a foot, catching one of the guards, square in the groin. A shriek of pain from the guard told Jim Andrea's aim had been perfect. The other guard began hitting him.

Using the noise to mask what he was doing Jim motioned to Dorf to pull the hinges. After pulling them, Dorf grabbed the bars of the window and silently moved the door off its hinges, lifting it, and setting it aside. The other guard had recovered enough to stamp hard on Andrea's knee. He was raising his foot for another kick when strong hands plucked him off the ground and hurled him head-first against the stone wall of the prison cell.

His partner fared no better. From behind Wade kicked him solidly in the groin hard enough to lift him from the floor. The sound he made was horrible, a high-pitched squeal, cut off as he lost consciousness from a quick blow to the side of his head. Through cracked, blackened swollen, and bleeding lips Andrea grinned crookedly up at the two men removing the shackles from his hands. They were swollen and white, bloody around the wrists, and his arms fell limply at his side when they were released. For a few minutes he slumped forward, gritting his teeth against the pain.

Jim popped open an ampoule of Morphine and punched the needle into Andrea's arm, squeezing the bulb tightly to release the drug. A moment later Andrea leaned back against the wall as the pain miraculously stopped. During this operation Jim took note of the state of Andrea's body.

"Thank you, my friend," Andrea groaned quietly.

"C.G. You've got the most trauma training. Let's see if we can do something for Andrea," John said quietly. C.G. nodded and opened his medical kit, taking John's as well. He began to work on the contusions and cuts, starting with Andrea's face and working down.

The two guards who had abused Andrea were beginning to stir. Vince and FM looked at one another, since they were standing guard over them, and both men put aside their weapons and knelt down beside the captives. Jim heard sudden yells of pain and looked over to see Vince and FM breaking fingers. After the fingers they each snapped the left wrist of the prisoners. Eyes opened in shock the two men tried to bite back their screams, but they could not. Calmly Vince and FM stood up. They looked at Jim with blank faces, then at Andrea, and back again at Jim and he understood. He nodded curtly.

"Company coming, Shep!" Mark Drumheiser, who was watching the corridor turned his head to speak into the room.

"How many?" Jim asked quietly.

"Two. One does a good impression of the Rock of Gibraltar: the other is middle-aged and small. Looks like Mr. Scalini and his watchdog, Leo," Mark replied.

"Got it, Shep." Wade said quietly, stepping through the door to join Mark. He had his Mac 10 extended and the laser sight on. The laser sight centered on Leo's chest and the huge man stopped in his tracks. Antonio Scalini moved a few tentative steps forward and paused. He took in the outfits and professional movements.

"So. The local police called in GIGN," he said softly. "You have invaded my home. Do you know who I am?" he said authoritatively. Leo raised his hands when the red dot didn't move from his chest, and the man holding the gun did not look away.

"He comes often in the night to listen to me scream," Andrea commented dreamily, his eyes closed. His voice was barely a whisper. C.G. passed the information to Jim quietly.

"We are not Groupe d'Intervention Gendarmeria Nationale," Jim said, stepping out into the corridor. "We are Americans, and you kidnapped our uncle and crewmember, Andrea Orvieto. In answer to your question; yes! We know exactly who and what you are. Jim held Scalini's eyes for a moment and then spoke in perfect Italian. *"Piacere di fare la sua conoscenza po' pervertire. Po' fancuilla. Po' femminile."*

"Come, prego?" Antonio spit between clenched teeth. "I am Don Antonio Scalini! If I say you die, you die!" he said in English.

"Sono morte, viola del pensiero." Jim clipped the words curtly, his green eyes hard.

"I think that upset him, boss," Mark commented with a grin. "What did you say?" Mark spoke Italian, but he knew that many of the crew didn't.

"I called him a pervert, a maiden, and a woman. Then I told him I was death and called him a pansy," Jim replied evenly, keeping Scalini's eyes.

"He definitely didn't like that!" Mark said with a chuckle, and Jim heard the rest of his crew chuckling in the background. The result was as he expected. Scalini drew himself up on his toes, prepared to speak, but Jim spoke first.

"You're a little behind there, Tony," Jim said calmly. "We've only begun, and when we're done, we will walk out of here and no one will learn of us, or of our presence here. As far as you and your giant friend are concerned, we are ghosts, leaving no evidence of our presence other than the obvious wounds we inflict."

"You are very brave with all your guns. Put them down and face me like a man!" Scalini spat, leaning forward, his fists clenched as though he himself would do the fighting. Jim laughed. For a moment he thought about this megalomaniac, and the words he'd just spoken. It was obvious that Scalini was over the edge mentally.

"Actually, you want Leo to have a crack at us," Jim said. "Alright. I'm going to take all of Leo's guns and weapons, and then I'm going to show you that you are powerless, and that what I say is absolutely true," Jim turned his attention on Leo.

"Leo, carefully remove your weapons. Start with the FN Five-seveN under your left arm."

Leo started, wondering how the man knew what weapons he carried. Carefully he pulled the small 5.7-mm pistol from its holster and dropped it on the floor. If looks could kill, Jim would be dead right now, but Jim ignored the stare.

"Good boy. Now take the knives from both sleeves," Jim commanded.

Leo obeyed, noting that the red dot on his chest hadn't wavered at all. He was sweating, hoping Jim would allow him a chance to fight. Leo was vicious, believing that no one could take him in a fight, fair or not. Already he was considering how he would kill Jim first.

"Okay, now take both of the .38s in your ankle holsters and add them to the pile, and then the knife hanging just behind your neck. Carefully remove the two throwing knives tucked into your belt buckle and last, take the Glock 17 you have tucked into your belt behind your back and put it on the pile."

Leo's eyes opened wide as Jim went through every weapon he carried. It was unnerving how calm the man was. Even more frightening was that the man seemed to know every weapon he carried, where he carried it, and what it was! *How had he come by such intelligence?*

"Mark, secure the pansy," Jim commanded quietly. Mark went to Scalini and carefully patted him down, relieving him of his only weapon, an FN Five-seveN in his bathrobe pocket. Without ceremony Mark took his arm and dragged him into the cell.

Watching Leo, Jim removed his vest, utility belt, weapons, laying all of them aside carefully. Finally, he removed his headset communication gear and helmet and put them on the floor. He motioned Leo to proceed him into the prison cell, and Leo, with his hands up, did as he was instructed. Wade never moved that sight from Leo's body, and the man knew that Wade would shoot him the moment he stepped out of line.

Inside the cell there was plenty of room. Jim's team moved to the sides to stay out of the way, saying nothing, showing nothing in their faces. Leo looked around at them, and stopped with Dorf, who seemed to be the most powerful man in the room. He was a little surprised that he was not required to fight Dorf, but he still had no doubts about his skills in fighting.

When Jim nodded Wade lowered his weapon and like a raging bull Leo charged at Jim, expecting the smaller man to spin away to the left or right. Having measured and weighed Jim in his mind Leo expected his height and weight to be an advantage. At six-feet two-inches in height and two hundred plus pounds in weight Jim would be no match for Leo's four-inch advantage and seventy or eighty pounds of pure bull muscle. With his extensive training he knew that he had an advantage in a fight against most men. Hurting people was something he loved. Most men didn't. Correctly he read Jim, knowing he was one of the honorable ones, one who didn't like hurting people. That too was an advantage. At least those were his thoughts.

The blow, when it came, surprised Leo, stopping his charge and standing him straight up. Jim lashed out with his left leg, hooking Leo behind the right knee, slamming him to the floor back first. Leo's head rang from the blow and all the air rushed out of his lungs. Desperately he rolled, not away, but into Jim, only to see his opponent completing a front flip over him, and then his back was turned to his enemy. In fury he lashed back with a leg, hoping to find Jim, but his leg found only air and he leaped to his feet, spinning around, desperately looking for his elusive enemy. Remembering the power of that blow he thought quickly. He wasn't nearly quick enough.

Jim's foot slammed into the side of his neck, physically flipping him over to land again on the hard rock floor of the cavern, dazed and confused. A savvy fighter, he didn't stop moving, rolling away and to his feet again, this time keeping Jim in sight. He was a hard man, and had taken two hard hits, but he had plenty of stamina left. Feinting to his left he drove a straight kick at Jim's chest, but without wind he was slower than he intended.

The American seemed to flow forward, catching and stopping his kick, and his right foot slammed into Leo's groin. Too late he tensed the muscles of his powerful thighs, and the toe of that military boot connected with his genitals with stunning force. Gasping in pain and surprised he ground his teeth. Jim pivoted and kicked his left leg out from beneath him. His face hit the rock first, breaking his nose and several of his teeth and he bellowed in rage and pain.

Jim, still holding a leg twisted the right leg and slammed his left foot down hard on Leo's femur, tearing the greater trochanter and neck of the femur from the hip, and snapping the femur near the center. Leo screamed in pain, jerked away and tried to stand. Jim kicked his right arm out from under him and he fell awkwardly. Stepping in Jim grasped his left hand, turned it in painfully, lifted and twisted the arm back and with his knee snapped the humerus. The bone erupted from Leo's tortured flesh spraying blood. Finally, Jim's foot connected with the side of his neck and he knew no more.

Antonio Scalini stared in horror at the broken body of his champion. He had seen Leo wade into a crowd of a dozen men bent on killing him and come out victorious! Jim knelt on Leo's back, ruthlessly strapping his hands together, back-to-back, with plastic restraint ties. He did the same with Leo's feet. Finally, he looked up at Antonio, and for the first time in his life Antonio understood terror.

His mind was numbed, and he saw himself suffering what he had done to dozens of unfortunate people. Somehow, instinctively, he knew that he would never hold that power again. The thought unnerved him completely and he fought desperately for the bravado that had served him so well over the years.

John and Wade brought Jim's gear to him and Jim silently put on everything until his gear was complete. The minutes dragged out and Antonio shook and sweated, his heart racing, the fear building until he could barely stand it.

"Take his clothes off," Jim ordered, putting his headset back on and the helmet in place.

Vince and C.G. grasped Antonio and tore every ounce of clothing from his aged flaccid body. Antonio's face flamed at the shame and humiliation of standing naked in front of these men. *How many men did I humiliate in this fashion? Andrea was the last!* His thoughts raced. He was shackled with the same shackles he'd used for Andrea, naked and helpless, shivering from the cold and fear. In his mind he did not think things could get any worse, but movement from the men surrounding him proved him wrong. Color slowly drained from his face as each man pulled a deadly knife, with a flat black blade, only the sharpened edges gleaming in the flickering light of the room.

"Today we're going to teach you a lesson," Jim stated calmly, matter-of-factly. "From this day forward you will behave yourself. You will not engage in any illegal activity. At no time will you threaten or hurt any person for any reason. If you do, we will hear of it and we will hunt you down and finish this lesson in a way that will shock your world. There is no death for you, only humiliation and fear!"

Nodding to C.G. and Vince Jim watched dispassionately as they each grabbed a lower leg and lifted his feet from the floor. Jim produced a hard, plastic rod, three eights of an inch in diameter, about six inches long. Wondering how something that small could hurt him Scalini felt the first blow on the bottom of his feet, wincing with the pain. Surprised and frightened by the sudden and building pain with each blow it got worse until he was screaming. His feet felt like someone was holding them to a hot flame!

Finally, mercifully, it stopped, and the two men simply dropped his legs. His whole body shook with the pain but there was more. Jim found nerves and put pressure on those nerves until Scalini was weeping and begging for his life, sure he was going to die. Terrified beyond reason Scalini smelled urine and feces and knew it was his own. Finally, Jim knelt in front of him, filling all his vision was that sharp point of a Cold Steel Recon Tanto knife, and Jim held it almost against his right eye.

"You will tell no one who did this. When you are rescued you may go home or anywhere else, but you leave this island forever. Remember, I know you. I can find you wherever you go. There isn't a hole deep enough that you can crawl into that I cannot find you. And you will always be reminded of what is to come if you disobey, every time you look into a mirror."

Antonio stared at the knife blade in terror, and suddenly it flicked down, slicing his eyelid in half! For a moment he thought his eye had been cut out, unable to see through the blood, but as he thrashed about in pain, he realized somehow that it was still there. Strong hands seized him and held him still, and with his good eye he watched each soldier approach, and each make a painful cut until he was sure he would bleed to death. After the last cut they sheathed their knives and stood looking down at him, knowing the pain from them over the weeks of healing would be ample reminder of what he'd suffered. It was quite obvious that the pain was growing exponentially. Scalini was panting from the pain.

Andrea asked for a slip of paper, and he wrote upon it in an unsteady hand and then pinned it to Scalini's chest. On the note were the simple words: *In Memory of My Beloved Caterina.*

Jim understood. Once, a long time ago, Andrea loved a young woman who lived on his home island of Crete. But Caterina's father was a grasping soul, seeking to raise himself above others through contacts with the Mafia. When he learned that Antonio Scalini thought his daughter was beautiful, he arranged a marriage for her, sure that she would live a life of luxury, even if she was never loved.

Andrea didn't know anything about Antonio, except that he was wealthy. Thinking that Caterina would benefit by marrying into a wealthy family, he withdrew from her, to her father's secret delight. Caterina had never expressed her love for Andrea, but she loved him desperately. Shortly after her marriage she realized that Antonio was a psychopath, and she lived in fear. After a year of marriage, she wrote to Andrea, pleading with him to rescue her. That was what brought Andrea to Corsica, where Antonio brought her to live, imprisoning her in the house on that hill.

Yet Andrea was too late. Antonio learned that his wife had written and in a fit of rage killed her. No body was ever found. Antonio claimed that Andrea kidnapped her, but he was able to prove that he had not yet reached the island or been a part of that. And so, Andrea stayed, and watched, and when he learned enough, he contacted the F.B.I. in America, who followed up on his tip and caught Antonio red-handed. Antonio went to prison for ten years, and though he believed Andrea had been involved in turning him over to the authorities, he could never prove it.

Their bitter feud lasted many years, and Andrea, working mostly for British Intelligence as an informant, was never connected to Antonio's failed ventures. Antonio never moved against Andrea until now. Perhaps in his old age he thought he was beyond the reach of justice. He would long rue the day that he had kidnapped and tortured Andrea Orvieto. But he would never tell anyone about the Americans who came to his home. This he knew deep in his heart. His fear shamed him, and he realized that he was indeed helpless. The cuts began to burn, and he felt bile rising in his throat. The men left him there, his vomit covering most of the front of his body, alone in the darkness, helpless, feeling as though at any moment he might die.

Jim made sure Andrea was comfortable and stable and then opened both of Scalini's safes, photographing every piece of paper and every lire-note that was contained in them. It was Zeke, handing papers to Jim to photograph, who whistled while reading a page of names, obviously men and women who had accepted bribes for services. He pointed to a name near the middle and Jim's eyebrows rose. It was the name of an American, a high-ranking military officer, a name that was on Jim's list of suspects in the new terrorist activities at home. His eyes met Zeke's.

I'll photograph it, and then I want you to redact that name from the list," Jim said after a moment of thought. Zeke nodded and did as directed.

Mark and Dorf went through the caverns leading down to the sea and photographed everything in the various chambers and caverns that they discovered. Once they were finished, they led the teams through the tunnels, leaving the house through the cave, launched the Rigid Raider, and silently faded into the early morning darkness.

Unable to sleep, Windy remained on the deck, and was surprised when the boat suddenly appeared at the stern. He quickly counted heads and sighed when he counted thirteen. Everyone had returned. Jim happened to be watching him and he grinned as he climbed to the deck.

"Worried some of us might not have come back?" he asked quietly.

"Well, yes!" Windy admitted. "That's always a possibility, isn't it?" he asked.

"It is," Jim said, watching as two of the men carried Andrea's stretcher down to sickbay while the others secured the Rigid Raider in its cradle and then washed it down, washing the salt residue away, even scrubbing down the deck beneath. Windy did not speak while this went on but worked shoulder to shoulder with the men as they cleaned. Finally, Jim looked down at him as the job was completed.

"How do you live with it?" Windy asked, almost afraid of the question.

"We accept it. That's why we train so hard every day, going over the basics again and again until they become second nature. One mistake could kill anyone of us, or several of us. Discipline and training will give us an edge, a better chance of survival. We've all been wounded, so we all know the reality of our own mortality. That too gives us an edge. If our edge is sharp enough, we'll come back.

Windy followed them down into the weapons room where they stripped down their weapons, cleaned and oiled them, before storing them properly in their containers. He noted that they used a specific cleaner on their knives and sheaths and asked why.

"Cleans away the blood and DNA evidence." C.G. answered gruffly. Windy blanched, noting that every knife had been taken and cleaned.

The men didn't chatter during this time. They were serious about what they were doing. Not until everything was satisfactory and stored properly, and the men were walking together toward the galley did they relax. Windy saw in this their dedication to detail and professionalism and was duly impressed.

Jim and John split off to visit Andrea in sickbay while the rest of the men went tiredly to the galley. Windy served them cold drinks or coffee and listened to the talk about the mission. They didn't talk about what they did, they talked about how their equipment had worked, and how the team had performed, which irritated Windy who wanted to know all that had taken place.

When the Captain and his brother returned from their brief visit to Andrea Jim invited the men into the conference room for a debriefing. He asked Windy to bring him an iced tea and to bring John a cup of coffee. Windy was quick to fill his order and sat at an empty space in the conference room as the men dissected their evening activities.

Jim went through every part of the mission, asking the men to comment on everything pertaining to equipment and weapons, and Windy learned much about the workings of the military mind when it came to an actual mission. They had to think of so many different things, be prepared for anything, and as he listened to them dissect the mission, he realized that men who participated in special operations were a breed apart. When Jim had satisfied his list of questions Frank Miller spoke up.

"Why'd you decide to fight Leo, boss?" FM asked softly. Every man looked at Jim who thought a few moments before answering. The question caught Windy by surprise.

"Men like Leo have a code. I didn't want him coming after any of my crew, or Andrea. So, I made sure that he knew what to expect if he did," Jim looked around the room, meeting the eyes of his men. FM nodded.

"He won't," FM said with a chuckle. "Up until tonight he thought he was invincible. I watched the way he went after you, even when he was hurt. That type always learns too late that nobody is invincible. After tonight he'll know he can die, and that knowledge will either drive him over the edge or sober him."

"Time will tell," Wade said, nodding in agreement. "I am convinced he was sobered by what happened. Jim didn't just beat him. He incapacitated him first, and Leo knew that had Jim wanted to, he could easily have taken his life."

CHAPTER 15

Unexpected Gift

Chief Inspector Étienne Marchand picked up the receiver of his telephone and listened to the excited voice speaking from the Scalini house. One of the daily women who came in early to cook breakfast for the family was the caller. For ten years the Scalini family had been a thorn in his side, but that was why he'd volunteered for this post.

Antonio, unlike his father, was a mean little psychopath with connections to a family that influenced the governments of France and Italy equally. Instinctively he knew that he had been handed a unique opportunity. A family member would not have called in the police. The daily cook was acting on impulse, which was fortunate for Chief Inspector Marchand.

He put down the receiver and then lifted it again, punching in the number for their local medical clinic. An ambulance, and medical personnel, were needed at the Scalini home, but they were to wait until the police gave them permission to enter the compound. The head nurse at the clinic heard and understood. Looking across the room at his second in command, Jacques Martineau, Étienne grinned. Martineau had been here when Étienne came, and served faithfully these ten years.

"There is an emergency at the Scalini home. Get all the men on active duty immediately and tell them to meet us there," he ordered.

"We are going in first?" Jacques asked, surprised.

"We have been invited. I do not anticipate any danger. But tell the men to hurry," Étienne replied.

Jacques called in the duty sergeant and gave the orders for all the men to be activated and sent to the Scalini home immediately. He stressed that the Chief Inspector was taking him alone into the compound first. The sergeant understood and hurried to get the men organized and moving. Some would need to be called, awakened, and informed. Others were already at the station, some getting ready to go home, others getting ready to start their day.

Jacques drove the Citroën through the open gate and parked at the front door entrance. Étienne got out of the car and saw the daily cook waving frantically from the front door. Straightening his uniform coat, he stepped around the car and walked with Jacques up the steps and into the house.

"Quickly! It is terrible!" the cook said breathlessly. She led them into the kitchen, down the steps into the basement and pointed at the opening in the wine rack. "The master is down there! He is hurt badly. You must go to him quickly!" she panted.

Étienne studied the wine rack opening, and then nodded for Jacques to follow him into the corridor. He could clearly hear someone weeping, and painful groans from someone else. Quickening his pace, he found the cell door, removed and set aside, and looking in he gasped. Don Antonio Scalini was unconscious, shackled to the far wall, his face and body bloody from a sliced eyelid and a dozen nasty cuts and covered with foul-smelling bile. The hands above his head were white and swollen. Two of his men lay lashed securely with restraint ties, one weeping, the other moaning in pain.

Leo also lay on the floor, but he was silent. His eyes were open, and he blinked when Chief Inspector Marchand stepped into the room. Other than that, he made no sound, and did not move. Étienne saw why he didn't move and sucked in a horrified breath. Pulling his radio from his belt he called for immediate backup and medical help. He sent Jacques up to escort everyone down.

Moving over to Antonio he squatted down and studied the cut on the eyelid. There were other cuts on the body that would be excruciating. One eye was open, because the eyelid had been neatly sliced in two. The other eye was closed. Antonio was breathing shallowly and looked to be in shock. Pinned to his chest, the pin going right through the skin was Andrea's note. Gently and carefully Étienne unlocked the shackles and stretched Antonio out, then lifted his feet, resting them on a wad of clothes that were probably Antonio's.

Men poured into the room, policemen and emergency medical technicians and the village doctor. She moved from patient to patient, administering Morphine. Quickly diagnosing that Antonio was in shock she directed the emergency medical team in treating him. Looking hard at Étienne she ordered that all four men be moved immediately to the clinic. The Chief Inspector smiled politely and nodded his head in the affirmative.

Étienne directed two men to explore the caves. He went upstairs and began searching the house. On the second floor they found the rest of the men asleep, and they were alarmed when they were unable to wake them. Almost overlooking the gas canister Étienne bent down and lifted it, raised his eyebrows, and produced an evidence bag. Another was found in the room with the other enforcers that Antonio retained. Whistling happily, he called the doctor and asked her to return to examine and move the men to the clinic.

A safe in Antonio's bedroom, and one in his office lay open. Étienne raised his eyebrows again. On a table and the bed everything in the safe had been laid out carefully, as if someone wished to photograph it. It was the same in the office. Taking advantage of the situation Étienne ordered his forensic team to photograph this evidence as well. There was more evidence than he had anticipated finding in a lifetime!

People began to stir, the women and children, awakened by the noise and activity. None of them suggested that the police leave. They huddled in fearful silence in the living room, where the night guard still sat unconscious in his chair. Even when he was removed, they said nothing. Étienne questioned them and learned that they heard nothing during the night and were unaware of what had happened. When he told them, he noted that the women looked at each other in surprise, seeming somehow to relax. Perhaps they lived here in fear. Vexed at the lack of information he moved on to the daily help only to discover that the gate was open, and the front door. They had entered unsuspecting.

It wasn't until near evening that his men finished their investigation and began the exodus. Taking advantage of the absence of anyone to object, Étienne had searched the entire house, the garage, and outbuildings. What was hidden in the caverns below the house was enough to ensure that Antonio served a long sentence in prison. That coupled with the evidence from the opened safes was a major coup for Marchand. But he was an experienced police officer, and there were no answers yet to his questions.

At the clinic he learned from the two men that a dozen commandos were responsible for the attack. One of the men believed they were GIGN because of the precision of their attack and their weapons. Étienne knew that to be impossible. GIGN would alert him if they were moving against Scalini. From Leo he learned that a single American soldier had inflicted his wounds, while the other eleven watched. Leo was shaken to the core, having been defeated so soundly by just one man. They were soldiers, Leo was positive about that. They came to rescue Andrea Orvieto.

From a terrified Antonio he learned nothing. Where there had been bravado and bluster there were now tears, and cringing terror. Scalini begged him not to ask any questions as if afraid he might slip and give information he might regret. It was a very thoughtful Étienne who exited the clinic and made his way slowly to his office, several doors down. Looking at all the evidence that had been gathered, and the clues he had before him, he made a decision after sitting and thinking for half an hour. Perhaps, he thought, he would get some answers. He called Jacques into his office.

"Call down to the harbor and ask the harbormaster to prepare the patrol boat. We are going to pay a visit to our American sailors on their ship." He said without inflection. Smiling as he said it his eyes danced with some inner thought.

"Bring It Up Coral?" Jacques asked, somewhat surprised. "Her registry is out of Boston, Massachusetts in America. She is a deep-sea salvage and rescue boat, owned by two brothers. I do not think there are soldiers aboard."

"We shall see," Étienne replied with a tired smile. "I would like to question Andrea Orvieto, and I believe he will be on board that boat."

Coming alongside the American vessel Marchand was impressed. Gleaming with fresh paint she floated proudly in the water. Men were busy on the deck. Marchand counted six of them, two scrubbing down what looked like a submersible, one checking the helicopter lashed to the deck, two oiling chains, and one standing at the side as if to greet them.

"Permission to come on board," Étienne made the request in passable English and was pleased when the man replied in perfect French.

"Please, you are welcome. The Captain is expecting you. Follow me, if you please, and I will take you to him," Mark replied.

Mark led them right up to the bridge, opened the door, and motioned for them to precede him. Once everyone was inside Mark snapped off a smart salute.

"The men you were expecting, sir," he said.

"Thanks, Mark." Jim responded. "I'm Jim Shepherd, the Captain of this vessel. Welcome," he too spoke in French. "I expect you are here to see Andrea Orvieto. He's a member of my crew and is at present in sickbay. If you'll follow me, I'll take you down there."

"I am Chief Inspector Étienne Marchand, and this is my second, Jacques Martin," Marchand introduced himself with a slight bow and shook hands with Jim. Jacques did likewise.

"I am honored to make your acquaintance," Jim replied, leading them down the steps two decks to the sickbay. "This is our ship's physician, Dr. Charles Wozniac, and our chief nurse, Millie," he followed by way of introduction. "I believe you already know Andrea," he added.

"Étienne, my friend!" Andrea said with feeling as Marchand came to his bedside. "Now you can stop worrying about me, eh? I am rescued!"

"That is good news. For three days I tried every avenue to get help, but none was available, my friend! I know you know that to be true. But enough of that! I have many questions, many unanswered questions! Are you feeling well enough to answer some questions?" Marchand asked. He looked over at the doctor as he spoke, and Charles nodded with a smile.

"Andrea is a tough old buzzard," he said when Jim translated the question. Jim translated that answer into French and Marchand smiled.

From Andrea he learned that Antonio kidnapped him to extort money from the sale of his fishing business. Andrea explained that he was joining his nephews in the salvage business. He told the inspector that one of the soldiers who rescued him gave him Morphine at the time of his rescue and he remembered very little other than the fact that his rescuers were soldiers. Describing their outfits, and the weapons they carried, he added that they were elite troops. He had awakened in the care of Dr. Wozniac and his lovely wife, simply overjoyed to know he was in good hands and rescued from the clutches of Antonio Scalini.

Étienne listened and watched as Andrea spoke. When his missive was finished, the Chief Inspector closed his notebook and looked thoughtfully at Jim.

"Would you permit me to search your vessel?" he asked after a long pause.

"But of course!" Jim replied enthusiastically. "I can accompany you, or you can search it on your own. Whichever you prefer!"

Marchand thought about that. "Perhaps Jacques can look around on his own, and you can take me through your vessel," he suggested.

Jim was as good as his word. He took Marchand through the entire vessel, from top to bottom, showing the Chief Inspector everything but the hidden weapons room. Impressed with the modern technology of the bridge and engine room, and the equipment for salvage, he listened as Jim enthusiastically described everything in detail. It was nearing evening when he met with Jacques again. Jacques shook his head marginally in the negative. There were no soldiers on board, no uniforms, and no military weapons. When they were alone for a moment Jacques leaned in and whispered.

"There are no weapons on this vessel, other than three shotguns for skeet shooting, and a handgun in the Captain's desk drawer," Jacques whispered. "No one even lifted an eyebrow if I opened cabinets or drawers," he stopped speaking as Jim approached the pair, and he smiled at the Captain. Impressed with the neatness and orderliness of the boat he thought much of Jim.

"I would like to invite both of you to dine with us this evening, Chief Inspector," Jim suggested, when Jacques had moved away from Étienne's ear.

"We would be delighted," Marchand responded. "I will send our boat back to shore and call for it when we are finished."

"We can take you ashore in our boat. It would be an honor," Jim said.

So, Marchand and Jacques found themselves in the dining room, where they met the entire crew. Marchand could easily pick out the twelve men who could have rescued Andrea. The fact remained, however, that no weapons were found on the vessel. He had been shown the interior of the submersible, the helicopter, and both boats. Jim opened lockers everywhere to show him how neatly the men stored their equipment. Yet he knew that they must be here, somewhere.

After a superb dinner he stood on the afterdeck with Jim while some of the crew lowered the HSB into the water.

"I am glad that Andrea was rescued," Marchand said, at last, breaking the silence. "I am also glad that I can report that I have searched this vessel, and that there are no unusual weapons on board, and no military unit hidden somewhere. The men who brought Andrea here, did you see them?"

"Yes, I did," Jim replied evenly. "They were elite troops, soldiers who believe in a strict code, good and decent men. You would have liked them."

"Yes. I believe I would. There are few men who can reach into the secret criminal world of men like Antonio Scalini unscathed. Their reach is deadly, but just. Such men will always be welcome here. They have done us a great service. I myself requested a GIGN unit to help rescue Andrea, but my request was denied. I hope you understand that," Marchand said.

"Chief Inspector, you are a good man. You see much. Andrea told me as much this morning. I am glad that we could meet under these circumstances. If I can ever be of service to you, feel free to call," Jim handed him a business card.

"Perhaps I too can be of assistance to you and your fine crew some day in the future. Please let them know that they are welcome in our village anytime." Chief Inspector Marchand shook Jim's hand warmly, bowed his head once in farewell, and stepped into the HSB. He and Jacques chose to stand beside Jack in the front of the boat as the engines roared to life and Jack spun the wheel expertly, moving away from the ship and making a short arch around her stern to head for the harbor docks.

Étienne put a hand on the spotlight beside the windshield. His fingers explored the base and took note of the strength of the mount. He smiled to himself and said nothing until Jack had deposited both of them at the dock. Together the two policemen watched the boat pull away and head back to the ship. As they walked up the wooden platform to the quay where their vehicle was parked, he spoke.

"That was a formidable crew," he said softly, listening to the echo of his footsteps. Jacques remained silent waiting for his superior to complete his thoughts. "It was a twelve-man unit, elite troops, and all twelve of them were on that ship. We sat with them and ate with them."

"But the weapons!" Jacques exclaimed. "I searched that vessel from top to bottom Chief Inspector."

"Yet I am sure they were there. I doubt if anyone will ever discover their secret, even if they had a week to search the vessel. No, Jacques, my friend, these are dangerous men, but they are on our side. Whoever they are, whatever they are, they will help us if we are ever in need. We too will help them. If you get any requests for aid from them, you will respond immediately and provide it!" Étienne commanded emphatically.

He gave a little laugh as he waited by his door for Jacques to unlock it from the driver's side. For the first time in ten years he felt that a great weight had been lifted from his shoulders. Then he sighed. The reports would take weeks to generate, and months would pass before this incident would finally be put behind them. Then would come the trial for Scalini and for Leo. Both would be put in prison for a long time if he was careful with the evidence. That was the nature of his work, and he loved it. He opened his door and sat down, a satisfied man who had received a great gift. On the short ride to the station he remained silent.

Early the next morning activity on the afterdeck centered on getting the CH-53D Sea Stallion helicopter ready for flight. Andrea was being airlifted to Nice along with Dr. Wozniac, Millie, and the flight crew. Dorf would pilot the craft, and Mark would be the copilot. John and Wade accompanied them as part of the flight crew. Once the rotors were unfolded and the pre-starting checks were completed Dorf fired up the engines and began the preflight checks.

With a cream and turquoise fuselage and the *Bring It Up* emblem painted neatly on the tail boom, she looked more like the Super Cobra than the Sea Stallion to those who were used to seeing it painted a dull gray. It was registered as a research and rescue helicopter. Andrea was helped on board; the rear door was closed, and Dorf lifted off. He pointed the helicopter on a course of 315 degrees northwest, climbing to an altitude of one thousand feet. The flight in would take a little over ninety minutes.

Weather cooperated that day, and the Sea Stallion returned in the late afternoon. At the controls Dorf looked down through his landing window and set the wheels on the deck gently. C.G. and Vince were quick to duck beneath the craft and chain it down properly. Even though there was no wind in the harbor, and very little swell, they had been trained to do this quickly in case of bad weather. A soldier always appreciated good practice and they carefully hurried through the procedure. Reaching up to turn everything off Dorf sighed, glad to be back on the ship.

Doc radioed ahead that Andrea's MRI showed no concussions and no serious damage from his severe beating. He would be sore for several weeks, but he would recover completely. As he made his way slowly down the ramp in the rear of the helicopter C.G. reached up to give him a hand.

"Take it easy Papa Orvieto," he said loudly enough to be heard above the rotor noise.

And so, Andrea received his nickname from the crew. Thereafter the men simply called him Papa. He didn't seem to mind the designation. That evening he made his way slowly to the kitchen to eat with the rest of the crew. After being introduced to all of them he sat down with Jim, John, Wade, Doc, and Millie at one of the tables and enjoyed a delicious supper of swordfish.

Andrea was meeting the crew officially for the first time. Already impressed with Doc and Millie, he gazed around, letting his eyes tell him things about the men in this room. He knew there were twelve men who formed the special operations team. One by one he identified them, and when he was finished, he asked Jim if he was correct. Jim was surprised that Andrea had picked all twelve.

"How did you know the twins were part of the unit?" he asked.

"They don't look like they would be at first, Nephew," Andrea said in his heavily accented English. "But there is something about them, something that links them to this elite force. It is more an air of readiness than anything I can put my finger on. But it is there!" Andrea finished, waving his fork in front of Jim's face.

"I'd like to introduce you to your bunkmate when you're finished," Jim said.

"The thin man who is about my age, is it not?" Andrea asked, pointing a butter knife at Jim Warner.

"Yes. That's Master Chief Warner, our mechanic. His wife died about nine months ago and he's still getting over that. He's glad to be back at sea, and he's done a magnificent job for us," Jim answered.

To Jim's great surprise and pleasure, Andrea and Jim Warner hit it off from the moment they were introduced, and from that time on the two were almost inseparable. Their friendship was good for both of them, helping them to rise above their past tragedies. Both men seemed to understand each other and their individual tragedies.

Later Andrea explained to Jim and John what changed Master Chief Warner. Andrea drew out of him the story of his wife's death, understanding immediately what was haunting the man. He was a soldier, and risked his life often, and yet it was his innocent wife who faced death so bravely. He felt guilt and shame. Andrea knew, because he had felt the same things with his beloved Caterina. In talking about it he helped Jim Warner finally put to rest his guilt and learn to live with himself.

Life was uncertain, always, and good and bad suffered alike when it came to death. It was not meaningless. There was meaning to every life, and therefore meaning to every death. Sometimes the meaning was clear, and sometimes it was hidden. It was not in the hands of man to determine the length of life, or how he would die. That lay in the hands of God.

CHAPTER 16

Saba's Barge

At ten the next morning Zeke sounded general call throughout the ship. Every hand made his way to the conference room. Zeke, Sparks, and Smitty spared no expense when it came to the conference room design and equipment. At each place, and there were thirty-six places at the table, a laptop computer was attached to the teak table, and snuggly nestled in a drawer under the teak table, that slid out for easy access, was a keyboard and mouse.

Zeke's laptop was connected to the mainframe computer system in the navigation room on the bridge. From his laptop Zeke could display anything he wanted on the others. Yet each computer was also independent, allowing the operator to access any information he or she might desire. To Windy, who studied the setup, it was a masterful design.

Jim was seated at the head of the table. John and Wade sat on either side of him, and by rank or ordinance the crew was seated on either side of the table. The kitchen crew found themselves seated across from each other furthest away from the Captain. That they were there at all was considered by each a great privilege. Since they owned a partnership in the company, they deserved to be there, and Jim was a firm believer that great ideas could come from the most surprising source.

"I want to begin this morning's business by introducing the last member of our present crew. This is Andrea Orvieto, a senior partner in the firm. As you can see by his uniform, he holds the rank of Chief Petty Officer. Having lived on the ocean, and especially in the Mediterranean area all his life, he will be an important addition to our current and future endeavors. Andrea speaks Greek, Italian, English, and French, and he knows the ports, islands, and especially the customs of the countries that share the shoreline to the Med," Jim finished the introduction with a smile at his uncle.

For a minute various voices welcomed Andrea aboard, while he returned the greetings. Looking to his left Jim lifted an eyebrow to Zeke who nodded in return, put his fingers to his laptop, and began to work his magic with the computer. Jim called everyone's attention to himself by simply straightening in his seat.

"The time has come for us to tackle our first operation as a salvage company. As you know, we need to have a bona fide cover for our presence here. That will be established with one success, in such a way that no one will doubt what we do. Zeke is going to help me with this presentation, so I would like everyone to follow along on your computer, but don't hesitate to ask questions for clarification. On each monitor you will be able to see some of the data that we have gathered to help us. As we do that together, let me give you some history.

"Sheba, or the kingdom of the Sabeans, embraced the greater part of the Yemen, or Arabia Felix." Jim said. On the monitors in front of each person a map appeared of that area. Jim continued. "At the time Solomon ruled Israel, Saba was the queen of Sheba. History records that she undertook a journey to Jerusalem to convince herself of the truth of the reports that reached her about Solomon. She proposed to test his wisdom by enigmas. Biblical history of this is found in I Kings 10:1–13; and II Chronicles 9:1–12."

Those Scripture references appeared on the computer monitors and Jim was quiet for a moment while everyone read. Then he picked up the story once again.

"A large number of inscriptions have been uncovered in southwestern Arabia, written in the Sabaean characters. They show, among other things, that, besides the famous kingdom of Sheba, there was another monarchy called Ma'in, hence the classical and now current term 'Minean.'" Pictures of those inscriptions flashed on the monitors one at a time while everyone listened to Jim's monologue.

"The Sabeans were governed by priest-kings according to Psalm 72:10. Historical verification of this is confirmed by archaeological evidence gathered to date in this area. The ruins of their capital city, Mariaba (Mareb), reveal the advancement of their culture.

"According to Saba, Solomon was able to answer all her riddles; and the demonstration of his wisdom, with the wonders of his retinue, his table, and palace, filled her with amazement. You can see the number of archaeological records that accompanied that famous visit. Her own words, spoken with astonishment to Solomon, are recorded. 'What her eyes now saw she had not heard the half.' After an exchange of valuable presents, she returned to her own country.

"Jesus spoke of her as the 'Queen of the South' in Matthew 12:42. Reference is made of the commerce that took the road from Sheba along the western borders of Arabia in Job 6:19; Isaiah 60:6; Jeremiah 6:20; and Ezekiel 27:22–23, along with various pieces of information excavated from the Sabeans own historical record.

"We know that during Saba's reign most of the Western Sinai Peninsula, and everything but the southern tip was under her influence. In ancient times Dedah, Havilah, Uzal, and Sheba would have been considered within her kingdom."

The monitors in front of each crewmember now showed a map with those cities listed, the tiny dot in front of each name pulsating from light to dark on the screen to make them easier to see. Jim continued.

"The Minean kingdom would have comprised Ophir and Hazarmaveth." Those cities now appeared on the map. Then the map changed to a larger one.

"Saba journeyed to Egypt first, visiting Memphis, Tanis, and then setting sail for Tire and Sidon in the Phoenician empire, before sailing south again to Joppa in the Philistine kingdom." Her journey, now a red line, growing on the map showed her route.

"Somewhere between Pelusium (Sin) and Azzah (Gaza), her fleet encountered a terrible storm, and one of the royal barges was lost. According to her own records, the barge was loaded with gifts for Solomon from the copper mines and treasuries of Egypt. Once she finished her visit to Solomon, she returned by the old trade route on a historical fact-finding trip to her own country.

"What little there is to know about that lost ship was recorded by her treasurer, an amazing artist and, fortunately for us, a stickler for detail. He recorded the journey on a skin, complete with an ancient map, and on another skin, he wrote his account. It was later transferred to a pillar in Mareb, in a temple there. Only part of the record was recovered from that dig.

"The skins, however, were discovered three hundred years ago. They were stolen, and then sold to a collector from Egypt. He died, and his relatives, unaware that he had hidden them in a secret drawer of his writing desk, sold it at an auction. A relative of Andrea's bought that writing desk, and passed it down from generation to generation, until Andrea's father decided to build a replica of it, before throwing out the old one.

"Andrea's father took the desk apart, piece by piece, to duplicate it, and discovered the hidden compartment and the skins. Being a wise man, he sent portions of what was written in the account to various universities around the world. Two of them were in England, three were in the United States, and two were in Jerusalem and Cairo. Fearing that these records might lead to a great treasure he took amazing precautions.

"Those who translated the inscription never saw more than a paragraph. There were questions, of course, as to where the inscriptions came from. Andrea's father was able to keep hidden the fact that he had the entire record. He passed both on to Andrea, who then showed them to my own father some years ago. Our family plan was to go into business together in deep-sea rescue and salvage, bringing up the barge or its contents.

"That dream is now a reality. Our first venture will be to locate and salvage the royal barge of Sheba that was lost in that storm," Jim sat back and watched the faces around the table.

"The value of a find of this nature would be enormous!" Doc Wozniac said with some energy. "Has anyone estimated it?"

"No, Doctor. If the records are correct, and the artifacts are not damaged from being immersed in saltwater for centuries, Zeke's estimate ran into eight figures. But we don't really know until we bring the barge up. However, we have to find it first."

"You're planning to bring up a wooden boat that's been under the water for centuries? Are you in earnest?" Mark Drumheiser was the speaker.

"Deadly earnest," Jim replied. "We think it can be done if the vessel wasn't broken up too badly in the storm."

"We've studied how many of the successful salvage operations of wooden vessels were accomplished in other parts of the world, and even some here. We have the technology and know-how to do it." Wade chimed in. "I am convinced it is not only possible, but quite likely we will succeed, if, of course, we find the vessel."

"Now that you know the plan, what we need to do is determine what is necessary to first locate the wreck, and then salvage her. Each and every one of you has a contribution to this endeavor, especially as we set in motion a plan of operation. You may come in here at any time, log onto your computer, and study every piece of information we have. If you have an idea, I want to hear it. I don't care how outlandish it may be, I want to hear it. I mean that. Just log onto the intership mail program and write it down in my mail," Jim looked around the table at each person, and then fixed his eyes on the kitchen crew.

"You guys who do such a great job of feeding this crew have something to contribute too. Don't think just because you don't have experience in this field you have nothing to offer. I want to hear from each one of you," he switched to Doc and Millie. "That goes for the medical team too."

"What's our time frame?" C.G. asked.

"We set sail for Cairo tomorrow at high tide, which occurs at 04:17 hours. If we push it, we can reach Cairo in four days. We are not going to push it that hard. Smitty has the freedom to make this a leisurely trip of fourteen days for two reasons. One, I want Andrea to be fully recovered of his bruises when we get to Cairo. Second, we need the time to think this one through together," Jim replied.

"Smitty says we're going to stop at Napoli, Athens, Tel Aviv, and finally at Cairo. There is a special bonus for each of you. At each stop you will be able to visit these historic cities and enjoy yourselves. That includes everyone!" Jim added.

"Awesome!" Windy breathed out loud.

"Well said," Jim said with a grin. "Let's get this tub ready to sail by tomorrow morning, then." He stood to let everyone know that the meeting was over. The eleven men of his team stood as he did, saluting him.

The action did not go unnoticed. Andrea nodded in appreciation. These men respected his nephew, and they were the kind of men from whom respect would be difficult to earn. Windy noticed how the men respected the Captain too, even his younger brother. He suddenly felt sorry that he hadn't risen and saluted as well, determining that he would first learn how to salute properly, and then salute the Captain when it was appropriate. Abe and Sturdy would help him discover when that was.

Later in the afternoon, after a refreshing nap, Andrea wandered out on deck to see what was happening. He had no specific duties yet, and he was not expected to partake in any until he was physically ready. Around the ship groups of men worked at cleaning, painting, or checking equipment. Andrea saw Dorf looking over some work that C.G. and Vince had just completed, checking it off his list on a clipboard he held in his huge hand. Then his eyes widened.

At the stern of the ship, dipping a brush into a can of grease, Jim carefully coated the gears for the bollard cable release. Someone, presumably the Captain himself, had just finished cleaning them carefully and he was now applying the grease. There was another can at his feet, probably the cleansing liquid used by so many mariners to fight rust.

Andrea looked around to see if he could spot John. He smiled to himself when he found his younger nephew painting a freshly scoured rust spot on one of the helicopter pontoons. That the two highest-ranking officers on this vessel were willing to do menial labor of this kind spoke highly of them. On this boat everyone worked, and he could appreciate that. Andrea now knew why Jim's men respected him. Jim was willing to do whatever he asked his men to do.

"How's everything back here, Captain?" Dorf asked, stopping to watch Jim apply more grease.

"This grease was a good choice, Dorf," Jim answered, standing up and wiping a sleeve over his forehead. "There wasn't much rust at all on the gears. Where'd you find this cleanser, by the way? It works a treat!"

"TRT recommended it, Shep," Dorf supplied, looking around to see who was ready for him next. TRT was the nickname they'd stuck on Master Chief Warner. "He's had a lot of experience," Dorf added in admiration.

"That he has. Let him know I noticed, will you Dorf?" Jim said. "I'm going to head in and clean up," he added, carefully collecting his cans and brushes.

"Righto, Shep. Looks like JR's ready for inspection. The two of you going up to visit that police officer?" Dorf replied.

"Yeah. I'd like Driver to take us in on the HSB after dinner," Jim answered.

"Done, boss," Dorf replied with a nod, walking off to inspect John's paint job on the pontoon.

Jim took his equipment down into the bowels of the ship to clean the brushes and hang them properly, placing the correctly sealed cans in their assigned spots. Once he was finished with that, he took off his bright orange waterproof jumpsuit and made his way to his cabin to clean up.

The Captain's cabin was as it should be on such a vessel. He actually occupied a suite of three rooms. One was a bedroom with a small bathroom adjoining. All the rooms had a bathroom similar in size and utility. Each bathroom had a fold down sink, a toilet, and a four-foot square shower. All of these were stainless steel, and each person or pair was responsible for keeping those units spotless.

The bedroom and bathroom portion of his suite exited onto a corner balcony, looking forward. Doc and Millie occupied the suite that had the other balcony on the port side. From the corridor going in Jim passed through his office first. Between the office and the bedroom was his private study. Each wall was covered in bookshelves and three comfortable chairs sat in the middle of the room in a semi-circle, with two reading tables between them, complete with reading lamps.

After washing, and then cleaning his shower unit, Jim put his towel in the hamper and padded naked into his bedroom. Opening his closet, he dressed in his civilian clothing, which for him meant crisp clean underwear, ironed before it was folded and stowed away, black dress pants, also carefully ironed, and a long-sleeved gray cotton shirt. He didn't pick out a tie. Over his black socks he pulled on a pair of Rocky Gor-Tex retractable hiking boots that he particularly liked.

Satisfied that he looked as he should, he checked to make sure his room was tidy, and made his way down to the galley for a glass of iced tea. He chatted with Abe and Sturdy, while Wendall and Bob walked back and forth setting up the salad bar for dinner. Abe had some ideas for buying supplies in Rome, which he shared with Jim, more to see if Jim was interested in the idea, than for any other reason. Jim's eyes lit up when he heard the ideas, and he licked his lips in anticipation.

"I never expected to have gourmet cooking for the men, Abe, but you and your crew do a bang-up job of it. We could start a cruise line with this kind of food!" Jim encouraged, meaning every word. Abe beamed at him and Sturdy grinned down from his great height, nodding his head.

Back in his office Jim took care of the paperwork for the day. He was putting the last page in a file folder to put in his file drawer when Andrea wandered in his open door.

"Do you always work with your door open?" Andrea asked, looking around with interest at the office.

"The crew knows that I am always available. I like for them to wander in and talk. It gives me a feel for how things are going on the ship. How about you, uncle? What are your feelings, now that you're on board?" Jim queried.

Andrea sat on the bench built into the wall across from Jim's desk. Jim smiled when Andrea's eyes opened in surprise. The seat was quite comfortable. Seeing the smile Andrea grinned back.

"I think this is a good crew. Most of the men are experienced seamen, and those who aren't, and I've only seen two, are catching on quickly," Andrea replied. As he spoke, he glanced around the neat office, noting that the desk was clean and orderly.

"Which two?" Jim asked.

"The men call them C.G. and Vince, so I am guessing that is Clancy and Vincent, the two Marines," Andrea said, rubbing the stubble on his chin from a day's growth of beard. "There are two in the kitchen that are new to the sea also I think," he added.

"Correct. You go to the head of the class," Jim's eyes danced with pleasure.

"I never got the chance to thank you properly for saving my life, nephew," Andrea confessed, his brown eyes intense, his forehead wrinkled in thought.

"Was it very bad?" Jim asked, watching Andrea run his big, scarred hands through his thick hair.

"I knew you would come, but I wasn't sure you would get there in time. Scalini has grown bold recently, and I was sure he had crossed a line somewhere in his psyche that would allow him to kill me. All I could do was hold on and hope. And you did come. For that, I truly thank you," Andrea spoke slowly, his eyes fixed somewhere in the past, remembering the pain and fear.

"Do you think our warning was enough?" Jim asked.

"Oh that! Yes!" Andrea laughed, remembering the look of terror on Scalini's face. "Antonio was always a coward at heart. He will not put a foot wrong for a very long time. Then he will only dip his toe in the water to see what might happen."

"I'm going in to see Marchand after dinner tonight. He will let me know if Scalini puts a foot wrong," Jim said quietly.

"And then, nephew?" Andrea asked his eyes suddenly focused on Jim.

"Exactly what I said," Jim replied, his green eyes suddenly as hard as granite.

Andrea shivered a little at that look, but he nodded his head in agreement. "Yes. A man like Scalini does not understand anything else. And he does not appreciate how it makes those who teach the lesson hurt either. You do not like hurting other men. This is as it should be. But in this world, there are those who cannot be treated by the systems in place, eh?" Andrea added softly.

"As you say. There are those who need special justice. It can never be a personal vendetta! That would make the one giving the lesson just as bad. Do you agree?" Jim followed.

"Yes. I agree," Andrea stood up. "I think I will visit the good doctor and his wife now, so they can tell me I am making progress," he grinned. "They will, of course, be correct."

After dinner Jim and John walked out to the afterdeck where the boat had already been hoisted into the water. Jack Boswell was at the wheel, wearing a short-sleeved T-shirt with a popular sports logo on the front, and a pair of faded jeans and tennis shoes. He waved them into the boat, and once both were in place he cast off and expertly shuttled them to the harbor dock. After securing the boat the three walked to the local police station.

Étienne Marchand looked up with pleasure as they entered his office. Jumping up to his feet he slipped around his desk to shake hands with all three men. He was beaming with an open smile.

"You leave in the morning, is this not correct?" he asked as he motioned for them to sit.

"You are well informed," Jim answered in French, which was the language in which Marchand was most comfortable. Sometimes, Jim surprised himself that he could slip into a foreign language like this and feel no discomfort.

"The harbor master is a good friend. He told me you paid your fees and logged your plans to travel to Roma," Marchand replied.

"I thought as much," Jim nodded. "And your investigation. It proceeds?" he asked politely.

"Faugh!" Marchand said, waving a hand. "It will take me months to sift through everything. You have done us a great service, a great service."

"Perhaps you would be kind enough to call me or email me if Antonio Scalini puts a foot wrong in the future," Jim said quietly. "It was explained to him in very careful terms what would happen if he did," he added.

"Ah!" Marchand responded, nodding his head in understanding. "There would be . . . consequences if he did, no?"

"Quite," Jim answered in the affirmative.

"Yes, I think I can do that. Perhaps, if it is necessary, you will allow me to assist?" Marchand raised both eyebrows as he asked.

"I think that would be in order," Jim replied with a smile. Marchand was surprised at the acceptance of his suggestion, and the honesty he heard in the answer. These men would not be coming back to kill Scalini, if he ever got out of prison. It would be another lesson that would leave him broken completely.

"Then, gentlemen, I wish you a safe journey and success," Marchand said with a grand gesture and a sincere smile.

"The friendship we have begun here is a good omen," John said.

"Will you join me for a drink to your success?" Marchand inquired.

"It would be a pleasure," Jim and John said together.

Leaving the office Marchand led them to the hotel where they sat around a table, surrounded by locals, in the hotel bar. Marchand ordered a wine from the St. Estephe label. Once the four glasses were poured, he toasted them, and each sipped from his glass. It was an excellent vintage, and though none of the men from *Bring It Up* drank much in the way of alcoholic beverages, the three men at the table recognized that this was a fine wine. Jim let the flavors develop on his tongue and nodded his head.

They sat and talked to the villagers and Marchand for an hour, nursing that one glass of wine, and finally took their leave. Étienne insisted in seeing them off from the dock, and when they tried to pay for their slip the harbormaster refused. With thanks and smiles all around they returned to the ship.

Bona Fide Cover

Smitty hadn't set their travel plans for pure pleasure alone. Admiral Rook was visiting Napoli, Athens, and Tel Aviv. Sir Edward forwarded Rook's schedule to them shortly after they arrived at Solenzara. After much discussion the team decided that Rook need to see Jim, John, and Wade, needed to become curious about what they were doing, and after examination dismiss them as a threat once he was convinced of their bona fide cover. Admiral Runion enjoyed Jim's suggestion for his own involvement in this little scenario, agreeing to do his part.

Bring It Up dropped anchor in Napoli harbor two days later. Jim, John, and Wade stayed on board for the first two days, making arrangements for the entire crew to visit the historic city, and even stay in a fine hotel for the night. When the crew returned, Jim, John, and Wade went ashore. There they found a rented Mercedes Benz, cream in color, rented for their use by Zeke and left where they could easily find it. It was parked exactly where he said it would be. Wade took the wheel and drove into the city, following careful directions.

Finding a parking space proved to be time consuming, but the car was parked and locked before the appointed time of their clandestine meeting. Just outside the offices of the Admiral of the Italian Navy was a small café, well liked by Americans and Italians alike. It was there that the three men took a table where they could be clearly seen from the steps of the office building, waiting for Admiral Runion to appear with Admiral Rook.

Both men appeared, perhaps ten minutes later than planned. By this time Jim, John, and Wade were enjoying a local dish with unfeigned gusto. None of them were looking around when the two Admirals appeared. It was Admiral Runion who spotted them.

"Well now! James and John Shepherd, and Wade Adams, as I live and breathe! What in the world are you doing here?" he asked. Not waiting for Admiral Rook to react he hailed the three men as he made his way down the steps. Admiral Rook was forced to follow. Jim looked up when he heard his name being called and looked around, finally settling on Admiral Runion. Leaping from his seat he walked toward the Admiral to greet him properly.

"Admiral Runion!" he said, as if surprised. "Hey John, Wade! This was my boss in the Navy!" he said. They both rose to their feet and shook hands with the Admiral as Jim led him to the table. Anyone watching would easily assume this meeting was by chance. Runion never let on that he met John and Wade before either.

"So, what in the world are you boys doing in Napoli?" Charles Runion asked.

"We stopped in for some supplies," Jim said simply. "Our cook wanted to pick up some very special items. He's a gourmet cook. Maybe you remember him. His name is Charles Lincoln, but his nickname is Abe."

"Of course! So, he's cooking for your crew! I take it that means you've started your new business. Tell me how that is going, and have you decided on your first conquest in treasure hunting?" Admiral Runion smiled as he replied.

"Yes. As a matter of fact, we're working on something specific," Jim said.

"Do you know Admiral Rook?" Charles said, turning to the Admiral who was trying to get his attention to avoid this very thing. Admiral Runion seemed as though suddenly aware of the chill that settled over everyone. His smile faded and he looked from the Admiral to the men standing beside the table, reading their body language correctly.

"Hello Lyle." Jim said coolly, not offering a hand to shake. Wade and John stared daggers at the Admiral.

"I'm missing something. What's wrong here?" Admiral Runion asked.

"It's Admiral Rook, if you please!" Admiral Rook spat.

"You don't deserve the designation." Jim said flatly, and Admiral Runion hid a smile as Rook took a small step back. "If this is Lyle Rook, he's the one responsible for withholding valuable intelligence from John's Marine Recon unit. A lot of good men died because of that!" Jim's answer was terse and filled with anger, his green eyes boring into those of Admiral Rook.

"How dare you!" Lyle Rook sputtered.

"Don't even try to start covering your fat little ass, Lyle!" John said quietly. He and Wade had gone suddenly still, and Admiral Rook took another step back. Admiral Runion looked back and forth between them. Rook did not know that Runion knew the whole story, and he wanted to keep Runion ignorant. He managed to pull himself together enough to grab the Admiral and pull him away.

"I won't stand for this! Let's go, Admiral!" he said, pulling Runion away. Admiral Runion winked at the boys as he allowed himself to be pulled away. When Rook looked back Wade made shooing motions with his hands.

"Run away, little man!" he taunted. Rook's face turned beet red and the three men laughed cruelly. His pace quickened as he put space between them, aware that he had been badly frightened by them.

Once the two men were out of earshot they sat back down and finished a delicious lunch. After they paid their check, and left a nice tip for the waiter, they stood up and looked the way Admiral Rook had taken. After a moment of silence John spoke.

"You can run, Admiral. Run fast. Your past is about to hit you like a force five hurricane!" Jim heard, resting a hand on his brother's shoulder with a gentle squeeze and shake of agreement. John's muscles were tight with tension.

"We'll get him. I promise that!" Jim said quietly. When John didn't reply Jim dropped his hand and led them back to the car. None of them wanted to stay in Napoli for any reason after that, so they drove the car to the rental agency, paid the fee, and took a cab to the ship. After paying for the slip rental they boarded the HSB that was waiting with Driver at the wheel, standing quietly as the boat roared out of the bay to their ship.

FM and Paul Warner were waiting to hoist the boat out of the water and secure it on the cradle on the deck. They grinned as the three men climbed out of the boat and down the ladder to the deck.

"By the looks on your faces I can see you saw Admiral Rook," Frank said quietly.

"We can expect to get boarded and inspected any time," Jim replied, releasing the tension in his own body suddenly. John and Wade were doing the same.

"I'm worried about seeing him in Athens, Jim," John said quietly as they made their way forward. "I nearly went for him. It took all my self control to keep my hands off his fat neck!"

"Still close, isn't it?" Jim asked, touching John's arm lightly. "I'm sorry. I almost went for him too!"

"It would have been fun!" Wade said with a laugh. "Did you notice his terror? The little turd was crapping his drawers!"

"It will be more fun to be there when Admiral Runion lays all the evidence in front of him before witnesses!" John said suddenly. "I'll try not to throttle him in Athens," John grinned.

"He'll probably order our arrest when he sees us there!" Wade commented sarcastically.

"I'll send a message to our attorney, just in case he does!" Jim said with a smile.

"If he does that, it will be one more nail in his coffin," John said quietly.

"Let's not provoke him, even if he does have us arrested. It will make him even angrier when we appear at his unmasking." Wade said with real relish. "If he doesn't know we were the ones who gathered most of the evidence against him the victory will be even sweeter!" Wade added with real relish. They gave each other high-five hand slaps in anticipation of the day.

Admiral Rook, alerted and afraid, moved quickly. A Napoli police boat approached *Bring It Up Coral* within an hour of their return. The crew, having been alerted, was ready. As before, when a polite request to come aboard was made, Mark replied in perfect Italian, welcoming the official onto the ship. He led him to Jim's office. Abe was in the office, going over the purchases he'd made in Napoli when the official arrived. Showing some interest in that purchase the police official asked to see the receipts, looked them over carefully and thanked Abe for shopping in his city. Abe smiled at him.

Jim permitted a search of the vessel and when he had satisfied the Roman official that *Bring It Up Coral* was a bona fide deep-sea salvage boat with nothing to hide, the official left with apologies. On shore he assured Admiral Rook that there was nothing suspicious about the boat. Unlike Marchand, he had not noticed anything particular about the crew. Rook accepted the man's report knowing that a complete search had been carried out. Still harboring doubts, he left with a resolve to keep an eye on the Shepherds and their crew. John and Wade knew he was responsible for withholding that intelligence, and that not only surprised, but alarmed him. The Admiral had been sure he'd covered his tracks, and that no one knew of his duplicity. Jim, John and Wade would bear watching.

Keeping their timetable Smitty had them dropping anchor outside of Piraeus two days after Admiral Rook arrived in the city of Athens. This time the entire crew boarded a bus and took a tour of the city. Sir Edward Marsh had several agents in Athens, using them to plan for the most innocent of meetings between the Admiral and the crew of *Bring It Up Coral*. As he suspected, though none of the men were wearing any kind of uniform, Admiral Rook was drawn to them because they were all speaking English. Only after looking them over for a moment did he notice Jim, John, and Wade in the group. He hoped they hadn't seen him.

It was Dorf who by plan drew everyone's attention to the Admiral and his little group.

"Hey! The American Navy is here boys!" he said loudly. Everyone turned and saw Admiral Rook and four other Navy personnel with him. Admiral Rook saw Jim take hold of Dorf's arm and whisper something to him. Dorf's face drained of color and then became mottled with anger as he glanced at the Admiral. Dorf, Abe, and Sturdy all moved to stand between the Admiral and the Shepherds. It was suddenly as if a wall of solid rock was there, intimidating and real. Admiral Rook said nothing, but after taking one frightened look at those three giants he herded the officers accompanying him away.

"Coward!" Dorf said loud enough for the Admiral to hear. Jim grinned.

"You have to admit that the three of you are a little scary looking!" he commented, his green eyes dancing with humor. "The tour's moving on, let's not get left behind."

A few minutes later a Greek policeman stopped the tour guide and inquired about the crew of *Bring It Up Coral*. The tour guide assured him that they joined the group in Piraeus and had not left it. Satisfied the officer left, never aware that several in the crew spoke fluent Greek and knew every word he said. Admiral Rook was none to pleased by the meeting but had to accept the fact that it had been accidental. Jim was not surprised that Greek officials once again searched his ship.

Bring It Up Coral departed before the Admiral's frigate this time, and the *Coral* was at anchor when Rook's ship dropped anchor two hundred yards away. A helicopter took off from the flight deck shortly after making anchor and passed directly over *Bring It Up Coral*. Admiral Rook looked down at a busy crew, washing down the deck. The boat was immaculate, which made Jim a good Captain who kept everything ship shape. Grunting with displeasure he looked away toward the approaching shore.

It was easy to spot the giant Sturdy from the ship, carrying packages under one huge arm, talking animatedly to the muscle-bound cook. Admiral Rook made inquiries and discovered that the two had been purchasing food items in quantities large enough to feed a crew of twenty. More and more he was convinced that the Shepherds were not a threat to him.

Bring It Up Coral dropped anchor off the coast of Egypt at Al-Iskandriyah, or Alexandria. Jack Boswell, Jim Shepherd, and Mark Drumheiser were the first to leave the ship, taking the HSB up the Nile River, through the locks, to the city of Cairo. Ira Lehman recommended an expert on the historical period that covered Solomon's reign who taught graduate students at the Fort Brydon Museum of Antiquities. His name was Alistair Gregg. Jack dropped his two passengers off in Cairo and returned to the ship to shuttle others ashore to explore the wonders of Egypt.

Making a good impression on Alistair Gregg was paramount to their quest, so both men wore their white dress uniforms. Both wore a crisp, spotless white short-sleeved shirt with a reinforced mandarin collar trimmed in gold. *Bring It Up's* logo Peregrine Falcon decorated either side of Jim's collar, signifying his rank as a Captain. The epaulets on the shoulder of his white jacket bore the four double braids of gold and four golden stars. The logo bird flew in the double braids at the top. His dress shoes were highly polished and tied in a sheepshank. The navy blue and gold striping on his pant legs the finishing touch of an immaculate uniform.

Mark bore the single silver bar of a Lieutenant Junior Grade, and the single and double braid on his epaulet. His mandarin collar was not trimmed in gold and he wore white rubber soled deck shoes. Walking stride for stride they marched in unison into the museum and were ushered into the presence of Dr. Gregg promptly.

Alistair Gregg was perhaps an inch taller than Mark, perhaps five feet five inches tall, extremely thin, with long wisps of white hair making a vain attempt to cover his bald head. His eyes were blue, sparkling with excitement, and his handshake was vigorous and full of energy. He might be nearing sixty years of age, Jim thought, but he had one of those perpetually young faces. Energy seemed to course through his body as he greeted them.

"Welcome, gentlemen!" he greeted them, bouncing up and down on his toes, his eyes twinkling with pleasure, as the twenty odd students gathered around a table covered by artifacts stared in curious astonishment. "That will be all for today class. Continue to work on dating these finds," he instructed his class without looking at them. "Won't you gentlemen come with me to my office."

His office was a surprise to both men. It was immaculate, sparkling clean, with a table for a desk, the top polished and empty of anything but a blotter and a phone. Comfortable chairs in one corner surrounded a round coffee table with a black stone top, also spotlessly clean. Overhead fluorescent lights made the room seem bright and cheery, and the windows bore bright curtains with a floral design that tied in all the colors in the room. He was watching the two men with obvious interest as they took their first look at his office.

"You expected a dark corner filled with books, papers, artifacts, with barely room to move, eh?" he asked, his Scottish accent pronounced. "That's the next room, although it is not dark, and it is not messy," he led them into his private library and study, a room with no windows, every wall covered in bookshelves from floor to ceiling, again well lighted, with a table in place of a desk. The table did have three stacks of books on its polished top, but they were neatly stacked, as were the folders in the center of the blotter.

"Ira called me this morning and told me a little about your company, Captain Shepherd," Alistair said, leading them back to the comfortable chairs. A young and very pretty Egyptian girl appeared with a tray that held a pitcher of lemonade and three tall glasses, filled with cubed ice. She poured each man a glass of lemonade, put the tray in the center of the coffee table, and left without uttering a word. Jim and Mark thanked her and their host for the refreshing drink, picking up their glasses to sip the refreshing liquid.

"You are, I am told, planning to search for Saba's missing barge. Are you in earnest?" Alistair asked after taking a long drink.

"Deadly earnest," Jim replied quietly.

"How can I help you?" Alistair asked.

"Dr. Gregg, we are interested in the shipping lanes of that time period, and the hull designs that were common. Storms, usual and unusual, natural currents, and salinity are also of interest. Since evaporation at the surface of the Mediterranean greatly exceeds gain by rainfall, the dense saline water may have allowed the craft to travel further before settling to the bottom. Anything you can tell us about that period of time will be carefully sifted and weighed in determining our search grids and methods of discovering the barge," Mark said quickly.

"Please, call me Alistair," the little man said pleasantly.

"If you will call me Jim, and my friend, Mark," Jim replied with a smile.

"Good-oh!" Alistair agreed. "You do realize that you are asking me to teach you everything I know about my favorite subject?" he added.

Mark lifted a laptop, opened it, and attached a microphone that had a clip Dr. Gregg could clip to his collar. Dr. Gregg threw his head back and laughed. Then he leaned forward, while Mark quickly set up to record every word. The same girl brought a lunch of cucumber sandwiches and melon, which the men ate while listening to Dr. Gregg lecture. Gregg took bites between bits of information. At the end of the day he invited the two to stay in his home while he continued his monologue. They accepted. Jim was aware that Dr. Gregg was going to help them more than anyone else in their quest. The man's memory was vast and precise.

For eight days Dr. Gregg gave them at least six hours of time. Sometimes he taught, sometimes he showed them what was in the museum from that time period, and at other times they studied ancient charts and he read from ancient tablets and papyri. He was delighted to find two students so willing to soak up every tidbit of information he had. Their questions were intelligent, and his estimation of these men rose by the hour. By the end of their eight days together they were on strong friendly footing.

"If, or I should say when you find her, will you allow me to log the artifacts and study them?" Alistair asked, as he walked both men to the pier where the HSB waited to take them back to the ship.

"We're going to do one better, Alistair," Jim surprised him. "We have housing for ten people on board *Bring It Up* that is currently not in use. Once we locate the wreck, you find nine of your best and brightest students, and we'll send our helicopter to bring all of you out to the boat and help us every step of the way!" Jim found himself smiling at the good Doctor's response.

"I'll begin preparing my nine students immediately!" Alistair said with glee. "I must say I never expected you to make such an offer!"

"We have learned that success is attained by using the brightest and best minds available for advice and aid. For your expert help we offer the chance to catalog and publish our discovery. Along with that, each of your nine students will receive regular seaman's wages, and you will receive a consultation fee. Our attorney has already drawn up the contracts and will be sending them to you." Jim replied evenly.

"You know, I actually believe you may succeed, young man!" Alistair said, pumping the Captain's hand with energy once again.

Jim and Mark stepped into the HSB, receiving a salute from Jack, and returning it smartly. They waved at the professor as the boat pulled away from the dock and smiled as the little man hurried back toward his beloved museum. Early in his career Jim learned that many counselors ensure success. Mark filled Jack in on their eight-day stay as they made their way down the Nile to the sea. He was as excited as Dr. Gregg, and Jim shared that excitement. Both men believed they now had a very good chance of success. It seemed that forces were moving to help them.

CHAPTER 18

Preparation for Success

It was good to be back on the ship. Mark, who had entered the information from his sessions with Dr. Gregg, downloaded everything into the main computer with Zeke's help. Zeke looked at the three hundred-page document with a quizzical expression on his face. Looking up at Mark who stood next to him watching he spoke sarcastically.

"Talked a lot, didn't he?" he smirked.

"You have no idea." Mark said with feeling, rolling his eyes at his friend's antics. "But the man was a walking encyclopedia, and he gave us information it might have taken years to uncover."

"I take it you liked the man?" Zeke asked, looking closely at Mark.

"Very much!" Mark replied. Absently he watched the document finish loading. "Make sure everyone gets a copy to read, will you, please?" he said when the program was finished.

Zeke nodded. "Done," he acquiesced with a smile. "I was getting tired of reading comic books anyway," he added.

"Oh! You read?" Mark asked too innocently.

"I like the pictures," Zeke replied with a straight face. "All those pretty colors, and tall super-heroes with bulging muscles and interesting clothes can be very exciting."

Mark laughed. He had yet to ruffle Zeke in a verbal contest and doubted he ever would. Shaking his head, he turned to go. "Well, I'm going to go down to the galley and get some real food for a change," he said with feeling, leaving the computer center.

When they weighed anchor and prepared to get underway a small yacht left the harbor, following. A military unit takes note of everything, and the yacht was studied, and a search for ownership submitted. It was shadowing them, always a nautical mile away, and twice Jim spotted someone on deck with binoculars. In Athens they'd spotted the yacht on their tail, but it had kept its distance. Now it was closely shadowing them.

Searching for a lost vessel, thousands of years after it disappeared, is a lot like looking for a needle in a haystack. Every day, for one hundred and fourteen days, *Bring It Up Coral* cruised at a speed of three knots, towing three deep-sea remote search vehicles, each with battery operated dive lights and several cameras. Each of the search vehicles also carried some highly advanced geological survey equipment, using sound waves to identify elements up to ninety feet beneath the ocean floor.

Every square yard of the grids was recorded and cartographed onto a growing map of the floor of the Mediterranean Sea in that area. Routine, discipline, and hard work were the watchwords of the crew. This was called mowing the yard, as the boat moved from grid to grid in the search. It was tedious, often frustrating, but never boring. There was always something, every day, discovered on the bottom of the ocean to learn about, or to mark for return and study. Often, they paused over a sunken vessel to take photographs.

To help alleviate some of the daily tedium Jim Warner started a Bible study on Sundays, always a day of rest for the crew, which became quite popular with not just a select few, but everyone on the crew. Abe and Sturdy participated with him and the three of them took turns teaching. It was not at all like attending church, there was no music, but the discussions were lively, and the men were permitted to ask any questions. This seemed to improve the crew's ability to handle their weekly workload immensely, and Captain Shepherd noted that every single crewmember attended the studies.

There were those, he knew, who did not understand the depth of faith expressed by the three teachers when it came to the Bible. Jim was one of them. Raised in a Catholic church he never doubted the existence of God. It was the veracity of the Bible he didn't understand, and he had been taught somewhere along the way that the Bible was full of mistakes. Recently he read a copy of Phillip E. Johnson's *Darwin on Trial*. Johnson, an attorney, certainly demonstrated that there simply is no vast body of empirical data supporting the theory of evolution. Reading that book simply enforced what he already believed. People wrote things that weren't true all the time.

But there was something different about his Master Chief, and his two cooks. During the course of their study Jim learned that it was a personal relationship with God. Since he had never experienced anything like that, he was even more curious. During the week the crewmembers talked often about the studies they were enjoying, and Jim learned that some of his men had the same depth of faith expressed by the Master Chief. Perhaps it was the simplicity and wholesomeness of their faith that impressed him so much.

There were, he knew, many religions in the world. Some were more popular than others, some more powerful. One difference he noted in thinking about the religions he was aware of is that this one began with God making Himself known to man. All of the others began with man, or time. Prophecy was something else too. The Biblical record on prophecy was impressive, and no other religion included detailed prophecy like Judaism and Christianity.

He began to prowl through the ship's library, noting that Master Chief Warner had influence even here. There was an entire section on Christianity. At random Jim picked up Francis Schaeffer's *True Spirituality* and tried to read it. For the first time in his life he was faced with a book that he could not understand. There were truths here that he could not fathom, and it made him a little angry and a little afraid at the same time. Angry because he felt the frustration of not understanding, and afraid, because he guessed that what this man wrote came from that same depth of relationship with God, and that somehow it was of utmost importance to his life. He could not shake that sense of urgency either.

In the evenings, after the meal, the men enjoyed game tournaments. There were chess tournaments, poker tournaments, Mile Bornes tournaments, Rook tournaments, Risk tournaments, Balderdash tournaments, Trivia tournaments, and Monopoly tournaments. Yet even here Jim heard the men discussing that day's Bible lesson, realizing that the three men teaching the lessons were inspiring the men on a level he desired as well.

Everyone on the crew responded well to the various tournaments and it counteracted the impatience and tedium that often comes with such a search. Crewmembers and Team members looked forward to the games that night and the lounge was filled with laughter, cries of dismay and whoops of victory.

Jim and John were finalists in the Rook tournament, playing against Andrea and Jim Warner. The brothers finally defeated their foes and were claimed the champions of that game. Jim also won the Chess tournament, much to John's dismay, defeating his brother in 16 moves in a classic discovered checkmate, after ending in a draw five games in a row. John sat staring at the board for a moment and then chided himself for missing the danger. However, he took the defeat with good grace.

Abe won the poker championship. Dr. Wozniac won the Balderdash tournament because he knew many of the words and their proper definitions. Aunt Millie won the Monopoly tournament, bankrupting the final three opponents. FM won the Trivia tournament, and Wade won the Risk tournament. Every game was played with the usual fierce competition of deeply bonded friends, and losses were taken with chagrin and good humor. Although the days dragged on, the crew kept its edge, and Jim was glad Abe suggested the tournaments.

A new tournament schedule was posted, and the fun started again. Popular card games were added to the list, including Millie's suggestion of Bridge, which none of the men knew how to play. She and her husband taught the game skillfully, taking the tournament as well. Jim wasn't surprised by that turn of events but was happy to add one more challenging game to his repertoire.

On the eve of their one hundred and fourteenth day of searching Jim sat with Master Chief Warner and Andrea for dinner. Mark Drumheiser was at the table with Dorf. Jack Boswell made the sixth. Jim expressed his frustrations about understanding Schaffer's book to Master Chief Warner, expecting vague platitudes in return.

"Jim, there are things in that book that will never be opened up to you until you put your faith in Jesus Christ," Master Chief Warner said seriously.

"I believe in God!" Jim replied, somewhat surprised.

"Yes, I know, Shep. I'm not talking about God at the moment. I'm talking about His Son, Jesus. You see, that book and every book of the Bible, because that's what that book is based on, will come alive for you when you finally trust Christ. And before you say anything, let me explain how that is done," Warner replied earnestly. "You have to realize that you are a sinner before a holy God, and that because of your sin you can never have a relationship with Him."

"I agree with that. At least, I was taught that when I was a kid going to Catholic Church," Jim said, nodding his head and listening carefully to his Master Chief's next words.

"Well, God knew that none of us could ever do anything worthy of saving us, or of having this relationship with Him. So, because He loved us, and wanted to have a relationship with us, He sent Jesus into the world to take our punishment, and to pay the price of our sin." Chief Warner said. "It would be like you, knowing that someone was going to kill John, and to save him, taking the bullet meant for him, even though you understood he should die."

"I'm following you." Jim said, suddenly aware that several of the men at the next table were listening carefully too. Some of them had their eyes closed, as if they were praying, and he thought that perhaps they were praying for him at that moment. It was perhaps that which broke his heart and let understanding flood his mind.

Suddenly he remembered all the verses from all those lessons long ago about Jesus and His love for man. The fact that someone loved him enough to die for him was something Jim understood very well. It all made sense.

"Now, what Jesus wants is for you to say, I trust you to be my Savior. I'm sorry for my sins, and I want you to become such an important part of my life that I become the man you intended for me to become all along. Today I choose to follow you, Jesus," Master Chief said.

"And then what?" Jim asked, leaning forward, his green eyes intense with the desire to understand. He knew somehow that this conversation was going to change his life forever, and he could not stop. There was a deep need to continue.

"And then you belong to Him. You might not feel any different, but your name will be written in a book in heaven, and His Holy Spirit will enter you, and begin to open your mind. That's the way it happened with me. I gave my life to Christ when I was twenty, and I spent the rest of the day more depressed than I had ever been. I thought something magnificent would happen, you know? Bells, whistles, angels appearing, whatever! But that night, when I opened my Bible, I understood something for the first time, and I knew then that what He promised was true," Jim Warner shared quietly.

"Don't I have to go to a priest and confess my sins, or something?" Jim asked, sitting back, his face drawn in concentration.

"You can, if you want to. Although your priest may die from the shock of your appearing at confession!" Warner said with a smile, getting a hearty laugh from Jim and those listening. "But the Bible says that Jesus is our High Priest. You can confess them to Him, and He'll take care of it. He's actually the only One who can!" Jim Warner replied. He pulled a small tattered New Testament out of his shirt pocket and opened the book of Hebrews, showing Jim the verse. "You can do that right now, right here, if you want to. I'd be honored to help," Master Chief Warner added. Looking intently at his chief mechanic Jim realized that there were tears in his eyes, tears for him.

So intent on what was happening, Jim no longer knew who was watching, who was praying, or that anything around him was going on. Mark Drumheiser put his hand on Jim's shoulder. "I'll help too," he said simply.

"You too?" Jim asked, surprised.

"Absolutely, Shep. I studied Martial Arts, searching for truth, and discovered that none of them satisfied. The girl I was dating at that time always went to church and was always talking about her walk with God. So, one Sunday I called her and went to church with her. For some reason I really heard the message that time, it got through, and I gave my life to Christ. Everything changed for me, then, and I've never regretted the decision." Mark replied.

"He led me to faith in Christ, Shep," Dorf added, a little awkwardly.

"Then I guess it's time I did the same," Jim admitted quietly. He felt tears on his cheeks and was not ashamed, for perhaps the first time in his life. Knowing those tears were something from deep inside his heart that was moved suddenly he wiped them away, bowed his head, and asked Christ to be his Savior. The words seemed to come naturally. When he looked up there were tears in every eye at his table, and in the eyes of some of the men at other tables as well. Andrea was wiping his face with a handkerchief and nodding.

Late that night Jim began reading that book again, discovering that Master Chief Warner had been correct. It made sense now, even though he didn't actually feel any different, or fully understand the deeper things, he knew that he was in a new and exciting relationship. For the first night in many years Jim Shepherd bowed his head and talked to God.

He wasn't sure how to do it, so he just said what was on his heart. Somehow, in the middle of that prayer, he knew that God was listening carefully to every word. Frightened that he might ask for something he shouldn't, he decided to stop, thank God, and find out how to pray properly to a Holy God before he tried that again. In time he would look back and laugh at that reaction.

As if God wanted to emphasize His pleasure in this new relationship at nine o'clock the next morning the port remote search vehicle registered a heavy deposit of gold and other precious metals. Zeke was staring at the computer monitors as the images were sent from deep under the sea and he grabbed his send button and called for all stop. Everyone heard the excitement in his voice. Some of the men gathered on either side of the boat, as if they could penetrate the darkness and depths and see what lay below. Jim and John were in the bridge and they pushed through the glass door to the CIC with eager faces. Looking at the computer display they noted that many precious metals and stones were identified by the sound waves and their hopes rocketed.

"Close reach, port side, Captain!" Zeke said in excitement. "We've got a heavy deposit of gold, 321 degrees northwest by west. Look at all this other stuff! Even if it's not Saba's barge, it is a significant find!"

Jim pressed his send button. "Now hear this. We have a deposit of gold, 321 degrees northwest by west of our current mark. Prepare the bathyscaphe," Jim and John grinned at each other as whoops of delight sounded from outside. Together they turned and left the computer center. Smitty was busy in the compass bridge calculating their exact position, while Wade reversed the ship slowly, once the cameras and equipment were on deck, to the spot where the gold had first been marked.

"You should oversee the launching of the bathyscaphe," Jim said to John. "I'll stay up here and monitor things from the CIC. Wade, you have the bridge."

"On my way Shep," John said, slapping his brother on the shoulder as he hurried out the door.

"Lieutenant Commander has the bridge," Wade said into his headset.

From his vantage point high above the afterdeck Jim watched the men work around the bathyscaphe. Developed by the Swedish submarine designers, Kockums, this vehicle is nicknamed *Steel Crab*. It was perhaps the ugliest submersible Jim had ever seen, and it really did resemble a crab. At least the two manipulator arms, and various other attached tools gave it that appearance. Grinning as he thought it might be a cross between an octopus and a crab, he continued to watch the activity.

The reinforced hull was shaped so that without the arms and sphere below it would have looked like a flying saucer. Hanging beneath it was a sphere made of a thick plastic designed to withstand the extreme pressures and changes of temperature. Most of the men called it the fishbowl. Mounted on clear plastic platforms so that they seemed suspended in the air were three stations for the men who would dive in her.

Jack Boswell would drive the bathyscaphe. Frank Miller would monitor and operate the life support systems and electric motors. Bill Kline would serve as the third occupant. His job would be to keep in contact with the mother ship and operate the lights, sonar, and special electronics. They were, at the present moment, going through the checklist, much like any pilot would. Jim could see them in their bright yellow thermal wetsuits, complete with thermal boots, bright orange in color, as were the gloves they would wear if necessary.

Outside the men were attaching all the hoses and cables that would provide energy, life support, and communications. Dorf was directing the crew in setting up the crane that would lift the bathyscaphe off its cradle and lower it into the water. Once it was secured to the deck and tested the cables and hoses attached to the bathyscaphe were threaded through a special pulley to keep them from becoming entangled in the lifting and lowering process. Last to be connected was the bollard cable, capable of lowering the sphere five hundred fathoms, or three thousand feet.

At this juncture they didn't know the exact depth of the ocean floor. The bathyscaphe could eject the hoses and cables if necessary and operate without them, working off a series of batteries. Connected to the mother ship the men could stay down indefinitely, having the added security those cables provided. Safety was important to these men. That was why John double-checked everything before giving his approval for the mission.

Two hours later Jim Warner sat at the controls of the crane, gently lifting the bathyscaphe into the air, and then slowly swinging it out over the gentle swells. His hands moved over the controls as only one who understood the purpose of each could. Setting the bathyscaphe into the water gently he waited while the divers checked everything once more before beginning. Communicating with the men inside all the lights and arms were tested, everything working as designed. At Jim's command when the divers had moved away, the crane began letting out cable as the bathyscaphe vented air and took on water, slowly sinking from sight.

CHAPTER 19

Discovery

S parks read out the depth as they went down, moving his eyes between the sonar bouncing off the bottom and his instruments. Once they passed four hundred feet the lights were turned on, though complete darkness did not close around them until they passed the six-hundred and fifty-foot mark. At nine hundred feet Jack began to slow their descent as Sparks read off the distance to the floor of the sea. Expertly directing the four directional screws Jack brought them to a halt just one fathom from the bottom.

Under the powerful beams of the searchlights everything appeared in shades of green. Sparks began using the specialized equipment, similar to that on the remote search vehicles, using sound waves to identify layers beneath the silt. Locking on to the strongest signal, again identified as heavy gold deposits, Sparks directed Jack in positioning the bathyscaphe over the site. When he was sure that they were in position he called for all stop, and Jack manipulated the controls with such skill that the sub settled immediately above the deposit.

Six long thin aluminum alloy arms extended from the sides of the bathyscaphe, thirty-six feet straight out, then bent at an elbow, eighteen feet to a forty-five-degree angle. Slowly the bathyscaphe settled on those four points and settled with the glass bubble only one fathom, or six feet, from the bottom. Jack cut the electric feeds to the screws that moved the bathyscaphe, the sudden silence settling around them like a soft net.

"*Bring It Up Coral*, this is *Steel Crab*, over," Sparks spoke into the radio microphone he now held up to his mouth.

"*Steel Crab*, this is *Bring It Up Coral*. Your signal is five by five. Can you give us a sit rep, and remember, Uncle Zeke is watching you!" Zeke's voice boomed over the speakers. Sparks quickly turned the volume switch down so that Zeke's voice was sounding like one's voice did in such situations, as though he were speaking in a tin can.

"We are sitting on the bottom directly above the strongest reading of gold. Depth is nine hundred and forty-seven-feet, water temperature is a cool 47 degrees Fahrenheit or 27 degrees Celsius to you brain box science type fellows. The bubble is one fathom off the bottom, and we have clear vision to about six and a half fathoms distance. FM is setting up the "sandbox" as I speak." Sparks replied.

The "sandbox" was a square net, twelve feet square, with six-foot high net walls. Setting it up involved using the longest manipulator arm, lifting it out and away from the bathyscaphe, and then pulling the inflate cord as the arm retracted. There were "posts" that filled with air to form the box, and weights that held it to the bottom.

Watching the net inflate and settle perfectly Frank continued to retract the manipulator arm. Next he pried open a spring latch that released a flexible hose, about three feet in diameter, that opened like an accordion to a length of twenty-six feet. Using the manipulator arm he set the weighted end onto the "sandbox" near wall, and then attached the other end to an air pump designed to blow silt away from their position.

On board the mother ship Jim Warner was busy lowering the powerful pump that could displace ten tons of silt in one hour. Frank pushed a switch that released a balloon, unwinding a long nylon cord all the way to the surface. The divers attached the pump to the hook on the end of the cord and released the air from the balloon. Pump and cord were reeled in towards the bathyscaphe until Frank could snag it with one of the arms.

Sparks whistled as Frank grabbed it the first time, never letting it settle into the silt. "Nice job FM!" he said.

"I used to play shortstop," Frank replied with a straight face.

Frank used both hands and his arms in a special device to manipulate the arms and claws and in minutes had the pump positioned properly. Sparks picked up the microphone and spoke.

"We gotta do a little spring cleaning down here. Somebody want to plug in our vacuum cleaner up there?" he requested.

FM was busy with another hose attached to a special arm, and now connected to the pump. Anything the pump accidentally deposited in the net would be caught there, and when the net was pulled up by the mother ship, the sand would be washed away.

In moments a cloud of silt billowed into the "sandbox." A very gentle current carried the loose silt away from the bathyscaphe and allowed the occupants a clear view of what they were uncovering. For several long minutes no one spoke. Those who could looked into monitors to see what would be uncovered, while others stood still, in an attitude of expectation, waiting to hear if they had indeed found their target. It was as if a stasis field had fallen around them, so intent were they on the voices from the bottom. At the bottom, it was Jack Boswell who gave a visual description to those waiting above. His calm voice described in detail what he was seeing for the benefit of those listening.

"There appears to be the hull of a wooden boat beneath us, and yes, we are clearing enough off to identify the type of boat. We have a possible match . . . shit! Excuse my French! There are dead people down here!" Jack's voice sounded strained. "Oh, God! They were chained galley slaves!"

On the monitors in the computer center Jim stared in horror at a complete skeleton, arms stretched out as if in supplication, shaking in the current against a rusty leg iron that still held it in place. The expanding gasses in the body must have pulled it out of the hole in the side of the ship. Suddenly the rusted chain broke away and the spectral figure seemed to swim out of view.

As the silt was removed part of the deck came into view and Jim's heartbeat increased in excitement. It was almost as if he were seeing one of the many pictures of the barge unfold before his eyes. Fifty minutes passed, as the entire deck was swept clean. It was covered with white limestone secreted by calcareous algae. Some of it chipped away in the suction and tiny puffs of black arose, like smoke, which Jim knew was the carbonized wood of the ship's planking.

Working carefully the crew of *Steel Crab* uncovered almost ninety percent of the barge. Damage to the hull was minimal and Wade, who had been studying the pictures sent up from the depths commented on the possibility of raising the entire barge, intact.

Suddenly the picture went dark. Seconds later the tinny voice of Jack came over the speaker, announcing that the current had changed, and the silt was now blowing back over the boat. They would have to set up another "sandbox" before they could continue. While they worked on that Wade called Mark Drumheiser and Dorf Bernard to the bridge.

"We're going to need some special gear to make this work. We've got to blow the bottom loose without damaging any of the planking, which will be a delicate job. Then we need to design a sling and net combination to pass under the barge. We'll need cables at eight points, and divers on the surface ready to put airbags under this whole thing to support it just beneath the surface."

"Okay. We can do that," Dorf said, nodding his head in confidence. "I'll get everyone started on working the whole thing out. You'll have to direct the construction, Wade. Let's make sure that we do this right the first time so we're sure of success!"

"I'm on it. Let me draw some plans up and I'll be down when they're finished," Wade replied.

"*Steel Crab*, this is *Bring It Up* One speaking," Jim said into the radio to the bathyscaphe. "Be advised that we are rigging a net and sling arrangement to raise the entire barge. Let's try to get some details to work with."

"Roger that, Shep," Jack replied. He looked up at Sparks. "You have any ideas?" he asked with a grin. They were all grinning. The long days of research and work were finished, and now the wreck was found.

"Yes. All we have to do is position ourselves so that Zeke can get every angle of the barge on his computer screen. He'll be able to measure it if we give him something for reference," Sparks suggested.

Frank looked down from the highest seat in the bubble. "We have a fathom length of steel pipe we can lay on silt in front of the barge."

"Great! Let's do that," Sparks replied.

Jack moved the bathyscaphe into a position where Frank could drop the pipe, then moved away until the entire barge could be seen from one camera. "What about light? We're losing a lot of light the further away we move," he said conversationally as he manipulated the controls.

"Hey Zeke, can you still see the barge on your screen?" Sparks asked into his microphone.

"Roger that, bro," Zeke answered immediately. "The image is good enough that I can enhance it. I heard the length of the pipe, so I can use that to determine a very close estimate of the size of this baby."

The crew on the bathyscaphe continued their work of sucking silt away from the barge, working now to expose as much of the hull as possible without actually moving it or causing it to move. Jack was working the controls and when Sparks looked down at him, he noticed that sweat was running down his forehead and his knuckles were white.

"What's up, Driver? You look a little stressed," Sparks said.

"The current down here can't make up its mind what direction it wants to pull us. This would be a deadly current to any divers," Jack said, keeping his concentration on holding the bathyscaphe where it was. "Last time it felt like this the current changed directions," he added, for Frank's benefit.

"All stop on suction," Frank said suddenly. On the mother ship Jim Warner heard the command and hit the switch to stop the pump. As before, a cloud of silt plunged the bathyscaphe bubble into darkness. Sparks looked at Driver with renewed respect. He'd called it just by the feel of the current. For several moments they were unable to see anything outside the glass.

"Let's switch to the first sandbox to finish," Frank said when the cloud of silt bled away. Once again, the flat desert of silt stretched out a few fathoms, blue green in color, showing some rock formations that had not been seen before. There was also something else visible.

"Hey, think this guy wants a ride?" Jack asked sarcastically as the skeleton appeared, stretched out in a sitting position on the sea floor, one arm straight out to his side with his thumb bones sticking straight up.

Sparks shook his head with a chuckle. "I knew hitchhikers were a problem these days, but this is ridiculous!"

"I'm going to try to bag the skeleton," Frank said. Two arms suddenly extended out from the hull, scooping the skeleton into a net. The men laughed when the skeleton's arms folded with its hands now behind the head, as if it were resting comfortably. Suddenly Sparks leaned forward and looked closely at the skeleton.

"Hey! That's a female skeleton!" he exclaimed.

Sparks fingers flew on the keyboard and a camera zoomed in on the pelvic area of the bones. Sure enough, the men could identify it as a female. To make double sure they scanned the ribs and counted them, confirming their discovery.

"A woman galley slave?" Sparks asked, his voice hushed. "How barbaric! Why would they use women?"

"A queen's barge," Jim said softly into the microphone, looking at the pictures sent to the ship. "Remember, the Sabeans were governed by priest-kings. The most beautiful woman became their queen. Many of those religions enslaved women as easily as men, using them harder."

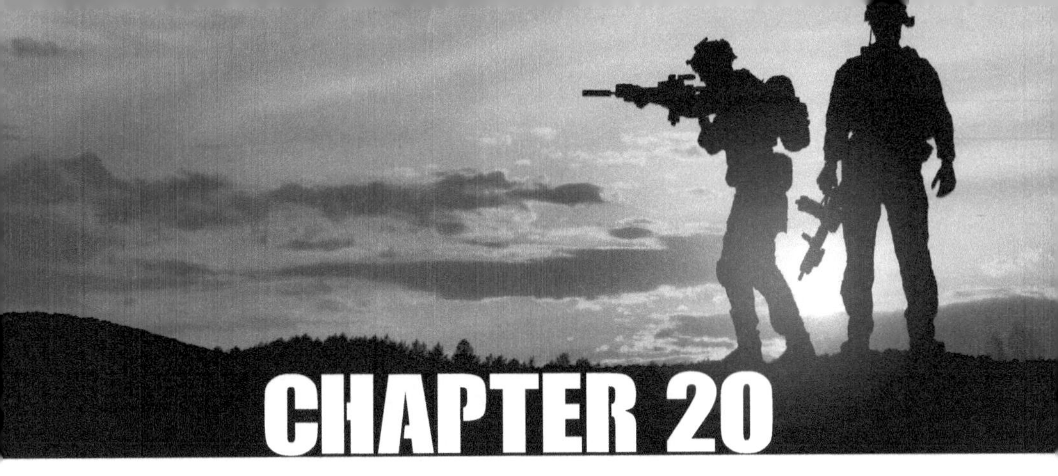

CHAPTER 20

Raising Saba's Barge

L ater that afternoon Jim sent Dorf, Mark, and John to pick up Dr. Gregg and his students in the Sea Stallion. Dr. Gregg had carefully selected nine hardworking, dedicated students for this honor. Five of them were women, two from America, one from England, and two from Greece. A young Englishman, a Frenchman, and two German male students were also selected. Alistair Gregg was amused often by the oddities of his students.

Martha Gimmel was the tallest of his students, an English girl who was just over five feet ten inches in height; very slender in build, and fairly pretty with light blue eyes and silky brown hair. Hugo Forry, one of the German students, was barely a quarter of an inch shorter, but tended to stay away from her for that reason. Rolf was muscular, while Louis was ripcord thin with the build of a marathon bicyclist. Lloyd Norris, the English gentlemen in his group seemed the most balanced of them all, and the others tended to listen to him.

Dorf towered over them as he ushered them into the helicopter and Dr. Gregg almost laughed as he watched his students stare at the giant. In his short sleeve shirt, his huge tightly muscled arms were obvious. People did tend to stare at someone who was tall, so he was used to it. He grinned at everyone and welcomed them, instructed them in belting in, and then took his place behind the controls in the pilot's seat.

As soon as the chopper lifted off, some of the students began to wonder if this was really going to be exciting, or sickening. Helicopters don't handle like airplanes, and they handle wind currents differently. However, once Dorf had the nose pointed in the direction of the ship and reached his top speed of one hundred and three miles per hour most of the bump and swing was gone. Two of the students were sick enough to throw up, but managed to keep everything down, at least until the helicopter circled the ship and settled in place for a smooth landing on the afterdeck. At that point they lost their lunch in a most undignified manner.

Once the wheels were down C.G. and Vince rolled underneath to shackle the helicopter to the deck with chains. When that was completed and the chains were tightened, they rolled out and signaled Dorf. He cut the engines and in the silence that followed the crew could hear the unfortunate pair coughing and gagging.

Mark hustled back and opened the door, ushering everyone out, and sending the two who had vomited down to sickbay. C.G. took them down. Dorf and Mark paused long enough to clean the mess with coffee grounds first, and then paper towels, followed by detergent and water.

The other students forgot the incident immediately. The activity on board the ship was far more interesting. John led them up to the bridge where they gathered in the CIC and stared in wonder at the pictures on the monitors from the depths.

"Welcome to *Bring It Up Coral*," Jim said, coming onto the bridge. He had changed into his white uniform, without the jacket, to meet his guests. "I'm Captain Shepherd, or just Shep if you want," he said, looking them over. At that moment C.G. ushered the other two from sickbay, where the doctor had checked them to make sure they were recovering properly. Dr. Wozniac accompanied them to the deck.

"I'm going to ask Mark to give you a tour of the ship. He's the Lieutenant that flew the chopper, and he will help you with any of your needs. Mark," Jim said, stepping aside. Mark gave him a smart salute, ushering the doctor and the students out to settle them in their rooms, and familiarize them with the ship. Doc Wozniac left them to the tour and returned to his wife.

Walking through the ship Mark answered questions in a straightforward manner. The men were assigned two rooms, both with four bunks, two small study desks, and storage space for their clothing. The women chose to divide into two groups, the Greek girls rooming together, and the girls from America with Martha, the English girl. Dr. Gregg received his own cabin, of course.

As evening approached the Bathyscaphe was winched to the surface with all the other equipment, and then carefully cleaned and stored properly. Dinner was a festive affair. Since there were guests, every crewmember showered and changed into uniform to look his best. Jim did not require this, but he was proud of his men for taking the initiative. Even Andrea wore his uniform.

Abe and Sturdy served steak and lobster for dinner that evening, with steamed vegetables and a salad bar. Jim, to give the students a chance to meet the crew, divided them in pairs and put them at different tables. Dr. Gregg and Katirina Vassar sat at the Captain's table. Katirina was surprised when Andrea welcomed her in her own language. Alistair Gregg chatted with everyone at the table, proving to be a charming guest with a pleasant sense of humor.

Late that night Louis and Dr. Gregg were talking quietly near the bow. Nodding his head in satisfaction, Jim looked up at the sky for a moment and breathed a prayer of simple thanks to God for this day. He felt hot tears fill his eyes and blinked them back in surprise. The depth of feeling he had for this new relationship was already much deeper than he had imagined, and it both pleased and frightened him. Walking quietly, he descended the stairs to his cabin and read his Bible for a short period of time before switching off his light.

On the deck, finished with their technical talk of the upcoming discovery, Louis stood quietly, watching Dorf and Mark as they checked everything on deck to be sure it was secure. One was a muscular giant, a fearsome man in many ways, disciplined and graceful in his movements despite his size. And Mark walked like a cat.

"Professor," Louis said quietly. "Who are these men?"

"They are men who spend their lives on the sea, Louis, men who risk their lives to rescue ships or boats in trouble, risking their lives to salvage ancient wrecks. Their Captain is a strange man, a soldier perhaps, but a man with the soul of a true historian. That is all I know. Why do you ask?" Dr. Gregg answered. There had been that something in the Frenchman's tone that said there was something more.

"Have you watched the way they move and work? My father was a soldier, and I traveled many places with him. I know how soldiers move and act, and these men are soldiers, or were soldiers. I do not know exactly what I am seeing, but there is something," Louis shook his head, as if frustrated at not knowing.

"Soldiers do not spend several months researching and then finding a sunken vessel to salvage, my young friend. Perhaps they were soldiers. Now, I think they are exactly what they claim to be. On the sea discipline is necessary, and with this Captain I would assume he expects his crew to maintain a high level of physical training."

"Perhaps," Louis replied softly. "Perhaps that is the answer. They were soldiers, and now they are civilians who know the value of physical and mental discipline. If this is true, they will be a very successful crew. I can tell you this, sir, I would not do anything to upset any of these men! They may no longer be soldiers on active duty, but they are death walking!"

Once again *Steel Crab* descended to the wreck. On the deck of *Bring It Up Coral* everyone was busy. Up in the computer room it was crowded as the students and Dr. Gregg crammed themselves into every available space to watch the monitors. Zeke found himself between Page Summers and Rhonda Klessel. Page was fascinated by the computer equipment, while Rhonda watched the monitors exclusively. To fill in the time it took for the bathyscaphe to reach the bottom and set up the sand boxes Zeke showed excerpts from yesterday's dive, finishing with the skeleton looking like it was hitching a ride. His witty comments kept the atmosphere light-hearted and the students warmed to this handsome computer genius.

His mind was multitasking watching over the systems of the bathyscaphe and the progress of the pictures he was showing the eager students. Their laughter at the skeleton was rewarding, but his eye did not miss the slight rise of carbon monoxide in the bathyscaphe.

"*Steel Crab*, your carbon monoxide level is rising. Check your settings and give me a status report," Zeke said.

"Settings are normal. I'm checking the filters now," FM's voice was calm.

Frank twisted his frame in an awkward and almost painful contortion to reach the filter. He pulled it out and sighed. Defective filters were unusual, but this one was obviously not working at all. Pulling himself out of the tight space he found another then screwed himself into the area again to replace it. As soon as it was in place the monoxide level began to drop.

"Defective filter," FM said into his headphone. "Thanks for keeping an eye out for us."

"Uncle Zeke is always watching you!" Zeke said with a grin.

Once again, the removal of the silt around the vessel occupied the crew of the bathyscaphe while the students above watched in fascination as more and more of the hull was exposed. The hours passed quickly, and when lunch was announced everyone was surprised. Only one of the students had risen in time for breakfast, but Abe, preparing for such an occasion, left fruit, milk cartons, and fruit drink out. Few had taken anything, and they were famished.

While the crew ate in shifts the crew of *Steel Crab* grabbed an MRE and then got back to work. FM was drilling the holes for the cables that now lay stretched on the starboard side of the vessel. After finishing the drilling, he inserted padded sleeves that would eventually be filled with air to protect the wood from damage from the cable.

Once that was completed, he fed the cables through the sleeves, holding the near end with one arm, while feeding the cable eye through. He went slowly, inch by inch, to avoid as much damage as possible. Once he had all eight cables stretched out with equal lengths at each end, he grabbed the cables hanging down from a steel frame that was hooked to the main cable from the ship's crane.

Steel Crab was no longer tethered to the ship by that cable. Driver kept the bathyscaphe in a position where FM could work the arms and tools without interference from any of the cables that still attached them to the ship.

Sparks watched with appreciation as FM expertly fed the hooks into the cable eyes, attaching the pin and clip in place to hold them. FM grinned at him when he finished.

"These controls are amazing!" FM said as he finished. "Once I got used to them just a few motions of my arm, hand, or fingers was all it took!"

Shortly after mid-afternoon everything was in place to set the charges which would, if correctly calculated, allow the hull to lift free of the bottom mud. A net was stretched to the starboard side that would be secured between the hull and the cables as well, so that nothing would be lost in raising the vessel to the surface.

As the students filed out onto the deck the bathyscaphe was just being lifted to its cradle on the deck, near the rear of the helicopter. They paused to watch the men climb out. All around the vessel men worked, spraying it clean, checking everything. Even inside the bathyscaphe men worked, preparing it for another dive.

None of the crew thought this unusual. It was necessary, and since each one of them owned part of the company, it was important.

As this was going on the deep-water sea sleds were placed strategically around the sunken ship, their bright lights illuminating everything, their cameras sending back digital images of amazing clarity to the monitors above. Wade knelt on the deck, a series of toggle switches in a steel box, perhaps eighteen inches long, three inches deep, and an inch and a half wide. The explosive charges were connected to those switches.

John stood above him, and on the crane, TRT sat ready at the controls. Raising his hand in a signal John motioned for TRT to take up the slack in the main cable. Watching the cable John suddenly closed his hand to indicate all stop. Quivering with tension the cable was now in place.

Wade began to flip the switches, holding a stopwatch in his left hand, and using his right to flip each switch when it was time. There was no noise on the surface, and nothing to show that the charges had gone off as planned until bubbles rose to the surface. Zeke, at the computer terminal watched the silt rise with each explosion, watching the bottom of the sea ripple. The last puff of silt went up. For several seconds nothing happened, and then suddenly the hull lifted from the mud, shedding a cloud of silt that blinded the cameras.

"Vessel free!" Zeke said into his microphone.

Once the silt settled and he could see clearly, he spoke again. "We have visual. Let's take her up one fathom and see how she takes it!" His voice was filled with excitement.

John nodded to Master Chief Warner, who carefully and slowly reeled in six feet of cable, braking at exactly one fathom. Zeke studied the pictures, and Wade, who was now standing behind him in the computer room, nodded silently. It was Wade who gave the next command.

"Slow lift three fathoms," He commanded quietly.

Most of the people who were not needed at the moment were standing at the railing, looking into the blue green Mediterranean waters, waiting with mounting excitement. Jim Warner lifted the vessel slowly another eighteen feet and then braked. Wade and Zeke studied the vessel as the cameras followed it up. Nothing much had changed, although Wade could see that even with the air sleeves the lifting was pinching the monkey rail, main rail or sheer, and the plank sheer molding. The deck was not buckling at those points, so he decided it was safe to begin the slow and steady ascent to the surface.

"Okay, TRT. Let's bring her up at about one third speed," Wade said.

Wade wanted to be out on the deck, watching the sunken vessel appear at the surface. With a sigh he continued to watch the crawling lift from the monitors, carefully sweeping his eyes over every part of the vessel, making sure that everything was as it should be.

"The air sleeves were a good idea," Zeke said conversationally, as he sat back and watched several different things at once.

"Next time I'm going to devise rails to go across the top, so they don't pinch. I should have thought of that," Wade chastised himself, looking at his design critically.

"Live and learn," Zeke replied matter-of-factly. "Passing four hundred feet, no significant changes," he added.

Just then a skull appeared at one of the square oar ports, looking as though its owner was peering out. Slowly it moved back out of vision. Zeke looked over his shoulder at Wade with a grin.

"Guess it's the first time he's seen the light in a while," The grin faded as Zeke thought about being chained to a boat that was sinking. He looked back to the computer systems.

"Bring it up to about thirty feet and stop," Wade said into his headset.

"Roger that," Master Chief Warner replied evenly. "Zeke, my instruments say that we're at one hundred and sixty feet at my mark. Mark. How do you read?" TRT added.

"Mark is correct," Zeke confirmed.

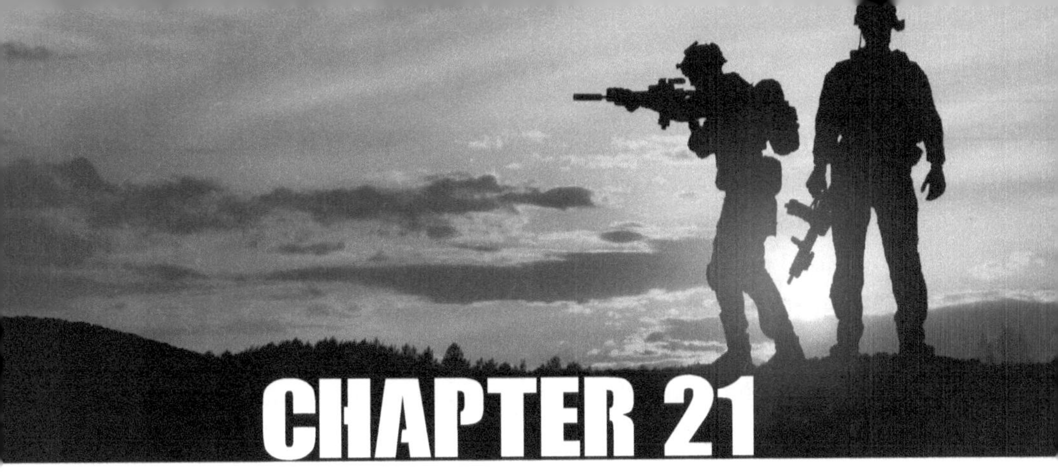

CHAPTER 21

History Uncovered

As the vessel came up bubbles broke the surface, and then the dark object was visible. Chief Warner brought it to a dead stop thirty feet below the surface. Wade sighed, and then grinned at Zeke. The two gave a "high-five" hand slap and then Wade was moving quickly out and down to the deck.

"Three divers into the water for photographs," Wade ordered as he stepped onto the afterdeck. Dorf, Mark, and Smitty were already suited up. They dropped backwards off the diving platform and slowly sank to the vessel. Each man had a camera. Circling the outside of the vessel Dorf took a total of one hundred and twenty still shots. Smitty photographed the deck and structures that were still visible, taking almost as many shots as Dorf. Mark found a large hole in the upper deck and slowly lowered himself into the bowels of the dead ship.

Mud covered everything. He reached into the mud, expecting his hand to sink several inches, but encountered something hard immediately. Slowly he moved his hands around, blind now because of the black cloud surrounding him, until he pulled up a square object. He kicked up carefully, the object tucked under his right arm, his left arm feeling for the guide rope. Grasping it he pulled himself out onto the deck and swam to the surface.

Lifting it carefully onto the dive platform he slid his mask up and grinned up at C.G.

"I think I found something!" he said, his eyes bright with excitement. "It's heavy!"

C.G. grunted as he lifted it carefully into a net, suspended from above. The net was then winched up to the deck, and the steel arm from which it hung rotated electronically one hundred and eighty degrees. The net was lowered, and the object removed.

Dr. Gregg carefully began to wash away the debris, using a salt-water solution, gently brushing with a soft bristle brush until the ivory surface of a box was revealed. The ivory had been carved into stylized lotus flower on the sides, and open palm-leaf on the top. The bottom was smooth. Louis took photographs, and Hugo and Rolf carefully pried the top open

In silence everyone stared down into the water-filled box at a golden figure, representing some Egyptian Pharaoh, with a necklace of glazed stealite, and precious gems, mostly hiddenite and kunzite, greens and violets to offset the stealite. The figure was sitting, as on a floor, on a gold platform, with a scepter resting on his right shoulder, held in his right hand, and his left hand over a scroll resting on his knees. A Pharaoh's crown sat upon his head.

With shaking hands Dr. Gregg slowly lifted it out of the water, and he began cleaning it. When he was finished the gold gleamed in the sunlight of the late afternoon, the gemstones gleaming on the necklace, sunlight seeming to dance within them.

"Captain Shepherd, this one piece should fund your entire project!" Dr. Gregg breathed. "And this is certainly an indication that we have the correct vessel," he added, suddenly laughing, his eyes shining.

Jim looked at his brother, and they hugged, suddenly laughing, slapping crewmembers on the back, shaking hands and congratulating each other. Then the work began in earnest. The wreck was lifted to just six feet beneath the surface, allowing the students to help in unloading the treasures within. As if glad to release its prisoners, the Mediterranean remained calm, all through the night. Barely a breeze rippled the surface as the crew worked, slowly emptying the hull of the wreck.

Some of the students had moved to a temporary wash tank set up on the deck. They were brushing away mud, uncovering treasures, cataloging everything carefully, and photographing each piece from several different angles. Those who were not at the tank were in the wreck, or on the diving platform, passing items from the water to the deck. Near midnight they were dropping with fatigue, and only went to their berths when ordered by Captain Shepherd. They slept only a few hours, up well before dawn, hustling down to the deck to continue their work, sharing their eagerness with everyone on the crew.

Late that afternoon Jim stood beside Zeke in the computer center, looking through the list of cataloged items. Saba had certainly collected an amazing array of treasures on her journey. From the Mesopotamian period a stone frieze, according to Dr. Gregg an artifact from the temple of Ninhursag, Tell 'Ubaid was uncovered. It depicted a dairy industry. In the same chest were cylinder seals, some made of gypsum, some made of aragonite, and one made of greenstone. The greenstone seal belonged to Hash-hamer, governor of the city of Ishkum-Sin. The owner was pictured, holding the hand of a goddess facing Ur-Nammu, king of Ur. Between the goddess and the king was a crescent moon, turned ninety degrees to the left so that it looked like a smile in the sky. This was the symbol of the god Nanna.

A clay tablet that had been a pictographic record of something was so worn that only a few symbols remained visible on its surface. The symbols were clear enough however to guarantee the piece a prominent place in the museum. Dr. Gregg thought it might be a record of daily rations for a military unit covering a five-day period. He was very excited about the piece.

Another chest held a three-pronged headdress and jewelry, probably prepared for Saba to wear to her grave. The remains of a lyre, the sounding box showing the "standard of Ur," peace side, and war side. The instrument had what appeared to be a bull's head at the front, but the upper frame was nearly gone.

Twelve helmets made of gold, probably provided for her personal bodyguard as a gift, filled twelve separate small boxes made of ivory. The helmets included a diadem, a braided bun, a carved ear with a hole for hearing, and were ornately decorated. Jim donated one to the museum, and one to Dr. Gregg personally, to help fund further research. Dr. Gregg was speechless, weeping openly.

One of the Satraps she visited in Egypt presented Saba with an inlaid gold bracelet, with the god Horus depicted as a child between two cobras, floating above a lotus. The hieroglyphic inscription inside the bracelet told the story to any who could decipher it. Dr. Gregg gave each of the women students the opportunity to wear it, but none of them had small enough wrists to close and latch it.

There were numerous gold rings, many of glazed stealite on a swivel, rings that were used to mark a wax seal on a missive. Several depicted Ankh, the symbol of life, in front of a sphinx. There were also gold rings with a polished Scarab skeleton. Wooden models of workers filled two crates, once painted, now just smooth bare wood. Only a few had pigments of color still attached. A Shabti box and dummy Canopic jars had been presented to the queen as well. There were crates of carved golden animals, probably used for money, still in excellent condition. Golden statues of various gods filled other boxes, others made of ivory, some made of aragonite, and several made of copper. Each box was hand made with marvelous skill. Jim thought the students got as much pleasure from the boxes themselves as the treasure within. That was as it should be, he thought.

Then there were the gemstones. In crystallography, crystals are divided into seven systems (isometric, tetragonal, hexagonal, trigonal, orthorhombic, monoclinic and triclinic). To Jim's amazement, there were seven small jewelry boxes, all cast silver, dedicated to each system. There were diamonds, rubies, sapphires, emeralds, spinel, tourmaline, amethyst, chrysoprase, precious opal, jade, lapis lazuli, malachite, gahnite, smaragdite, and obsidian.

Each student was allowed to pick one gem as a gift of thanks from the crew. Some, Jim noticed, chose the more expensive stones, while others looked for what they liked, planning to have the stone set as a memento of this occasion. Zeke watched Jim go through the list, item by item, and spoke when Jim closed the booklet.

"We certainly established our name in deep sea salvage. The proceeds from this stuff will pay for this boat, all the salaries, all the excess equipment, and leave us enough to operate for another forty years, with regular salary raises!" Zeke was obviously pleased. "What the heck do we do as a swan song to this!"

"Every year we'll do research on a lost treasure ship. In between we'll do some rescue. The rest of the time we'll spend nailing a certain Admiral's hide to the wall." Jim replied with surprising passion. "Then, in about five years, we'll train a replacement crew to take our places, and retire to a simpler and less hazardous life at sea," Jim added that with a grin.

CHAPTER 22

Sins Uncovered

"**O**h! I forgot to tell you. I tracked down the registration on that yacht that's been shadowing us. It's registered to a company called Mercury. Sir Edward says they smell wrong, but he doesn't have anything concrete to give us. I hacked into their mainframe and discovered that three women run the company, all graduates of Harvard, all from the Middle East. You flagged them back in Boston," Jim looked at Zeke quizzically, remembering the three young women.

"They're daughters of some very powerful oil sheiks we don't like at all," Zeke handed Jim a computer report and watched his Captain carefully read it. When Jim looked up, he continued. "They are an export firm that seems legitimate. However, when I hacked them, I discovered that their clandestine operations are all directed at their fathers!

"You also need to know that for the past few hours they have maneuvered their vessel carefully so that we can only see the bow, and their rear deck is hidden. That in itself is unusual," Zeke finished his report.

"Interesting," Jim murmured, looking quickly through the report again. "Let's do a reconnaissance tonight, see what they're up to on that yacht," Jim handed the report back to Zeke. "Please put that on my desk. Tell Driver and Smitty to suit up at 03:00. We'll go in under water. I'll meet them on the diving platform. Make sure none of the kids see us go," Jim waved a salute as he left the computer center.

Abe and Sturdy prepared a special meal that evening, Greek cuisine, which everyone enjoyed. Driver and Smitty sat with Jim that evening, along with Lorin Monair, Doc and Millie, and Andrea. Lorin took to Millie immediately, and the two of them chattered all during the meal, leaving Jim free to think. Jack talked to Doc and Andrea, and Smitty occasionally added a comment. When the meal was finished Jim nodded to Driver and Smitty.

They met in his office for privacy. Jim let them read Zeke's report, which was on his desk as ordered. For a half an hour they discussed boarding the yacht and what Jim wanted. Leaving one at a time the two men made their way to their berths to sleep for a while. Jim stretched out on the cot in his office after setting his alarm to wake him at two in the morning.

Wade had the night watch. He was, of course, aware of what was planned. Keeping an eye on their guests he made sure all of them were in bed. When he saw Jim making his way to the hatch cover into the center hold, he pressed his microphone button twice, to signal that all was clear. Jim responded in kind to assure him he'd heard the transmission.

For this trip the three men suited up in their covert infiltration units, which included no bubbles breathing equipment, a waterproof bag, navigation swimboard, neoprene helmet, storage pouches, facemasks, and a combat dry suit. Each man chose one Ontario Navy Knife, and their favorite pistol. Jack Boswell liked the H&K P-10 because of its light weight. Jim liked the H&K Mark 23, a heavier gun and heavier caliber. Smitty picked up one of the Beretta M92F pistols. Each also carried one of the Mac 5/10's as their main combat weapon.

Smitty had two stun grenades. Driver carried two gas grenades that looked much like a hockey puck, putting anyone taking one breath into a deep sleep that lasted for up to 16 hours. Most men woke up between sixteen and seventeen hours after inhaling the gas. When they were ready, they made their way to the diving platform and silently slid into the water. Their navigational swimboards were silent and made the thousand-yard trip uneventful and quick. It was exactly three in the morning when Jim and his team surfaced at different points.

Smitty and Driver kept their Mac 10's trained on the boat while Jim climbed onto the wooden platform at the stern so carefully the boat did not change its rocking motion with the gentle swell. In complete silence he dropped his rebreather system into the water, hanging it on the platform so it would not sink. He put on his facemask and combat dry suit, taken from the waterproof bag. Once he was fully dressed and armed, he slipped silently over the stern into the yacht.

A single guard sat in a padded chase, snoring softly. Tightly bound to a wooden chair, a woman sat, her head resting on her chest. Jim pulled a small bottle from his pocket, put it under the guard's nose, and then covered his own. He sprayed a small jet of the gas in the grenades. The man snored on.

Walking like a cat Jim put a hand on the woman's mouth before she could waken and scream. Her eyes shot open with real terror and she struggled vainly, opening scabs around the cruel bonds that held her. Jim leaned down and whispered softly in her ear.

"Easy does it, ma'am. We're the good guys." Perhaps it was his American accent, or the way he spoke, but she stopped struggling and moaned softly into his glove. He discretely patted her shoulder, giving her a dose of morphine to ease the pain.

Stepping around so she could see him, and then removing his mask for a moment, he took note of her, his eyes quickly taking in everything she'd suffered. Her eyes took him in as well, then the guard sleeping so peacefully on the chase. She rolled her eyes as if to warn him. Jim grinned.

"He's out cold," he whispered. "I'm going to take my hand away now. Don't talk yet, please." Taking his hand away he watched her struggle to breathe against the tight ropes as she relaxed slightly.

"Two more of my men are coming on board. How many people are on this boat?" Jim whispered. He put his ear close to her mouth.

"Four men, including the guard up here," she whispered hoarsely. An English accent came with those whispered words, and he could tell she'd been screaming until her vocal cords were severely damaged. It was obvious that it hurt to talk. Anger against the men who did this to this poor woman flooded through him. It was obvious she had been beaten and tortured.

Jim nodded as Smitty and Driver ghosted over the stern, as silent as he had been. They moved below, found the three other occupants of the yacht, and put them to sleep. Since they were all in the same room, having drunken themselves into a stupor earlier that evening, it was easy. Following orders, they gave only a minimum dose of the gas to knock them out completely, returning topside to Jim.

"You two search this boat from stem to stern. I want to know everything about it. The lady on the deck needs some help," Jim ordered.

"On the job, boss!" Smitty said with a grin. He and Driver moved off, still making no sound, and showing no lights to curious eyes from outside.

Up on the deck Jim took a good look at the girl. She spoke English with a definite British accent. Her hair was greasy, matted and tangled, suggesting she had been a prisoner for some time. She was thin, almost gaunt, and filthy. The smell of urine and feces lingered around her suggesting they did not allow her to use a bathroom. Then his eyes rested on her feet, encased in hardened cement blocks that rose halfway to her knees, her toes sticking out. Once again, he knelt in front of her, his mask off, his voice soft as he spoke, his eyes locked on hers.

"The men below are unconscious. They will not awaken for some time. We can talk, but not loudly. Voices carry over the water," Jim spoke easily, keeping his focus on her. She was naked, but he kept his eyes on hers. "My name is Jim. When are they going to dump you in the water?"

"There's a boat coming in an hour. It's a rubber boat, very quiet. Three men come, bringing supplies and orders. One of them is going to drown me," she began to sob, softly.

"Why do they want to kill you?" Jim asked, reaching behind her and putting his hand over hers, and using the other one to wipe her nose with a cloth, as gently as possible.

"They kidnapped me. They kidnap western European girls often, at least four times a year to listen to them talk. Once they know about your family, they send trained killers to wipe them out, right after the ransom is collected," her voice broke and she wept for a few seconds and with a sinking heart Jim knew this story was going to be bad. "They wait then, and while letting this cement dry around your legs they show you the pictures," she began to sob again, deep soul wrenching sobs of utter loss. This time Jim found himself holding her, stroking her greasy hair with one hand, saying nothing. After a while she quieted, and he released her.

Driver appeared, moving his head so that Jim joined him. He showed Jim the photos. Having seen the look in Driver's eyes he knew his own were now filled with rage. He breathed slowly, calming himself before giving Driver the order to copy the photos and put them back. Returning to the girl he knelt again.

"Time is running short, so I want you to listen carefully," Jim said. "I'm going to rescue you, but not until they've put you into the water. I'll be there, far enough below the surface so that they will not see. I'm going to put something in your mouth once you are in the water. Before you breathe, you must blow out. So, take a deep breath before they put you in. They will do this almost immediately, because they have to do it while it is still dark. I will be waiting."

"And then what?" she was angry, her eyes suddenly flashing. "I saw what they did to my family!" Fresh tears fell as she sobbed bitterly and again, he held her as best he could in her bound condition, his own heart fiercely ablaze with the need for justice.

"And then we find out how many of them are involved, how they work, and who their next victim is. After that, we bring them to justice," Jim said simply.

"Send them to prison! How does that pay for what they've done?" her cracked and whispering voice dripped with scorn. "Even if some are given the death penalty, most of them will eventually get out! They are worse than animals, and they deserve to die horrible deaths!"

"Justice doesn't always mean prison," Jim said quietly, his eyes boring into hers. She saw something in them that made her catch her breath, and if she could have, she would have recoiled from what she saw. "There will be no prisons for these animals. Their sins are uncovered, and proper action is required! This I promise! Remember, blow out before you breathe in."

He was gone as quickly and as silently as he had come. Two men came into her vision from below, dressed much like Jim had been. One paused over the guard on the chase, waving something under his nose. Both of the men looked at her, their eyes locking on hers, and nodding before moving again. Then they slipped over the stern and she heard no more.

Hope began to grow in her heart then, and she thought about the entire experience. Jim had studied her condition, but kept his eyes on hers, and the two men leaving did the same. They did not make her feel filthy, looking at her naked body, and there was something about them, something she couldn't quite place, that made her believe that perhaps men such as these could bring justice into balance. As they left, she could feel nothing change in the motion of the boat and wondered how they did that. Even the men that held her made the boat move with every motion.

CHAPTER 23

Rescue

It took the guard about fifteen minutes to wake up properly. When he did, he looked about in surprise, grunted and sprang to his feet. For a few moments he was noisily sick over the side of the boat. Recovering quickly, he stalked over to her and tested the ropes that bound her, laughing coarsely when she groaned from the fresh wave of pain. The morphine helped some, but it still hurt. Grasping her hair, he jerked her head back hard against the back of the chair.

"It will be soon now," he threatened, his face close to hers. She spat, but he was ready and quickly jerked out of the way. He slapped her hard enough to make her head spin, then laughed again. Spinning her chair, he pushed it forward until her chest rested against the side of the boat and she could look down into the dark water. "Get used to the view," he said, laughing again.

He left her there, which was torture because she could barely breathe, and the ropes cut into her. The cramps came back and she howled in pain before the guard tipped the chair back and stuffed a filthy oil-soaked rag into her mouth to muffle her screams. He was chuckling the whole time.

When she fainted, he pulled the rag out and put it aside. The sound of an outboard motor, barely discernable reached him, and he went to the stern. As always, there were three men in the boat. Two he thought little about, for they were like him. The other, the leader, he thought much about. Few men frightened him, and this was one of them. This one was as cold and deadly as a shark. Just his presence was enough to cause fear!

He was Middle Eastern, but the guard had never been able to put a finger on just where he came from. The man was six feet tall, maybe an inch more, thin and wiry in build, with whipcord strength and speed. His dark eyes never showed any emotion. They were like the eyes of a shark, penetrating and dead. Leaping over the stern he looked at the girl and back at the guard, his face never changing.

"Did you show her the pictures?" he asked in perfect English.

"Yes, over a period of two days, one at a time, just as you instructed," the guard answered respectfully. "She saw it all, everything that was done, how her family suffered and died."

"It is important that she die hating us and defeated," the man said simply, watching her as he spoke, seeing the hatred in her eyes. "It is time."

A knife appeared in his hand, as if by magic, and the guard swallowed nervously, hoping no one had noticed.

"I am Fezik al' Loudi," he said, looking into the girl's eyes. He grinned evilly as she recoiled from his face. All the signs were there. She had been weeping, and in pain. The hate radiated out from her. Sometimes the hate overshadowed the fear, as in this girl. With swift and sure movements, he cut the ropes that bound her, then quickly stuffed the oil-soaked rag into her mouth as the screams came from the release, the new cramps almost deforming her limbs.

He spun the chair and pulled it out from underneath her and she fell. The concrete blocks around her feet so heavy she could not move them. Someone pulled tape over the rag. She fought them as best she could, but they slapped her weak arms aside easily. It ended quickly.

Two men grabbed the concrete blocks hardened around her feet and lower leg and dragged her to the stern. They simply dropped them over the edge and her body followed. She tried to land standing, but her body tipped forward and her face hit the water hard. Fighting with all her strength she got her head up for a deep breath. The man dragged her out of the water and left her in a sitting position, the concrete pulling painfully at her knees, as they lowered them into the water quietly.

This time they took her wrists, breaking open the scabs and holding her up, so that from the waist up she was out of the water. Fezik al' Loudi urinated on her while the men stood laughing. When he was finished, he waved for them to let her go. They did, and she took a deep breath through her nose, smelling the sour urine and passed beneath the surface.

Twenty feet below the surface hands caught her. The tape was ripped off hard and fast, and the rag removed. Something hard and plastic went into her mouth and she blew out weakly, and then sucked in blessed air. Her ears hurt but shortly after she began breathing, they popped. She sensed movement, though hanging on to consciousness was difficult. She was being pulled feet first, but Jim was beside her, she could see him dimly through the water, and he was holding her hand gently in his.

Then she realized his other hand was clamped over her bleeding wrist. Another diver was on the other side, holding her in the same way. Sharks smelled blood, and there were sharks in these waters. These men were risking their lives to save her. What if the sharks attacked them as well? *Oh God, please, don't let them die saving me this way*! She lost consciousness at that point.

When consciousness came again a pair of dancing brown eyes hovered over her, set in a pretty face, wrinkled with age, and surrounded by a halo of curly white hair. The smile on that face was beautiful and sweet, and the patient found herself smiling back weakly.

"You've had a terrible ordeal, my dear. You are safe now, and in good hands. Rest, child. Try not to think about the painful things. We'll work through all this somehow, you'll see," Millie talked brightly as she moved around the hospital bed, checking that all was as it should be. Assured by that competent and smiling face the girl slipped into sleep again. When Millie was done, she stepped away from the bed and the smile slipped from her face. Tears rolled down her cheeks and she turned to her husband who opened his arms and gathered her in, sobbing against his chest.

Over her head Charles looked into Jim's eyes. What he saw there was almost frightening. There was a fury, and behind the fury a resolve so powerful that it seemed to radiate outward, like the heat from a lamp. There were no tears in Jim's eyes, though he'd shed some when he saw the full extent of the girl's condition. What there was in those eyes was death.

"I don't know how to deal with this," Dr. Wozniac said softly, burying his face in his wife's hair.

"I do," Jim said simply, his voice flat, his eyes suddenly blazing.

"Is killing them really the answer?" Dr. Wozniac asked.

"I don't think that's wrong in this instance!" Millie snorted, surprising him, her tears suddenly stopped. She looked up at him. "I don't think these men will understand anything less."

"This kind of terrorist does not surrender. The man who masterminded this is evil in a way none of us understands. I *will* stop him! If I can capture some of his men, I will, but I doubt if it will be possible," Jim said softly.

"No. I don't think so either," Doc agreed quietly, his eyes on Jim. "This time I don't think I'll even feel a little sorry for those men when they meet your team, Captain. When men such as those who hurt this poor child do violence, they take a deadly gamble. They gamble that their deeds will never be uncovered, and that God Himself will not notice their deeds or punish them. That's a deadly gamble indeed, and I think their marker just got called in."

Doc shook his head and squeezed his wife one more time before letting her go and returning to his patient. Her feet and lower legs were a mess, and it would take days before she would be able to walk, and weeks before the skin healed.

How long had they held her prisoner? They never let her use a bathroom. Perhaps she'd been tied to that chair for two or three weeks. Infection was a real danger from sitting in her own waste.

She was thin, too thin, and her blood tests showed that she was near losing the battle against the many dangers she faced. But he was pumping life-saving medicines into her to fight the infections. Her body would be whole again. *What about her mind?*

Shaking his head, he moved away to write in her chart and to think about how to treat some of the lesser things he'd left until now. By evening she would be able to wake up enough to tell them who she was, if Jim didn't have an identification before then. They did have a name. She'd whispered it twice. Fezik al' Loudi, whoever he was, had left an impression to fight its way through the fog of her brain. Her sleep had been broken by horrible night terrors as well.

Doc knew that Jim already had a complete dossier on al'Loudi. Jim had been holding it in his hand as they talked, and Doc had seen the name on the file cover. It was a thick file, so this was a very bad man, with many sins to his credit. This, Doc was sure, would be one of his last.

"Rest now, child," he said softly to her. "We will help you heal physically, mentally, and emotionally. This I promise," his wife nodded in agreement.

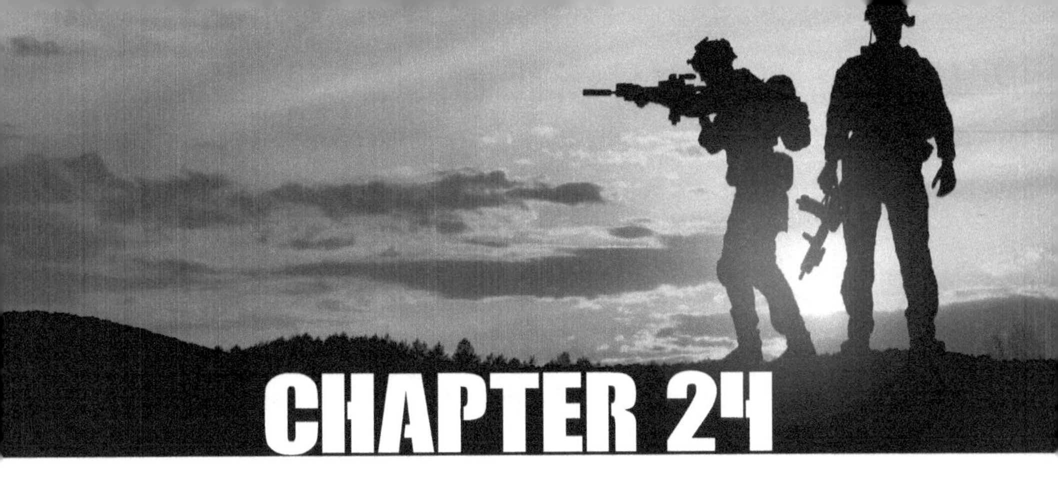

CHAPTER 24

Doing What It Takes

On deck Jim stood with Dr. Gregg. With the crew's approval he was entrusting the entire treasure of Saba's barge to this diminutive man. Gregg would arrange for the auction of the treasures for the company. Jim offered him fifteen percent of the total offered from the auction, but Gregg refused. Instead he angled to be part of another treasure hunt, one he had pursued for years now. Jim agreed with a grin, caught in the excitement of another discovery, and liking the professor very much.

Eventually it was time for the students, some reluctantly, to climb once more on board the helicopter. Doc Wozniac had provided those who had been sick before with a patch to help. They didn't seem too confident. Each passenger stepped around the boxes and crates holding the catalogued items from the barge, to find a seat and strap in under the careful eye of Dorf. Dorf, John, Wade, and Mark were the crew for this trip, with John in the pilot's seat, and Mark flying co-pilot. Wade was at the communications center and Dorf would act as host to their guests.

Dr. Gregg was the last to climb on board, pumping Jim's hand with unveiled excitement in his eyes. "I'll put together what I have and meet you in two weeks at the museum! By then the auction will be arranged, but I'll call about the result as soon as I get it. Thanks for everything, Captain Shepherd!"

To Dr. Gregg's delight Jim stepped back, drew himself to attention and saluted the Doctor. Then he saluted the students. They laughed and waved and then the whine of the rotors and the thump of the engines drowned out any other sounds. The huge bird lifted from the deck and headed toward Egypt. Jim stood for only a moment on the deck before heading up to the bridge.

On his way up he glanced toward the place where the yacht had remained watching them until they determined what had been salvaged and left. He found that odd. *Why did they want to know what we were searching for?* Andrea stood at the wheel, calmly waiting the order to get under way. It was not the first time he was piloting the ship, yet he still felt honored to be chosen for the job. As Jim entered the bridge, he turned from reviewing the instruments.

"The girl, she is recovering?" Andrea asked softly. It was not the question Jim had been expecting.

"Yes, Papa, she is, as well as can be expected." Andrea smiled as Jim used the nickname that had become his on the ship. Jim grinned back. "We're all going to help her get well, and we're going to let her see justice done!" Jim added grimly, the smile fading. He heard the iron in his voice, knowing that in his soul his intent was set. Nothing would do but to see his plan through. Not now. *Why?*

"There is great emotion with this one, yes? The pictures tell a story that is beyond understanding. I felt and saw in all the men this great emotion," Andrea watched the instruments as he spoke.

"Yes. That is dangerous. Some of the emotion will be replaced by determination. The anger must be carefully managed, so that we do not become distracted by it, or driven by it. But it must be allowed to motivate us!" Jim was silent for a moment, his mind somewhere else. Suddenly he looked back.

"Let's get underway and tow this barge back so the museum can attempt to display it," he commanded.

Andrea turned to the wheel, gave two sharp blasts on the horn to warn the crew that they were getting under way, and eased the tug into forward, gently pushing the throttles forward until the dial read six knots. Jim entered the compass bridge and found Smitty hard at work plotting their course and speed. He nodded to Smitty as he passed and entered the computer center. Zeke looked up from the array of monitors and equipment surrounding him and without pausing began to speak.

"Her name is Cecilia Merton. Her father is Roland Merton, who resided in Middleton in Teesdale, Cumbria. Mother Mary, two brothers Ronald and Jeffrey, eighteen and sixteen. Family found murdered in their home, no witnesses, and no leads. Middlesbrough's finest are working on it with help from London. No one saw anything or heard anything. They've been trying to locate Cecilia, a student, last address a school in Athine. Some of the students went to see the Holy Land and she's been missing for three weeks now."

Zeke paused, his eyes looking down and somehow inward. Then he looked up and Jim was surprised at the anger that flashed suddenly. "The woman at the murder scene was raped, and the boys were sodomized. The father was castrated and probably forced to watch while he slowly bled to death. Both boys had their testicles nailed to small boards before they were sodomized. The boards were then doused with gasoline and lit on fire. Forensics said it took a long time for them to die, Jim."

Jim just stared at Zeke as he finished speaking. In the pit of his stomach he felt sick, almost to the point of vomiting. *Could I do something like that to another human being? No! How do we apply justice here? There isn't anything that can do that! And she saw those pictures. She saw how her mother and father died, and how her brothers suffered!*

"I'll tell Doc," Jim whispered softly. But the flint in his stormy green eyes told Zeke everything he needed to know. The perpetrators of this crime would face justice. Zeke nodded quietly, handing the report to Jim.

Jim made his way down to sickbay and asked Doc if he could see him privately. When they were alone in the Doctor's small office

Jim handed him the report, complete with the photos that had been shown to Cecilia. Charles read it and his face went white.

"Didn't you tell me they showed her pictures of this?" Doc said his voice strained. Suddenly the good doctor ran for his bathroom, and Jim heard sounds of retching from behind the door.

Go ahead Doc. I feel the same way myself. Jim waited, keeping a tight reign on his own emotions and stomach. When Charles returned, he nodded at Jim, his eyes filled with tears.

"We'll get her through this, Jim. We have too," he declared.

"For the first time in my life that's what's most important," Jim said. "I never really gave much thought to victims before, other than to extend them the utmost courtesy. Somehow that's all changed. I need to help get her through this as much as you do, Doc. Whatever I can do, whenever you need me, I'm here! Hope that makes sense," Jim added.

"Millie will have to know," Doc said sadly.

"I know. I wanted you to break it to her. You know her better. I'm sorry," Jim added, meaning it.

"How long will it take us to get to Egypt towing the barge?" Doc asked.

"The better part of ten days," Jim replied. "Possibly a little more if we run into rough water."

"Okay, Jim. We'll brief the crew tonight. Have them all meet in the conference room. Millie will have to stay down here with her, in case she wakes up. I'll do the briefing," Doc replied.

Jim left without saying anything else and went to his own office to wade through the day's paperwork and update his logbook. For once he was glad to have this distraction and he diligently went through everything, finding himself just finishing up as the supper bell sounded on the speaker system. Perspective was difficult to find here, he knew, and while he worked he'd thought long and hard about that. He went down to the dining room with a lighter heart, though he was not hungry. *How can anyone eat after seeing those photos?*

John and Wade came into his office as he was finishing his work. They took seats, and for a few moments they simply stared at Jim. He wondered what could be on their minds.

"Why are we suddenly doing this?" John asked, leaning forward and resting his elbows on Jim's desk. "I can remember a time when we would deliver this package to the proper authorities and be on our way." Jim understood, and suddenly he knew how to answer, though the sudden knowledge both frightened and thrilled him. It was, he knew, the Holy Spirit.

"Because I have a relationship with Jesus Christ now," Jim said quietly. "I've accepted him as my Lord and Savior. For the first time in my life, the victim of these atrocities is more important than anything else," Jim sat back and watched his brother.

"Ah!" John responded, sitting back. He looked at his brother carefully.

"What's changed?" Wade asked, curious.

"I've changed," Jim said softly. "My heart has been softened and I can actually hear the Lord speaking to me through His Word."

"Abe and Sturdy say that," Wade nodded once. "I envy their faith; wish I could know God the way they seem to know Him," he sighed heavily.

"Me too," John admitted, his eyes now downcast. "How did it happen with you?" John asked, looking up. Jim paused a moment, sending up a desperate prayer, because more than anything else, he wanted his brother and best friend to know Jesus. To his surprise the Bible verses and words came easily.

Abe helped him prepare to witness by teaching him the Roman's Road to Salvation. He'd added a few verses to that from his own studies, and he shared simply his faith, quoting the verses, trying to explain the condition of sinful man and his inability to do anything about it, and Jesus' response to save man, even though not one of those he died to save could love Him in return.

"And all I have to do is admit that I'm a sinner, and ask Jesus to be my savior?" Wade's eyebrows climbed his forehead.

"That's what I did," Jim said simply. "He gave me the grace and the faith to believe. And for the first time in my life, I am talking with God every day, and understanding His word."

"I'm ready!" Wade said. "There's something about the faith of the guys who know Jesus this way that just appeals to me!" he admitted, looking at John.

"Yeah. I see that too," John sighed. "I'm ready too, because I've seen you change, Jim. Your faith is so simple, and yet so powerful it just pulls at my heart. How did you pray?"

With tears in his eyes, Jim told him, and listened as his brother and best friend submitted to the Lord Jesus and asked Him to be Savior and Lord.

They prayed together then, for Cecilia and their mission to track down the criminals that killed her family. Afterwards they spoke at length about justice. Despite the wonder of his brother and best friend coming to know the Lord, the horror of what had been done weighed heavily on all three men. The dinner bell rang, and they got up together, their eyes hard and hearts set to bring these men to justice.

Bob, whom everyone but the Captain called Stinky, was serving at table today. He noticed the Captain's demeanor and wondered what could be wrong. In fact, every member of the crew was quiet tonight and their appetites were not anywhere near normal. Growing concerned he poured a glass of tea for the Captain and after searching for the words he chose simplicity and spoke.

"Something wrong, sir?" he said. It was the first time Jim could remember Bob speaking first. Surprised he looked up at the man, seeing in those brown eyes only a sad curiosity, and perhaps concern.

"Yes, Bob, there is something wrong. We'll tell you all about it after dinner. We've come across something that makes our hearts heavy, Bob. No offense, the food and service are first rate, as always."

For a moment Bob just stared at him. *He's worried about whether I'm offended! Something terrible has happened and still he worries about the least of his crewmember's feelings.* Then he smiled.

"Thank you, sir. Always a pleasure," Bob said, and then turned away toward the kitchen.

Just about that moment the crew from the helicopter entered the dining room. Jim noted that they had taken time to clean up before coming to dinner. His crew constantly surprised and pleased him. Looking down at his plate he played with his food a little, then tried to eat some of it. He didn't remember tasting it, surprised when he noticed that the plate was empty.

After dinner the crew was asked to meet in the conference room, including everyone from the kitchen. Only Millie's place was empty around the table, but no one commented about it. Doc stood up, when everyone had been seated, and explained what had happened to Cecilia's family, and how she had been shown the pictures. He spent some time talking about the dangers of what this could do to her psychologically and spiritually. Jim watched the men read the report. Some faces drained of color, others hardened, and Windy, weeping openly, clutched his stomach as though he was going to vomit. Bob sat silent and mute, but tears ran down his face too.

Doctor Wozniac talked for two hours about how they were going to treat this poor girl. He explained how the crew must treat her at all times, gave them tips on what to do, what to say, what not to do, and what not to say. When he was finished, he sat down, and stared at his hands.

Jim Warner stood up. "Captain, with your permission, I would like to lead the men in a prayer for this girl, and for us. We're going to need His help with this," Jim nodded permission and listened carefully as Jim Warner led them in prayer. Every man bowed his head and listened, repeating the words in their hearts with deep feeling and even deeper need. When Warner finished, John and Wade announced that they had prayed to receive the Lord Jesus as Savior in Jim's office earlier that afternoon.

Jim didn't know what they expected, but there was a collective sigh, cheers, clapping, and congratulations. He wondered if his entire crew were believers, deciding that perhaps they were. In that moment he felt the presence of the Lord in the room in a tangible way, seeing in Abe and Sturdy's eyes tears of joy. Defining moments like that came few and far apart. Jim thanked the Lord.

Three days passed without incident. Going about their duties with their usual panache, the men kept the ship in pristine condition. Morale was high. Jim knew it was not because of the success of their search for the sunken barge, but because the men met every morning and evening to pray for Cecilia. Somehow those moments drew the men closer together than anything else.

On the second day Jim gave permission for Dorf and the crew to take the helicopter to shore to buy flowers for the hospital room. Every man on the crew presented Dorf with money until he was sure he had enough to purchase an entire greenhouse. Jim was pleased by the response, proud of his men.

"Just make sure the biggest arrangement is from me," Jim demanded, his neck burning and his cheeks hot with the sudden blush that appeared. Dorf noticed but hid his grin and nodded assent.

That evening Cecilia awoke to a room full of beautiful flowers. She stared in wonder at the multitude of colors and breathed in the scent of the flowers with pleasure. All bore cards expressing various messages of encouragement. Millie took pleasure in reading each card, showing her a picture of the person who sent it.

When she came to Bob's cryptic message of one word she paused. The word "Sorry" was all that adorned the card. Explaining Bob's past, and the way the kitchen crew was working with him seemed to impress Cecilia. Millie was surprised that Bob had come far enough to send flowers and include a card. She was rather proud of him.

Cecilia finally pointed to the largest arrangement, positioned so that she could clearly tell it was the finest and largest. Millie chuckled as she pulled the card. She'd been waiting for this moment with anticipation and was glad to finally share with Cecilia. The Captain had taken great pains to compose the card, neatly printed in his firm hand. Knowing the thought and effort that went into writing it she read the card quietly.

"Life can sometimes strip away everything, dealing us a hand that makes it seem as though the world must end. In those moments of shadow and brokenness, God remains steadfast, eternally good, with the power to fill the emptiness and loss with His love, mercy, and tenderness. There are none on this vessel who can offer anything more than a reflection of His love. I hope you put your trust in Him to help you through this time of fear, grief, and loss." Millie was rather proud of Captain Shepherd for that note.

What Cecelia thought of the missive Millie could not tell, but she saw the tears in the girl's eyes and patted her arm gently. Putting the card back with the flowers she got up and left the room.

Alone Cecilia stared at the flowers for a long time, thinking about the notes of encouragement and wrestling if she still believed God was steadfast, and eternally good. At the moment it seemed very difficult to believe that concept, though she wanted desperately to trust Him. Reasoning told her that she needed someone like God to help her, or she would drown in her sorrow.

On the third night she awoke in a cold sweat, trying to breathe, terrified. Jim sat at the bedside, suddenly taking her hand and speaking softly to her. She knew he was the Captain of this vessel. There was something about his hand that made her feel secure and suddenly comforted, even though it felt like holding a piece of oak. His voice was pleasant, deep and resonant, strong and comforting at the same time. When she calmed, she asked him what he was doing there.

"I have the watch tonight. Someone stays in this room every night in case you wake up and are frightened or need something. It's my turn. He explained quietly. Offering a cup of water with a straw he helped her take some before setting it on the table beside the bed. He seemed embarrassed to be there and she found herself trying to put him at ease.

Master Chief Warner and Andrea visited her often, sitting beside her bed and talking to her of this and that. Occasionally they read from the Bible, or shared a poem, mostly from memory. Abe and Sturdy were regular visitors too, praying with her every visit. To her surprise she found herself wanting to please these considerate men, to get better. Millie, of course, was almost always there, and

Cecilia began to talk to her about her feelings. Millie listened more than she talked, but she understood. When Cecilia shared how she felt about getting better to please her visitors Millie just smiled.

"They grow on you like that, my dear," she said, smoothing the sheet. "These men are hard men, and they have lived hard lives. They are often called upon to risk their lives, doing so willingly. For years they have served together in the military, living in a world of danger and death. Unlike some soldiers, they have never come to like it. They do what has to be done, but they do it because it has to be done, not because they want to. And now they are facing something far beyond their understanding, yet they will do their utmost to succeed."

"What are they facing?" Cecilia asked, not sure she understood. Millie just smiled. *They are learning to be gentle.* Millie smiled brighter at that thought.

CHAPTER 25

Healing Tears

On the fourth day Cecilia was able to stand for a few minutes, though her legs were unsteady. On the fifth day she took her first feeble steps, surprised that Jim was there to help, grasping his muscle corded forearms to steady herself, seeing the encouraging smile on his face as he gently moved backwards. The encouragement she received from the good doctor and his wife was warming. She learned that day from Andrea where the new cards and flowers came from, and how much trouble the men took to get them. Beginning to tend them with care, which was Andrea's plan, did wonders in her healing.

As he left the room Millie looked at him and winked. He winked back, his face breaking into a smile, all craggy lines and sunshine. Days came and went, and Cecilia grew stronger, coming down to the dining room after ten days in her hospital room for the first time. Blushing with pleasure at the comments from the men as she walked with Doc and Millie to their table.

Looking around with some interest she realized suddenly that she knew the names of every man in the room. Millie had shown her pictures and talked about them so much that she had somehow memorized their names. *Perhaps because I want to thank them, she thought. Or, perhaps because I want to know if they can do what Captain Shepherd said they would do.*

Her face grew serious as she looked at them closely. There was something about them, something she couldn't quite put her fingers on, an illusive trait. They were certainly military men; every one of them bore himself with a martial dignity. But there was something more.

When the food came it was one of her father's favorite dishes. Tears filled her eyes and she wept bitterly, trying to apologize through her handkerchief, while Millie held her tightly. Jim, who was sharing her table reached over and patted her shoulder gently. Millie looked over and caught something in his eyes, something hard, and was shocked by the intensity of that look. *He's thinking about the men who did this to this poor child. Well, this is one time I'm feeling much the same.*

Cecilia tried to apologize again, when she had finally stopped crying, but everyone at her table would have none of it. Gratefully she began to eat, finding that she was hungry. As she ate, she looked around and noticed that something in the room had changed. At first, she couldn't fathom what had happened, but then she began to see and to understand. There was a new atmosphere. It was a tangible thing, and every one of the soldiers and crew exuded it. Surprised, she realized it was an atmosphere of purpose and resolve so intense she could literally feel it.

It was in their eyes. She saw it and slowly came to understand what it was she couldn't grasp before. These men were sitting, talking, eating, but they were like coiled springs, ready to leap into action. Dangerous men, and the man sitting next to her, Captain Shepherd, the most dangerous of them all. She began to feel that perhaps these men could bring justice. But the thought of her family suffering brought new tears.

D r. Gregg met them at the museum of antiquities three days later with news of the upcoming auction. It was going to be held at Christie's auction rooms in King Street in London. The date was already booked for the first Wednesday in September. Every piece had been cleaned and restored and readied to ship to London. *Bring It Up Coral* would be taking the cargo. Dr. Gregg went as far as having each piece weighed, photographed, and valued. The sum was staggering.

Dorf and Wade took over the loading of the precious cargo while Jim and John spent several hours with Dr. Gregg discussing his research, centered around the loss of a steam locomotive shipped from New York to Cairo in 1909. According to Dr. Gregg, the locomotive was built in the Schenectady Steel Works, and was a 0-4-2, with a coal car and a luxury car, that seemed more like a palace on wheels. A very wealthy oil sheik from the Sinai area ordered it. Gregg wasn't as interested in the locomotive and luxury car as he was in the crates of $20 gold eagles that was said to be in the luxury car.

The last message anyone had from the steamship carrying this precious cargo included sighting the Balears islands, which put the ship off course, perhaps running from a German patrol. Nothing was ever heard from the steamship, and no trace has ever been discovered. John studied the data that Dr. Gregg had compiled and became excited.

"Who else knows about this?" he asked the professor.

"Some of my former students helped me research parts of it, but I never told them what we were looking for. Other than that, no one," Dr. Gregg shared, putting a finger beside his nose and winking at John. "One has to keep such secrets close to the vest, eh?"

"Has anyone else ever looked for this lost vessel?" John asked.

"Two," Gregg replied immediately. "One of my best students spent a year trying to find the wreck, giving up eventually. He lacked the funding and the proper equipment. A member of the Sheik's family tried about twenty years ago, spent nearly a million dollars looking, but the boat and crew he hired failed to find anything and eventually he too gave up."

"Okay. You finish up on the research while we're in London. I'll put my own team on it from another angle. When we return, we can discuss how we'll divide the find, if we are indeed successful," Jim said. He leaned down to look the professor in the eye. "Don't talk about this to anyone."

"No, indeed no!" Gregg said, his eyes grave.

Jim returned to the docks to find that the loading was completed. Dorf and Mark were making sure the crates and boxes were securely in place and strapped down in the hold. Wade was on the deck, waiting for them, while Andrea prepared the ship for departure. As the two senior officers walked up the gangplank Wade saluted them smartly.

"Cargo and passengers safely on board, sirs," he said cautiously.

"Passengers?" Jim queried, his eyebrows rising slightly.

"Yes sir. Lorin Monair, Page Summers, and Martha Gimmel asked for passage to England. Lloyd Norris also made the same request. I granted their request," Wade replied quickly.

"Well!" Jim said with a smile. "I guess they've earned a free ride to merry old England," Jim grinned as Wade sighed in relief. Then Wade caught the look in his eye.

He cuffed Jim on the shoulder. "Shep, you sly old dog!" he laughed. "J.R. said you wouldn't mind. But with the cargo and Cecilia on board, I thought it might present a problem." Jim grinned up at his huge friend with appreciation.

"It will be good for Cecilia to have some girls to talk to other than Millie," Jim commented thoughtfully, heading to the quarterdeck steps. He caught Andrea looking down at him from the bridge and waved with a thumb up.

Having guests on the boat made some of their training difficult. Jim had the team meeting between two and four in the morning to practice some of their more difficult skills. None of the men complained about having their night interrupted. They understood the need for this kind of practice, and they used every opportunity to fine-tune their skills. Jim kept them on the thin edge of perfection. At any time, he could have interchanged team members and each team would have operated as usual. He was proud of his men, and he let them know that often.

Windy and Stinky had taken an interest in some of the training, and they were coming along nicely. Windy claimed he was in better shape physically than he had ever been, and he looked it. Bob Stankus didn't say much, but he lost his flabbiness, lost weight, and began to build muscle on a body that hadn't seen physical exercise in years. Jim made sure that Bob knew he was doing well. Responding to positive influence, good food, and the right company, Bob Stankus was now a solid member of their crew. When some of the men suggested his nickname be changed Bob argued against it. He told the men that the name suited him.

Sturdy and Abe lifted weights in the gym with some of the men. They were working on keeping their bulk and strength, while the team members were working on keeping their edge on strength and speed combined. Sometimes the students came to the gym to watch, but most of the time they walked around the deck, enjoying the fine weather the Mediterranean provided.

Every day men worked on the ship, cleaning the decks, the windows, painting areas that showed rust. Chemicals were used to remove the rust before paint was applied. There was never a day that the ship did not look as though it had just been launched from the shipyard. Whenever the students talked to the crewmen they were treated with respect, though the men tended to keep working while talking.

Martha Gimmel was studying to be an archaeologist, and she had an amazing ability to notice little things. The grace with which the men moved was something that puzzled her at first. Most of the deck hands and seamen she observed did not move with such grace, regardless of the weather. Eventually she described it as a deadly grace, feeling that she had defined the crew in two words.

Lloyd noted that the Captain rarely wore anything signifying his rank, and worked as hard as any crewmember, often shoulder to shoulder with one or two of them. And the men did not seem to pull rank on each other. They preferred to call each other by their clever nicknames, and he had yet to hear one of the superior officers give a direct order. Instead, those men asked politely.

He had difficulty putting the nickname "TRT" to Jim Warner until he wandered into the engine room one afternoon and saw the Master Chief's plaque. Master Chief Warner waved at him and Lloyd saw he was covered in grease and oil. The name made sense after that. But Master Chief Warner never came to the table dirty, nor did any of the men. They always cleaned up for lunch and dinner, regardless of the fact that they would have to wash two outfits that evening instead of one.

Page Summers took part in their Bible studies in the evenings, but the other three students looked upon that as foolishness. Martha Gimmel made the mistake of commenting on it in a derogatory fashion one day. Captain Shepherd looked at her as she talked about evolution and the fact that science pretty much destroyed religion. Taking her hand, he led her down to the library and pulled Johnston's book *Darwin on Trial* off the shelf. He handed it to her.

"When you've read that, young lady, I have another for you. Then we'll talk about what you call science," Jim said quietly. She was surprised at the intensity of his eyes, deciding perhaps she had offended him in some way. When she tried to apologize, he merely waved at the book. "Just read it, please," he said. "I once felt much as you do."

Jim found her in the computer room the next day, researching some of the things she read in the book. Zeke was sitting with her, helping her find the information she sought. He left them to it and took his place in the bridge to spell Wade. Three days later Martha returned the book to Jim with an angry look in her eyes.

"I wish you never showed me this book!" she stated fiercely. "Everything I believed has been founded on deceit! Will the next book dash all my presuppositions like this one?"

"Yes," he said quietly. Once again, he took her to the library, where he replaced the first book and offered her the next one, *Reason in the Balance*. "This one will be worse," handing her the book he left her there, staring after him.

Once they passed Italy, Cecilia began to come out on the deck to walk with the other girls. There was a deep sadness in her eyes, and she walked often like one in a dream. Little by little she began to unbend, to feel again, though cautiously, afraid of what it might bring. Sometimes everything would weigh upon her so heavily that she burst into tears, often unexpectedly. One morning, early, as the Shepherds, Wade, and Andrea came to the bow to watch the sunrise, they found her sobbing at the forward railing.

John, never shy around girls, walked right up to her and put his arms around her, turning her so she sobbed into his chest. Over her head his eyes met Jim's, and there was a resolve in them, a resolve to bring justice to whomever had caused this grief. John saw mirrored in his brother's eyes the same resolve. Slowly they nodded to each other.

Andrea watched the interchange and shivered. John's eyes were gray, cold, like the grave, and Jim's were green, hard, and stormy. Almost he could pity the men who would face his nephew's wrath. Almost. Andrea took Cecilia gently from John, his gravely voice quietly telling her she was among friends, and she could cry as often and as much as she wanted. Jim noted that against Andrea she seemed to melt against his body and relax. He realized that there was a softness there that neither his brother nor he had yet attained.

I've been a soldier for what seems like a lifetime. And I haven't allowed myself to feel since Mary Ann ripped my heart apart when I was just a kid. Will I ever be able to feel again? Could I be like Andrea, could I find my way through this hardness to being vulnerable again? If I'm asking myself this, I must want to. Maybe God will help me find the way back.

Jim sighed, and gently patted Cecilia's shoulder. They stood there like that; watching the sun push back the blanket of night, erase the stars pinpoints of light. Slowly silver light gave way to softer shades of golden light, and finally the full glaring energy bringing daylight. All the clouds to the west were Altocumulus, suggesting another day of gentle sea and Mediterranean warmth. Jim watched it all unfold, sipping his iced tea, his hand resting on Cecilia's shoulder. With the scent of the fresh sea air he could also smell the scent of her hair, gently moving with the movement of the ship and the soft breeze.

Cecilia felt foolish. At first, she had been alone, so desperately alone in the world, all her loved ones gone, and now she was safe in the warm embrace of the old Greek everyone called Papa. Papa Orvieto. When John held her, she felt the hardness of his body, the tense muscles, and while he held her, they grew even harder. *He hates the men who did this to me. He will kill them.* Andrea had seen her shoulders stiffen, and he had taken her from John. Now she was aware of Jim's hand on her shoulder, big capable hands, calloused, strong, and somehow warm.

Andrea gave her a clean handkerchief. She blew her nose, still in his embrace, somehow missing that calloused hand that had been so warm on her shoulder. When she had mustered some self-control, she looked at the men who surrounded her. Content to remain in Andrea's embrace she gave them each a tenuous smile.

"I'm sorry," she apologized automatically.

"You shouldn't be," Jim assured her quietly, his stormy green eyes locked on hers. There was surprising warmth in them for a moment. *He knows what I'm feeling, but he hasn't allowed himself to feel that way in a long time.* The thought surprised her.

"Thanks," she said simply. "And thanks for the shoulder to cry on," she said to John, and then with a smile to Andrea. She stepped away from Andrea and looked out over the water. For a long moment they stood together, and she realized that she felt somehow that she belonged here. It surprised and frightened her. Somehow, with her family gone and nothing to return to, she felt that the ship had become her new home.

CHAPTER 27

"Where are we?" she asked, looking around. Far to the north and south she could see land.

"We are passing through the Straight of Sicily," Wade answered, looking down at her from his great height with gentle eyes.

"Who's driving the ship? I never see anyone at the wheel but one of you!" Cecilia asked.

"Captain Rob," Wade replied with a grin. "He's our IGS, Inertial Guidance System, or what you might call an automatic pilot."

"We come out here every morning to watch the sunrise," Jim added quietly, his eyes fixed to the east.

"I'm sorry I interrupted your meeting, then," Cecilia apologized, feeling foolish.

"No interruption," Jim said with a smile that almost took her breath away. "We're always glad of company, especially the company of a beautiful young woman." *She is beautiful, even with her hair hanging limp and her face ravaged from weeping.*

For a moment their eyes held each other, tentatively, and then Cecilia looked away. "Thank you," she said shyly. Andrea smiled. John and Wade exchanged winks. Cecilia didn't see any of that. Jim's neck grew crimson as the three looked at him.

One by one the men took their leave, until only she and Jim stood there, neither looking at the other. Jim reached out his hand and touched her arm gently. She looked up at him. The touch was surprisingly gentle, and she could see a softness in his eyes.

"I hope I didn't cause you any discomfort," he said haltingly, searching desperately for the right words. "You are welcome, anytime."

"Thank you, Captain," she too spoke shyly, her eyes still downcast.

"Please, call me Jim, or Shep like the rest of the crew. We're really not that formal here," Jim said.

"Then, thank you, Jim," she said with a smile, meeting his eyes.

They stood like that for a few minutes, his hand warm against her arm, cupping her elbow gently. Her eyes were blue, flecked with green, so that depending on what she wore they either looked blue or green. He liked them, and he noticed that the pupil of her eye was expanded. A man could get lost in those eyes. He grinned more at himself than at her.

"May I escort you down to breakfast?" he asked suddenly.

"I need to freshen up first. Would you save a seat for me at your table?" she replied, still feeling very shy.

"It will be a pleasure," he replied honestly. Standing on the bow he watched her walk to the port side door leading to the steps that would take her to her stateroom. For several moments he stood there, then made his own way down to the dining room.

Saving a seat for Cecilia was a simple matter of turning her plate over, indicating that that space was taken. He took his own plate up to the breakfast buffet, filling it with eggs, bacon, and sausage. Page Summers and Lorin Monair were also sitting at his table, along with Andrea and Jim Warner. Cecilia came in several minutes later, her hair braided, wearing light makeup. Some of the men noticed, and their second looks were contemplative.

She went right to Jim's table, picked up her plate, and walked over to the breakfast buffet. Choosing fruit, toast, and jam, she returned to the table and sat down after Jim rose to pull out her chair. Andrea and Jim Warner also stood as she approached the table. On this ship the men always stood when a woman came to the table. Jim noticed that she paused a moment before eating to say grace. She ate slowly, taking one bite of fruit at a time, and listened to the conversation going on around the table.

Windy filled coffee cups, and then brought milk and after that iced tea to Jim. Cecilia asked for orange juice. Jim Warner and Andrea drank a glass of red grape juice for breakfast every morning. The American girls drank water.

One morning Wade called Jim and John to the bridge. They were passing the Balears Islands. All three entered the computer center and watched as Zeke performed his magic. Lines appeared on the map, showing traditional shipping lanes, and then overlapping lines showing the shipping lanes that existed at the time the steamship went down. Another monitor showed the currents, and the usual weather patterns of the area were on yet another monitor.

Zeke's hands flew over the keyboards as more and more information came up. The Germans patrolled the waters heavily, and El Djazair, or Algiers had heavy traffic to Marseille. The French suffered great losses there during the war. England fared little better. The number of ships that disappeared during that time was enormous.

"Another needle in a haystack!" John muttered, looking at the figures.

"Yes, but the cast iron signature will be different from steel hulls," Wade replied. "We should be able to pinpoint the engine without too much difficulty, once we get near enough for a reading," he added the last with a wry grin.

"Well, gentlemen. You have a lot of work to do over the next month," Jim commented into the silence that followed. "Let's plot a search grid based on the last sighting and last message from the steamship. Zeke, learn everything you can about the weather that particular year to factor that in."

"On it Shep! Uncle Zeke sees all! He can even see into the past," Zeke was grinning as his fingers began to manipulate the keyboards around him.

John and Wade grinned at Jim as they walked out of the computer center and back to the bridge. "A hundred thousand $20 gold eagles!" Wade said. "Do you guys have any idea what that will be worth on today's market?"

"It will certainly cement our cover as a salvage operation!" John added.

"Don't get too cocky!" Jim said suddenly. "We need to keep our edge, maintaining our focus. Rook is no fool, and the people he is being influenced by are going to be suspicious of everyone. At no time can we afford to let down our guard!"

"Right you are, Shep!" John said with a grin. "But I think we have the edge there too. You've kept us sharp, and we'll keep sharp. But we can enjoy what we're doing too."

Jim grinned wickedly. "I'll certainly enjoy clipping Rook's feathers!"

"Semper Fi!" Wade said with emphasis.

"Jar head!" Jim teased.

"And proud of it!" Wade said, his smile broad, his eyes alight with pleasure.

"I'm sorry, sir," FM quipped from the wheel. "I've tried to train that stuff out of 'em, but I think they were brainwashed in boot camp or somethin'."

"Sorry, FM." Jim said with a laugh. "Once a Marine, always a Marine."

"You too?" FM said, his eyes round and his mouth turned into a pout. "It just isn't fair!"

"Just drive the boat!" Wade said, still laughing.

"It's a ship, Jar Head!" FM retorted. "See the HSB back there in its cradle? That's a boat. This is a ship!"

Twelve days later they passed through the Thames Barrier, the silver arches gleaming in the early afternoon sun, and berthed at Canary Warf. As arranged, four armored trucks waited at the dock to take their valuable cargo to Christie's. Cecilia stood on the deck, watching as the crew worked with the dockworkers to unload the crates from *Bring It Up Coral* and load them into the waiting armored trucks. Men moved up and down the ramp, loading the treasures with care, never hurrying.

Jim appeared at her side, watching the unloading with a critical eye. He looked down at her and was surprised to see fear in her eyes. Almost immediately he understood. She was afraid to leave the ship, to travel north to where her home had been. Afraid of facing what she would have to face she stood there, almost frozen in place.

"I took the liberty of asking a favor from a friend here in London," Jim said quietly. She looked up at him, half expectantly, half still terrified of what she had to face. "A man and a woman from Scotland Yard will be arriving shortly to escort you home, and to help with everything." He didn't tell her that the woman was a psychologist who worked with families like hers. She would learn that in time, and he hoped she would appreciate it.

"When you're through, if you want to return here you are more than welcome. In fact, I'm offering you a place on my crew," Jim added.

Her eyes filled with tears and she reached out and grasped his hands tightly in hers. "May I, really?" she breathed. "As odd as it seems, I don't feel that I have anywhere else to go!"

"I intend to see the men who attacked you and your family brought to justice. It would be good, I think, if you saw that accomplished," Jim replied.

Cecilia shivered suddenly. In his eyes she read the resolve, knowing that he would risk death itself to bring those men to justice. She remembered the deadly grace with which he moved at times and shivered again. Whatever those men had faced in the way of law enforcement, they had no idea what was coming.

"Are you cold?" Jim asked, noticing the shivers.

"A bit," she lied. *How do I tell him he frightens me; that I am frightened about the risks he will, must take?* "Thank you for arranging for someone to accompany me. I would like very much to return. When will we sail?" *How do I tell him he's the reason I want to return, that I don't care as much about justice for my family as I do for his safety? How do I crack that military barrier against emotions?*

"Two days after the auction, which is scheduled for September tenth. We will sail at high tide on the twelfth. My friends will bring you back to meet us," he added, watching her reaction.

"That would be splendid!" she said, her eyes once again filling with tears. She gave his hands a gentle shake and then let them go.

A man and woman stepped to the gangplank and the man actually asked permission to come on board. Jim grinned and waved them to come up the plank. He was surprised to note that the woman was young, no older than himself, and attractive. The man was thin and moved with an easy grace that suggested he kept himself in physical condition. His handshake was firm, and his brown eyes were penetrating.

"Inspector Roland Lancaster," he said introducing himself.

"I'm Amy Foster," the woman said, shaking his hand in turn.

Once the introductions were over the two Scotland Yard representatives escorted a reluctant Cecilia down the gangplank and into a waiting sedan. Jim watched her go and waved as the car pulled away. She waved back, looking lost and forlorn.

"I think, my nephew, that this girl will return. Do you think so?" Andrea asked, coming quietly to his side. Jim looked at his uncle for a moment, his stormy green eyes fading from hard resolve to something of a mystery.

"I hope so," he said quietly.

"Perhaps the men should enjoy some shore leave, a few nights on the town," Andrea suggested after a moment of silence.

"Let's get them together in the conference room," Jim said with a smile. He passed into the bowels of the ship, his mind still on Cecilia, already missing her company. Slowly the crew gathered until everyone sat around the table.

Jim grinned as he looked them over, glad that he could do something positive for them. "Our cargo is unloaded and safe, so the entire crew has three days shore leave. Each of you has a company credit card with a ten-thousand-dollar limit. The company will pay for your room and meals, but any presents or personal items you pick up will be your responsibility. Don't get into any trouble if you can help it. Zeke, please pass out the cell phones."

Zeke opened a box in front of him on the table and handed a cell phone to each member of the crew. They were tagged, and every crewmember's number was already programmed into the phones. Obviously, these were not ordinary phones.

"Use these if you need anything or need anybody. You can call home with these, or your favorite girlfriend," Jim smiled as a few of the men laughed. "You've earned your time off. Enjoy it."

"So, you'll be keeping in touch with Cecilia?" John grinned as his brother blushed crimson. The men laughed.

"Maybe you'd like to remain on board to guard the ship?" Jim tried to look angry and mean, but he burst out laughing at his brother. John had his lip out in a pout and was waving his hands. It felt good to laugh.

Charles, Millie, Paul Warner, and Andrea left first. They had plans for their three days, and being older than most of the crew, they tended to stick together. Jim was not surprised. Abe and Sturdy took the kitchen crew with them next. For a few minutes the rest of the men sat in silence.

"Where are we going?" Dorf asked in the quiet that followed.

"I take it that means we're going to stick together?" Jim replied wryly.

"Hey Shep, we're a team!" Sparks quipped.

"Uncle Zeke, do you think you can get us rooms at Brown's Hotel in Mayfair?" Jim asked with a smile.

"Oooh! Luxury, is it?" Zeke said, manipulating the keys on his laptop. Three minutes later they had rooms on two floors, doubling up, for the price of three-hundred-and-ninety-six-pounds sterling per night. Some of the men raised their eyebrows at the price, but most of them grinned with anticipation. They went to their cabins, dressed in casual clothes for London weather, and packed an overnight bag. Twenty minutes later they were hailing taxies to take them to the hotel.

Jim continued to surprise his team when he announced that they were eating dinner at Wheeler's in Old Compton Street, famous for lobster and other delicious seafood dishes. In honor of the occasion the men dressed in a manner appropriate for such dining. Most of them wore dress jeans, a sweater under a sport jacket, suitable for the cooler night air and appropriate dress for a fine restaurant.

Wheeler's often catered to large groups of people, but the twelve men who appeared that evening caused a few eyebrows to rise. By their dress they were obviously Americans, but not like the usual Americans who visited. These men were as odd a group as had ever dined there, but it was obvious to all who cared to notice that they were military men, well mannered, and obviously enjoying a visit to London's finer places.

Dinner was a success. Some of the men decided on a St. Estephe wine for the meal, though they drank less than a glass each. Others settled for water. The chef was certainly pleased by their appetites, and the waiters each received a proper tip at the end of the meal. When the group left most of those at the restaurant felt that America was coming along nicely in producing fine young men.

For three days the men stayed together, walked about London, visited some of the museums and shops, and enjoyed rest and relaxation. They were rarely in bed after nine in the evening, and up early each day. Every one of them took advantage of the health club gymnasium for exercise each day, and all of them ran, early in the morning together. It was a pleasant change for them, and every man enjoyed it to the fullest. When the time came to return to the ship, though, every man was ready to get back to work.

CHAPTER 28

A dmiral Rook sat in the back seat of his rented Mercedes and watched the men on *Bring It Up Coral* with the critical eye of a career naval officer. Every man on board was working hard, cleaning, painting, or helping load containers in the hold. Grunting with admiration he noted that the boat glistened in the morning sun. Every window was spotless, and there wasn't a hint of rust anywhere to be seen. Apparently owning a part of the company was strong incentive for hard work. He envied the men of that crew, especially after the major recovery of those treasurers.

Already he knew they were preparing to hunt another famous wreck, and even knew some of the equipment the company had purchased for their next venture. It was obvious to anyone that these men were salvage experts, young, adventurous, and so far, incredibly lucky. None of the crew had come anywhere near his operations, so he was satisfied that they were what they appeared to be. He motioned for his driver to pull away and sat back with a sigh. *Bring It Up* was a thorn he could live with, and if his men brought in the woman, he would know everything there was to know.

In the computer center of the ship Zeke watched with a grim smile as the Admiral's Mercedes pulled away. Carefully he had leaked the information about their purchases, so that only those items that were fitting for a salvage operation were noted. Everything else was still a protected secret. He pushed the send button on his headset.

"Rook is leaving. I think he's satisfied that we're not a threat," he said for every member of the team to hear.

At that moment the phone rang, and Zeke answered it. One eyebrow rose and a smile crossed his face as he forwarded the call to the Captain's tiny office. Jim picked up the receiver, his mind on the work at hand, but the voice at the other end caught all of his attention immediately.

"Hello, Jim?" It was Cecilia.

"Hey Cecilia!" he said with a smile. "Where are you?"

"I'm in a vestibule at Scotland Yard at the moment. Inspector Lancaster thinks I need an escort to the ship. We were followed today."

Jim heard the fear in her voice. "Okay. Sit tight. Give me the number there and I'll get back to you the moment I have things organized," he said quickly.

She gave him the number and he immediately hung up and called together the team. They listened carefully to him as he explained what was going on. Every one of the men listened attentively, and then the suggestions began. For half an hour they discussed various ideas until Jim and John chose the one that they liked the best. It was with a laugh that Jim spoke next, enjoying the charade he was about to play.

"Okay. Remember, we want to get lost so no one knows she's back on this boat," Jim said when the men had been assigned their jobs. Zeke looked up as they prepared to leave.

"Should I call Sir Edward, in case there are problems?" he asked.

"Only if we run into problems," Jim replied after a moment of thought. "I don't think we will. Can you find out who ordered this?"

Zeke nodded and his fingers began to dance over his keyboard. Smiling Jim left him to it.

Cecilia looked up with real pleasure when she heard Jim's voice outside the tiny vestibule she had occupied for the last hour. He came through the door with Inspector Lancaster and Cecilia looked into those stormy green eyes and saw with pleasure that he was glad to see her. He grasped both her hands in his for a moment, his whole face softened by the smile he bent upon her. Then he surprised her with a bear hug!

"We're going to take a little stroll to the tube, losing whoever is following you," Jim said softly. "I have ten of my men out there watching our backs, and they will help. Just do everything I tell you to do and we'll be out of here in no time, safe and sound. Okay?" For some reason, just the sound of his voice gave her comfort she hadn't expected. Sighing she dredged up a brave smile for him.

Cecilia nodded her head, biting her lower lip after the smile, a nervous habit she had. She looked at Inspector Lancaster who nodded. Thanking him for all his help she allowed Jim to lead her out of the offices of Scotland Yard and down the street toward the underground. They walked at a normal pace, as though they had no worries, and Jim kept up a conversation about what they were going to do to keep her mind off the danger.

In the underground Jim timed their steps so they had to dash for the train, just getting inside the doors. Jim saw the man following, miss the train, and pull a radio out of his pocket. After a look at the radio he knew who had ordered the tail on Cecilia. It was a U.S. Navy issued radio. There would be someone at the next station waiting for them, but they wouldn't be there. As planned, the train came to a stop halfway between the two stations, for just a moment. Jim winked at the people in the car as he led Cecilia off into the tunnel.

As they stepped out Jack and Sparks stepped to the door. "I'll bet they're eloping!" Jack said, loud enough for several nearby people to hear.

"Sure looks like it. Cute couple," Sparks replied, his Cockney accent perfect.

The conductor appeared, looking at the doors. Jack turned toward him and spread his hands. "I'm sorry, sir," He said, his North London accent at its best. "I just wanted to see if the doors would open."

"Don't do it again," the conductor snapped with some heat, turning back to head back to the front of the train and report to the engineer. He was shaking his head at the audacity of some people. Several of the people in the car smiled at the ruse. Jim knew that if anyone questioned the people on that specific car the details would be confusing at best.

Jim led Cecilia into an access corridor and up to the street level. Once he was sure no one official was watching he pushed up the grate, and the two climbed out onto the sidewalk. They hurried to a cab, sitting at the curb, waiting for them. Mark was at the wheel of the cab and he grinned as they got in. Jim waved and he took off, watching for anyone who followed. No one did.

At the next station Sparks and Jack watched with some amusement as a man hurried into the car they were exiting. He was looking for someone; that was obvious. Stepping off, he watched everyone leaving, and then got back on the train. His search for Jim and Cecilia would be in vain. They hurried to the surface with the other passengers, hailed a cab, and returned to the ship.

Two hours later *Bring It Up Coral* cast off his lines and headed out of the harbor. Cecilia stood on the bridge with Jim, John, and Wade. She was still smiling over the reports of the men who had returned. Whoever her pursuers were, they were still looking frantically for her all over London. Zeke, she knew, was working on getting a line on who had been following her. Feeling very safe, she enjoyed watching Jim and his crew as they made their way into the English Channel.

"Could I see you in my office for a few minutes?" Jim invited her, turning away from watching the channel traffic.

"Of course," she said, still smiling. He smiled back, opened the door and motioned for her to go through. He led her down onto the next deck and into his tiny office. She noticed that he left the door open and smiled again.

"Time to get to know what I can do on board your ship, isn't it Captain." Cecilia stated, her blue green eyes twinkling.

"Very perceptive. In a way yes," Jim replied. "The men who were following you belonged to Admiral Rook. Apparently, they thought if they could get you separated from all of us, they might squeeze some information out of you about what we are doing. We'll take care of Admiral Rook soon enough. But for now, you need to know a few things about this company."

"Now that will be interesting!" Cecilia said, her cheeks dimpling with another smile.

"Why do you say that?" Jim asked.

"Well, you are certainly a deep-sea salvage and rescue operation. That I've seen first-hand. But there is something else. You have international connections and carry some weight or influence. This is obviously a military group of men for the most part, even some of the kitchen crew. It's all very interesting," Cecilia answered. "There is something going on behind the scenes, something you are all very good at keeping secret, but it is there!"

"Very good," Jim said. "Let's start with you. I know very little about you. Are you still a student, or do you have a profession?"

"I just finished earning my second doctorate degree and was on holiday before deciding where to put my interests to work," Cecilia said, surprising Jim. "My doctorate degrees are in Archaeology and Chemistry. I also have a master's degree in forensic studies, vulcanology, and meteorology. Most of my life I've wanted to be a forensics expert because of an aunt who is very successful in Scotland Yard. That is what I was working toward."

For about three minutes Jim just sat and stared at her. She sat quite still in her chair, watching him digest the information she had given him. His eyes gave nothing away. Allowing him to work through his thoughts she waited patiently. At last he sat back, his right hand holding a pencil, lightly tapping an empty page in a spiral binder.

"It has to be the Lord," he said at last, his voice quiet, his eyes serious.

"I beg your pardon?" Cecilia said, arching her eyebrows.

"You've thrown your lot in with the perfect company to use your skills to their utmost!" Jim said with a slow smile.

He proceeded to tell her about his paramilitary unit, and their cover as a salvage and rescue operation. She listened intently to everything he said and things she had noticed began to fit into place. When he was finished, he offered her a position as part of the crew, and as an equal owner of the company, at a salary that had her head whirling. Adding that she would have to be cleared first made her smile.

Zeke was quick to verify everything she said in her interview, and to hold a phone interview with her aunt at Scotland Yard. He vetted everything and gave his report to Jim. Jim called a meeting in the conference room for the entire crew to decide if they wanted to add Cecilia to the roster.

When the crew was asked about adding Cecilia to the company the vote of acceptance was unanimous. Doc Wozniac suggested to Jim how to use Cecilia immediately, and with some reservations he followed the good doctor's advice.

"Cecilia, I need three things from you," Jim said to her, again meeting in his office. "First, I need a list of materials you want for your work. There is no limit, so get what you want and need. Zeke can handle all the payments on-line or write checks, which Dorf will sign. Please give me a copy of your signature to send to our banker friend. Also, please remember that the cost of what you want includes buying the very best equipment. We don't skimp on equipment!

"Second, Zeke is setting up a computer station for you to do research at, when you need it. He wants to know what you want, and more to the point, what law enforcement agencies you want to be able to tap for information.

"Last, I want you to begin gathering information on Mercury, and especially Fezik al'Loudi and his band of cutthroats. We need to be ready to move when they take their next victim. There's no way to stay detached from this one, but I want you to consult whenever you need to with whomever you need to. Don't let this consume you, Cecilia, if you can help it."

She reached out a slender hand, silencing him. "Don't worry, Jim. God will keep me from going off the deep end over this. I'll do everything in my power to protect the next girl, I promise. I was hoping that you would allow me to work on that, as a matter of fact. Visiting my home nearly destroyed me, but that wonderful psychiatrist you managed to have assigned to the case helped me move away from the precipice, and to get some focus. A visit to my Vicar helped some, and the Bible studies on this ship have done the most," she smiled at him. "Is that all?" somehow, she felt there was something else.

"Actually . . ." Jim spoke hesitantly. He was surprised he'd spoken but now had to continue. "I'd like something else, but it would be best to let nature take its course, and let God lead us," he wanted to tell her to spend every moment beside him, but he forbore.

Her smile was radiant and once again took his breath away as he lost himself in the deep pools of her mysterious eyes. The blush that radiated upwards from her neck was pretty.

"I could spend more time with you, so we could decide together on that matter!" she laughed when he jumped and blushed. But the look of anticipation and hope in his eyes told her volumes, and her heart was lost to this strange taciturn man who had come into her life in such a timely manner.

Dr. Gregg returned to *Bring It Up Coral* by flying from Egypt to Valencia, Spain. Again, he had eight students with him, four men, and four women. Thomas Moore would receive his doctorate degree in archaeology upon completion of this mission. He was British to the core, good looking with light blue eyes and sandy hair, a bit above average in height and obviously keen on physical training. At first, he was a little reticent to bond with the men of the crew, but soon unbent.

Adley Ferinc was a French student, working on a master's degree. His father had worked his entire life in a vineyard, where Adley learned to work hard and to enjoy life. He was not much bigger than Mark Drumheiser, with dark curly hair, dark dancing brown eyes, and a ready smile. One thing was evident; Adley loved his work and the adventure, right from the start.

Dick Persons was a visiting professor from the United States, near fifty in age, with dark hair, dark eyes, and well-tanned arms and legs. He claimed to be from Minnesota, but he had been teaching in California most of his college career. He too was earning his doctorate degree in archaeology, a little late in life perhaps, but ready to enjoy being away from the classroom for a year or two. He hit it off with Jim Warner and Andrea almost immediately. Jim and John found themselves liking this gregarious professor.

Jim suspected that Dr. Persons was an eternal student, always seeking another horizon to conquer in higher learning. He had two other doctorate degrees. One was in History and the other in Ancient Languages. Dr. Gregg certainly seemed impressed with the former Minnesota farm boy and his abilities.

"I would give him his degree at this moment, but he insists on completing all his work!" Alistair said with feeling.

Dave Curtis was a Canadian student, on a scholarship program. He was average; around five foot seven inches in height, thin, and athletic. His sandy colored hair and dark eyes decorated a handsome rugged face. A long-distance runner at heart, he felt confined by the ship, but was obviously enjoying his adventure. He took to running the steps with Jim's men in the early morning and proved capable of keeping pace.

Lisle Mirelle turned out to be a beautiful Belgian who spoke perfect English, turning every head on the ship. She had dark wavy hair, piercing blue eyes, and lips that just begged for a kiss, set in a beautiful oval face. She was not thin, like many girls liked to be, though not heavy either. That she loved life and the adoration of the men around her was obvious. She carried herself with poise, and she was well on her way to earning a doctorate degree in anthropology.

Heidi VanHaaten, from Holland, was another pretty child. She was just out of High School, eighteen years old, and on her first real adventure. Her father arranged for her to study under Dr. Gregg because he was the curator of a museum, and he thought his daughter might enjoy a similar life. That she was the youngest member of the crew did not seem to bother her in the least.

Mary Ann Lewis and Barbara Stafford were dear friends, both from England, and both determined to make their mark as research specialists. They jumped at an opportunity to work for Dr. Gregg, and he seemed to enjoy their company. They were almost always together, discussing research. Both women were very attractive and very poised, English ladies from head to toe. Mary Ann was short, and Barbara was tall, both with an obvious bent toward being pranksters. Almost from the beginning of the journey they began to play pranks on the men.

Jim made all the introductions in the dining room after they were settled in their cabins, before Abe and Sturdy provided a fantastic seafood extravaganza. Cecilia took to Mary Ann and Barbara immediately, sitting at the Captain's table with them in animated conversation. Sitting beside her, Jim smiled as she talked animatedly to the two women. Doc Wozniac and Millie were also beaming.

Early in the morning work began in earnest. *Bring It Up Coral* left his berth before the sun was up, and Smitty worked with Dr. Gregg, Mary Ann, and Barbara on a search grid. Zeke and Cecilia worked in the computer center on their various tasks, Zeke finding

Cecilia good company. Jim worked with the crew on setting up the crane, then preparing the equipment for the search. Doc and Millie helped the students who were suffering from seasickness.

Though everyone was busy with the tasks at hand, none of the men on the team forgot their primary objective. Work went on at two levels, the visiting students and the good Dr. Gregg never aware of that second level of activity. Some of the training went on right under the student's noses, in the gymnasium in the form of Martial Arts exercise. Most of the other training went on in the early hours of the morning.

The same yacht that shadowed them off the coast of Israel was back, following in their wake at a respectful distance. Everyone on the crew recognized it, including Cecilia. She forced her emotions down and attacked her work with zeal. However, she did confide in Jim her fear. Somehow, she had come to trust sharing anything with him.

If he was surprised that she chose him he kept that to himself. The way he held her hands and gazed into her eyes made it easy to unload. He even folded her into his arms when she wept, making a conscious effort to be gentle, relaxed, and responsive.

For the first time in his life Jim unwound, allowing himself to enjoy this closeness. The scent of her soft hair filled his nostrils and the feel of her tiny body in his embrace made him feel fiercely protective. She was amazed at how safe she suddenly felt in that embrace. After several minutes they separated.

Two days of hard work and preparation readied them for the impending search. Andrea, John, and Wade took turns in the wheelhouse, following the grid pattern, while the three deep water search vehicles were towed behind the tug. On deck, in the computer room, compass bridge, and library work went on with precision and attention to detail.

There is nothing exciting about towing sea sleds in a grid pattern, or any of the other detailed work required. Days went by as their search area grew with no contacts of any kind. Again, the evening games and tournaments broke up the monotony of the work, delighting crew and guests alike.

Texas Hold 'em Poker proved the most popular card game. No one gambled money. Poker chips were handed out in equal numbers to each participant and they played until one player ended up with all the chips. Frank Miller was named the champion after twenty-eight days of eliminations. Jim won the Chess tournament, and Vince won the Rook tournament. Jack Boswell was the five-card draw Poker champion, and Heidi VanHaaten distinguished herself as the Phase 10 champion. Thomas Moore won the Uno championship that lasted the longest, stretching into thirty-two days.

Abe and Sturdy did their part by making one meal each day a special treat. There were days that everyone ate picnic style on the deck, enjoying delicious submarine sandwiches, and interesting salads, fruit and pies for dessert. Evening meals were sometimes formal events where everyone dressed up, and sometimes great fun with messy finger foods. Jim Shepherd was proud of his crew and the way they worked together to break the tedium of the search.

Two days after the search began the yacht began to shadow *Bring It Up Coral*. Four days into the search, Jim, John, Wade, and Zeke slipped aboard the yacht to discover what they could. Zeke was able to clone the cell phones on board and the others searched the boat from stem to stern after dosing the crew with their special sleeping gas. A few days later they learned that the crew and Mercury had not discovered that Cecilia was on board, but they were part of a regular routine of watching any and all salvage operations in the Mediterranean. As odd as that seemed, it only piqued their interest further in the organization.

Sir Edward, Ira and even Admiral Runion began checking the company carefully. Three women, daughters of very wealthy oil sheiks in the Middle East, ran it. None of the three seemed to be connected in any way other than their education, though sharing the same religion, they were of different sects. It was odd that the three women were working together. All three of them were graduates of Harvard School of Law and had united in an import and export business that proved very successful. Their interest in any and all salvage operations on the Med was well known and documented. They had agents in every office where salvage claims could be filed who called and gave the information immediately. As this was not illegal no one questioned it. However, the connection to the kidnapping ring within the company now made them suspect. Zeke pondered what they might be looking for, continuing to look closely at the women and their business.

After riding out a severe storm on the forty-third and forty-fourth days of their search, the deep-water search vehicles were lowered once more. Within minutes of beginning the day's search a heavy deposit of cast iron was detected. Everyone heard Zeke's excited voice in his or her earpieces.

"Contact! Cast iron, heavy deposit, surrounded by iron, possibly the hull of a sunken ship. Depth is two hundred and eighty-six feet. The wreck is resting on a ledge. The drop beyond the ledge is about another two hundred feet. Let's hope everything is on the ledge!"

While he spoke, Zeke was entering the coordinates in the computer. A marker buoy was dropped over the site, and the deep-water search vehicles were slowly brought to the surface. Both anchors were dropped a safe distance from the wreck, where no metal readings registered. Camera images of the wreck were already being studied as several of the crew made the bathyscaphe ready.

Driver, FM, and Sparks prepared to take the submersible down, checking all the equipment to make sure everything was working properly. This was the fifth sunken vessel they were going down to check. The others had been a disappointment, though expected because of the lack of a cast iron reading of any significance. Their hopes were not running any higher than usual. All three approached this as just another one of the many jobs they performed as part of the crew. To them it just wasn't worth getting too excited until they knew for sure they had reached their objective.

Jim Warner manipulated the crane, lifting the bathyscaphe out over the blue Mediterranean water. The sea was cooperating today with only gentle swells and a soft summer breeze. Once the bathyscaphe was in the water Dorf and Mark made sure all the lines were connected before thrusting themselves away from the submersible with powerful strokes. Jack pushed the switch that would flood the ballast tanks and take them below.

Most of the students were in the lounge where the monitors now showed the image from the various cameras on board the bathyscaphe on the flat screen HD televisions mounted on the walls for that purpose. Zeke added them recently for that very reason. They watched as Jack positioned the submersible over the strongest reading and descended. The current here was not strong and he was able to keep on course with tiny corrections. Suddenly the shadowy image of a ship appeared as they neared the bottom. There was enough light to see clearly, and with the lamps to help, the ship was suddenly vividly clear. One of the two smokestacks was broken, the other intact, it's ventilator still in place.

"It's a steamship," Frank said quietly.

"Cargo passenger liner," Jack added. "I'm going to make a pass over her from bow to stern. Let's see if we can get a length."

No one said anything as "Driver" as Jack liked to be called, made a sweeping turn and settled in on the starboard side. Too much covered the name of the ship printed on the forecastle. An eel slithered out of the ventilator cowl. Passing the mooring port and derrick they slowly glided by the foremast. Next came the wheelhouse. As they neared the stern, they passed the after deckhouse and came to the ensign staff, the flag long rotted away.

"I have three colors, black, gray and red," Sparks said.

"Unites States Lines," Cecilia commented in the quiet that followed that statement.

"*Steel Crab,* this is Uncle Zeke. I estimate length a little over four hundred and eighty-three feet. Also, heavy readings of cast iron under cargo hatch four. We're going to have to get some divers down there to enter the ship to see if the engine is on board. Can you clean off the name on the bow?"

"Heading forward for an attempt now," Driver replied.

An hour passed as everyone who was not assigned something watched the manipulator arms work at clearing the name. Water pressurized for the purpose slowly cleared the debris from the name. Eventually they could read *Moromac I.* Dr. Gregg sat back with a deep sigh. They had discovered their ship. He grinned at Mary Ann and Barbara, who both were looking at him with eyes shining in excitement.

On the main deck the men were working together to send down the saturation tank for sustained deep dives, and the NEWT Suit. Smitty was slated to wear the NEWT Suit. The NEWT Suit weighed eleven hundred pounds with Smitty inside. On the deck he couldn't move once he was inside the suit, but on the ocean floor this articulated, deepwater atmospheric diving system constructed of magnesium and fiberglass, would allow Smitty to work for hours at that depth while eliminating the need for decompression.

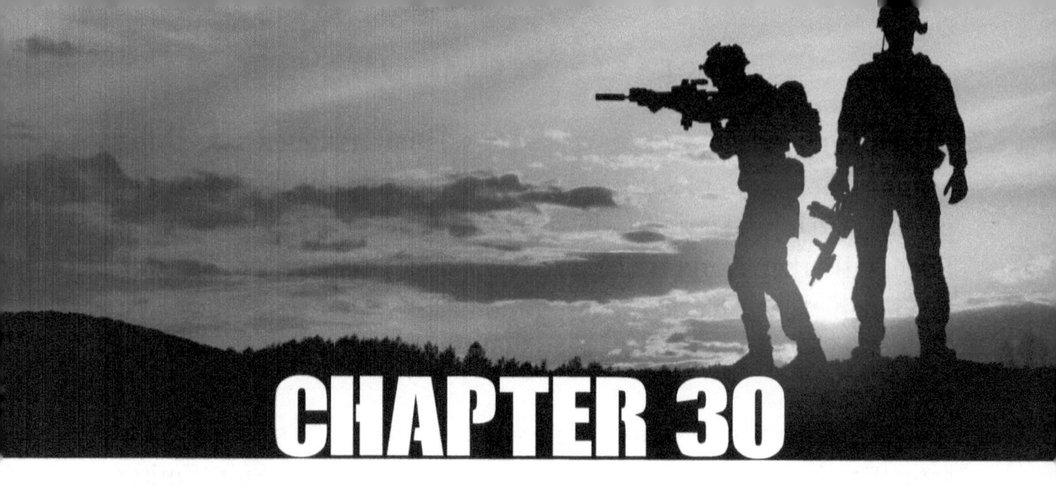

CHAPTER 30

D orf, Mark, C.G., Vince, and Zeke were going to go down with the saturation tank. This was one of their newest acquisitions, a cylinder, sixteen feet long and twelve feet in diameter. On one side there were four ports with underwater lamps mounted above and below each port. At one end a con tower entry was fixed to allow divers to enter and leave the tank. They would breathe a special mixture of helium and oxygen inside the pressurized chamber preventing the narcotic effects of inhaling nitrogen under pressure. The saturation tank allowed men to work underwater for long stretches of time without the danger of lung gases dissolving into the bloodstream, forming bubbles causing the bends. Decompression came at the end of the job.

Packed on board were enough MRE and NASA meal tubes, liquid bags, and water containers to keep the men below for fourteen days if necessary. None of the men who would be cramped in that small space wanted to be down that long, but they were prepared to face whatever the job required of them.

That evening the men who were going to be absent from the ship on the saturation tank were given special privileges to choose their favorite meal. Abe and Sturdy didn't mind this extra work, especially since every one of them chose a steak and lobster dinner. So that the men knew they were being treated special, the other crewmembers dined on chicken cordon bleu, steamed vegetables, garlic mashed potatoes and dinner salads. Quite a bit of teasing went on during the meal about the special treatment, all good-natured and fun. Everyone knew that great danger went with dives of this nature, and it was one of the ways the men dealt with the stress.

Near nine o'clock that night the five men climbed into the saturation tank, closed the hatch, and stretched out in their hammocks. In the morning, when their lungs were adjusted for the depth they would be diving, Master Chief Warner worked the crane, lowering them in stages to rest just off the port bow of the *Moromac I.* Vince switched on the outside lights and the ghostly bow of the wreck came into view.

"Hello *Moromac I,*" Vince said, pressing his nose against the cold Plexiglas port. "Meet the *Diving Can.*" Since the saturation tank really looked like a large can lying on its side on the bottom, the men had christened it with that name. The other four men took turns looking out at the ship before making a final check of all the systems and climbing into their hammocks. Getting a good rest was paramount to the success of this mission.

Shortly after sunrise and a hearty breakfast the crew set to work. The *Steel Crab* went into the water, and then Smitty in the NEWT Suit. In the *Diving Can* the five divers prepared for their first foray. Their diving masks were state of the art and allowed them to talk to one another and communicate with the ship, submersible and the NEWT Suit. Here the water was hovering around fifty degrees Fahrenheit, limiting the divers to about twenty minutes diving time for safety.

Working with the bathyscaphe and NEWT Suit the deck around the number four hatch was carefully cleaned. Smitty, using his pinchers and hydraulics was able to lift one section of the hatch, while the bathyscaphe manipulator arm lifted the other. Silence fell as everyone paused to look at the scene below. Incandescent dive lights showed the ghostly outline of a steam engine, heavily chained, still upright in the cargo hold. Behind it they could see the shadow of the coal car.

Dorf and Mark led the other three divers into the hold and for a few moments they circled the heavily rusted engine. Some of the parts would have to be replaced to restore it, but it looked as though it could be completely restored. Cameras recorded every detail, sending the photos up to the ship, where they were displayed for all to see. Dr. Gregg was watching the camera pictures from one of the deep-water search vehicles following the divers with rapt attention.

"This is a life-long dream, suddenly materializing before me!" he breathed reverently. "It's a 0-4-2, and was made in Schenectady, New York. It will be the only one of its kind on this side of the Atlantic!"

Slowly Dorf and Mark moved to one side of the train, while C.G., Vince, and Zeke moved to the other. They kicked gently, trying not to stir up too much silt, and made their way to the coal car, and finally to the luxury car behind it. The luxury car was still upright, though a few containers had crashed into it either during the attack or while it was sinking. Mark made his way to the door and peered into the interior.

"Hey guys!" he said with excitement. "You're not going to believe this! I think we'll be able to bring this baby up intact."

"Can you see what's inside?" Dr. Gregg said into the microphone on the desk in front of him.

"Are you thinking that the gold will be in the car?" Mark asked.

"I doubt it, but it could be possible," Dr. Gregg replied. "I would imagine the gold was either packed in crates or containers or placed in the ship's safe."

"Dorf and I will check the safe and see what we'll need to open it," Mark said.

"Zeke, C.G., and Vince, you guys start getting these containers ready to lift out of here. See if you can get that other hatch open too," Mark ordered. He and Dorf kicked upward to find the safe, leaving the other three behind.

"We're going to have to cut away a good portion of the deck to get the engine, coal car, and luxury car out," Zeke commented.

"We should do that, and then shift all these crates and containers first," he added.

"Roger that. You guys head back to the *Can* and warm up. We'll cut away the deck," Driver drawled into his radio.

"Mark and Dorf, you guys hear that?" Vince inquired.

"Roger. We'll find the safe, inspect it, and be back shortly," Dorf replied.

"Tell Abe to send down some hot soup!" C.G. quipped. Everyone laughed.

True to their word, Mark and Dorf returned before their twenty-minute limit passed, shivering, lips blue with cold. All five attacked MREs with tomato soup for an appetizer. Two hours would pass before it would be safe for them to return to the ship. They settled in, wrapping in thermal blankets, resting in their hammocks.

Smitty used a torch on one side of the deck, while the *Steel Crab* burned away at the other side. Frank was operating the torch, his eyes fixed on what he was doing, while Driver expertly moved the submersible to keep up with the burn. Every ten feet a steel hook and chain would be attached to the cut deck and the gang chain unit hooked to *Bring It Up Coral's* crane and cable so that when the cutting was finished, the deck would not fall into the hold.

Ninety minutes later Smitty made the last cut and the deck now hung suspended by chains. Guiding a cable through the upper hooks Smitty radioed for Master Chief Warner to lift slowly, and the crane gently lifted the deck. Using the manipulator arms and the bathyscaphe the deck was jockeyed away from the stern and dropped just as gently to the ocean floor.

Joining them from the *Can* the five divers began to help load crates and containers to be hauled to the surface. Master Chief Warner didn't hurry, because he was always safety conscious. Still, in an amazingly short period of time the rear deck of Bring It Up was littered with crates and containers. These were being opened and searched by Dr. Gregg and his group.

Below, the divers returned to the *Can*, rested for two hours, and made their final dive of the day with the intention of opening the safe. Using a new version of waterproof primacord Smitty blew the hinges while the men hovered a deck above. Even there the explosion rocked them and left their ears ringing. Sound travels with great force beneath the surface of the water. The steel deck protecting them from the shock wave kept them conscious and unharmed. Even with that protection the explosion had been violent. Various fish darted away from the ship.

When they returned to the safe Dorf, using his great strength and a six-foot long pry bar eased the door open from the hinge side until it suddenly fell away. Everyone was careful not to get trapped beneath that weight and sighed when it banged home against the deck floor.

"The safe is open," Dorf reported to the others. "We're going to return to the *Can* in five minutes. We'll give everyone a report tomorrow morning!"

Busy with the crates and containers on the deck Dr. Gregg hardly noticed the interruption or the impending wait. His team was busy cataloging amazing items from the late 1800s and the early 1900 era. There were lamps, fine china, and even some marble top tables in one group of crates. The tables were too rotted to recover, but the marble tops were in great condition and would probably net the museum a nice share of the sale of such materials.

One container had been filled with lady's hats, all of them long gone, but a few of the boxes remained with pictures. Several containers were filled with nickel and copper in rods and sheets. Though the copper was worn by the saltwater, it was still a viable metal and would bring a tremendous price. For that matter the nickel was in almost perfect condition, hardly pitted at all it had been so carefully packed. Jim was pleased by the early haul and knew that more was to come.

CHAPTER 31

In the computer room Cecilia had been working hard researching Mercury. The more she dug the more convinced she became that this company was a serious threat, but to whom was somewhat of a toss-up. The girls hated their parents, especially their fathers, who would not allow them to work in the companies they controlled, despite their legal training and abilities. Already Cecilia was aware of two very well-prepared sabotage missions on the oil pipelines owned by two of the three sheiks.

These women were serious about what they were doing. Sir Edward uncovered a small private security force that was more an army than anything else. Fezik al'Loudi was a primary trainer for the armed group. His background was about what she expected. He'd been tossed out of military units in several countries because of his brutality and lust for blood. She still wasn't sure if the three women who ran the business knew about al'Loudi's sideline in kidnapping.

One interesting thing that came out of her research was a list of missing girls who could have been taken by Fezik and his sycophants. A thread that ran through that list was that the women were all well educated, many having earned master's and doctorate degrees. She met with Jim that evening in his office to share what she had learned.

"What's your take on that last bit?" Jim asked, his fingertips together under his chin, elbows resting on the arms of his chair.

"Either he hates working for these women, but instead of biting the hand that writes his paychecks, he takes it out on other young educated women, or he's discovered that most well educated girls come from wealthy families. Maybe it's a bit of both," she said after a pause. "Either way, the connection is bona fide.

"Do you have any leads on the next possible victim?" Jim asked.

"I may," Cecilia said quietly. Jim watched her eyes, but they stayed steady. She was dealing well with her trauma and memories. "Five of the girls who were kidnapped had one thing in common. Their families were slaughtered, though never in the same way, and they all came from England, France, Sweden, or Italy. There are none from America or other countries yet. In that group there is one other thing in common. All of them made their original travel plans through Cook's in London." Jim took in that information thoughtfully, not surprised at all, but contemplating what it might mean.

"Get on to Sir Edward and have him forward any girls on holiday who just finished earning high degrees and come from wealthy families with ties to those countries and Cooks of London," Jim commanded after a moment of thought. "We may just catch these vermin through that link."

"How will you deal with them when you do catch them?" Cecilia asked quietly. She almost recoiled at the hardness that came into Jim's eyes at that moment.

"I'm making preparations for that. You'll know when the time comes," he assured her, his voice suddenly as hard as those eyes.

Deadly preparations, I'll wager! How can this man be so urbane, so focused on business one moment, and the next become death stalking? And why do I find that so intriguing? "I'll leave that to you, then," she said lightly.

When she got up to go, he was still staring at a spot on the wall, his eyes as cold as the grave, and she shivered. Fezik al'Loudi did not believe that such men existed in the world today. Few terrorists did. It would be his mistake and possibly the last one he would ever make. Cecilia smiled suddenly.

Jim likes me; I can see it in his eyes. I think I've met the man I can't resist, though he's so unlike anything I ever dreamed of finding! A cold shower is needed at this moment! She was laughing at herself as she entered her cabin, and Doc watched with a twinkle in his eye.

Cecilia was not fully recovered from her horrible ordeal, or the loss of her family. Purpose and business brought unexpected benefits in healing those kinds of wounds. He chuckled as he turned back into his own cabin to catch his wife in a playful embrace and dance her across the floor.

"Charles!" Millie gasped, giggling. "What's gotten into you?"

"If you must know, I think Jim and Cecilia are attracted to each other. I think that's quite interesting," he replied, kissing her nose and then lips gently. "Neither of them expected to be attracted to each other either, I'll wager! Falling in love is a good thing. I certainly never regretted it!"

"Well, you'll have to tell me about her sometime," Millie said, pressing her face against his chest. He swatted her on the bottom and grinned.

If discipline ruled the crew during the search, now that they had the treasure within reach it seemed that attention to detail and discipline became even more focused. Thomas Moore watched the crew work with a critical eye and knew that he was watching perhaps the most dedicated group of men he had ever seen. They seemed to know what each other were thinking and no man turned his hand from the smallest or most insignificant task. Any task that needed to be done was done immediately and thoroughly.

The submersible and NEWT Suit were on their way down again when the first call came in from the divers entering the vault of the ship. C.G. came up with the idea of looking for the keys to the lock boxes and within five minutes the keys were located. The divers wasted no time opening boxes and removing the contents to be placed in nylon bags. After eighteen minutes of searching they returned to the saturation tank for a two-hour rest. Again, the discipline of the men surprised those watching, because the diving crew did not open their bags and paw through the treasures they found. They drank down some hot tea and lay down on their bunks to rest.

As the day wore on it became evident that the gold was not in the vault, and after emptying it the divers returned to the train. A safe was discovered inside the luxury car. Dorf and C.G. tipped it up so that Mark could lay straps beneath the heavy container. The straps were fastened to the top and then a cable hooked to the straps. Guiding the safe out the door as the cable was reeled in was done with great care, until at last the safe hung suspended in the water, making its slow ascent to the surface.

Once on deck the safe was cleaned and then opened. Every member of the SEAL team knew a great deal about opening safes, and Jim had some of the best equipment available for the job. This safe was fairly easy to open because of its age and simple design. Inside they found the $20 gold eagles, still in their original bags holding ten each. The bags were rotted from the water and only three of them could be saved. Dr. Gregg stood beside Jim as the last of the gold pieces were packed away and stored in the hold.

"I have dreamed of finding this most of my adult life," Dr. Gregg sighed. "All the research, all the waiting, it was worth it."

Thirty-six days of hard work followed. Jim requested a barge for the engine, coal car, and luxury car and it was delivered by tug within three days. After all the weeks of hard work and tedium the salvage was almost complete. Finally, the steam engine was winched on board the barge and strapped to the deck. *Bring It Up Coral* didn't seem to mind towing the extra weight as he powered back across the Mediterranean to Egypt.

Those days were spent cataloging the treasures taken from the sunken steamship. Everyone on the crew was fascinated with this part of the work, because history was before them, in a very tangible way through things they could touch. Studying those items gave them a sense of values for that era and everyone discussed them with respect.

"It seems that we've made another fortune in salvage, Shep," Vince announced, standing next to the Captain after a long day's work. They were in the buffet line for dinner, waiting as Sturdy carved a huge roast prime rib, expertly placing the slices on plates in eager hungry hands. Jim looked back at Vince with a grin.

"Our investment advisor seems to be doing better than we are! We'll soon have so much money we won't know what to do with all of it!" he said as he stepped up to Sturdy. The giant looked down at him with a huge grin.

"Rare, with the bone on, Shep," he rumbled, putting the thick piece of beef on the Captain's plate.

"Thanks, Sturdy," Jim said. He waited for Vince and the two walked back to one of the empty tables and sat down. Almost immediately John, Wade, C.G., and Andrea sat down at their table. Most of them caught Jim's news of how well Worthington was investing their fortune.

"So, what do independently wealthy deep-sea salvage guys do?" Andrea asked, then popped a piece of the tender roast beef into his mouth and chewed with enjoyment. For a few moments everyone at the table did the same, quietly chewing the delicious meat. Finally, Jim swallowed and spoke.

"First, we take care of this business, then we let the world know we are researching another wreck, and we visit various ports to do that research. We'll actually do some of that along the way," Jim said quietly. "If we don't have to go out on a rescue mission, we focus on our man and begin the task of taking him down.

"After that we increase our team, purchase the best equipment for the job, and stay on the cutting edge of perfection!" Jim looked at the men around him as they nodded agreement.

Bring It Up Coral and his crew made front-page news and even drew the interest of Omni magazine. His treasure this time drew some undesired attention. The family of the sheik who bought the train and gold demanded that their property be returned. State departments from three countries descended on Jim, but Ken Worthington came to the rescue with a legal team that made it quite clear what maritime law was on salvage rights. Once that was clear pressure was withdrawn and the sheik's family, to everyone's surprise, out bid everyone at the auction and retrieved the family's long-lost treasure.

Dr. Gregg and his eight students were the pride of the education department, seeming to enjoy the short-lived notoriety for what it was, and nothing more. Heidi VanHaaten returned home to begin working with her father in the museum at home. Mary Ann Lewis and Barbara Stafford became permanently attached to Dr. Gregg's research staff. Jim was sure they would be back, and he smiled, remembering some of their pranks and antics on the ship. He would welcome them. As for Dr. Gregg, he would always be welcome!

The lovely Belgian Lisle Mirelle returned to her home country and eventually left to teach at Oxford in England. Adley Ferinc and Dave Curtis returned to their homes with a better understanding of different cultures around the world, and Dick Persons went back to teaching in California, glad to have enjoyed the experience and better prepared to teach.

CHAPTER 32

Zeke made sure that anyone interested in the company became aware that they were now researching another sunken vessel from the past, in search of another treasure long thought lost for all time. Three days of shore leave followed the end of unloading all the treasurers, and returning the ship to its pristine condition, ready for the next job.

Jim and Cecilia spent those three days wandering through museums, shops, and churches, discovering information about each other that both thrilled and confused them. Jim knew he had strong feelings for this lovely young woman, thinking that perhaps she felt the same about him. It frightened him to think of entering a relationship because as a Christian man he was sure his responsibilities would be more stringent. Yet he yearned for the relationship, sought it eagerly, surprising himself each day.

Bring It Up Coral set a course for Rome after those three days of rest. Jim walked through the vessel on their second evening out from Egypt and took note with no little pride that his ship still gleamed and sparkled like new. His men were taking great care of the ship, and their pride in ownership showed everywhere he looked.

None of the men on the crew seemed to mind the mundane tasks of keeping the boat in pristine condition. Cecilia began to help with little things and soon became the person in charge of caring for the women's facilities, which were hardly ever used on most decks. Those simple tasks seemed to give her pleasure, and her energy in her other work became more focused. As far as Zeke was concerned, spending a great deal of time with her in the computer center, she was worth every penny of her salary. Cecilia had a knack for research and a keen grasp of facts.

Sir Edward Marsh assigned two under cover agents, both female, to a group of girls traveling together, to keep a sharp eye on two of them, both prime targets for Fezik al'Loudi and his band of cutthroats. MI6 was convinced that one of those two girls had been targeted through Cooks Travel. They were even convinced that they knew who was passing the information along. Within two weeks they would be proven correct.

For the men who believed that there was a higher being who often made things happen exactly according to His plan it was no mystery. Others pondered how fate often wove two threads together in such unique ways. For Cecilia, it was the former, for she had a strong faith in God. It had been that faith that carried her through her ordeal, and it gave her strength now. Yet she worried about Jim, and how he would respond once they were on the trail of the kidnappers.

Bring It Up Coral was berthed in the port of Napoli, within sight of Stazione Marittima, where the all too familiar yacht from Mercury was also at anchor. Arriving in the morning the crew tied the ship up to their dock, paid the port fees, and set about their business. Cecilia, dressed in her white uniform, had been designated an Ensign and bore the designation of a Science Officer. She was on the observation deck with a pair of binoculars studying the yacht and the surrounding marina.

That very morning, she had awakened knowing that today she would be required to face her worst fears. She turned first to God in prayer then sat for a few moments thinking everything through. Jim and his crew were there and that gave her strength. Yet she prayed for them for she worried that one or more could be injured or even killed in the line of duty. Surprised at the thought turning her stomach even more than facing Al' Loudi she was able to find a little amusement in the situation.

Jim knew little about women's intuition, but he trusted his instincts. He felt that Cecilia was probably on to something from her research and so listened carefully and prepared his men for action. They would work in their usual teams of four, two making the trip to London or Iceland, depending on which girl was kidnapped. The third team would take care of the yacht and its crew, securing the release of the kidnapped girl.

Zeke, having cloned the cell phones from the yacht, was confident that he could intercept all their messages, and that he could block any calls when the time came. All that required was putting a disk into the systems around Napoli that recognized cell phones and patched calls through. Calls to those numbers would need a special prefix number or would send the message that the phones were in use or not in service. Local police assets were in place to help with entry to the cell towers. It seemed to the administrative crew that every possible scenario had been considered, every "i" dotted, and every "t" crossed.

Abe and Sturdy took their crew on shore and began buying food and staples for the kitchen. Master Chief Warner and Andrea went ashore to purchase some tools, barrels of oil, and other engine room supplies. Jim watched them walk down the gangplank. Master Chief Warner led the way, his five-foot seven inch one hundred-and forty-five-pound frame still erect as he walked with purpose. Behind him Andrea seemed to tower over him, five inches taller, and a hundred pounds heavier. Andrea's shoulders were rounded and strong from his years of hard work on the sea. They were talking as they walked, and Jim could hear Andrea's laugh floating up to them as they reached the quay.

"They are loading supplies," Cecilia's tight voice brought him back to what they were doing. He lifted his own binoculars and watched as two men loaded heavy bags onto the skiff that would take them out to the yacht. The bags were familiar, and they were filled with ready-mix cement.

"No doubt about their plans now," Jim said quietly. He looked down at Cecilia who gazed back at him, her eyes filled with emotions so strong they seemed at war within her. He reached out and took her hand in his and squeezed gently. She seemed to take strength from that contact and breathed deeply. "We'll put a stop to this, Cecilia. This time we put an end to it," Jim spoke softly, keeping the anger that threatened to erupt carefully hidden from her, or at least he thought he'd been successful.

He would never forget his first sight of her, bound cruelly to a chair, her legs encased in cement, her hair a greasy tangled mess, skin raw and pale. Now she looked the picture of health, with a healthy tan, and the sun had bleached her brown hair to an almost golden color. Huge hazel eyes stared up into his, and those, he decided had not changed all that much. They were no longer filled with pain, but they were still filled with resolve.

They turned back to watch as the skiff was loaded with other supplies. Two cases of beer and a case of Vodka were the last to be loaded. The men fired up the outboard engine and putted out to their yacht, and two more men helped bring the supplies on board. Jim switched to a camera with a telephoto lens almost as long as his arm. He took pictures of all four men, then removed the memory chip from the camera and took it down to Zeke.

Not much happened until nearly midnight. Cecilia, who could not rest, spent most of her time on the observation deck either pacing or watching for something. At eleven o'clock in the evening she asked Jim to join her, using her communication headgear, which she was still getting used to.

"When they kidnapped me it happened fast, so fast I hardly knew what was happening. I think I was gassed, because it was almost a full day before I woke up. I know I had a terrible headache afterwards. And I was violently sick too, vomiting from the effects," she broke off, the horror of those moments washing over her and tears ran down her cheeks. "I was terrified when I woke up and they were all there looking at me. I was tied to that chair, and my feet were already in the cement, and it was nearly set. They took pleasure in hurting me. They never asked me any questions, they just hurt me until I passed out," her voice had dwindled to a near whisper.

Wade, who had been sharing the watch with Cecilia, looked across her head at Jim. Both men had bleak expressions on their faces and both of them knew what the other was thinking. It was a time for reckoning. Jim put his arm protectively around Cecilia's shoulders and she seemed to melt into him, needing his protection. Wade smiled and turned back to watch the shore.

"Are you thinking we need to move fast on the boat?" Jim asked quietly.

"No. They'll wait until she wakes up to start hurting her," Cecilia sighed again, putting her own arm around Jim's waist. "I just can't stand the waiting. Actually, I wanted to ask you if you thought they might try to bring her out from somewhere else, since the Marina is pretty busy," she questioned, suddenly pulling away, wiping her eyes with a handkerchief, and then turning toward him. "Sorry," she apologized simply.

"We thought the same thing. We figure they'll bring her from somewhere along the Via Reggia di Portici. There are fewer lights there, and the warehouses are closed. Earlier John and C.G. took a walk and discovered a powerboat that is registered to Mercury, tied to one of their export ships. They're watching it now," he replied.

Forty minutes later John's voice came over the radio sets. "Hey Beer Bottle, you copy me?" John's voice was clear. Beer Bottle was the name they affectionately called Wade. His full name was Wade Samuel Adams, and since Samuel Adams was the name of a popular beer, they nicknamed him Beer Bottle. He didn't seem to mind the moniker, even though he never drank beer. He was so used to hearing it, he rarely even thought about the name anymore. It was simply his.

"Hey JR, this is Beer Bottle. I read you five by five. Watcha got?" he replied, pressing the talk button on his earpiece.

"Blondie's gone missing. I saw her get on a boat. It's a real party here. Seems that several lovely young ladies have been impressed into service on the other boat. Wish I could be on board. Some of them look real pretty," John offered.

"Roger that, JR. Message received and understood. Gotta keep your post and leave the pretty ladies alone. Work first, bud," Wade replied. His eyes were bleak as he looked at Jim. John's code had been easy to decipher and they both knew what it meant.

"God damned white slavery!" Jim swore. Immediately he was sorry for his choice of words, and he looked down at Cecilia chagrined. "I'm so sorry!" he said quickly. "Please forgive my poor choice of words."

"Actually, I'm sure God does damn white slavery, or slavery of any kind," Cecilia said, enjoying the moment. It wasn't often she saw Jim so unsettled. She reached up and patted his cheek. "We won't need to wash out your mouth this time," she said with a twinkle in her eye. Wade laughed.

"What do we do about those girls?" Cecilia asked, her face suddenly serious.

"The one's on the ship are not our problem. We'll alert Petros Kladas and let him alert the Italians. Our mission is with this girl and her family," Jim replied. "She remains our priority."

They heard the sound of a boat approaching and sure enough it pulled up to the yacht and a huge man climbed on board, carrying the girl over his shoulder Two other men clamored aboard after him. One was al'Loudi. He issued orders that they couldn't hear, and the girl was taken below.

Fezik al'Loudi did not spend much time on the boat. He issued orders and then went back to his powerboat with the two men who first accompanied him. Once they pulled away the Yacht slipped anchor and quietly moved off into the night. Zeke activated the computer homing chip he had planted on the boat earlier. It was designed much like the chips used to track stolen money by the FBI. He could pinpoint the exact location of the yacht at any time via satellite. Phase one was complete.

"Beer Bottle, this is JR," John's voice cut into their thoughts. "Devil boy just returned with his goons. They have a rented BMW and are heading away now." Devil boy was the designation they had given al'Loudi.

"Roger. RTB (return to base) immediately," Jim ordered. He hurried down to his office and made a few calls, putting assets in place and making plans. When he was finished, he sighed audibly.

At one o'clock in the morning eight men and one woman arrived at Aeroporto Capodichino where a Gulfstream G-3 waited. Petros Kladas provided the jet and was there in person to greet Jim.

"Petros!" Jim said when they exited the rented Jaguars. "It is great to see you."

"Since it is so late, and I am not officially here, I thought perhaps we should meet. When you return from this mission just leave the jet here. I will see that it is retrieved. Your tip on the white slavery ring was perfectly timed. One of the girls taken in that raid is the daughter of one of my government's officials. That shows that this character thinks he is untouchable. Be careful.

"The Italians have invited us to participate in the take down, as you say," Petros said with a satisfied grunt. "Because I am here it will look like an international incident which is the result of our two government's police forces working together in an investigation. You should be clear of any suspicion." For a moment Petros looked out over the empty and quiet airport, sighing deeply. Nodding once he looked back at Jim, who spoke.

"That's good news, and I thank you. Time your take down for early morning," Jim added. "That should give our target ample time to get to his intended mission."

"Come back unharmed, my friend," Petros said, patting his shoulder with a heavy hand.

Jim nodded and his crew began loading the jet. Petros faded into the background and disappeared out some side door. The two pilots were both Greek nationals, both part of Petros Kladas secret service, and both competent. They spoke English fluently and asked no inappropriate questions. Jim liked them immediately, and because he wanted good relations with Kladas and his intelligence group, he immediately invited the men to accompany them on the mission. They agreed with alacrity, and Jim suspected they might have insisted anyway. He was glad to have them along, because they would guard Cecilia while watching the take down in Iceland.

The kidnapped girl came from a very wealthy family in the city of Reykjavik. Her father, Eugen Vilhelmson was a transplanted Swede who owned a fleet of fishing vessels that fished the icy North Atlantic waters. From Stockholm to Iceland his fleet of aqua blue, black, and red boats were famous. He was one of the few who really cared about the ocean, and consequently was careful not to fish too heavily in one area. Respected and liked by most he now lived in Iceland where he conducted his business from an imposing office structure near the north end of the city. His palatial home was near the outskirts of the city, set among some lovely rolling hills, where he lived with his wife, and their four children.

Evie was their oldest, the girl who had been kidnapped. She had one younger sister, Charlotte, who was just sixteen, and two thirteen-year-old twin brothers. Already Icelandic officials were moving them from their home to a secure location, a heavily guarded suite at one of the larger hotels in the city. Evie's father would meet with Jim's team there, and then take them to his home, arriving before al'Loudi who had taken a commercial flight. No one was surprised that the men who traveled with al'Loudi all traveled coach under assumed names.

The Gulfstream gave them the advantage of time, arriving four hours before al'Loudi's flight. Official cars met them at the airport and a fifteen-passenger van brought them to the hotel. Jim and Cecilia would go up and meet with the family while the team remained with the van. The officials with them made the introductions in the hotel suite.

Eugen and Emma were frightened for their daughter, huddled together with their children seated around them equally agitated, even more so because of their parents. Jim took in the situation in one glance and strode forward to shake hands with Eugen who stood nearly six feet six inches in height.

"Mr. Vilhelmson, I'm Jim Shepherd and I'm here to tell you that your daughter is safe. No harm will befall her and the men who took her will be dealt with," he confided, his voice full of confidence, his handshake firm.

Eugen calmed down marginally and introduced his family. Jim bowed to Emma and Charlotte, and he shook hands with the boys. They were already over six feet in height and looked like they might match or surpass their father's height. Both were angry and shy but put at ease somehow by Jim's demeanor. Eugen noted that and began to relax more. His wife and daughter however remained in states of shock and dismay.

"We need to leave now sir, to get set up," Jim said, turning back to Eugen. His no nonsense attitude and ready for business look convinced Eugen. He nodded, untangled himself from his wife and nodded to the boys who surrounded her.

"We go," he said simply.

Team 1, with Jim in charge, took their places in the house with Eugen. He was a little larger than life, wearing a bulletproof vest underneath his shirt, but the suit coat made it almost invisible. Zeke, Frank, and Sparks were invisible, as was Jim. The two Greek Intelligence men were with Jim. Team 2, with Wade in charge, waited outside, also invisible, ready to come in behind al'Loudi, once they had dealt with any outside guards. Zeke was monitoring radio bands in case al' Loudi used radios for contact.

In the past, al'Loudi struck quickly, in the early evening, when the whole family was likely to be together. Jim was depending on him keeping to his usual tactics, since they had worked so well before. He was not disappointed. At six o'clock, the usual time the family sat down for dinner, his team of six men arrived. Zeke already knew of their arrival, since al' Loudi was using a telephone to check on the family. He alerted the others.

Eugen took the call and lied masterfully, telling al' Loudi that he was having dinner with his family and could not talk. Al' Loudi hung up with a wicked smile on his lips.

Cecilia, waiting with the two Greek operatives in the living room, which adjoined the dining room, listened as the men prepared to deal with the impending threat. She had her own part to play, and she was more than anxious for the time to come.

Fezik al' Loudi studied the house critically. There was nothing to suggest that Eugen had called in the police. He had passed no suspicious vans that could be doing reconnaissance, no police vehicles, and saw only the usual vehicles that should be in the driveway of the home. Nodding to himself he left one man on guard outside and burst into the home through the windows of the dining room, his men coming through the door and other windows to maximize surprise.

He was startled to see only Eugen there at the kitchen counter. He looked around the room but saw nothing. He lifted a silenced pistol and pointed it at the stunned Eugen.

"Where is the money? Where is your family?" he asked in English. "I will ask you only once, and then I will shoot you if you do not answer."

Four men suddenly appeared in the room, as if by magic, wearing the body armor of professional soldiers and SWAT teams around the world. The four men around al' Loudi, who were just turning to meet the threat, went down immediately, three shots in the head spraying brains and bone everywhere. Before he could react, Jim brought the stock of his P-10 down on al'Loudi's wrist, sending the pistol to the floor. For his part, al' Loudi was stunned. Three men had their weapons trained on him, he could see the laser sights connecting his head with those weapons, and he froze.

That was Cecilia's cue, and she stepped out of the living room with her two companions on either side of her. They carried deadly looking pistols with silencers attached, holding them professionally, aimed at him. Neither of the two men looked away from him, moving slowly, keeping their weapons trained on the target. He swallowed, and then recognized Cecilia.

"No! You are dead!" he hissed. He turned to Jim. "Who are you?"

"Mr. Vilhelmson's family is safe, presently waiting him to join them to let them know he is safe. I'm sure they would like to know that, aren't you, Eugen?" Cecilia's voice was level and controlled, though inside she was struggling to keep it that way. Only Jim's implacable presence lent her the strength she needed, that and her sense of the presence of her Lord and Savior. Fezik al'Loudi was the most-evil man she had ever met, and even though he was surrounded by guns, she still felt the danger that seemed to radiate from him. Then she looked at Jim and somehow knew that al'Loudi was no threat. That calmed her. Amazing even herself she smiled at Eugen.

Wade and his crew came in a moment later, training their laser sights on al' Loudi. "One guard, dead," Wade announced quietly into the silence.

"Mr. Vilhelmson, I think Cecilia is correct. You should go to your family, sir," Jim said quietly.

CHAPTER 33

Fezik dived for his gun as Eugen stood up, but he never reached it. His captors had been careless not to kick it away, and he was positive he could reach it. With only one slim chance he tossed the dice, diving toward the weapon, ready to die, and ready to kill. The shots he expected never came. Instead a foot connected with his ribs with enough force to lift him into the air and spin him over a chair. Jim calmly reached down and picked up the pistol and dismantled it quickly.

"One moment before I leave," Eugen said, walking over to al' Loudi. The huge man picked up the stunned kidnapper like a rag doll and then smashed a huge fist into al'Loudi's face, sending him crashing over furniture to lie in a heap. Eugen shook out his hand.

"For my daughter," he said simply, nodding at Jim. Jim smiled and nodded back, understanding.

"We'll handle the rest. You shouldn't be here for that," Jim said.

"No. I think that is for her to see," Eugen said, nodding at Cecilia. His keen business sense had allowed him to read much. Jim just nodded and Eugen left quietly. He stepped outside his front door to find the guard lying there, his head an ugly mess of blood.

Stepping gingerly over the dead body he climbed into his Bentley and drove away.

When al'Loudi regained consciousness he found himself lying on the floor. The men around him no longer had their weapons pointed at him. Slowly he lifted himself up. His nose was smashed, broken, swollen, and painful and one eye was swelling shut. Jim leaned over him, his face a study of amusement and sarcasm.

"You're not having a very good evening, Fezik. Your face looks awful, but then it wasn't much to look at in the first place." The men laughed at Jim's words.

Fezik pulled his knife and lunged for Jim. He had one goal now, to kill this man before the others killed him. Although he prided himself in his quickness and abilities as a knife fighter his thrust never reached his intended victim. A hand that possessed the strength of a vice, and the speed of a striking cobra, grabbed his wrist and twisted his arm painfully behind his back. The knife was plucked from his fingers with seeming ease.

"You may be good against women and children, Fezik, but you're pretty useless against real men," Jim commented quietly. He continued twisting the arm and then his left hand smashed into the humerus, which snapped, exploding from al'Loudi's flesh at the same time he screamed in pain. Jim's hand came down again snapping the radius and ulna cleanly.

Jim lifted al'Loudi easily and threw him into a ladder-backed chair. The man was panting, trying to control the pain, the shock settling in. A hand grabbed a fistful of hair and al'Loudi's head was jerked back.

"The girls in the ship, where were they bound?" Jim asked. His voice was almost conversational. It frightened al'Loudi, because where he expected anger there was only calm, and that warned him. He was in for a bad time. Still, he was not quite convinced yet that he was powerless in the hands of these men. His agile mind worked, and he answered after a short pause.

"If I tell you, will you let me live?" he asked.

"You will tell me whether you live or not," Jim replied. Fezik stared into Jim's eyes, and what he saw there shriveled his courage until he was ashamed of himself. *How could any man alive frighten me like this? What is this implacable force that emanates from this man? In all the battles I have fought I have never seen this!*

Screwing up his courage Fezik set his jaw, as if to resist. Perhaps it was the smile that he saw flicker across Jim's lips for a moment, as though the man read what he was doing. Whatever it was he cried out, lifting his good hand as if to defend himself. Jim turned to his men and grinned.

"Here is the great Fezik al'Loudi, beater of women and children, coward and thief. He calls himself a terrorist, but he is less than a man," the last words were delivered eye to eye.

The taunt hit home and Fezik knew with a sinking heart that he would eventually talk. Still, he determined to make these men struggle for their answers. How little he understood the minds of the men who stood over him. One of them stepped forward with a syringe. He plunged the needle into al'Loudi's arm after swabbing it with alcohol and depressed the plunger.

"What have you given me?" he gasped.

"Just a little something to help you remember all the correct answers to our questions," Sparks said, stepping back.

Jim let go of al' Loudi and stepped back. All eight men stood around him, just watching, saying nothing. For almost ten minutes al'Loudi sat there cradling his broken arm, sweating, waiting. The waiting was the worst part. He felt wetness spread between his legs and shame filled him.

"Where are the women on the ship being sent?" Jim asked quietly.

"To Bombay, to be sold. Kamir Ahmed is the agent who is purchasing them. He pays top dollar for virgins," Fezik couldn't understand what was happening. He was telling them everything! Trying to stop he looked away, but his mouth kept speaking.

"My employers do not know about this trading of human cargo. They are so busy trying to figure out how to kill all the male members of their families that they have no time to notice what is going on under their noses," Fezik's eyes grew wide.

"What have you done to me to make me talk like this?" he cried. "If they discover that I have spoken they will have me killed! The Russian they call Black Death will kill us all! I am an evil man and have killed many, but even I do not kill as he does, and even I do not wade in the blood, even drink it from a warm heart after a kill. His twenty soldiers are the most dangerous men alive! Please, you are killing me!"

"I know who he's talking about, sir," Zeke said quietly. "Had his own private army hiring out to anyone who was willing to pay in Africa. An SAS operative put a bullet in his head that should have killed him. Somehow a Swedish doctor saved him, but he can't feel anything. He doesn't feel pain, cold, heat, anything at all. He's a bad hombre for sure, Captain. When he was able to move about, he killed the doctor who saved his life and disappeared. He's had a lot of training and done some of his own."

"Yes, I remember reading about him," Jim said softly.

"Fezik, who is your contact at Cooks?" Jim asked.

"A woman. Elizabeth Forry. She does not know she is passing the information. She has a boyfriend; I pay him well to extract the information I need," Fezik replied.

"And why are you shadowing salvage operations in the Mediterranean?" Jim asked.

"A doctor Hess from South America is paying a great deal of money to know if a German U-boat without identifying numbers is ever discovered. He has a small army, ready to attack the ship that brings up the cargo and steal it. The women I work for believe that this is a chemical or biological weapon from the Second World War. They want it to trade with the doctor, to use it on their families." By this time Fezik was as placid as a wet rag, draped in the chair, slowly losing consciousness. Jim slapped him, waking him fully.

"The day of reckoning has come, Fezik al'Loudi. It is not a day in which you will die, but rather the beginning of a lifetime of wishing you could die. Perhaps the Russian will finish it for you, but I doubt if he will ever find you.

"Your hand will never be raised against an innocent again. Your mouth will never utter threats or curses. But you will know who you are, and what you were, only to live out the rest of your life as a vegetable. To live you will need others, and though you may not wish it, they will feed and care for you. You will want to tell them to stop, but you won't be able to do so, and they will not. You will want to tell them about the pain, but you will not be able to. This is true justice, Fezik al'Loudi."

Jim turned to Cecilia. "Would you mind waiting outside?" he asked gently.

"No!" she surprised herself. "This I will watch. Let him see me watching and remember that those he thought helpless are not," she spoke with confidence. Jim saw the determination in her eyes and nodded slowly.

"It will be bad," he said, his voice full of sadness. She knew then that he was not acting in anger, that this would somehow take all of his courage. Her hand automatically went out and held his for a moment.

"For all the innocent girls in the past, and those who might have been in the future," she said simply.

Jim knew where and how to strike. For a moment he hesitated, as he held al'Loudi away from the back of the chair. Then, with precision, he struck, just below the axis at the cervical vertebra. Fezik al'Loudi did not make a sound, but his body simply melted. He could neither speak nor cry out, and his body from the neck down was now completely devoid of motion of any kind. Cecilia watched, holding al'Loudi's eyes, and then quietly went and stood beside Jim, holding his hand in hers. Looking into his eyes she saw the great sadness he felt for this act, and she leaned against him.

Wade and C.G. lifted the limp body and carried it outside. The two Greek operatives said nothing, following along in the wake of the team. Technically, they disapproved of anyone taking the law into their own hands. Secretly they were pleased these men had decided to do so. In a way, they saw this as another means of justice. No one had suggested killing al'Loudi outright, and this was certainly a more fitting punishment than putting him in a prison cell. A large van met them, and an ambulance. Fezik's body was placed on a stretcher and he was taken to the hospital. Jim spoke for a long time with the Icelandic police, and finally, with Eugen's influence, they caved.

As the Gulfstream jet prepared for take off an ambulance arrived, and a stretcher was transferred on board. The jet sped down the runway and into the crisp clear air, heading south. Cecilia sat next to Jim, surprising him, and once again took his hand in hers, holding it for most of the trip. If the other men noticed, none made any indication.

Once back at Napoli the team hurried to the ship. John was waiting at the head of the gangplank with Evie, wrapped in a blanket, looking frightened, lost, and dazed. Jim stopped at the top and took her hands in his. He bent down and looked into her blue eyes, as Cecilia folded her in her arms.

"Evie, your parents, your sister and brothers, all are safe and well. I left them a few hours ago. The men who did this, the monsters that did this, have all been taken. There is nothing to fear from them, ever again," he said quietly. "You are safe now, and I'm sure your father will be sending for you today."

"Did you bring him?" she asked, her voice trembling, but her eyes suddenly flashing.

Jim stepped aside and the men carrying the stretcher went on into the ship to the medical wing. She looked down at the man who had kidnapped her and to Jim's surprise she turned away and vomited on the deck, almost falling to her knees before John could catch her. She was weeping now, uncontrollably. Cecilia took her away from the men and walked her down to her stateroom. Looking back once she was not surprised to see Jim and John working together to clean the vomit from the deck.

"How did it go for your team?" Jim asked John as the rest of the men filed down to put away their gear. John walked beside Jim.

"We took them down as planned. Evie never even woke up. When she did, she was here, in sickbay, and Doc and Millie had a time getting her calmed down. Al'Loudi frightened her silly. He told her he was going to Iceland to kill her family, and how he was going to do it. One of his men provided photos from other kills," John said.

"He'll never do that again," Jim replied, sighing sadly.

"How was your take down?" John asked.

"By the numbers. Our team is cresting the wave of perfection, JR. Every shot was perfectly placed," Jim replied.

"The trick is keeping us there," John mused as they walked into the weapons room. He helped his brother put all his equipment away and they joined the rest of the team in the galley for a subdued reunion. Millie came in shortly after they all sat down and walked up to Jim.   He looked expectantly at her, wondering what she might need. She stood there a moment, looking into his eyes, and then nodded.

"Well done," she said quietly. "Horrible, but well done. He's no longer with us. Petros Kladas collected him while you were below. If you need to talk, I'm available." With that she turned around and walked away.

"I don't think al'Loudi was very popular," Dorf said quietly.

"It still seems wrong!" Jim suddenly said loudly enough for everyone to hear. "I hated every minute of it and will hate it as long as I live!"

"Jim, what would happen if we turned him over to the authorities?" Mark asked. "Prison? Life? Perhaps, perhaps not! Certainly not a fitting punishment for the crimes this man has committed against innocent victims. And you didn't make the decision alone, Jim. Every one of us cast our vote for this. We all decided. We were the jury, if you will. It wasn't all you, Shep."

Jim thought for a few minutes, remembering that this was the first time they'd done this. He wondered if it would always feel wrong because his men were the ones bringing justice. They had all voted, and each decided that a lifetime without being able to communicate or move was a much better punishment than death, and much more certain than incarceration. People escaped from prison all the time. Finally, he sighed and nodded.

"No, you're right, Mark. Thanks. In battle we took orders and carried them out. This time we decided the plan and carried it out and it felt different. I'll have to get used to that," Jim said, nodding at Mark. "What we did was fitting punishment for this scum. I may have trouble putting it behind me, but I will. We have some other scum to catch, and twenty-six Marines are counting on us to do just that," Jim said, squaring his shoulders. He grinned. "To bad we can't do the same to him!" he said.

"Hear! Hear!" the men said in unison, raising their glasses to each other. Jim went to his bed in a better frame of mind after their meeting, especially after Jim Warner led them all in prayer.

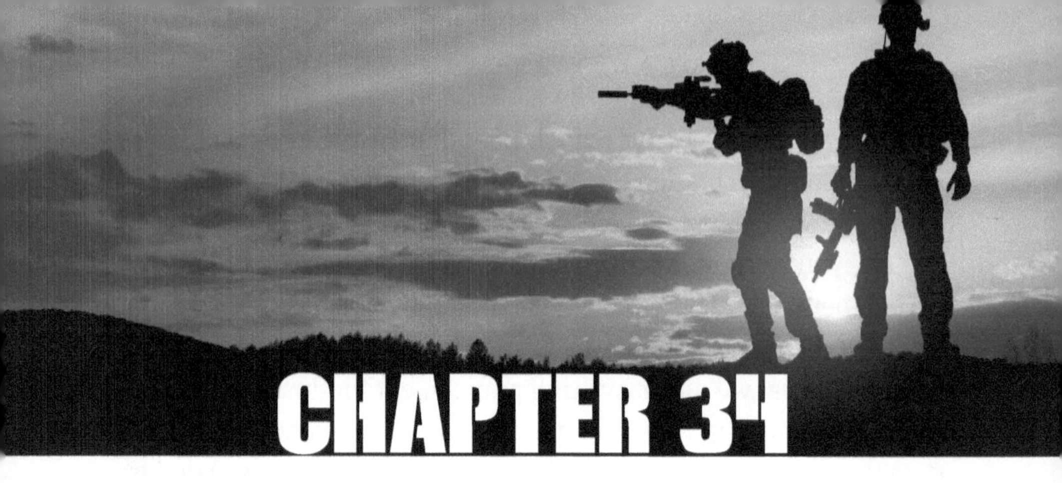

CHAPTER 34

"Emergency call just came in, Shep!" Jim reached out and turned the light on, taking a look at the clock on his bedside table. It was just after three in the morning.

"Give me the facts, Dorf," Jim said into the ships phone.

"Container ship sailed from Naples at eleven last night. An explosion went off in one of the holds. She's taking on water too fast for the bilges and emergency pumps to keep up. We're the closest ship, and it's a standard Lloyds contract. Smitty is heading up to plot our fastest course."

"Wake the crew, let's get cracking," Jim replied, hanging up the phone and throwing the covers off.

Minutes later he was shrugging into his waterproof work coveralls as he made the last three steps to the bridge. He walked through the door, pulling his zipper up to his chest, and passed straight into the compass bridge. Smitty was already there, and he and Wade were plotting the fastest course to the wreck. Jim nodded to the two men as they looked up and stood beside the chart table, watching them figure it all out.

Ten minutes later John pushed the throttles to the stops and the ship leaped forward, climbing in speed until she was coursing through the water at a steady twenty knots. Jim stood at his usual place on the bridge, behind and to the left of John at the wheel. Wade was still in the compass bridge with Smitty.

"Okay gentlemen, listen up!" Jim said over the headsets. "We have a container ship going down approximately four hours out. She's going to be close to going under by the time we get there, so we're going to send the chopper out ahead of us. The chopper will pick up the crew. We'll mark the location of the wreck and salvage her once the crew is safely on board. It's a standard Lloyd's contract, so we should make a good bit of money on this one. Any questions?"

"Who does she belong to, and what happened?" Master Chief Warner asked.

"It's an American company, shipping Alpha Romeo, Ferrari, Fiat, Lancia, and Mazaratti automobiles to New York harbor. The crew thinks one of the cars had a bomb in it, and that the bombing was deliberate. That's all I know for now. When we bring up the ship and her cargo we'll know more," Jim replied.

"Terrorists?" Mark asked.

"I don't know. It could be. Let's just wait and see," Jim replied.

Three hours out they launched the helicopter with Dorf, Mark, Wade, C.G., Vince, and Jack Boswell on board. Dorf kept a running commentary on the rescue operation with the ship. She was still afloat, but only moments from going under when *Bring It Up Coral* arrived. Working swiftly the crew got their emergency pumps working, getting ahead of the water flow and stabilizing the situation. Dorf landed the chopper and after everything was secure, he led the diving team beneath the ship to work on a temporary patch.

Most of the container ship's crew were exhausted from their ordeal and chose to sleep for several hours. Eventually some of them came out on deck and offered to help where they could. Working hard for nearly twelve hours the crew finally had a temporary patch in place and was able to remove the emergency pumps and return them to *Bring It Up Coral*. By then, the Mediterranean was working up a storm, and in that arena storms could come fast.

Mark, Dorf, C.G., and Vince stayed on the crippled container ship. Her Captain, a hard, old salt came back on board, wanting to drive the ship while she was being towed. Mark explained that special expertise was needed for operating a towed ship of this size and when the Captain wouldn't budge Dorf was called upon to convince him that he could stand in the bridge, but Mark or Dorf would be driving the boat. Dorf's imposing size and quiet implacable voice convinced the Captain that this was the best course to follow.

The bollard pull was attached to the bow of the container ship and the tow began. As they slowly gained speed Dorf expertly matched the speed of the tug, keeping the towline slack, two thirds of it under water at about a depth of four feet. *Bring It Up Coral* was designed to pull a ship through the worst that nature could throw and keep it up for days if necessary. In the engine room Master Chief Warner listened to the steady throb of the diesel engines and kept a wary eye on the gauges. Frank was there to help him.

Andrea was in the bridge, a pair of binoculars to his face, keeping an eye out for anything that might be floating in front of them. John was at the wheel, keeping their speed at six knots, which seemed to handle the developing swells best. Occasionally Dorf would radio ahead that the towline was approaching the surface, and John would pull the throttles back until Dorf radioed that everything had settled down. After three warnings they were still moving at a speed of six knots, but everything seemed to be going well. Jim was on the deck, holding a lifeline, when the unexpected happened.

A violent squall hit them from the west, joining the storm that was pushing them from the southwest. A wave washed over the deck, taking Jim's feet out from under him, but his hands held the line tightly and he was able to stand almost immediately. He could see the container ship take the hit and begin to slide, rocking heavily. Two containers broke free from their straps on the deck and went over the side.

"Two containers down, two containers down, the ship is yawing, increase speed immediately!" Jim yelled into his headset. John reacted immediately, slowly increasing the rpm's while Dorf cut his engines entirely. The line leaped out of the water and snapped tight, humming in the wind, and slowly the huge container ship came back into place behind the tug. Dorf began to increase his speed slowly until the line again dipped beneath the surface.

"I wouldn't have known what to do in that situation!" the Captain of the damaged container ship said, letting out a deep sigh as if he had been holding his breath. He was shaking his head and looking at Dorf with a new respect.

"Tugs have been lost because the ship they were towing ran over them that way," Dorf said evenly. If he had been at all nervous it didn't show. He lifted a hand to his earpiece.

"Mark, you okay?" he asked. "C.G., Vince, you guys still with us?"

"O sure! Ask about Mark first. He's in the hold checking the patch, out of the rain. C.G. and I nearly got run over by those containers, but let's make sure Mark is okay first!" it was Vince talking, and Dorf could almost hear his grin through the wire.

"Well I'm not okay!" Mark's voice came on then, sounding angry and frustrated. "That roll dumped me in some of this sludge down here and I'm covered with it! Now I ask you, what girl in port is going to want to give me a hug? All you gotta do is drive in a straight line, but no! Putz!"

Every crewmember chuckled. The sludge down there was filled with oil, dirt, grease, and saltwater. Mark would be a mess when he came back on the boat. Jim depressed his speaker button.

"It must be those cat-like reflexes." he said with a short laugh. He and Mark had been discussing those reflexes in some Martial Arts training the day before. Mark laughed, remembering the conversation and shook his head.

"Hope nobody was video-taping that move!" he said.

"Film at eleven. Uncle Zeke is watching you!" Zeke said.

"Shut up, you brain box!" Mark retorted.

"That's the problem with officers in the Navy. They never recognize real talent," Zeke replied sadly, shaking his head. "No matter how hard I try I just can't win! I catch the gymnast with his backside raised to the ceiling and his arms windmilling wildly, and he calls me a brain box."

"You're actually taping me?" Mark asked, surprised.

"I installed a small camera to keep an eye on the patch in case you got busy somewhere else. I think we'll save this footage for the archives," Zeke snorted with a nasty grin. "We can pull it out and watch it whenever you get too big for those boots you wear!"

Everyone laughed, the tension slowly ebbing away as a near disaster was avoided. Jim kept his watch for another hour while wave after wave sought to tear him away from the lifeline and wash him over the side. Enjoying the challenge, he kept alert and in good spirits.

"I think someone's laundry is blowing around astern," Andrea said into his headset. He had looked down at Jim for a few seconds to make sure he was still safe, before returning to his vigil of the waters in front of them. To him Jim looked like he was literally blowing in the wind, his feet high up above the deck and facing the side.

"It's me, Papa Orvieto. I'm just hanging around back here," Jim quipped sarcastically. "And yes, I'm doing my laundry the old-fashioned way, using the deck of the ship as a washboard!"

"You're too thin!" Andrea said with a chuckle. "You need to eat more, like Papa Orvieto. Then the waves would not toss you about so."

Hours passed, until finally the storm blew itself out, moving to the northwest again and leaving the two ships behind in churning waters. Frank Miller relieved Jim at the stern watch. He was hanging onto the lifeline, like Jim, when they came together. The two watched a dolphin slide across the deck, making a sound very much like a gleeful "whee" as it nosed into the water on the other side.

"If a shark does that I'm out of here!" Frank said.

"Well, if one does, don't give it a leg up," Jim replied with a straight face.

"Very funny, boss, very funny!" FM said sarcastically.

Another Dolphin shot across the deck, and a third. It seemed to be a game with them, and the two men watched them with smiles for a moment. Moments like this were precious to men of the sea, and they both loved watching the dolphins at play. Jim turned away and headed in to get dried off and work in his office. He showered, dressed in his tan work uniform, and sat down at his desk with a happy heart.

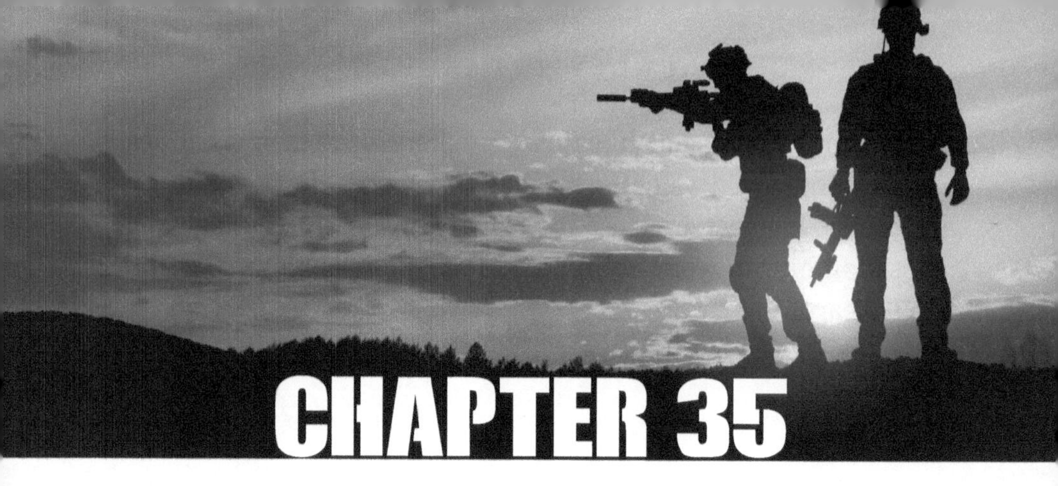

CHAPTER 35

Cecilia came in with a sheaf of papers. "Here are the papers from Lloyds, I've already filled them out so that all you need do is sign them," she handed the sheaf to him.

"Cecilia, we didn't hire you to be a secretary!" Jim chastised, smiling in spite of himself at the work that was completed.

"No, but you need one," she retorted, smiling too. "I wasn't that busy, but I really do think you need to add to your office staff. That is what businessmen do, and you are, whether you want to admit it or not, a very successful, very real businessman."

"Let's make a note of that, and talk about it at the next business meeting," Jim said, writing it down as he spoke. "May I escort you to dinner, after I sign these documents?" he asked.

Cecilia happened to be looking down at him when his eyes rose and caught hers. There was something in them that told her he was almost afraid she might say no. And there was a memory too, one that he probably rarely even admitted, and never talked about.

"Who was she?" Cecilia asked, immediately shocked and ashamed that she had spoken without thought.

"To whom are we referring?" Jim asked, his eyes even more troubled.

"The girl who broke your heart," Cecilia said, sitting down suddenly in the chair facing his desk. "The girl who hurt you." Quite suddenly she wanted to tear her hair out, and she laughed at herself.

"Her name was Mary Ann Baxter, and she was my High School sweetheart," Jim found himself answering. "I thought we were in love, at least I was. When she found out I wasn't going to college, but into the Military, she dumped me very loudly and very publicly. Over the years I've come to realize that she was in love with the idea of being married to the team's most valuable player, a sports superstar, who would take her out of Boston and away from the ocean. I did have several scholarships offered to schools in the west."

"Were you the team's most valuable player?" she asked, suddenly interested in his past.

"In football and wrestling I was. Wade was in basketball, and John was in track and field and baseball. We played every sport we could. Wade didn't wrestle, and neither did John, they played basketball. But in other sports we were usually together," Jim replied.

"Why so set on the Military?" Cecilia asked, as they rose to go to dinner.

"Our dad always wanted us to be Marines. He thought it would be the best training for us, before going to school. He died mysteriously at sea when we were seniors, and we wanted to do it mostly for his memory," Jim admitted, his eyes suddenly full of those memories.

"I'm sorry I brought that up," Cecilia said, suddenly wrapping her arm around his and giving it a squeeze.

"It's okay. I don't talk about these things often. You have a gift for pulling things out of people, I think," he replied, smiling down at her.

"Some people," she replied with a strange secret smile.

Outdoing themselves, the kitchen crew fed everyone an excellent steak and shrimp dinner. Several of the *Bring It Up Coral* crew made sure that the four men from their crew on the container ship knew exactly what was being served. Those poor men were eating poorer fare on their boat, sharing cooking duties, which were actually well liked by the men. Still, it wasn't steak and shrimp. Several members of the container ship crew asked if they could sign on.

Jim made sure the kitchen crew knew he was pleased with their efforts before returning to the bridge with Cecilia, who still seemed to be attached to his arm. He didn't mind, and he didn't even mind the looks he got from other crewmembers. Cecilia might not be a fashion model, but she was quite dazzlingly beautiful in her own right, and Jim was finding himself more and more attracted to her. When she finally let go to enter the computer center he sighed. She heard it and wore that secret smile again.

"We're an hour out from the shipyard at Naples," Wade said his eyes fixed on the water in front of him. Jack Boswell was holding the binoculars and keeping an eye on the water in front so they wouldn't hit anything floating. Smitty was glued to the radar screen for the same reason.

"We will lay over for two nights and a day before returning for the containers," Jim said, relaying a decision he'd made during dinner. "Everybody needs the rest." Looking out the windows he saw that the sea was still rough from the storm.

"Roger that, Shep," Wade agreed. "You should rent one of those Vespa's and take Cecilia to see the city," he added, turning to look at Jim.

"Not a bad idea!" Jim said with a grin. "I'll have to ask her. She might want to go with someone else."

Wade grinned and turned back to the wheel. Under his breath he muttered, "Fat chance of that!" Jim heard it and smiled again.

Without further incident, they towed the container ship into the port, and the pilot was able to take her in on her own power to the dry dock for repairs. Cecilia joined Jim, John, Wade, and Mark in the hold to determine what had happened, so they could make a report before the local authorities did their own research. Cecilia showed her real talent as a forensic expert in that hold.

"This bomb was designed to explode outwards, tearing out the side of the ship. Whoever did this planned to sink this vessel." They were standing knee deep in water, inside the container from which the blast had occurred. "I think they used plastique, probably C-4, and a fulminate of mercury detonator," she held up a tiny piece of glass with some mercury still attached to it. "It was a lot of C-4. Probably three or four bricks, under the middle car, so the blast would radiate down and then out."

Jim had the ship's manifest and was checking for the container they were standing in. He found it. "This one had a total of twelve Ferrari's inside," he looked around; counting the cars that had been tossed about and were in disarray, toward the back of the container. The steel runners stacked on top of each other were mangled and bent upwards, the cars below with rooftops flattened.

"This was one of the first crates loaded." Jim went on. "They were sure of their placement by making sure this crate was up front."

"Anything interesting about the company or the destination of these vehicles?" Wade asked, suddenly.

Jim returned to the manifest and read. "Hmmm!" he said, looking up. "Every vehicle on this ship was designated to a series of automobile dealerships, all owned by a Jewish man who has offices right here in Naples."

"Really. Perhaps we should pay his office a visit tomorrow," John suggested softly.

"Let Sir Edward and Admiral Runion handle that," Jim said. "Sir Edward can see that the proper local officials visit this office, and Admiral Runion can send the appropriate FBI agents to the dealers in America. We're supposed to be nothing more than salvage experts. It might arouse suspicion if we showed up there asking questions."

"Good point," Wade nodded.

Cecilia digested the information, making a mental note to remember for the future. It wouldn't do to bring attention to them, and she wasn't about to endanger their cover. She asked the obvious question. "Where were the dealerships located that these vehicles were destined to be delivered?" Cecilia asked, curious, shivering a little from the cold water around her legs.

"Mostly in New York city and New Jersey cities," Jim answered.

"Well, we got what we need. Let's get back to the ship," John said.

They walked in companionable silence back to *Bring It Up Coral*. As they climbed the gangplank Jim noted that a yacht had anchored in the harbor since they landed. He went up the bridge and asked Zeke to check it out. Sure enough, it belonged to Mercury. He left orders for the night crew to keep a close eye on the yacht and on their own vessel. Then, bone weary, he walked down to his quarters, undressed, hung his uniform carefully in his locker, and put his laundry in the hamper.

At breakfast the next morning Jim turned over the plate to his left without giving it much thought. Cecilia joined his table moments later with a bright smile, picked up her plate and joined the line at the breakfast buffet. Realizing that he had automatically assumed Cecilia would join him, Jim felt a stirring uneasiness in his mind. Before he had time to really think about it, she was there, and he was standing, pulling out her chair, and welcoming her.

"I hope you don't think I was too forward in saving you a place." Jim said quietly, leaning down close to her ear. Her hair smelled wonderful and he found himself desiring to hold her in his arms. Feeling that he was falling too quickly he sat down, disconcerted.

"I would have been disappointed if you had not saved me a place," Cecilia said looking at him, her eyes deep pools that held his, unresisting, for a few moments. *He's afraid of getting too close to me. And I'm afraid of getting too close to him. Well, nature will take its course. This might be one wild ride!* She smiled at that last thought, and suddenly Jim was at ease again. They said grace together before digging into their respective breakfasts.

Cecilia liked to eat oatmeal and fruit for breakfast. Jim was a bacon and eggs man, and this morning there were sausages and slices of ham to compliment that. He drank a large glass of ice-cold milk that Stinky brought out to the table almost the moment he sat down. Along with that was a glass of one hundred percent fruit juice, also chilled and over ice. Cecilia drank tea exclusively at breakfast.

"Would you like to see Napoli on the back of a Vespa?" Jim asked when he had cleared most of his huge plate.

"Oh, that sounds like fun!" Jim hadn't noticed Zeke sit down at the table with his brother Sparks. His face turned red at Zeke's quip, but he smiled.

"I was asking the young lady beside me, Mr. Kline," Jim said. Cecilia laughed, and her eyes were dancing with pleasure.

"And I would have responded in exactly the same manner, had I not been interrupted!" she said.

"Please accept my humble apologies," Zeke said, half rising, and bowing. "I am chagrined that I interrupted you!"

"You are impossible!" Cecilia laughed.

They rented the Vespa from a small shop on Corso Umberto and after exploring the streets of Napoli turned south and rode along the coast all the way to Sorrento, where they ate, before returning. It was a turning point in their relationship, and they talked at great lengths about their pasts, and their immediate future.

When they returned to the ship it was dark and Jim walked Cecilia up to the observation deck. No one was up there, and they stood beside the railing and talked more, enjoying the lights of Napoli, the yachts and ships around them, and the sounds of the city approaching its evening character. Later they walked down to Cecilia's stateroom, where Jim kissed her goodnight, a chaste kiss on the cheek and a whispered thanks. She was wearing that secretive smile when she turned away and entered her room.

CHAPTER 36

Early in the morning two days later *Bring It Up Coral* moved sedately out of the harbor just after high tide. Although it was still dark, the yacht shadowed them, keeping a distance of about a thousand yards. John took note of the yacht's position and made a mental note to mention it at breakfast. An hour later, Captain Rob, their IGS autopilot named after their father, propelled the ship forward at a steady twelve knots. John left the bridge and went down for breakfast. The IGS was designed to warn anyone away from the bridge of impending danger early enough for a human pilot to reach the bridge.

Two days later they were anchored over the two missing containers and preparing to drop the submersible into the water. Once again Jack took his place at the controls, Sparks and FM in the fishbowl with him. Dorf and Mark were in the water checking all the lines for any problems. Dorf thunked the fishbowl with his huge hand twice to let them know that everything was as it should be. Moments later the submersible slid beneath the surface, using the sensitive metal detecting gear to locate the containers.

C.G., who had been training for this moment, climbed into the NEWT Suit. He and Vince had both been working hard to be certified as deep water divers and checked out on all the diving equipment. They flipped a coin to see who got to go down first, and C.G. won. He was grinning widely as he climbed into the suit, excited for his first real dive and work.

Air rushed into his suit when the helmet was fastened down and he stood quietly, waiting to be lifted into the water. On the deck he couldn't move the heavy suit, but beneath the surface he could move quite easily, if slowly. Master Chief Warner told him to prepare for lift, and suddenly the heavy suit rose into the air, carrying his body with it.

It was still new enough for him to enjoy every moment of the descent. The other divers often felt bored making a long descent, but C.G. was fascinated by everything. In time it might become routine, and wouldn't be as much fun, but he doubted it. To him everything he was experiencing was awesome and new!

He considered target practice. When they first received the MP-10s the feel of the weapon, and its inherent accuracy thrilled him. Now, after firing thousands of rounds in practice, changing the barrel, and making some adjustments, it was routine. It wasn't novel anymore. For now, he was content to be in the suit making his first serious dive. Consciously he kept his eyes on the gauges inside his suit and followed his descent, adjusting his air supply as he went deeper. All those long hours of training came to mind as the suit descended into the depths.

The first container had tipped on its side, but it was still sealed. It wasn't watertight, so it would be full of water. They would use the water to stabilize the container on the way up, and then drain most of the water away before lifting it clear of the surface. That was for the crew above. C.G. guided the straps for lifting into place and signaled Master Chief Warner to hoist away. The container lifted clear and settled into an upright position.

As C.G. approached the second container, he could see that it had landed upright, but one corner of it seemed to be resting on a rock sticking out of the bottom. At least it looked like a rock, but when he stepped on it, he detected the sound of metal on metal, the bottom of his weighted boots connecting with something that gave off a slight metallic sound.

"Hey!" he exclaimed, stepping back and looking down. "I stepped on something metal, under the container. It's covered by crud but I'm sure it's metal!" his voice was filled with excitement. The manipulator arm of the submersible suddenly came into gentle contact with his left arm and lifted and pushed him aside.

"Step aside sailor," he heard FM drawl over the radio.

"Don't get so pushy," C.G. said with a grin, looking up and into the fishbowl hanging beneath the submersible. All three men were visible there.

"What's going on down there?" that was the voice of Zeke.

"Some ugly crab-like thing just got fresh with me," C.G. said. "I might have to wrestle it."

"I wouldn't. Your suit could spring a leak, and then where would you be?" Zeke laughed.

"Okay. I'll remain a gentleman," C.G. replied.

"Now that I've got to see!" FM said with a chuckle.

While the talk was going on FM was using the arm to clear away the growth. Everyone down there watched with anticipation as the debris slowly disappeared and they could see what lay beneath. In a moment they could see gray metal.

"Hey, I think I have a submarine conning tower here?" it was more of a question than a statement, but it certainly looked like that was what was sticking out of the silt on the bottom. His eyes swept over the familiar shape as he studied it.

"That's my submarine. I found it first!" C.G. whined, sounding for all the world like a petulant child. Everyone laughed.

"Checking definition now," Sparks said, using the detecting gear to map out the shape and size of their find. Minutes passed by until Sparks spoke again. "We'll have to lift the container clear. Are these radios secure?" he asked.

"Yes, they're encrypted. Anyone listening in will not be able to understand anything being said," Jim replied.

"Okay, Shep. I'll take your word for it, since I seem to remember reading something about that in the instruction manual," Sparks replied. "I have the configuration of a German U-boat, at least the rear half of it. Get that wiz kid on the computers working on salvage rights for this!"

"Roger that, *Steel Crab*. As soon as the first container is secure, we'll send down the straps to lift the second container free. Meanwhile the wires are burning," Jim replied.

An hour later the second container was securely strapped, and the cable was lifting it slowly away from the bottom. C.G. helped set up the sandbox and position the giant vacuum hose over the conning tower. Master Chief Warner had wisely sent the power attachment for that equipment down with the straps so that the clearing away could commence.

Standing off to one side C.G. watched as the silt began to billow over at the sandbox and the shape of the submarine began to appear. It was a U-boat, and furthermore, it had a huge hole in its side, indicating how it happened to be there at the bottom.

Sometime later Jim noted that the yacht that had been shadowing them was departing at full speed. Curious, he pressed the speak button on his headset. "Zeke, the Mercury yacht just left. Do you know anything about it?"

"Uncle Zeke is always watching, Captain!" Zeke replied from his computer terminal. "Remember we cloned their phones. A call came in earlier alerting them to our request for salvage rights. They're on their way to a nearby port to pick up a ten-man team. We are to bring up the sub, and discover it's secrets, and if the sub is carrying what they want, the ten-man team will board us after dark and steal it."

"How will they know what it contains?" Jim replied, his interest suddenly piqued.

"Someone from Hess pharmaceuticals will make a move, sending out a fighting unit to steal whatever it is. Mercury wants to steal it first, so they can negotiate with the pharmaceutical company," Zeke replied. "They're watching Hess pharmaceuticals."

"So, we now have two fighting units that are going to try to steal whatever we recover from this submarine?" Jim replied, somewhat surprised.

"Sounds like that's correct, Captain. It will make for an interesting couple of days," Zeke replied laconically.

"My aren't we bloodthirsty today?" Jim said into his headset. "Maybe you should try decaf." After the laughter that followed, Jim continued. "Monitor them, and let's see if we can steal a satellite photo of Hess pharmaceuticals and some background."

"I'll run the name through some data bases, Shep," Cecilia said from beside Zeke.

"Right then. You two are the best, so go to it," Jim replied with a smile.

"Ooh, it's nice to be appreciated!" Zeke said into his headset. "I hope the rest of you heard that!" he added.

"Great, we'll never hear the end of it!" FM said into his radio.

"Hey, Doc, can you give him something that'll give him laryngitis?" his brother Sparks added.

"He'd just text message all of us," Vince said.

"Just remember! Uncle Zeke does not get even, he always gets ahead!" Zeke said with dignity.

"Hey, Captain, anyway we can get Mary Ann and Barbara back on the ship?" Dorf quipped. Mary Ann and Barbara had kept the crew laughing with their pranks during their stay on board, and twice had pulled pranks on Zeke, neither of which he knew about until he was the victim. It had been Mary Ann who had noticed loudly at dinner that apparently Uncle Zeke didn't see everything after all. Rare moments like that were well remembered by everyone.

"I think we'll have enough excitement with the Mercury and Hess outfits thrown into the mix, guys," Jim said in reply.

"Besides, we all know how women distract us on board a ship!" Andrea said into his headset.

Zeke watched Cecilia turn a bright red and laughed. Andrea was watching Jim and getting about the same results. He laughed loudly. Jim grinned in embarrassed silence, and then went back to work. He could feel the flush on his face even as he spoke.

"Listen up *Steel Crab*," he said tightly. "That sub may have something on board that isn't safe. Treat it with every caution. Acknowledge, please."

"Acknowledged boss," FM said from the submersible. "We'll treat it real careful."

"Really carefully!" Cecilia spoke. "When using an adverb, use it correctly. The proper grammar is: We'll treat it really carefully."

"Yeesh!" FM replied. Then, mimicking her accent he replied. "Yes, Miss Cecilia. I'll practice my grammar, I promise. Please don't make me write it a hundred times on the chalkboard!" Laughter broke out at that interchange.

Everyone took a break for dinner after Vince and the NEWT Suit were lifted to the surface. Vince helped hook up the cables to the submarine before being lifted topside himself. After dinner the crew returned to work, and worked long into the night, lifting the submarine from the bottom and slowly bringing it to just beneath the surface. Once it was securely in place the submersible was lifted to the deck and everyone grabbed a few hours of sleep.

Dorf and Mark had the watch and noticed the return of the Mercury yacht as dawn first touched the sky with its magnificent aerial paintbrush. Mark kept a close eye on the boat but noted that the men seemed busy getting ready to get some rest. By the time the sun reached the eastern horizon only one man was visible on deck, watching the boat through binoculars.

After breakfast the men went back to work on the sub. Dorf and Mark got to rest for a few hours. Jack took C.G. and Vince down to search the sub. Their findings were amazing. Describing the torpedo room door and vents told Jim that something dangerous rested inside that room. No one welded an inner hatch and ventilation duct unless there was danger, and danger of a specific type.

"Okay men. Don't try to get into that area. My guess is that we have something biological inside," Jim said, after hearing the description.

"The outside hatch is not sealed," C.G. reported from atop the sub. Jim could see him hovering there.

"Roger that, C.G." Jim replied.

After an hour-long search the divers came up and stood on deck watching as FM and Master Chief Warner winched the ancient vessel out of the water. It hung there in the air for several minutes while the water from inside drained away. Then, after nearly seventy-five years, the U-boat lay at rest somewhere other than beneath the sea. A long silence followed the settling of the boat on the cradle the men had prepared on the deck for it.

First, once the boat was on the deck, a team of men attacked it with pressurized water hoses, washing away much of the muck and sea life clinging to it. Jim was glad to note that the identification numbers of the sub were worn away after so many years and the work of Acorn barnacles, or, they had never been there in the first place. He walked around the sub, noting the two huge holes on either side.

"It looks like she hit two mines," Jim said to Wade, as the latter joined him.

"Probably set by her own side. They mined these waters pretty heavily in the war," Wade replied, looking at the damage with the eye of an engineer. "Took her down fast. She probably hit one, and then was blown into the other one on the opposite side. Sometimes those mines broke free," he added.

"How deep do you suppose she was when that happened?" Jim asked.

Wade looked closely. "Some of the mines were set to trap submarines trying to slip past the mine fields. I've heard they were anchored at different depths, sometimes as deep as one hundred and eighty-five feet. I'll have to check the records from this area, but that is my best guess."

"So, the poor guys never had a chance?" Jim said softly.

"Yeah! Horrible way to die, but probably pretty quick," Wade replied.

John and C.G. appeared at that moment. John was holding a shallow pan in front of him, and in the pan was the ships log. Because it was written in ink, it probably wouldn't have much to give them any clue about the last voyage of this strange boat. Master Chief Warner and FM signaled that they were ready to open the top hatch.

Jim turned away from the interesting discovery of the log and made his way up the ladder. All the testing had been done and the hatch was still sealed tightly. This chamber, and this one alone had experienced no damage from water. Jim watched as Vince and Sparks, dressed in biohazard suits, slowly lifted the hatch open and checked the equipment that tested the air inside the hold. The equipment he was holding would identify any substance that was harmful to man. For a moment it seemed as though the entire crew held its breath.

"No traces of anything other than stale air," Sparks said finally.

No one suggested taking off the biohazard suits. Clearly visible at the bottom of the ladder was a fifty-gallon drum, sealed with lead and tar. Climbing down gingerly the two men tested everything around the drum to be sure nothing was leaking, and even tested with a Geiger counter. Nothing registered. The only thing that told them was that the drum was still sealed. What lay inside may not be!

"Let's hope it's still intact," Jim breathed. Some of the men nodded.

Careful now, the two men in the biohazard suits used vice-grip pliers and small pry bars to remove the top. Once this was completed the tools were handed up to be cleaned. Inside the drum sand and decomposed straw had settled to about two thirds of the depth.

Sparks sank his gloved fingers gently into the sand and encountered a canister beneath the surface. He felt around it and then carefully lifted it free of the sand. It was clearly marked biohazard. Vince was already waving the various tester ends around the canister, but nothing registered. It was still tightly sealed.

"Is it small enough to fit inside a normal bucket?" Jim asked quietly.

"Yes, Shep," Vince replied.

"Alright. Put it on the floor and climb back out and try to look like you're puzzled. We'll send a cleaning crew down with buckets and hoses and they can bring it up. In the meantime, Master Chief, get me a sealed container large enough to cover this one. I want a newer seal on that package before we move it too far," Jim said tersely. "We're taking no chances!" The men nodded in agreement.

Master Chief Warner was already moving down the ladder, with FM in tow. They had some hazardous waste containers in the engine room that were perfect for what Jim wanted. Another group of men grabbed buckets and hoses and made their way into the hold while the two with biohazard suits removed them outside the hatch cover on the top of the sub.

Jim was leaving nothing to chance. He had the container carried down to the weapons room and put in a safe there. Meanwhile everyone on the ship prepared to head back into port with the containers to complete their contract. Due to the professional expertise of his crew *Bring It Up Coral* made a tidy profit on this venture that would add one more bona fide check mark to their cover.

Before evening set in the ship was moving back toward Naples with the Mercury yacht tagging along behind. Dinner that evening was a festive affair as the men celebrated yet another coup in their salvage endeavor. Yet even as they sailed forces were set in motion that would put them all in harms way. Chance favors the prepared mind and their fate would lie in the decision of a mind well prepared for the challenge. Fate, fickle mistress that she was, lay in the future, unknown, yet to be experienced. Jim thought about that for a moment, and then decided that God knew everything that was going to happen, and He, awesome omniscient God that he was, would know exactly what to do.

CHAPTER 37

Mediterranean storms were often unexpected, violent, and unpredictable. This one didn't disappoint anyone. Coming from the west it literally built in minutes and flung all its full fury on the unfortunate ships in its path. Mercury's yacht was not designed to run fast through the storm and fell behind quickly. Taking advantage of the distance Jim asked Dorf and Mark if they were willing to take the CH-53D Sea Stallion on an unscheduled flight.

"She's fully capable of handling this storm," Dorf assured Jim with a grin. "You want to get that container off the ship, and have it analyzed, don't you?" he asked quickly. In his own mind the existence of that canister was sinister and the danger to the crew imminent.

"Yes," Jim said simply. "I spoke to Sir Edward and he's sending a special unit down to help the Italians out. They can meet you at Capodichino. You two stay with the container and see that the contents are destroyed correctly. Once the container is sterilized bring it back and we'll see what develops."

"You want the contents destroyed?" Mark asked, surprised.

"Yes. Whatever it is it's a threat to everyone," Jim replied. For a moment Mark considered that and then nodded approval.

"Consider it done," He said emphatically.

Working with the crewmen to prepare and launch the helicopter was exciting in the storm. Everyone got very wet, and there were a few bumps and bruises from waves sweeping them along the deck to crash into things. Dorf and Mark took off in the worst part of the storm and Jim watched the helicopter for a few minutes as it drew away, picking up speed, seeming to diminish in size until it was lost in the rain and wind.

"That was well done!" Jim said to the crew once they were back inside. "Is anyone injured? Some of us got tossed around out there."

"Really?" FM said sarcastically. "I hadn't noticed."

"FM's okay!" Sparks quipped. FM just glared at him.

Once Jim was cleaned up and in dry clothing he sat down at his desk, preparing to wade through his paperwork when Cecilia appeared at his door. Somehow her tan uniform seemed to accent every part of her that appealed to Jim and he found himself swallowing and staring at her like a teen-age boy. Sure that she would notice his discomfort he worked hard at trying to appear at ease. He grinned and she smiled in return.

"Doc wants to see you about the cut over your eye, and I have bad news. I'll tell you on the way to sick bay," she said, stepping back and waiting until he rose and walked out into the passageway.

"My cut is fine," he said. "It stopped bleeding."

Cecilia looked critically at the cut on his forehead and shook her head. "It needs a few stitches from the look of it. Come on, I'll hold your hand," Cecilia was teasing, of course, and Jim laughed.

"That sounds pleasant," he replied, taking her hand in his. She pulled hers away.

"Not until you're experiencing pain!" she scolded.

"Oh! Ouch!" Jim said, mockingly, placing his hand over the cut, which made it start to seep blood again. Cecilia punched him, her eyes sparkling with laughter.

"Picking on a wounded soldier is low," Jim said in mock sorrow. "How I am abused, a poor wounded seaman, bleeding and bruised. Have you no pity?"

"None," she replied, taking his hand and pulling him along.

Dr. Wozniac was used to men like Jim, and he worked quickly to sew up the cut on his forehead, numbing the area with a quick shot and then beginning the work with a deft hand. Cecilia sat perched on one of the beds smiling at everyone, her eyes twinkling occasionally at Millie who stood by to assist. She loved these people, not just because they had been so kind and helpful, but because they were the best kind of people. Jim sat stoically through the whole ordeal.

"So, what's the bad news?" he asked, showing no reaction as the first stitch was threaded.

"Admiral Rook is meeting you in Naples to investigate your find," Cecilia said, her blue-green eyes watching Jim for any reaction. Jim raised an eyebrow and Doc tisked, brushing it back down with his little finger even as he continued working.

"Admiral Rook can take his investigation and shove it!" Jim said irritably. "Who does he think he is, anyway?"

"He claims there's some maritime law that allows him to examine the wreck," Cecilia said, shrugging her shoulders. "I checked the law to be sure, but it's pretty vague. I don't think he can push it."

"He'll certainly push it," Jim said with a grimace, sliding his eyes to Doc. "You enjoying this?" he asked sarcastically.

"Oh yes!" Doc said grinning back. "I'm creating a work of art. Your scar will add to your manly charm," his voice dripped with sarcasm.

"First, I get abused by the ship's forensic expert, and now the doctor is purposely butchering me. You want to get into this too, Aunt Millie?" Jim asked with a grin.

"I'll get some foul-tasting medicine to force down your throat," she said with a twinkle in her eye.

"Your Captain retires, bested, madam!" he said, trying to bow.

"Hold still you pirate!" Doc snapped, pushing him back.

"There!" Doc announced, tying off the last stitch. "Now let's have a look at the rest of you. Take your shirt off."

Jim unbuttoned his shirt and slid it off, then pulled off his tank-top undershirt. Cecilia had never seen him with his shirt off and raised her eyebrows, her eyes now filled with mirth.

"My, what a hairy creature!" she said to Millie. Jim blushed.

"He's got more on his back," Doc said, examining that area and checking a particularly large bruise. "You're lucky you didn't break a rib!" he added. His deft fingers probed carefully, and Jim winced twice, but other than that seemed to have suffered no more than the bruise.

Cecilia wandered around to his back and laughed. "You should get a hot wax treatment," she said, her clipped English accent and droll way of speaking sounding like music in Jim's ears.

"I need it to keep warm," he replied, shrugging back into his undershirt and then putting on his uniform shirt. He buttoned it, turned his back on his audience, and tucked everything in, and then turned back to them.

"May I go now, or do I need to stay for some more abuse?" Jim asked with a grin.

"I do have some Cod liver oil. Would you like to take some?" Millie asked.

Jim hugged her with his right arm, and with his left motioned for Cecilia to follow him. "Thanks, but no. I think I'll live," he said. "Thanks Doc."

"Do you want a bandage over that cut?" Doc asked.

"No, it looks more impressive just hanging out there for everybody to see," Jim replied, winking at the doctor and whisking Cecilia out the door.

Jim walked Cecilia all the way to the computer center on the compass deck. Smitty looked up and waved as they passed through the chart room and went through the glass door to the computer center. Jim could see he had been working on plotting their course and sketched a wave in return. Zeke looked up as they entered and grunted.

"Do we repel boarders?" he asked, his eyes going back to the monitors displayed in front and around him.

"With lethal force, if necessary," Jim said grimly.

"Oooh, someone's had too much caffeine this morning!" Zeke said with a wicked grin.

"Call the team together in the conference room, thirty minutes," Jim said cryptically.

"Aye, aye, Captain!" Zeke said with a salute.

"Can you access the computer on the *Farragut*?" Jim asked. The *Farragut* was a guided missile frigate, 5,368 tons, a five-hundred-and-twelve-foot ship that could make over thirty knots. Admiral Rook had assigned the ship to himself. She was launched in 1961 and was soon destined for retirement.

"Do birds fly?" Zeke queried with mock dismay. "Not only can I access the computer on that ancient tub, I can do it so that they will never know I was there. What do you want?"

"Everything," Jim replied, looking at Zeke, his face suddenly still. Zeke knew that look.

"He probably doesn't keep his private stuff in there, but we'll get everything. I can access his laptop. He's using a new IBM clone model, one of those generic brands that everyone seems to think can do it all. When he goes on-line, I can freeze his computer for about twenty-five seconds and download everything he has stored in the memory," Zeke said.

"You can do that?" Cecilia asked, astonished. "I didn't think it was possible."

"Child's play, my dear," Zeke said with a wicked grin. "You do know why he's doing this?"

"Yes," Jim replied. "He heard about the salvage rights and found a way to board our ship to see things for himself. It's his way of telling us he's the big man."

"Both computers then," Zeke said, turning back to his keyboards.

"Do them both and have some fun," Jim said after a moment of thought. "Let me know what you get."

In the conference room Jim explained his plans to the team. John, Wade, C.G. and Vince would guard the gangplank and personally deny Admiral Rook access to the ship. Jack, Frank, and Smitty would provide back up with Jim.

"We use shotguns with beanbag shot," Jim said quietly. "But only if necessary!" he cautioned the four Marines who would hold the gangplank.

"It won't be," John said lightly. "The man's a coward."

"Yes, but the men who accompany him might not be," Jim cautioned.

"Sneak thieves and weasels," Frank said with a grin.

"Right on FM!" Jack said with a grin.

"Everybody knows what to do," Jim said, grinning himself.

"Semper Fi!" Vince said, raising a fist.

"Ooh rah!" C.G., Wade, and John replied.

"Jarheads!" FM said, shaking his head. "They're all the same."

"Ooh rah!" Jack said.

"Do shut up!" FM replied in mock disgust.

When they entered the harbor, the team went down to the weapons room and gathered the shotguns. For the beanbag shot they had Mossberg 590 Tactical 12-gauge shotguns. Each man loaded nine shells into the shotguns but did not pump one into the chamber. Making sure the rifles were set on safe, the men filed up to the deck.

Andrea was at the wheel. Expertly he guided the ship into the assigned slot at the loading docks, following the instructions of the harbor pilot who had boarded the ship upon entry of the harbor. The pilot watched nervously as the eight men positioned themselves, noting the guns.

"You are expecting trouble?" he asked Andrea.

"Just a nosey Admiral from the American Navy," Andrea said with a grin.

"The one from the *Farragut*?" the pilot asked with a grimace.

"That's the one," Andrea assured him.

"Then I shall turn a blind eye to what I am seeing," the man replied. Both had been speaking in Italian. Andrea grinned.

"I see you've met the man," he said.

"It was not a pleasant experience," the pilot shared.

"It never is," Andrea said quietly. "It never is."

Once the ship was in position Frank threw the bowline to a waiting dockworker, and Smitty threw the stern line. Both lines were made fast to the heavy iron cleats bolted to the dock. Admiral Rook stood off to one side with six sailors standing at attention behind him. He watched as Wade manipulated the controls to lower the gangplank to the dock and began moving toward it, waving the longshoremen waiting to unload the two containers aside. They looked at him with undisguised disgust. Jim noted that they said some rude things, but the men with the Admiral did not respond.

Halfway up the ramp Admiral Rook stopped, his eyes narrowed, looking at the four men who now faced him at the top. All four held shotguns but he didn't think they meant to use them. Shrugging he began walking up the ramp again and stopped when shells were pumped into the chamber. That was a sound that would stop any man in his tracks.

"Stand aside, I'm boarding your vessel!" he commanded.

"You don't have the Captain's permission to board this vessel," John replied calmly. "This is a private vessel and you have no authority to board this vessel without the express permission of the ship's Captain."

"I am an Admiral of the United States Navy!" Rook sputtered. "No one talks to me that way, no one! Now get out of my way!" he took one step and halted again as all four shotguns lowered, now pointing directly at him.

"Detail!" he snapped looking down at the six men on the dock. "Get up here and remove these men so I can board this vessel!" he commanded.

Four more shotgun slides were heard, and Jim and his three men appeared to either side of John and his team. For a moment the six sailors hesitated, and then stepped forward in twos, their faces betraying the hesitation and fear.

"This is a private vessel, and I am the Captain. You do not have my permission to board this vessel. My men will repel boarders with extreme assertiveness!" Jim snapped.

When the sailors continued onto the ramp six shotguns rang out. The beanbag shots were accurate at this distance and all six went down. Two of them, the first two, had taken hits in the forehead and were unconscious. The others were crying out in pain as they sat or lay on the ground. One had taken a shot to the groin, and he was rocking back and forth on his knees making high-pitched keening sounds. Another had been hit in the thigh. The last two had taken hits to the shoulders, near the neck, and lay on their backs holding a hand over the spot where the beanbag hit.

Jim walked down the plank to stand in front of Admiral Rook, his shotgun lowering until it was pointed right at the Admiral's groin. "Get off my ship," Jim threatened quietly.

Admiral Rook paled, looking into those stormy green eyes. Slowly he backed down the ramp until he ran against one of the unconscious men. He turned and looked down. Then he looked at the rest of his detail.

"Get up, get up!" he snapped. "Get these two bodies out of my way," he turned back to Jim. You haven't heard the last of this!" he snapped at Jim.

Jim's shot took him in the groin and the Admiral was hurled backwards, bent over, landing hard on his knees and face, his hands grasping, and his mouth open in a silent scream of pain. Never in his entire career had he felt such pain and agony. Laying there gasping in pain he was unaware of anything else until rough hands seized him, lifted him, and half carried, half dragged him to his car.

"Clear the gangplank!" Jim ordered.

Smitty collected the rifles while the other men rushed down. Wade grabbed the Admiral and was none to gentle in removing him to his car. There he dumped the Admiral on the ground unceremonially. The two unconscious men were stirring, and they were set down gently, their backs to the car. Vince was helping the man shot in the thigh limp to the car, and C.G. had the man shot in the groin, bent over, guiding him carefully.

"Best to get some ice on that," he said with some sympathy.

The men returned, collected their weapons, and John took Jim's shotgun down to the weapons room, while Jim remained to arrange for the removal of the containers. At the head of the gangplank he found the harbor pilot.

"You have made an enemy today, I think," the pilot said quietly. Without thinking about it he had spoken in Italian and was surprised to hear Jim reply in that language.

"He was an enemy before today," Jim said. "I hope there will be no trouble over this."

"Not from us," the Italian replied with a smile. "What did you shoot them with?"

"Beanbags," Jim replied.

"Ah! I have heard of this type of ammunition. Very effective!" the pilot added.

"I did warn him," Jim replied.

"Yes, senior. I heard you. It is your ship," the pilot replied.

With a cheerful wave the pilot took his leave, watching the men around the Admiral's car slowly crawling into the vehicle. One of the two with wounded shoulders was going to drive. The white Lincoln moved away slowly, heading to the military dock where their ship was moored. *There will be trouble now, but not for us.* With that cheerful thought the pilot returned to his office to tell the tale, which quickly spread throughout the town.

"Let's have a dummy container ready for the Admiral's next visit," Jim said into his communication gear.

"I'm on it, Shep," the voice of Jim Warner replied. "What do you want inside?"

"How about a Vodka Martini?" Jim replied with a smile.

"You are bad!" Master Chief Warner retorted.

"Where are you going to keep this container?" John asked, coming up the steps out of the hold.

"In our biohazard storage unit," Jim replied with a grin. "Anyone who wants it will know right where to go."

"I know where I'm going!" Wade said as he trudged up the steps. "I'm going for a nice dinner!"

"Nope!" Jim said with a wicked grin. "You've got guard duty. John and I will ask Abe to put something aside for you.

Shaking his head Wade threw up his hands in mock surrender, turning back down to the weapons room to get his shotgun. He loaded it with bean bag shot and took up a position on the observation deck, high above everything, where he could keep an eye on things all around the boat. Jim and John sent Windy up with a plate of food for him. Windy reported that Wade was pacing the deck with a murderous expression on his face.

CHAPTER 38

Dorf and Mark returned and landed the CH-53D easily, since the waters in the harbor were as calm as a millpond. Once the craft was secured and the rotor blades folded properly and strapped, the two men reported to Jim, who was finally seated at his desk and wading through the much-hated paperwork that plagued every ship's captain. He was glad for the interruption.

"Hey Shep!" Dorf said by way of greeting, dropping tiredly into one of the chairs facing the Captain's desk. Mark sat with grace beside the giant. Dorf leaned forward and handed Jim a file folder with three pieces of paper inside. It was the analysis of the contents of the biohazard container. Jim opened the file carefully and glanced through the three sheets, his face grim.

"Sir Edward sent down some techno weenie from England's version of the CDC. He had enough equipment to take up an entire hangar! But he was fast, once the equipment was up and running. That's a detailed analysis of the stuff we found. Dude claims the only way to destroy this stuff was in an incinerator. We had to drive to the university to destroy it in their lab incinerator. That container never left our sight, and it's a good thing if I understand that paperwork," Dorf added as he sat back with a sigh.

Jim grinned at the way the giant dwarfed his furniture. Dorf was an interesting mix of social styles. He was primarily an amiable in social style, but also a driver, which was a fascinating combination. Jim, primarily a driver with analytical as his secondary style had some weaknesses that Dorf didn't have to worry about. Dorf was easygoing as well as determined, and he didn't suffer from the impatience Jim often experienced with the crew. He finished reading the report and whistled softly.

"So, this Dr. Leonard Hess developed a mutated form of the Ebola bacteria and was ready to launch a new plague upon the world. We need to do some research on this guy, and his offspring. I'll get Cecilia on it with Zeke," he said.

"Didn't you tell us you ran into a Hess family in Boston that gave you the willies?" Mark asked, suddenly.

"That's right, owner of a pharmaceutical empire and suspected of being one of the main suppliers of illegal drugs in South America. The oldest daughter runs the corporation. She has the reputation of being ruthless," Jim replied, remembering.

"It might be interesting to determine if that firm has an antidote to this bacteria strain. Something like that would send it to the top among pharmaceutical firms," Mark mused. For a moment the men looked at each other, no one making any comment as that thought permeated. Finally, Jim spoke.

"Damn!" Jim swore, something he did rarely because of his upbringing and respect for his mother. "Could it be that easy?"

"Releasing a bacterium like that one would have killed millions though!" Dorf said.

At that moment their headgear came to life. It was Wade, still on guard on the observation deck.

"Shep! We have a contingency from the United States Navy entering the yard," his voice was clipped.

"Who's on the bridge?" Jim asked.

"I am here, Nephew," Andrea replied gruffly. "I have ordered the lines released and am ready to take the ship out," he had anticipated Jim's next move.

"Thanks, Poppa!" Jim grinned, realizing how much Andrea had become one of the team. "Take her out to sea and drop anchor when we've entered international waters. We need some time to think about this. That container was much more valuable than we originally thought. An idiot like Rook will get innocent American's killed over it if we're not careful."

"Roger, Captain," Andrea said, pushing the throttles forward.

"Don't forget to ask for a pilot to board us quickly, once we're away," Jim added.

"I have already done so. The pilot will meet us immediately," Andrea replied.

On shore Admiral Rook swore as *Bring It Up Coral* left the dock before his men could reach it. He watched the pilot boat swing along side, and a pilot climb aboard with the help of crewmembers. The ship made a gentle turn and headed out to sea. Around the Admiral the men kept their eyes down. He swore and gestured and paced up and down the dock sputtering in rage. Suddenly he spun on his heels and headed back to the convoy of vehicles.

"Quick, back to the ship!" he commanded. "We're going to board that ship whether they like it or not!" he snapped.

"Uh, sir . . . uh, that's probably not a good idea," it was one of the senior officers who blurted out the statement before he could take it back.

"It's not a good idea to obey your Admiral?" Rook asked quietly and dangerously.

"That's not what I meant, sir, and you know it!" the commander replied with some heat. "Boarding an American vessel in international waters is illegal, and you know it!"

"It's not illegal when it's a matter of national security, and I'm declaring a matter of national security on this one, Commander. Any questions?" Rook spat, his own rage going up a notch. That Commander Cummings was correct irritated the Admiral, but he wasn't about to budge on this one. He was going to teach those Shepherds a lesson!

"No sir," the Commander replied with a sigh, knowing when he was powerless.

On board the *Farragut* there were unexpected problems in getting under way. Any attempt to access the main computer and start up the guidance systems seemed to be interpreted by the computer as an order to fire missiles.

Several of the computer experts were working on the problem. They suspected that Zeke Kline was responsible for this little fracas, but had no way of proving it, and wouldn't have told the Admiral anyway. Most of the men hated the man, and served him only because they had to, and then only as far as they needed to stay out of trouble.

Rook, of course, berated them, yelled at them, and stormed in and out of the computer center interrupting their work again and again. After a four-hour delay they were able to reboot the system and get the ship under way. It was then that Admiral Rook stepped up to the main speakers of the ship and prepared to deliver a scathing speech to the crew. He'd been working up to this moment, his ire ratcheting to a place where his face was beet red. What happened next would long be remembered by that crew.

Zeke planned for precisely this series of events, knowing the Admiral had to hear himself shouting commands to his crew. To everyone's horror the Admiral's voice came out of the speaker's sounding very much like Disney's Donald Duck. It took a great deal of self control from the men on the bridge to keep their faces straight, although the red color in their necks and cheeks gave them away. Any other voice using the microphone came out clearly.

Rook stood there, his face beet red, his veins popping out in his neck, furious and powerless to fix the problem. Even his communication experts could not discover the cause. Rook suspected that they weren't trying very hard, but he couldn't say that. He retired to his quarters.

Jim took advantage of those four hours to study the docks and the position of the *Farragut*. He was sure that a mercenary force would attack the ship once it was learned that Admiral Rook had taken custody of the container. His team was ready to move as soon as the container had been removed to protect the crew of Rook's ship. At his request, a row of empty containers slowly appeared on the dock, forming a protected cover to get anyone evacuating the ship to safety without being shot from above. For now, they watched the approach of the guided missile carrier while cleaning the deck. There were no weapons anywhere to be seen among the crewmembers as they worked at their usual jobs. If any were nervous about the approach of the ship it didn't show, which did nothing to improve the temper of the Admiral.

Cecilia poked her head out of the computer center and looked for Jim. He was scheduled to be on the bridge, and was, in full dress uniform. She caught her breath looking at him. He was a handsome man in a very rugged way, with his stormy green eyes, black hair, and strong features. The cleft in his chin gave his face the suggestion of virility and strength, not to mention the corded muscles in his neck and arms. Getting her emotions under control she cleared her throat.

"Captain," she said.

"Ma'am?" he had taken to calling her that in front of the other officers. She grinned.

"A Mercury private jet just landed at the airport, and another plane landed with flight plans from Lima, Peru. It was chartered on short notice. I think it may belong to a group from Hess Labs," she watched him digest the information.

Jim nodded to her, smiled once, and then looked at Wade and at John, who were sharing the bridge with him at the moment. "Alert the team, have them ready to move the moment Admiral Rook takes possession of the container. Let's see if we can warn one of his officers of the impending danger without him noticing."

"Team, we are on yellow alert," Wade said into the communication headset. Cecilia wore one now, a request that Jim had made early on. She listened to the men responding, each using his own special nickname. These men were close, they understood each other, and they worked so well together that they knew what each one was going to do without talking. The only reason the men responded was training. Wade needed to know that every member received the message. Noting that none of the men stepped upon another in announcing he had received the message she sighed. In many ways she wasn't up to speed in understanding how these men worked. She watched and learned.

Suddenly she realized that her new friends were going into battle again, and that any one of them would be in harms way. Despite her knowledge of their training and capabilities, she retreated into herself a little, afraid of what may occur. When she sat down Zeke looked over at her and accurately read her mood and thoughts.

"Funny thing about operations," he said, his eyes roving over his many monitors. "The Captain is a master strategist, but he knows the rules. Once the operation begins the situation is fluid and requires constant adaptation. There aren't any men like Captain Shepherd when it comes to that. He's a legend in the Corps and in the Navy. He seems to know just the right thing to do at just the right time. We've had men wounded, but we've never lost a man. Put your mind at rest. If it is possible, we will all come back. But also expect the unexpected. Prepare yourself to support the team, regardless of circumstances. With that frame of mind, you'll be able to function."

He seemed preoccupied with his work on the computers, but Cecilia knew he was also noting every movement she made. Able to read her like a book he had given her the one thing she needed most. Detailed instructions of how to prepare for this helped her considerably, and she sighed, put her mind into gear, and began to make preparations for meeting this challenge head on. Zeke nodded silently to himself. She would do.

Jim watched silently as the *Farragut* dropped anchor across their bows, where they sat in the gentle swells. A skiff was lowered and powered over. All the men were dressed in their uniforms and welcomed the Admiral aboard as soon as he asked permission. He had learned a bitter lesson. Once aboard however, his usual manner took over.

"You have a canister taken from that U-boat. I want it," he demanded like a petulant child.

"You asked permission to board my boat. You are not in charge here, Admiral. This is my ship, and on my ship, you keep a civil tongue in your head, and you ask nicely if you want something," Jim said, his eyes boring into those of the Admiral. Admiral Rook stepped back at that look and sputtered.

"How dare you threaten me!" he said.

"No one threatened you, you pernicious miscreant. You come on my ship and spout your flatulent, turgid, mouthings of a mental pigmy as if vomiting your pompous opinion of yourself all over everyone here will overwhelm us. All it really does is make us sick. If you are polite and ask politely, I will gladly turn over the canister we hold in our biohazard container into your keeping. It's that simple," Jim stood quietly, holding the Admiral's eye, saying nothing. He'd practiced that line several times and saw the grins on faces around him but schooled his face to hardness.

"I will remind you that I am a superior officer, sir!" the Admiral said, trying to save face.

"Not really. You may be a higher-ranking officer, but I'm not in the Navy, and this is still my ship. Here I hold the authority, as you well know from your studies of maritime law. Your vain pretensions do not move me. You're running out of time, Admiral. Ask or I will have you physically removed from this vessel," Jim's tone and body language said much more than his words and the Admiral wilted.

"Oh, alright!" he said peevishly. "If you must have it, I most humbly request that you turn over the canister in question to my crew. There! Is that acceptable?"

"No. You're still acting like a stuffed shirt and if you say another word aboard my ship, I will personally slap that offensive demeanor right off your face. Do you understand?" Jim leaned forward a little and Admiral Rook swallowed hard. He nodded, recoiling from that veiled threat, aware that the men with him had seen his movement and hating himself.

"Fine. Commander, please escort the highest-ranking officer of this party, other than this flagrant excuse for an Admiral, and two seamen to our biohazard storage unit and hand over the canister,"

Jim said, looking at John who saluted and motioned for Commander Cummings, from the *Farragut* to follow him. Cummings motioned for two seamen to follow him while Jim remained, holding Admiral Rook with his stormy stare.

Admiral Rook drew himself up and prepared to deliver a scathing speech but remembered in time what Jim had said previously. He knew beyond a doubt that this young man would literally slap him down if he spoke, so with a scowl he walked over to the railing and stared back at his ship.

Public humiliation did not sit well with him and he vowed that these men would pay. Then he noticed C.G. and Vince on one side of him, and Wade on the other. One look in their eyes told him he would never raise a hand against them. Fear and guilt fought within. Fear won the day.

Fearful he went back to his men and stood among them, saying nothing, looking at no one. Red faced the men did not look at the Admiral either. Some of them had laughter dancing in their eyes and they winked at the men of *Bring It Up Coral* when the Admiral could not see. Every one of them wished they could dress down this most disliked Admiral personally like that. They were still in the Navy, and many of them wished to continue their career, so they held their tongues, and enjoyed the moment.

On the way down to the container John outlined the dangers to Commander Cummings. The Commander had heard of Sergey Vasilevich Botenkov. The threat of two teams moving on his ship bothered him and he thanked John for the information. John warned him that Van Poole liked using explosives, and he would probably plant explosives on the hull of the *Farragut*. The canister was turned over and the men left on the launch making their way back to the guided missile carrier. Jim watched them leave with a strange smile on his lips.

"I think you boys frightened the poor Admiral more than I did!" he said, looking at Wade, C.G., and Vince.

"Well, Captain, we knew you had him confused with all those big words you used to describe him, so we figured all we could do was try a little intimidation. What in thunder is a pernicious miscreant?" C.G. asked, grinning.

"A dangerous troublemaker." Jim said quietly.

"And where did those other words come from?" Vince asked. "I never heard you use them before."

"I looked them up in a Thesaurus." Jim admitted laughingly. "It pays to use the right words for the right occasion. Now, let's go green. Andrea, take us back to our berth forthwith, please," Jim said into his intercom.

"Did I see a stain on the front of the Admiral's pants?" Andrea said into his com link. "If not, it was a close thing, I think," Andrea added with a laugh.

"Now that would be something to behold," Wade said with a laugh.

CHAPTER 39

In the weapons hold the men packed their gear in carrying bags. They would leave the ship by twos and threes, making their way to their positions under the light of day. Jim figured that the two teams would attack at night. Whatever team Hess had gathered would be first to attack, and then Sergey and his team would take the canister from them. It was the way he would do it himself, and he knew a little about Sergey and the way he operated.

Cecilia had done her homework and she knew the leader of the Hess team: a Dutchman named Van Poole. Van Poole was wanted in six different countries for his atrocities as a Neo-Nazi. What made him very dangerous was that he had been trained as an anti-terrorist in Holland, and he was known as a demolition's expert with uncanny skill. Van Poole would surely rig charges on the *Farragut* forcing an evacuation. During the evacuation he could easily catch the crew in a crossfire killing most of them. All of this meant real danger for the men on that ship, and the men of *Bring It Up Coral*.

When Admiral Rook returned to the dock, he ignored Commander Cummings suggestion of strengthening the guard and preparing for a possible attack. Commander Cummings, who was a career officer, knew when he was beaten and retreated without getting himself into any real trouble. As he walked out on the deck, he noted that there were several containers sitting on the dock that hadn't been there when they left. The containers were empty; both ends open, stacked so that they formed a corridor from the dock into one of the warehouses.

He smiled. Captain Shepherd was giving them a safe evacuation route from the ship if that became necessary. The fact that the containers were there told him that it would be. Quietly he began to alert the men to the danger, and if the Admiral saw the change in his crew, he ignored it. No one really noticed the twelve men who moved onto the dock and into the various warehouses in groups of four either.

Jim chose the warehouses to occupy because he knew which ones the enemy would choose. These three offered the best views to the ship and the best shots at the crew. Therefore, the enemy would come and occupy them in force after nightfall. But the night belonged to his team. Once the shooting began his men would move and take out the enemy. Some would escape, and the canister would make its journey to one of the enemy headquarters. A homing chip would identify that location to his team.

Waiting is always the hardest for a soldier who knows that battle is coming. All twelve men were well hidden, each in a separate crate made of wood, so that a search of the warehouse would leave them undetected. Since they were alone it was harder to maintain vigilance and discipline, to be quiet and mentally prepared. Radio silence was the order for the evening until the actual shooting began.

Shortly after midnight Van Poole's team arrived at the warehouses. There were eight men assigned to each warehouse. Once he knew they were in position Jim silently moved out of his crate, making almost no noise, and clicked his radio microphone twice to alert the others that he was doing a reconnoiter to pinpoint the enemy positions.

Wisely, he waited until he heard the enemy passing through, inspecting the floor to make sure there were no people there, to change into his night gear. It was hot in the box, and he didn't want his sweat smell to give him away. Moving cautiously, he became one with the shadows and found all four snipers and their spotters, right where he thought they would be. As he stood, looking at one pair, he noted the telltale bubbles of divers breaking the surface in the moonlight near the *Farragut*. Explosives were being attached to the hull.

Rather than change locations and risk being seen he clicked his microphone three times to alert the troops that action was about to begin. He heard Wade and John doing the same in their warehouses. Quietly Jim pulled up his MP-10 and looked through the dioplar sights. He kept the laser guidance off. From this distance he could drop both snipers quickly.

The MP was a very popular successor to the MP5SD. The entire stock is made from polymer material, giving great strength allied to low weight. It was a .45 caliber weapon with all the features of its 9 mm predecessor. Now Jim waited, among the shadows, a shadow of death.

Suddenly the quiet of night was shattered by the alarms on the *Farragut*. Multiple explosive devices had been detected and the abandon ship whistle code was sounding. Men burst from the ship, fully armed, and knelt at the bottom of the gangplank to provide cover fire. Jim was sure that Admiral Rook would be first off the ship, and he didn't want the snipers to kill him.

The sniper in his sights tightened his finger on the trigger and Jim put three shots into the back of his head as he fired his first shots of the night. Because Jim's bullets arrived first, the shot was a miss. Looking with surprise at his partner the spotter took the next three shots in the side of his head and dropped as silently. Jim could hear the suppressed fire of other MP-5/10s and knew that his team was taking out the snipers.

Leaving his position, he ran down to the first floor to provide cover fire for the crew from the forces that would necessarily be on the ground. Stymied by the containers, enemy troops on the ground were confused, and instead of catching the crew in a crossfire they were themselves easily identified by the flashes from their guns.

Jim's team began to take them down with deadly accuracy, and some of the Navy gunners added their help.

Men began to pour into the warehouse where Jim was laying down cover fire, taking up positions, firing at the enemy. When enough were there Jim and his three team members slipped out the back, circled behind the enemy, doing terrible damage. Van Poole didn't care about the men on shore. His team was there to take the canister. As expected, no guards were posted, and Van Poole blew the safe and removed the canister. With speed and efficiency, he departed the guided missile carrier and detonated his charges.

Admiral Rook stood in the warehouse, surrounded by guards, and watched his ship lurch into the air. Then the force of the explosion hit the warehouse, shattering glass and showering everyone inside. Several men experienced cuts and bruises as the explosion knocked them down and rolled them around in the glass. Stunned the Admiral watched his ship from the floor as it settled in the water and began to sink.

"It was that Captain Shepherd who did this!" he stammered.

"Really sir? Why was he here, laying down cover fire, killing the snipers in these buildings who were supposed to kill your crew? Why is he out there risking his life to continue to protect us? We've been attacked, just like he said we would be, probably by Van Poole and his group. The explosions certainly indicate that!" Commander Cummings growled, his eyes hard. At that moment he truly hated Admiral Rook.

"If it wasn't for Captain Shepherd and his men many of our crew would be dead right now. Remember, I warned you, sir. You refused to listen, for whatever reason. Who do you think arranged for those containers to be lined up there and filter right into this warehouse?" Commander Cummings turned away.

Admiral Rook knew he was right. Captain Shepherd and his crew had saved him, and what was more, they had saved his crew. It was a debt he would rather never have, and he knew deep down inside that he would ignore it. Somehow, he felt ashamed and was instantly angry. How this group of men constantly irritated him was a matter for later.

"Thank him for me," was what Admiral Rook should have said after a moment of thought. Instead he said something else entirely. "Remind him that all his planning did not save the canister. I'm sure that is the reason for the explosives and evacuation. That container is now in enemy hands!"

"Quite right Admiral!" Jim's voice said from the darkness. He stepped out, a deadly shadow, and men stepped back when they saw him, before they recovered. "The canister is surely gone. I am sorry about the damage to your ship. She'll take a while to be seaworthy again."

"How did you know about this?" Admiral Rook asked.

"One of my crew did some background work on the sub, discovering that it was taking a shipment of something out for a Dr. Leonard Hess, a pet scientist of Adolf Hitler, who worked mostly here in Italy. That led to the discovery of an elite force under the direction of Paul Van Poole, a Neo-Nazi. I am a bit surprised by that. Hess didn't think much of the Third Reich or of Hitler, according to his journals. That his descendants would turn to a Neo-Nazi was something I didn't expect," Jim shook his head for a moment.

"That of course led us to check out if any agents were watching to see if a U-boat was salvaged. We traced an agent in every salvage registration office around the Mediterranean, sir. And in the course of that investigation we discovered another group doing the same thing. This group is called Mercury, and their elite forces leader is none other than Sergey Vasilevich Botenkov. I have no doubt that he will steal the canister in short order."

"You uncovered all that?" Admiral Rook asked, surprised.

"I was a Navy SEAL Captain, sir. I do know how to uncover such operations. I hope you don't mind my using my former training to protect my crew and our salvage cargo," Jim replied with a smile.

"Where is my canister and what's in it? Do you know that, you arrogant sod?" Admiral Rook demanded suddenly.

"When we first discovered the canister, we knew it was trouble. We flew it in ahead of our ship and some techno guys examined it and determined what it was. As far as I know they were able to identify the substance in the container. You can check with the Italian government on that better than I can, sir," Jim replied.

"You knew the canister we had was dangerous and you let my crew take it? You put us all in harms way!" Admiral Rook sputtered.

Jim stepped forward, his eyes suddenly hard and cruel. Admiral Rook raised his hands as though to fend off a blow, stepping back, frightened.

"No, Admiral! You put your crew in danger by taking it, and then you ignored our warnings through Commander Cummings of the impending danger. I have everything on tape and in my log. You also put my crew in danger, something you've done before, and for that you will pay dearly! You make me sick, now get out of my sight!"

Admiral Rook fled, his guard following, wondering why they were trying to keep the little creep alive. It was their job, and they believed in doing their jobs with honor. One of them turned as they left and sketched a weak wave at Jim. Then he turned to his job, tasteless as it was, and did it with honor.

"I'm sorry for that, Captain Shepherd," Commander Cummings said, sighing.

"No need, Commander. Your men did us all proud tonight. Do you have any casualties?" Jim replied, looking around. Like many he had cuts from flying glass, but he didn't see any dead bodies.

"Just cuts and bruises from the explosion and glass," Commander Cummings replied.

"Who is that man over there by the door?" Jim asked, pointing out a medium sized man who was holding his M-16A in a relaxed position.

"Petty Officer Duncan, one of our deck machinists," Commander Cummings said quietly. "Why do you ask?"

"He saved your life, twice. And he saved the lives of one of my crew too. I'd like to thank him, with your permission," Jim replied soberly.

"You saw this?" Commander Cummings said with some surprise.

"Yes." Jim nodded.

"Follow me," Commander Cummings replied, heading over to the sailor, now quietly watching the dock area where bodies were being counted.

"Mr. Duncan," Commander Cummings said quietly. Duncan turned around, straightened up immediately, and saluted.

"Sir!" He said.

"Thank you!" Commander Cummings said softly, shaking hands with the surprised Petty Officer.

"Let me add my thanks for saving the life of one of my crew," Jim said, shaking hands in turn. "That was quite a shot!"

"You saw that, sir?" Duncan said, amazed.

"And both times you saved Commander Cummings' life." Jim replied loudly enough for others to hear, though not in an abnormal tone of voice. "It was my honor to work with you."

"Just doing my duty, sir," Duncan said, embarrassed.

"That's what makes a great soldier, Duncan. That's what makes us alike," Jim said quietly, watching Duncan's face turn red. He had just paid the young man a high compliment, purposely. "We do our duty, as unsavory as it sometimes is, or honorable as it more often is, as tonight, and expect nothing in return. America was built upon such honor!"

Dorf appeared suddenly, towering over them. "This the guy who saved my life?" he rumbled. He pumped Duncan's hand. "Thanks, man. I never saw that scum sneaking up on me! Imagine my surprise when I heard his head explode!"

"Well, you do make a big target," Duncan said with a grin. His lips were rimmed with white in his red face.

"That I do!" Dorf replied with a laugh. "I owe you a brew, or whatever your favorite drink is, anytime!" Dorf added, leaving as suddenly as he had come.

"Well, I have to go. I thought I'd put all this soldier stuff behind me," Jim replied turning away also. "We have to return our gear," he added, suggesting the idea that the gear was borrowed.

"My crew is in debt to you, Jim," Commander Cummings said, walking along beside him. "Once Admiral Rook is off my ship, and I think that will be soon now, all you have to do is call."

"Thanks," Jim said, shaking hands once again with Commander Cummings. He would put in a good word with Admiral Runion about this man, and Petty Officer Duncan. With a grin and a wave, he disappeared into the night, lost from view almost immediately.

CHAPTER 40

Jim was not surprised to have the Italian port authority politely ask if he could search his vessel. Admiral Rook wanted to know if the gear they wore the night before was on board or borrowed. Of course, he couldn't search the boat himself, so he appealed to the port authority under false pretext.

Rook had been surprised when Jim did not use the press that descended on the docks as a means to accuse him of negligence. Realizing that he would have done just that didn't improve his temper. His ship was crippled, and he knew the Navy would not spend the money to repair it. Instead he was faced with explaining a terrorist attack on his ship and the loss of the canister.

Appearing distracted with a sheaf of papers on his desk Jim grunted his approval. Four hours later the man left with his underlings to report to Admiral Rook that there were no weapons or outfits described on the ship. Silently Jim thanked Master Chief Warner and Wade for their design of the false wall in the hold that hid their weapons room. Every search had come up empty and no one ever questioned the bulkhead wall. It really was invisible, as things hidden in plain sight often were.

Shortly after the expected search preparations got under way to leave. Once they were at sea Jim went down to the dining room to find his plate turned over and Cecilia waiting for him. Her smile dazzled him and feeling suddenly clumsy and unsure he picked up his plate, nearly dropped it, and then pulled out her chair so quickly he nearly dumped her on the floor.

Cecilia recovered nicely and smiling that secret smile walked in front of him to the buffet. Today there were three choices of sandwiches, potato salad and cold slaw, a pasta salad with broccoli and dried cranberries, and kosher dill pickles. Abe also made a batch of his own sweet pickles, a favorite among the crew.

"Zeke wants to see you in the CIC after lunch," Cecilia said, watching Jim put some kosher dill pickles and sweet pickles on his plate.

"Will you hold my hand? Zeke frightens me!" Jim said, as Zeke came to stand beside him.

"It's the size of my biceps!" Zeke said, striking a pose. Abe, across the table, struck the same pose and nodded.

"That has to be it!" he said, as if impressed.

"Hey! Who put a chef's uniform on this Hummer?" Zeke said loudly. "Oh! It's you Abe! Sorry!" he added insincerely.

Jim loved the bantering of his crew, and often wished he could join in himself. He rarely did. Smiling after the laughter died down around the buffet, he returned to his table to eat with Cecilia and thought little about Zeke's request until he walked her into the CIC.

"Ole Rookie's been a very bad boy!" Zeke said.

"How so?" Jim asked.

"He's been emailing some undesirables trying to get a lead on Sergey. So far, he's contacted four known terrorist moneymen for help. He wants that canister back, to save face."

"Hope he likes his martinis shaken, not stirred!" Cecilia quipped.

Zeke looked at her, his face showing nothing. "That's our James Bond, not yours!" he said hotly. Cecilia laughed at him.

"Is there any way he can detect you're monitoring his email accounts?" Jim asked.

"Captain! Please!" Zeke pleaded as though dismayed. "Uncle Zeke sees all, and no one knows he has been there!"

Jim grinned. "Keep on it. We want enough evidence to bury this guy, and to give a certain Admiral an iron leash to hold him with."

"The canister is in Marrakech," Zeke added, looking back to his computer monitors. "It seems that Sergey was able to take it away after all. I wonder if Van Poole is still alive?"

"Not if Sergey has the canister," Jim said grimly. Zeke nodded.

Jim suddenly turned to Cecilia. "By the way, thanks for the idea!" he said mysteriously.

"What idea?" she asked, interested.

"I'll tell you later," he said, his green eyes sparkling with laughter. "You're a genius!" he added, walking back onto the bridge. He waved at Smitty on the compass bridge.

"I always wanted to visit Mallorca!" he said, opening the glass door for a moment. "Let's set a course to Palma for a little vacation time."

"Isn't there supposed to be three Spanish ships lost near Cabo Blanco?" Smitty asked, his eyes on his chart.

"Actually, between the islands of Conejera and Cabrera. We'll do some research. There is supposed to be huge shipment of Inca gold on those ships." Jim replied evenly.

"No one has ever found any evidence of them," Wade said calmly from the helm. Then he added a single word. "Yet."

"We get lucky sometimes," Jim replied with a grin. He switched to Italian and spoke fluently to the pilot who was guiding them out of the harbor. The Italian had never heard of the lost treasure ships and was intrigued. He would talk, Jim knew, and his cover would be established. *And maybe we will get lucky. If we do, we're going to sail around the world, just to say we did it.* That too had been a dream of theirs from boyhood. They might even invite family members and girl friends for the trip!

Mark, who had the watch, pointed out a Mercury yacht following them when Jim joined him on the observation deck. Jim merely nodded. It was to be expected. He stood for a few moments without saying anything and then turned to Mark with a serious expression on his face.

"How do you hurt someone who doesn't feel pain?" he asked.

"By hurt, I expect you mean disable?" Mark said quietly, keeping his eyes to the binoculars and sweeping the seas before the ship.

"Pretty much," Jim said. He sighed. Mark knew to whom his Captain was referring, and he thought carefully before replying.

"He wouldn't feel broken bones, although he'd lose the use of the limbs. Even without pain you can't make a broken arm or leg move. Still, that wouldn't necessarily distract him. My guess is to go for the spine and paralyze him. It's either that or kill him," Mark replied after a moment of thought. "I'm in favor of paralyzing him and then killing him, if you want to know," Mark looked at the Captain.

"Botenkov frightened Fezik al'Loudi. He must be a monster," Jim said.

"I've heard a few things, probably the same as you," Mark admitted.

"Yeah. Like removing the bones from the legs and arms of that Russian Colonel who tried to track him down and arrest him. He did that while the man was alive and conscious, and kept him alive until he healed enough to be returned to his home. His wife woke up and found him lying there, weeping, unable to move anything but his head. He died shortly after that. Merciful, really."

"He's one of the people we have to stop, Jim," Mark said, stopping his vigilance long enough to look Jim in the eye.

"After this we're going to take a vacation," Jim said quietly. "Maybe we'll sail around the world if we find those Spanish ships and their gold."

"This is different, isn't it?" Mark asked, his eyes back on the sea before them. "In the Navy we took orders, knew what we were supposed to do, and did it. Conscience wasn't a problem then. But now we have to decide what to do, and sometimes that requires hard choices. As long as you hate it, you're safe, Jim. Keep hating it."

"You hate it too, don't you?" Jim asked.

"Yeah. But I also know it has to be done. The military solution is the only one we can use against animals like Botenkov, al'Loudi, and Van Poole. People like them are so evil and depraved that in defense of the innocent people of the world we must rise up against them. The trouble is our world is too skewed from what's right to see it anymore.

"They call themselves civilized and define it as something else. Babies die, women die, children die, old men and women are butchered, but we're civilized, so we let the butchers live and continue to butcher. I hate it just like you do, but my conscience is clear before God. We don't decide alone, we all vote, and if it is not unanimous, we don't do it. You set that rule in place for your own protection. Be guided by it, Jim." It was the longest speech Mark had ever made and Jim smiled.

"Thanks, Mark. I needed the pep talk and reminder," Jim admitted after a moment of thought. "What we do is necessary. Amoral people have no respect for humanity, our world, or its Creator. I need to remember that!" he nodded and walked away.

Mallorca was a beautiful place to visit, especially that time of year. Late fall was the perfect time to visit. Calm waters, wonderful weather that wasn't too hot, and the city of Palma to discover pleased everyone. Once again Jim called upon his friend Dr. Alistair Gregg and his two assistants Mary Ann Lewis and Barbara Stafford. It didn't take long for Dr. Gregg to clear his schedule and they arrived in Palma traveling first class, to their delight, shortly after Jim's invitation, excited to help research the three sunken ships from the Spanish Armada.

Ira Lehman's Mossad agents were keeping watch on the Mercury operation. Jim knew it was only a matter of time before they were called upon to retrieve the lost canister. He wanted the canister for another reason, but that would have to wait. Meanwhile he busied himself researching, with Cecilia, and then wandering the town with her, hand in hand. He was falling in love with this girl, and he knew it.

That sent a shiver of fear through him. In High School he had dated the girl he thought was the prettiest in the whole school. Her name was Mary Ann, and she was not at all like the Mary Ann who worked with Dr. Gregg. The Mary Ann of his past had been beautiful and knew it, and to have the attention of one of the school's best athletes was something that appealed to her vanity.

She had dreams of leaving Boston, which she hated. She hated the cold of winter, the heat and intense humidity of summer. Most of all, she hated the smell of the harbor and the sea. Her dreams were full of scholarship offers from west coast schools. Jim would go to Iowa State, Nebraska, or Oklahoma University. He might even get into one of the University of California schools. She'd been to the Pacific coast once, and she loved it. Jim loved her to distraction, learning too late that her love was not for him, but for using him to escape Boston. He'd been helpless when she'd attacked him in public, knowing he could do and say little. He also knew that Cecilia was different, but that didn't erase the fear.

Although Mary Ann knew Jim had plans to work for his father and to enter the Marine Corps, she was confident she could change his mind in time. All through his junior year, and halfway through his senior year she tried. When at last she realized that he was determined to join the Marines straight out of High School, and then work for his father out of Boston Harbor she broke off their relationship in the most dramatic way possible, at lunch hour, in front of many witnesses.

Since then Jim had difficulty trusting women, and he dated few. Now he was in love again, only this time it was different. Cecilia loved him too, she had declared it only recently, and he knew it to be true. Cecilia didn't ask him to be someone else, or to go somewhere else. She seemed content to accept him as he was and to go with him wherever his journeys took him. If his mood was better than usual, no one made a comment. But everyone on the ship was pleased to see the romance budding.

One evening, a week after their arrival, he returned to the ship late with Cecilia tiredly resting on his arm. Looking up he saw

John and Wade waiting for him. Cecilia saw them too and with a sigh straightened up.

"I guess you're needed," she said with a tired smile. "Me, I'm going to bed. Tell me about it in the morning."

He kissed her lightly on the lips and let her go. All three men watched her walk away, and this was not lost on Jim. Whatever they had to tell him was serious. They didn't want her to hear it. When she was out of hearing distance John put his arm on Jim's elbow, guiding him up to the bridge. On the way he talked quickly and quietly.

"Ira called. His two men disappeared two hours ago, and he fears for their lives. He's emailed all the information and pictures they gathered over the past week to us. He wants us to rescue them, if they're still alive." John opened the door to the CIC and Zeke looked up. Every printer was working on images, and Zeke already had most of it loaded in his laptop.

"We need to move, Jim." Zeke said.

Jim nodded and gave the order for the team to gather in the conference room. He went through the galley to get a glass of iced tea from Windy before joining the team. Once they were all seated Zeke began taking them through the Mercury information, frame-by-frame, report by report.

Ira's men were thorough. They had detailed pictures of everything. Their last report that morning, suggested that they had been noted and were in danger. All reports had ceased later that afternoon.

The women of Mercury had an interesting military set-up in their main warehouse. The first three floors were strictly storage, but the fourth and fifth floors were housing and training areas for Sergey's mercenaries. How those two agents got pictures of that compound was a question Jim hoped he could ask. The sixth floor of the warehouse was weapons and ammunition storage. There were cameras on the rooftop, throughout the compound, and alarm systems that seemed state of the art.

"We have to go in tonight. I don't think the men will live through the night, if they are still alive. Not with Sergey's reputation," Mark suggested.

"Agreed," Jim replied tersely. "We'll take the CH-53D and fly in. Let's roll!" He said.

"What about our plan?" Wade asked.

"We'll strategize on the chopper. We have no time," Jim said as he led the way to the weapons room.

Thirty minutes later they were "feet wet" over the ocean and headed for North Africa. The trip to Marrakech took three hours, with one refueling in flight courtesy of Ira, just off the coast. A mile from the Mercury compound Dorf set the chopper down in an Israeli facility. Ira was there with the necessary equipment.

Moments after landing Sparks was working on a Pinch, a device that replicated the electro magnetic pulse of a nuclear explosion, taking out every electrical device in its path without the boom. Since the compound at Mercury headquarters ran on a diesel generator, they could fry the circuits and plunge the compound into darkness. Even battery-operated emergency lighting would fail. How Ira got the Pinch was something no one asked, though Sparks really wished he could take it back to the ship with them. He made a mental note to purchase one at their earliest convenience.

Ten minutes later the compound and most of the city went dark. Since it was so widespread the Mercury troops would not think it an attack on them, or at least Jim hoped that would be the case. High above the compound twelve men glided silently through the sky, landing seconds after the lights were extinguished. All of them landed lightly, some on the roof, others in parts of the compound. Within thirty seconds none could be detected by the naked eye.

Zeke, Sparks, and FM followed Jim to the office, where Zeke was allowed to work his magic with the computer systems of the compound, crippling them completely after downloading everything in their memories. The electrical problem would be blamed for the loss of information.

Zeke used a battery pack to fire up the computers. According to his ongoing description of the pack it would last for several hours. His fingers flew over the keyboards of the computers as he looked through them during the download of materials. Thirty minutes later the men began their attack on the warehouse.

Sparks was able to bypass the alarm system that might become operational again. Stealthily they crept into the warehouse, their night goggles showing a pale green display of everything clearly. Jim divided his forces, sending four up the north steps, and taking four up the south steps. The other four were coming in through the roof. C.G. and Vince would take care of the weapons and ammunition on that floor, detonating the explosives once they were safely away.

Someone screamed in agony as they mounted the steps, covering any sound. It had to be one of Ira's agents. Jim took his time now, planting each foot carefully, staying to the edges of the steps to avoid any creaking. As the screams continued Jim's resolve grew and he steeled himself for what he was about to witness.

On the fourth floor they came to a stop, peering into the main exercise and training gymnasium that had been built there. Most of Sergey's men were gathered around the two prisoners, and Sergey was standing before them, a bloody knife in one hand. Even the three women were there, watching, silent, unmoved by the horror before them. Gas lamps provided light for the group huddled near the center of the floor.

Two clicks sounded in his left ear, and two more in his right. Both the other teams were in place and ready. Jim clicked once, and four flashbangs went off in the room. Jim kicked the door all the way open and followed, one second after the blast, and saw Sergey bringing up the knife to kill the two Mossad agents. He fired on the run, careful to put three bullets in Sergey's right hand, and watched with satisfaction as the knife fell away.

Sergey looked at his hand in amazement and turned to face the attack. Jim's team acted quickly, lethally, and with the military precision expected. Sergey turned to find every one of his men on the floor, each one dead from head wounds. Like a crazed animal he flew into motion, pulling at the pistol at his side as he charged Jim.

Botenkov was good; one of the best Russia had ever trained. He was perhaps the most dangerous man Jim had ever faced in single combat. Yet even Sergey Vasilevich Botenkov was no match for Jim Shepherd that night. He'd seen the bloody pulp Botenkov had made of the two agents. As his pistol came out Jim grasped his wrist, twisted it back and up and broke his arm in three places in the blink of an eye. Even as the pistol fell useless to the floor Jim moved behind Sergey and struck, his knuckle burying itself at just the precise point, and Botenkov collapsed on the floor like a rag doll.

Mark watched Jim flow into battle, noting the deadly quickness, the perfect balance. It happened so quickly that few of the men saw it, and only one of the women. Botenkov had been alarmed to see his target slide around him so quickly, hearing the bones of his arm snapping, and then nothing as he sank to the floor. He knew he was paralyzed, and that he had been defeated easily. He wanted to scream but could not.

In the silence that followed Jim looked around at his men, to be sure none were injured. Dorf was looking at a tear in his sleeve, checking to be sure there was no blood beneath. His fingers came away dry. Jim could tell the arm hurt, but the Kevlar sleeves they wore had done their job. FM was limping a little from a turned ankle. He'd dived to the side just in time to avoid being shot. Everyone else was accounted for.

Jim turned back to the two agents, who were staring at him, tears leaking down their cheeks, amazed to be alive, surprised to be rescued. Both were shaking in the aftermath. He smiled at them and walked over to look at what had been done to them. Both were badly beaten, faces swollen and flesh torn. One of them, the one who had screamed moments before was bleeding from his mouth. Jim opened his mouth and sucked in his breath. Botenkov had cut several teeth out by slicing away part of the man's gums with his knife.

Mark was there with a morphine ampoule and in minutes the agent was asleep and out of pain. Jack packed the mouth with a bandage as best he could to stop the bleeding. He worked quickly and deftly with the emergency medical pack. Wade and John were covering the three women, who had yet to speak. One of them finally did as she watched them work over the two prisoners.

"They are Hebrew scum!" she spat. "Why do you worry about them? You are not Hebrew. Who are you?"

So far, not one of the men had spoken a word. Jim nodded to FM who sauntered up to the women and handcuffed all three of them, despite their struggles and threats. Dorf lifted the sleeping prisoner and gently carried him down the steps and out of the compound. Wade and John helped the other between them. As they walked away C.G. and Vince paused, finishing the connections to detonate the explosives.

Botenkov remained on the floor, unable to move, and as FM passed by, he showed him the detonator. It was a fitting end for such a monster. FM knew he would have to wait until everyone was clear, every second an agony as he waited for death. Suddenly FM felt sick, and he knew it was because such evil should not exist in the world.

No one spoke to the women and the silence of these deadly men frightened them more than they wanted to admit. Yet they still believed themselves to be untouchable. So great was their arrogance that they believed they were above the laws of man. Jim knew this, and also knew that the silence would weigh more heavily than accusations or speech. He smiled as they slowly lost that arrogance.

CHAPTER 41

J im carried the canister, which he retrieved from the office while
Zeke was working on the computers. The three women looked
at it more than once and finally one of them spoke.

"You are from the Navy ship?"

She could see nothing of their faces, because of the masks they
wore. Only their eyes showed. When Jim turned his on the women
they recoiled and the one who had spoken fell silent. Jim was more
than angry at these women. Their greed prejudice, and hatred was
beyond description. No one spoke to them as they moved through
the darkness, the women wondering where the walk would end. At
the gates of the Israeli compound the women stopped dead in their
tracks.

"So. You Hebrews have violated our business, killed our people,
and you think you will take us to trial? We are lawyers, all three
of us, and we will be out of prison before you can imagine." She
looked at them to see if they would react to that, but they didn't.

Ira opened the gate personally and smiled at the three women.
If they were surprised to see him, none showed it. He ignored the
women, and had his agents placed carefully on stretchers and carried

to the hospital. Once the ambulance sped away, he turned to the men, nodded once, and motioned for the women to follow him.

"I spit on your Mossad!" one of the women said with venom in her voice. "What can you do to us? Nothing!"

"O, I plan to do nothing," Ira said with a smile. "I'll let your fathers decide your fate. I'm sure they'll find your plans to disrupt their lives quite revealing," he added.

Jim was watching them and saw their shoulders slump in defeat. Once their fathers knew of their plot to kill all the male members of their families they would be punished appropriately. He didn't even wonder what that might be. It was deserved. Knowing the people of that part of the world he thought it would be very harsh, if not fatal. Satisfied that he had completed his mission he headed for the helicopter, which the women did not see, glad to be finished.

Once again, he had taken his men into a situation that only a team such as his could handle. He was proud of them. Each man had carried out his duties flawlessly, and no one had been seriously injured. His team was definitely riding the crest of the wave of perfection when it came to military precision. Training made sure of that. Training left nothing to chance. Chance, Jim knew, was fickle, and his thoughts about chance had changed dramatically in his newfound faith.

Once he thought that chance favored those prepared. Now he understood that there was no such thing as fate, or chance. God was Sovereign and He was in control. Had it been Jim's day to die he would have died today, going quietly into the arms of his Savior and Lord. There was great comfort in that, and great strength. He knew that one trusted God, did the best one could, and left the results up to the Lord.

He listened to the men laughing and joking, the pressure releasing slowly, the realization that once again they had faced death with courage and resolve. They were at their peak, and it would only last a few more years. All of them knew that. For now, what and who they were was enough.

In the conference room they debriefed, discussing the mission in detail, and going over everything with care. It was decided that purchasing a pinch was a great idea for future missions. Last they looked at the devastation of the Mercury compound. The warehouse was completely obliterated in the blast.

Most of the next day the men rested, and on the following day Jim and Cecilia returned to the research. They sat side by side, their arms and shoulders touching, looking through microfiche, books, maps, and anything else relating to their search. For some reason Cecilia seemed to need to feel his touch that day, and he thought it might be because he'd been on another mission. Since everyone on the crew had been filled in on the mission, she already knew just about everything, and she had asked no questions. Nor, he thought with an inner smile, had she asked him to stop taking risks.

No one knew that his team had the canister again, except Ira, who had promised not to talk about it. Jim had plans for that canister, but he had to wait a few months before he could carry them off. By then, he hoped, his team would have gathered all the information needed to satisfy Admiral Runion, the President, and anyone else.

Admiral Lyle Rook would be put on a very short leash and his political aspirations would end. It would be that, Jim thought, which would hurt the Admiral the most. His dreams would be crushed and all chances of ever holding a political office of importance would be denied. His contacts known he would have little recourse.

After dinner that night the crew gathered in the conference room to share the information they had gathered, and to brainstorm. Dr. Gregg sat at one end with Mary Ann and Barbara on either side. The company had flown them out first class, and they attacked their task with excitement. All three of them beamed with pleasure, suggesting that they had unearthed something important.

Cecilia sat next to Barbara, missing sitting next to Jim. At the head of the conference table Jim took his seat. Cecilia noted that every member of the crew stood when he entered the room, saluted, and then sat after he had seated himself. Again, she was impressed by the loyalty and respect these men held for their Captain. Hers, she felt, was more than mere loyalty, but becoming a deep and abiding love. Confused she sat down and tried to settle her mind.

Not wasting any time Jim started the discussion by explaining how they would conduct this particular session. Jim was trained in working with a team, knowing that amongst his team there were those who needed such instructions and details in order to feel secure.

He abhorred details, and slow deliberate work. A man of action, he made decisions instantly, and wanted the bottom line quickly. During his years as an officer he had trained himself to recognize and work with analytical people who needed slow deliberate detailed meetings.

Because there were women in the room, the other men kept their voices softer than usual, especially those who were expressive in nature. Jim was proud of his men, pleased that they had such respect for each other and for those who were helping them. Some of the men had noted that Millie always flinched when someone raised a voice, even in jest. The men had quickly adjusted, for her sake, when she was present. Millie noticed it, was pleased, and let everyone know that.

Jim glanced at her now, sitting next to her husband, her soft brown eyes twinkling with anticipation and pleasure as the work began in earnest. Jim wondered if she might be as excited about finding this treasure as the rest of the crew. It was possible.

Dr. Gregg had indeed unearthed something of importance. When his turn came, he leaned forward in his chair, taking his favorite teaching pose, and began to lecture them, in an animated and interesting style that held everyone's attention.

"I had the girls searching through the available logbooks of Spanish Captains who sailed during the time of the disappearance of our three vessels. They were skimming, mind you, through the records, both of them linguists who fortunately speak and read both Spanish and Portuguese. One Captain made mention of the loss and actually gave us a better idea of where to look than anything else we have come across!" he said with delight. He motioned for Barbara Stafford to speak.

"On your laptops you will see excerpts from the log," she said, her delightful Eaton accent carrying clearly across the room.

"Note that the Captain fears that his own ships might be attacked and that he plans to avoid any of the waters around Espalmador. He also speaks of something that none of us knew before. At the height of the attack on the three galleons a sudden storm sent them to the bottom before the pirates could board them. All hands were lost and the treasures the ships carried were lost forever. Even one of the pirate vessels is said to have capsized in the storm."

"Ladies and gentlemen, I would say conclusively that we now have a better idea of where to search," Dr. Gregg said, spreading his thin arms wide.

"Given the typical currents and recorded weather patterns of the last forty years I think we can safely narrow that search down even more," Cecilia mentioned.

"Yes, but wooden ships would not sink as quickly as steel ships. The currents may have carried them some distance before they grounded on the bottom," Dorf said quietly.

"Do we have any data on the difference?" Wade asked suddenly. "I mean do we know anyone for instance that can tell us how long it might take for a galleon to sink, or even how such a craft might act in the water as it went down?"

"I know someone who might know the answer to that. He is the foremost expert on ships of that era, how they acted above and below the surface of the sea. If anyone knows the answer to that, he does!" Dr. Gregg informed them, his eyes flashing with excitement. "The Maritime Museum in Liverpool is run by a man who could direct us to any such information. I'm sure of it. Let me call him."

"There's a satellite phone in front of you," Jim said with a smile, sliding the instrument down the table to Dr. Gregg, who picked it up with a huge grin. Punching the international code Dr. Gregg input the number and waited. He glanced at his watch to make sure his friend would be at home at this time. In a few seconds he heard the extension at the other end lifted.

"Morrison residence," a young voice piped.

"Hello, this is Dr. Alistair Gregg from the Museum of Antiquities in Cairo calling for Dr. Peter Morrison. Is he there?" Dr. Gregg replied. He heard the child yell and a moment later Dr. Morrison picked up the phone in his study.

"I say, is it really you, Alistair?" he asked, real pleasure sounding in the greeting.

"In the flesh," Alistair replied. "I'm doing some research and one of my students asked me if there was any data on how quickly a Spanish galleon might sink," he said with a wink at Barbara and Mary Ann. "My student would like to know how water currents and even stormy waters might affect that sinking. You're the expert. What can you tell me, my friend?"

For about eleven minutes Dr. Morrison lectured Alistair on the data available, where it could be found, what it was, and who had compiled it. Finally, Dr. Gregg was able to get a word in.

"Thanks, old bean!" he said. "I'll call you later and tell you all about this one. It might just interest you!" he pushed the end button on the satellite phone and slid it back to Jim.

Zeke was able to access the actual database where the information originated, and half an hour later everyone understood the dynamics of a sinking galleon. Discussion went on for nearly two hours before Jim ended the meeting.

Bravely he offered to lead the men and women in prayer, before they left the room. Having never prayed aloud before he was nervous, but he was the Captain. More than anything he wanted God's blessing on his efforts and his prayer represented that.

Abe invited everyone into the kitchen for a snack of fruit, ice cream and cake, or just a beverage. Together the crew walked the short distance to the dining room in high spirits.

Early the next morning *Bring It Up Coral* slipped her moorings and headed out to sea. Dr. Gregg, Mary Ann, and Barbara were in the computer center with Zeke and Cecilia as they plotted the possible positions of the wreck, forming a grid search pattern for the ship to follow. On deck many of the crew worked hard getting the three deep-water search drones ready. Sparks checked the equipment to make sure everything was working properly. A diode on one of the motherboards failed, and he replaced it. Everything else was working properly.

After lunch, which everyone ate on deck since the weather was perfect for an on-deck picnic, the drones were lowered into the water and the ship began towing them through the grid search. Most of the crew that were not on duty waited in the observation room, watching the big screen televisions that displayed what Zeke saw on his computers, real time video of the ocean floor.

Like most searches of this nature days passed, routine was fixed, and discipline high. Even though everyone was anxious to follow the search no one shirked his or her duty. Not a rust spot went unnoticed. Men cleaned, polished, painted, repaired, and checked everything. At sea everything was important. Every day someone checked the lifeboats, their equipment, and the winches that would lower them into the water in case of an emergency. No one found that unusual or illogical. Monotonous though it might be their lives depended on their equipment, and they knew it.

Everyone on the crew and even their three guests joined in the daily Bible study held each morning at the mid-morning break. Abe and Sturdy, seasoned leaders in this type of thing, led the men into a detailed study of discipleship. They knew how to include everyone in the discussion time, and how to ask questions that got everyone thinking.

Jim found this study to be particularly challenging, enjoying it thoroughly. He understood following someone, for during his military career he had followed orders. But following Jesus Christ went even deeper. And it raised new questions in his mind about his role as a follower of Jesus. Unafraid to ask questions, he often challenged Abe and Sturdy so that they had to ask for time to look into the answer before replying to his queries.

At one point he asked Dr. Gregg how he had come to know Christ. The good doctor smiled at him. For some reason he seemed even more energized than ever.

"My studies did not lead me toward the Bible, but away. However! One cannot be a good archaeologist and ignore the evidence! The Bible is a reliable and true account of history and the prophecy in the Bible is always fulfilled to the letter. Unable to ignore that evidence I began to explore it and not long after gave my heart to Jesus. I was 51," he replied.

As usual, there were games to be played during the evenings to break the monotony of the search, contests that appealed to all the different tastes. Barbara Stafford surprised everyone by winning the five-card stud poker tournament. Jim ran a streak of good cards to win the Texas Hold 'em tournament by defeating Doc, who had drawn an inside straight only to discover that Jim had a pair of twos to match the other pair of twos that appeared on the flop and turn. They laughed a good deal at that hand, commenting on the luck of the draw.

Usually, Jim liked games that required his statistical skills, like chess or backgammon. He disliked games where luck played a major role. Luck could go against you as readily as it came in your favor at any moment. That was why he never trusted to luck on a mission. Although the situations he found himself in were often fluid, his choices were based on being prepared for all contingencies. Prepared minds overcame. He and Andrea played to a draw in the chess tournament, while Cecilia and John lost to them in the finals. He was amused that beating Cecilia bothered him so deeply. She laughed at him.

Three months turned into four as the search went on, until they were in their final grid of the pattern. Even then the crew took the idea of failure philosophically. The sea was a mystery, and sometimes hid its secrets jealously. Though they might fail they did not accept it. Each day seemed to spur them to work harder to achieve. In the end, it was that conscious effort that kept them searching.

During that time Jim and Cecilia grew closer in their relationship, almost frighteningly close if Jim were honest. Although he tried to moderate his time with her, he couldn't resist seeking her out, spending time with her, or having her at his side. She seemed to feel much the same way, and he marveled that such a beautiful woman would find him desirable. It was an effort to stay on top of everything, to juggle his responsibilities and his time with Cecilia, but Jim persevered.

Persistence pays off. As they were nearing the end of their last day the metal detectors on the search drones suddenly sent the signal everyone had been waiting for. A heavy deposit of gold, silver, and bronze marked the possible resting place of at least one of the ships. It was impossible for it to be an undersea mine, because gold and silver never formed together.

Since it was close to the end of the day, they dropped anchor ten yards from the largest deposit and celebrated with a night off. Abe and Sturdy cooked steak and lobster and as the night was beautiful for that time of year, most of the crew spent some time on the observation deck, sitting in small groups, talking and drinking their favorite beverages.

Doc and Millie stood by the railing watching the crewmembers as they relaxed together. Charles hugged Millie closely for a few minutes, enjoying her presence, and she hugged him back.

"You know, dear," Millie said, looking up at him, "We are very fortunate to be part of this venture. These men are all good friends. Look at Windy and Robert!" she indicated the two, sitting with Dorf, Mark, and Frank. She had refused to call Bob Stankus by his nickname. She thought it demeaning, though he certainly didn't seem to mind.

"Yes, that man has come far. He works as hard as anyone now, and I never hear a word of complaint. He looks us all in the eye now, speaking sometimes before being spoken to. Abe and Sturdy have done a wonderful job of rehabilitation," Doc mused.

"For the first time in his life, Robert has a job, and money, and he's not spending it on drink. He's clean in many ways, and I think he may even be a believer too." Millie said with pleasure.

"He's certainly careful when he goes ashore to stay with his friends. Although for the first time I saw him walking through Palma with other members of the crew. He works out in the gym and is learning how to keep himself in excellent physical condition." Doc added. "He's even advancing in martial arts, and he has earned a black belt in two of them according to Mark."

Jim, who had assigned himself the watch, came up beside them, putting the binoculars to his eyes to scan the horizons around the ship. He grinned at both of them.

"Do you miss being dogged by the Mercury yachts?" Millie asked, teasingly.

"No, we have a new tagalong," he replied, keeping the binoculars to his eyes.

"Really! Who?" Doc asked, turning to look in the direction the binoculars were pointed.

"I think Admiral Rook is having us watched," Jim said quietly. "There's a submarine out there about three hundred yards, just beneath the surface. I've seen her periscope pop up a few times tonight."

"He's actually wasting the taxpayer's money by having us shadowed by a submarine?" Doc asked, surprised.

"He's had a coastguard plane flying over us a few times too," Jim mentioned, looking at them again. "We're keeping records of all this for future reference. Zeke has photographic records and Admiral Runion has the orders sent to the sub recorded. Every misdeed is being carefully documented for the future," Jim put the binoculars down and looked at the two.

"Are there many like him in our Navy?" Millie asked sadly.

"Fortunately, no," Jim replied. "But he is gathering a following, and some of the men who are following him need watching too. Once he is stopped, they will have second thoughts and probably drop out of what is going on. A few will stay for the money and the power they think it will buy them. Those are the ones we will always watch carefully."

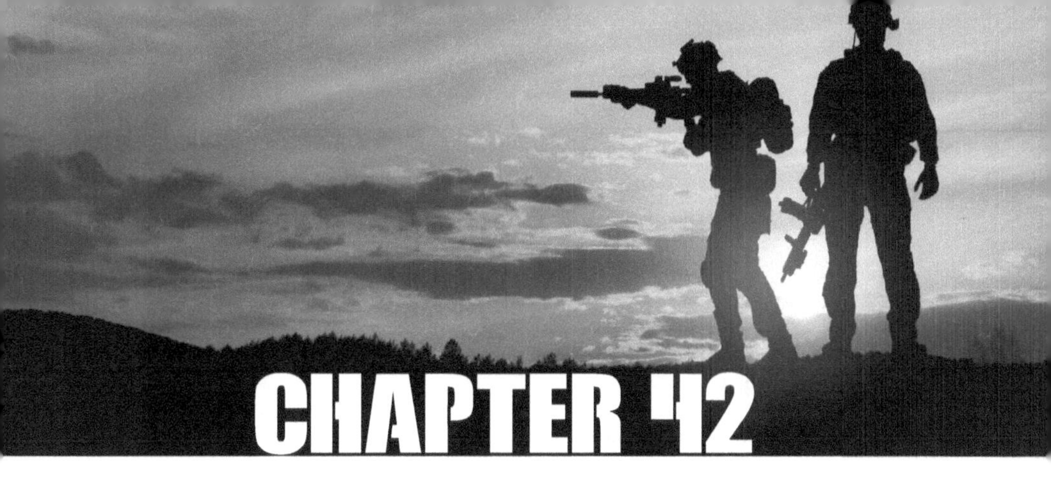

CHAPTER 42

FM and Sparks took Dr. Gregg down in the submersible early the next morning as a favor to the historian. Alistair had never been beneath the surface before, nor had he been in a submarine. He might have been concerned or alarmed by the tight quarters in the *Steel Crab* but was too fascinated by everything going on around him to notice those discomforts.

FM guided them down, putting them right on top of the largest deposit of gold and silver. During the trip down Sparks explained how the bathyscaphe worked, and Dr. Gregg listened with fascination, asking intelligent questions. At the bottom Alistair looked at the greenish ocean floor, discerning nothing that told him if a ship was there or not. Frank and Bill, who were now experienced at looking at the bottom of the sea differently, spotted the bow of the ship almost immediately.

She lay at about one hundred and forty feet below the surface, on the top of what appeared to be a ridge running along the ocean floor. Slanted to port, she was almost completely buried by silt and hidden by Acorn barnacles and other such creatures. Once FM pointed out the outline of the ship Alistair could see it, and he began to get very excited.

"Why are there no masts?" he asked, looking at the flat deck and seeing one of the reasons he'd missed the configuration.

"They were probably swept away by the storm or broken away by currents. I think there's one laying off to the side there," FM indicated, pointing.

"Yes, I see the shape now. What about the other two ships?" Dr. Gregg asked.

"We'll see," Sparks said, reading the equipment carefully.

FM took them over the second and third deposits, and they sent word to the ship that all three galleons were there. So was one of the pirate ships! One of them was stern down, bow pointing to the surface, against a wall that rose to about sixty-five feet below the surface. That wall had stopped it from ending up in really deep water. The other lay upside down, part of the keel broken away, but the rudder still in place.

"How many men died, I wonder," Dr. Gregg mused quietly.

"I imagine all hands went down. There are no survivors mentioned in any of the records we read," Zeke said over the headset.

A school of Flounder suddenly appeared, curious about the fishbowl and the strange creatures staring out at them. The three men watched them swim around the bowl for a moment before heading off in search of food. An angel shark cruised along the bottom, searching for flatfishes and crustaceans, strangely graceful, though it didn't look as if it would be able to produce such lovely motion.

A white-tipped shark followed the school of flounder.

"I'm glad I'm in here!" Dr. Gregg said, watching the white-tipped shark glide past, flicking its tail in sudden motions that sent it darting forward easily.

"Not much to fear from one of those," FM said. "Sharks tend to leave divers alone, as long as the diver doesn't do something stupid," he smiled at Dr. Gregg.

Once the salvage basket had been set up near the first ship the submersible rose to the surface. Dr. Gregg was exchanged for Driver for the tricky job of setting up the vacuum pump to clear away dirt and debris from the deck of the sunken vessel. Dorf, Mark, C.G., and Vince were the first four divers going down to work on the wreck.

"Any chance of bringing this one up?" Jim asked FM as the submersible once again hovered above the long-lost wreck.

"No way, Shep!" FM replied confidently, looking critically at what he could see of the ship. "She's got some huge holes, and the knees and ribs look like they're falling apart. We'll have to settle for the gold and silver and other artifacts that we can bring up. If we tried to bring this one up, she'd just fall to pieces," he grinned as he spoke, glad that the waiting was finally over and they had found another treasure.

Work began in earnest then as the divers arrived at the bottom and began to help clear away enough of the deck to break through. Here the water remained a chilly fifty-two degrees Fahrenheit, whether the winter mistral whips the Mediterranean or summer sun warms its surface. The divers worked fast, then rose at the recall signal—given by Jim in their earpieces and by Master Chief Warner in an underwater shot. The latter was a safety precaution in case the earpieces failed. If the divers stayed longer than seventeen minutes they had to decompress in stages. Each diver would make three dives that day, no more.

Smitty, in the NEWT Suit could stay down much longer, and he worked with Driver, FM, and Sparks in the submersible to clear as much away as possible to allow the divers to penetrate the vessel. By noon all the divers were finished with their days work, and the salvage basket was brought to the surface. There were cups, plates, flatware, and the first three chests discovered in the hold. Dr. Gregg and his two assistants were busy photographing and recording the finds.

Later that evening, after the submersible and NEWT Suit had been cleaned and locked down on the deck, Jim looked out at the growing number of boats that surrounded them. Word had leaked out that *Bring It Up Coral* had discovered the long-lost treasure, and many interested people rushed out to watch. Some of them were news people, and after politely asking for permission to board, were allowed each evening to view the treasures from below.

Winter was fast approaching, and they worked nearly a month over the four ships, pulling up what they could recover. To Dr. Gregg's delight, several unique Inca pieces were unearthed. Spanish armor, pitted and nearly destroyed by the ocean water, was displayed in growing quantities. The hilt of a very fancy rapier came up one day, bearing one jewel, but wound with true silver. The blade had long since rusted away, but the ivory and silver remained.

The jewel on the end of the hilt was an Emerald cabochon nearly seven carats. From that ship several pieces of jewelry including rings and necklaces were also obviously done by the same lapidary. Was he Inca or Spanish? Everyone wondered, and everyone remarked on the unusual cuts and sizes of the stones used. Whoever had owned the rapier had been wealthy, perhaps even the captain of the ship, or one of the commodores of the Spanish fleet.

Daily news crews came aboard to look over the finds. Most wrinkled their noses at the smell from the cleaning tanks and kept their distance. A few of the hardier souls stood shoulder to shoulder with crew members cleaning artifacts, gemstones, gold and silver pieces, jadeite and chrysocolla jewelry and individual stones. Amber, marble, and even quartz pieces were carved into beautiful images of animals, temples, and even a few of the Inca gods and religious rituals. Turquoise pieces, Lazulite, and Orthoclase, a variation of Amazonite with blue and pink colorations were also brought to light.

Even the pirate ship yielded a treasure trove. In the Captain's Cabin they found a huge wooden chest full of jewelry, precious gems, including a diamond studded tiara. Dr. Gregg was confident they could discover the name of the former owner of that particular find.

Eventually the work drew to a close and *Bring It Up Coral* weighed anchor and made for the United Kingdom. Dr. Gregg and his two assistants disembarked in Malaga and flew back to Cairo rewarded handsomely for their aid. Shared promises of future ventures together pleased everyone.

Dr. Gregg promised to look through everything that crossed his desk for possible searches and future voyages with Captain Shepherd. He did not lack for ideas and his two assistants would be busy with research, which was what they loved most.

Returning to England seemed anticlimactic. In a little over a year the company made three major discoveries, recovering vast treasures. Jim and the crew wondered what they would have to do to top that! Yet beneath the surface each man pondered the next great adventure at sea. Jim knew that like him his men were sold on this new way of life. Long hours of hard work and research would finally pay off in another discovery, and once more they would look at history that could be seen and touched, and better understand that period of time.

Dry-docking in Portsmouth meant unloading their treasures. Once that tedious task was completed the crew left the ship in the hands of Calvin Beardsley and his company for cleaning and repainting the hull. Zeke made reservations for them to occupy two floors of Brown's hotel in London, where they spent two weeks relaxing, visiting London, and meeting with Ken Worthington to discuss their financial situations.

Every member of the crew decided to accept a modest salary, leaving the rest of the money in the business for growth and development. Jim discussed the trip around the world with John and Wade before bringing it up to the crew. Such a trip appealed to everyone, especially the idea that they could stop wherever they wanted for however long they needed. The team knew that many places they visited might require their services. There was so much going on in the world related to terrorism they knew there would be no lack of opportunities to employ their particular services.

CHAPTER 43

Bring It Up as a company became the talk of the salvage community, and business offers poured in. Jim politely informed all those making offers that his company was a limited company and would not be sharing in any partnerships. Many of those who offered felt that their amazing finds were more luck than anything else, and once the tedium of empty searches settled in, they would be more interested. Every member of the crew, including Windy and Stinky, agreed with keeping the company limited.

In the midst of all that, Jim, John, and Wade met with Sir Edward and Admiral Runion in secret to outline their plan to use their evidence to put Admiral Rook on a very short leash. Both men were impressed by the amount of information this paramilitary team was able to gather against Admiral Rook, most of it admissible in court if necessary. Working together the team uncovered the entire organization in America, but they had yet to track down the money source. At the moment they all knew one thing. The money didn't come from the Middle East!

President Royce hosted another meeting in his underground rotunda and listened as Jim and Admiral Runion went through the reports. Discussing various options, listening to counsel from everyone, they finally decided on a course of action. As Jim followed Admiral Runion out of the underground meeting area he was smiling. So was Admiral Runion.

Admiral Rook accepted the invitation to attend a special party to celebrate the retirement of a prominent Naval attaché, a retired Admiral and close friend of the President of the United States. The invitation came from the President, and Rook decided it was time to maneuver for a post commensurate with his accomplishments and service to his country. Several letters went out from supporters of the Admiral, some of them from legitimate sources that had no knowledge of man's culpability.

President Royce enjoyed the letters, and the plans to put a dent in one of the most dangerous threats to American security. Admiral Rook was advised of the President's high spirits and encouraged by his chances to finally move forward in his plans to cultivate serious political power.

He met in secret with three men who were serious financial supporters, and movers of their own in world circles. That their security could be breached was something they did not think possible, and Admiral Rook guaranteed the highest security for himself in such situations. Of course, against men like Sparks and Zeke such security precautions were merely a challenge to be met and overcome.

Jim's team was able to record the meeting with a clear digital video and audio feed. Zeke managed to capture the contents of the laptop computers used by the men at the meeting through a clever technique he and Sparks invented together. The cost of the equipment to make this possible was made up in less than two hours of work.

Not only did the military purchase their technology immediately, but the added sweetener of receiving two percent of all funds seized by the various law enforcement bodies within the government from use of their equipment ensured continued refinements and further breakthroughs for the team's technology department. It was a major breakthrough and Jim made sure that officers that had previously refused requests from those two men knew what they missed.

After all the intelligence was gathered Jim sat with his team in silence, looking at the damning proof of Admiral Rook's part in the death of twenty-six Marines. Rook was paid handsomely for withholding the information John needed to get his team out alive. At the moment that money lay untouched in a numbered account in a bank on the Cayman Islands. The sum was twenty-five million dollars, paid in U.S. currency, and deposited on the day a certain middle eastern general experienced a coup against the ugly American forces lawlessly violating his country's sovereignty.

Of course, the fact that thirty Marines managed to kill two thousand and seven of his troops was suppressed in the reports that went out to the world. John remembered with horror seeing the bodies of his men mutilated in public. He still dreamed of it from time to time waking up in a cold sweat and swearing again his vengeance. Would it be sweet, or bitter? He didn't know. He only knew that he would avenge the deaths of his unit.

"I didn't know General Haaman was involved so deeply," Wade said, shaking his head. His cheeks were white with anger.

"We know now," C.G. said quietly. "And we know how to deal with him," he added, his eyes suddenly cold and dark as the grave.

"What do you mean, C.G.?" Jim asked quietly, his eyes intent on his friend.

"How embarrassed will his government be to learn that he is in bed with an American Admiral, and using government funds to enhance his own personal career? What about the blood money he was given for his part? I think if we leak this information to the right people, we won't have to lift a finger against him!" C.G. said. "And if not, we can always go in and take care of it ourselves. Of course, it would be much better if he were exposed and killed by his own government."

"How do the rest of you feel?" Jim asked, looking at John, Wade, and Vince.

"I think C.G. is right!" Wade said with a nasty grin.

"I think we should be there when he is arrested, somewhere where he can see us," John said slowly. "It would make the punishment even better. He would know that the enemy he thought he defeated ultimately rose up and destroyed him.”

“I think I don’t ever want any of you angry with me!” Cecilia said from her place. “You are quite right, John. He must see the four of you, the men he knows escaped.”

“I’ve got a suggestion,” this was Windy speaking. “May I speak?” he was not sure if he had the right. Jim smiled.

“We may not use every idea you share, but we will listen to every idea you have,” Jim assured him, nodding his approval.

“If he sees the four of them before he is arrested, he’s sure to try to kill them. Criminals of his type will always opt for self-preservation, and they will be a threat to him, real or perceived. Should he attempt to kill them, and not know he failed, the blow would be even more potent!” Windy said.

“Dang, Windy! Where you been all my life?” Vince said, nodding his head. “We could easily penetrate his organization and find out who his enforcers are. We could even fix it so their weapons are loaded with rubber bullets and pull a Hollywood fix on them! Heck! I’ll bet Ira would help us set the whole scene up!”

“When the trap falls, and they slap the bracelets on his slimy pudgy wrists, seeing us will make him crap his drawers!” John exclaimed, slapping the table with his hand. “I love this idea!”

“Okay!” Jim said, holding up his hand. “But we are going to have to carry this one off at the same time we take down the Admiral. Once Rook goes down, Haaman isn’t going to stick around to see if his political plans come to fruition. He’s going to cut and run. So, John will take most of the team to deal with Haaman, and I’ll take the remainder to deal with Rook. Both men will pay for their part in the deaths of good men, and we will personally make sure every family is well cared for in the future! We’ve done everything we need to except the final confrontation.”

“Ooh Rah!” John, Wade, C.G., and Vince said as one.

Smitty leaned over to Cecilia who had a puzzled look on her face. He knew she was puzzled by the Marine chant in unison and was happy to take a dig at his friends. “Eventually, they’ll teach

Marines to talk. Right now, they don't have to be that smart," he teased with a grin.

She laughed as the four Marines waggled a finger at Smitty. It was Vince who spoke. "Don't listen to him, he's all wet!" Vince warned. "Besides, those Navy boys are just jealous of our stylish haircuts and handsome physiques."

Vince, at six feet two inches and one hundred and ninety pounds was much bigger than Smitty, who was only five feet nine inches tall. But Smitty weighed one hundred and seventy-five pounds and certainly had much the same physique. Cecilia smiled as the two continued to banter back and forth and thought with some amusement that she was certainly surrounded by unusual men. They were powerful, and often reminded her of lions or tigers in the way they held themselves and the way they moved. She hadn't been kidding when she said she didn't want any of them angry with her. There was something frightening in their demeanor when they spoke of certain men. Personally, she had witnessed the military precision and power of these men in action!

But she was also pleased that they had not opted to kill General Haaman. They could, easily. She realized that and also knew that as soldiers they understood killing. Yet none seemed to like the idea. They weren't bloodthirsty like Fezik al'Loudi had been. Still, if needed, they could be. She shivered.

"They're soldiers of a very special type," Millie confessed, leaning over to talk to Cecilia. The two had become very close, and Cecilia looked upon the tiny woman as a favorite aunt or cousin. Millie continued. "Often, they are called upon to face terrible men, and sometimes to kill them. They rarely talk about it, and if they do, it's a job that needed to be done, a duty. Still, they suffer deep inside because they know the value of human life. That's why they protect it with such ferocity."

Cecilia's smile was sad as she listened. She nodded. "I'm glad we have such men in our world," she said quietly.

"Well said, my dear!" Millie replied, patting her hand.

John and Wade gathered the men together at one end of the conference room. Windy got up to leave and C.G. put a hand on his arm.

"Where do you think you're going?" he asked.

"I didn't want to be in the way," Windy said.

"This was your idea, Windy. Stick around and let's see how it ends up!" C.G. invited.

"You want me to stick around?" Windy asked, surprised.

"You may not be a soldier, bub, but you're one of us," Wade said, patting Windy on the shoulder as he passed.

Something inside of Windy swelled up until his eyes actually filled with tears. These men accepted him, not as a crewmember, but as one of them. Until now he hadn't quite put all that together. He looked over at Bob Stankus, quietly sitting by the wall. As their eyes met Bob understood some of what Windy was feeling. For the first time in a long time they were men again, they had that special value that all men crave, the sense of belonging, of achievement, of being part of something worthy and good.

Millie, who missed very little that went on among the men, noted the exchange. Those two men had changed dramatically during their year of service. She caught Sturdy's hand as he slid by her.

"You and Abe have done a very good job with those two," she said, nodding toward Windy and Stinky, now seated among the soldiers. Bob Stankus certainly had changed physically. He was no longer flabby and listless. Daily exercise with the men had shaped him into a leaner, stronger man who now moved with purpose, even if shyly. Windy almost bounced on his toes when he walked anywhere.

"All through His grace," Sturdy said, leaning down and speaking softly. "In another year or two they'll be ready to help us take in two or three more men. This kind of work is perfect for getting men back on their feet. There's no place to go, they can't exercise their bad habits, and the atmosphere is always conducive to hard work and the pride that comes from a job well done. Windy is almost ready to go off on his own again, though I doubt if he will. He's done a lot for Bob that we couldn't have done."

Cecilia liked this gentle giant and she put a hand on his forearm, patting it gently. "Jim told me about the work you do, and about Wendall and Bob. I'm convinced one of the reasons this crew is successful is because of their dedication to God first. You're a very important part of that."

"Thanks," Sturdy said, putting his huge hand over hers. Then he grinned. "Best not let Jim see us holding hands. I don't much feel like getting thrashed!"

"Yeah, like I could thrash you!" Jim said, coming up behind them. Sturdy had seen him there.

"Well you could, if you had a mind to," Sturdy admitted with a smile as he straightened.

Cecilia saw the look in the giant's eyes, and knew he was speaking the truth. Jim looked so small next to him, yet there was something indefinable about him, an inner strength perhaps, some hidden force that told her Sturdy was just being honest. It made her feel very secure and she saw Millie smiling at her and knew the other woman had read her thoughts. She winked at Millie.

"Makes me feel powerful the way I can wrap him around my little finger!" she said with a sudden laugh.

Sturdy threw his head back and laughed, slapping Jim on the back nearly propelling him over the table.

"Ouch!" Jim said, shrugging his shoulders. He was red in the face and grinning. "Take it easy on your poor old Captain!" He and Sturdy grasped hands, as though they might arm wrestle for a moment, and then touched shoulders. It was a very masculine gesture, yet it conveyed to Cecilia the depth of their respect for each other.

CHAPTER 44

John took his team to Beirut in Lebanon, including Abe, Windy, and Stinky. This would be the first time they would serve as part of the special unit, and though their parts were minor, they were important. Wendall and Bob were thrilled and frightened, a healthy mixture of emotions. Abe was there to ensure that they remembered to do exactly what they were supposed to do. Secretly, he was as thrilled as his two crewmembers.

Cecilia, Charles, Millie, Master Chief Warner, Frank, Andrea, and Sturdy waited in Baltimore with Jim. Like the other team, for the first time everyone would play a part. Charles and Millie were tickled to be included, and more than willing to do their part. Master Chief Warner was proud to be asked to serve, chuckling to himself when he thought of his role in this plan. Andrea too, though he had experience in dealing with criminals, enjoyed his role. His part would be child's play to him.

Ken Worthington met them at the airport in Baltimore, and in a rented limousine they made the trip to the house he built for them in River Oaks. It was a sprawling mansion at the end of Live Oak Drive, on river front property Worthington had picked up at a mere 1.2 million dollars. Using the money entrusted to him wisely, Ken invested in properties all over the eastern seaboard, buying and selling until he had doubled the real estate investment funds. With that money he hired a host of contractors to build the mansion, and in the time it took for construction, he doubled the fund again. Loving investments of any kind Ken quickly learned how to maximize his profits.

Cecilia was a little nervous because she was going to meet Gwyneth Orvieto Shepherd for the first time. Along with that, they were visiting a place she might one day call home, a place she had never seen. Jim asked his mother to move to the property and to hire a staff to keep the place up. As they entered the gate Jim looked with appreciation at the grounds. A gardener sat upon a John Deere tractor, a medium sized tractor pulling a gang mower, keeping the thirty acres of grass looking like a country club golf course. It was breathtaking.

Huge old oak trees were scattered on the property, and a smattering of Hickory, Walnut, and Box Elders. Close to the house there was a grove of Birch trees, and by the pond three huge Weeping Willows. Jim took it all in and for the first time in his young life perhaps he realized that he was indeed a wealthy man. As the limousine pulled up to the front of the house Jim spotted his mother coming out of the door.

A couple, perhaps in their mid-sixties, stood beside her, along with a group of younger women that ranged from their twenties to mid-forties. These made up the staff that kept the house. Even the gardener stopped mowing to come and meet the newcomers. As Jim stepped out of the limousine his mother ran into his arms and gave him a greeting only a mother could give.

After Jim had hugged her for almost a minute, he let her go, stepped back and looked at her. She looked vibrant. Her blue eyes sparkled, and her black hair, streaked with grey, looked wonderful. Turning to the others he introduced them.

"Mother, may I present some of the partners in my firm. This is Cecilia." A gentleman always introduced a lady first. He was surprised when the two embraced, moved that his mother seemed so pleased to meet this girl. Jim had written emails to his mother about her, asking advice, and she had correctly read between the lines. The two were in love, and this girl seemed perfect for her son.

"Uncle Andrea you already know," Jim said with a grin, as Andrea gave his sister a bear hug. Jim watched with a sense of both pleasure and loss as his uncle hugged his mother, glad they were together, but missing his father desperately. "This is Doctor Charles Wozniac and his wife Millie, the chief medical staff on our ship." Millie hugged Gwyneth and Charles kissed her hand.

"This is Master Chief James Warner," Jim watched as Warner followed Dr. Wozniac's example and kissed his mother's hand. "And this is Petty Officer First Class Thomas Martin Sturdevant. You may call him Sturdy. Everyone else does."

Gwyneth Shepherd looked up at the giant, just an inch shy of seven feet tall and smiled at him. "I've heard a great deal about you and your fine work, young man. I'm so glad to finally meet you." She said, as Sturdy engulfed her tiny hand in his and bowed over it. Obviously, he was enchanted with Mrs. Shepherd.

"And this is Chief Petty Officer Frank Miller, mother," Jim said, finishing the introductions. "We all call him FM for short." Frank stepped forward and took her hand gently in his.

"I'm very pleased to meet you, Mrs. Shepherd," Frank said. "May I say that you look absolutely radiant? I think you've missed your sons," he grinned.

"Now it's my turn to make introductions," Gwyneth said, her cheeks flushed with pleasure. "These folks have become more than just a staff. They're good friends and we're well on our way to becoming family!"

Jim was watching them as his mother spoke and he was pleased to see that they were deeply moved by her words. "This is Maisy Ellen, who manages the staff and house for me. And this is her husband Mitchell who doubles as a butler and chauffeur. He's also a retired policeman."

Mitchell and Maisy Ellen were a pair, according to his mother, perfectly suited to her liking. Mitchell, whom everyone called Much, was about two inches taller than Jim, heavy set in the way of a man who was once powerful in build. Much had come to America as a young man from Jamaica, with a young wife, eager to make his way. Working three part-time jobs he put himself through college, in a pre-law course, and then chose to become a policeman. He had served with honor until retirement. Maisy Ellen began working in a motel and worked her way into management, finally managing one of Washington's premier hotels until her husband retired. Both of them still spoke with that Jamaican lilt in their speech.

"This is Bob Sears, our grounds keeper," Gwyneth said proudly. Bob Sears was as round as he was tall, with twinkling brown eyes. His wife, Margaret, was introduced as well. Margaret was the chief cook, and though she was not thin she wasn't heavy either. She held her husband's hand while she was introduced and looked up at Jim with wide-eyed curiosity. Then she smiled.

"You can trust my cooking," she said, her silver hair bobbing. "Just look at my Bob and you can see I'm a good cook!" Bob laughed good-naturedly. Jim had felt the strength of his grip. The man might carry around a lot of weight, but he had once been fairly strong, and even in his late fifties he carried his weight well.

One of the women, nearing fifty, worked with Margaret in the kitchen. Her name was Alice. The two youngest were Ellen and Candice, or Ellie and Candy as Gwyneth called them. They took care of the daily cleaning under the care of the housekeeper Mrs. Duncan. Her name was Loraine, but no one thought to call her that. She was a widow and took her job seriously. But she was a happy soul too, and Ellie and Candy were pleased to be working with her.

Bob Sears had three young men who came in on Monday, Wednesday, and Saturday to work on the grounds. They were part of a youth program aimed at giving young inner-city youth hands on experience. Bob seemed to like teaching them how to care for growing things. Jim certainly had no complaints. There wasn't a weed visible in the huge garden in the back yard and around the pond.

Introductions made and a tour of the main part of the house and grounds finished, the crew settled into their rooms, showered and changed, and returned to the dining room for lunch. Mrs. Duncan, Ellie and Candy served lunch, weaving back and forth from the kitchen to the dining room with practiced ease. When everything had been served the staff sat down at one end of the table. At this house everyone ate together. Jim was pleased to see his mother had decided on this course of action. In many houses the staff would eat separately, but Gwyneth didn't put on airs, and she didn't look at the staff as servants, but as friends.

If the staff was nervous at first, by the end of lunch they were at ease. Captain Shepherd and his crewmembers were friendly, and treated them much like Mrs. Shepherd, the mistress of the house. Jim made a point to memorize their names, and he could see that this pleased them.

After lunch Jim took his team into the library, where they met with Ken Worthington to discuss some financial matters, and then together about their mission. After the meeting they all went down to the garage to look at the fleet of vehicles their company now owned.

For a few minutes they all stood and stared at the garage. It was Sturdy who broke the silence. "I've never seen a twelve-car garage before!" he said. "Struth!" That was one of his favorite bywords.

They entered a side door and looked down a line of vehicles that included mostly SUVs, with two luxury cars, proudly parked in the center of the line. One was a Rolls Royce Silver Cloud that Ken Worthington purchased as an investment. In mint condition, this 1952 model would only increase in value. Jim liked the cream exterior and tan convertible roof. He'd never driven a Rolls, and he looked forward to the adventure.

Next to the Rolls was a Cadillac Fleetwood Brougham, white with gold and chrome trim. It was brand new, and it was the car Gwyneth used to travel into town for shopping. She always took Ellie and Candy with her to help carry groceries, and to have lunch somewhere together. Gwyneth claimed it was like having the daughters she'd always wanted.

There were two Hummer H-2 vehicles, one white, one a pretty sky blue. There were four Jeep Rubicons, all white with tan soft tops and trim. The other four were BMW X5s, white, yellow, red, and silver in color. All of the SUVs had the company logo painted on the doors. In front of the cars the garage ran another twelve feet deep, with workbenches, toolboxes, compressors, and tools neatly placed. Bob Sears was neat and orderly. Jim Warner walked through the shop looking at everything with obvious pleasure. He even checked out the bathroom at the far end of the shop.

"This is perfect!" he said, coming out of the bathroom.

"Makes me want to find something wrong with one of these cars and get to work!" FM laughed.

CHAPTER 45

"Well, we all have things to do. Pick your car and have at it!" Jim said with a grin.

With excitement shining in their eyes FM, Sturdy, and Jim Warner each chose a BMW X5. Cecilia let Jim choose, and guessed right. He chose the Jeep Rubicon. Doc and Millie looked at one another, smiled, and then stepped into the Rolls. Garage doors opened quietly, and the vehicles backed out, turned, and slowly moved off down the long, paved driveway, lined by trees. Jim took a moment to let the Jeep warm up, leafing through the owner's manual, learning proper operations.

They unzipped the door tops and laid them on the floor behind them and then Jim backed the Jeep out and headed into the city. This was Cecilia's first trip to America, and she spent the trip fascinated by the busy scenery. After an hour of driving Jim drew up on the Naval Base, parked the Jeep, and led Cecilia into Admiral Runion's office.

Admiral Runion's new Lieutenant, Junior Grade, sat behind the desk. Jim was wearing gray dress pants, a darker shade of gray shirt with an oriental empire collar, and black cowboy boots. Cecilia wore a white pantsuit with a brightly colored scarf around her neck. Her shoes were white. She looked quite pretty in her outfit and the

Lieutenant, Junior Grade, didn't miss that fact. He was surprised however at the appearance of the three-thirty appointment. Captain Shepherd was, apparently, enjoying his privilege of wearing civilian clothes. Since he was visiting the Admiral, the Lieutenant was sure he would dress in a uniform. Jim noted the look the Lieutenant shot him.

"I'm not in the Navy anymore, Lieutenant," he said quietly. "We're old friends and this is not an official visit."

"Oh, of course!" the Lieutenant said, even more mystified. The appointment sheet was for a Captain Shepherd.

"I'm sorry sir," the secretary said. "I saw the Captain and thought you were still in service."

"I am a Captain, of my own ship. I run a deep-sea salvage and rescue business," Jim replied with a smile.

"You're that Captain Shepherd!" the man exclaimed. "I'm Lieutenant Junior Grade John Mooney," he added, shaking hands with Jim. Mooney was typical of the navy of his day, his skin untanned, his hands soft.

"This is one of my crewmembers, Ensign Cecilia Merton. She is a research specialist, historian, meteorologist, and forensics expert," Jim said, introducing Cecilia. He took that moment to study Mooney, and decided that the man had potential, which was, he was sure, why Admiral Runion chose him.

"Is that pirate Shepherd here yet?" Admiral Runion's voice boomed from his office. He appeared at the door, gave Cecilia a bear hug, and shook Jim's hand with both of his.

"Make sure no one disturbs us for one hour!" he said to his secretary as he led them into the office. Inside he motioned them into the leather chairs that had occupied that space for fifty years or more. He grinned as he sat down himself.

"Well, Miss Merton!" he said, watching her. "You seem to have fallen into our laps like manna from heaven!"

"Actually, I was dragged aboard the first time," Cecilia smiled.

"Yes, I saw the reports. Nasty that. Very sorry about your family. I read that you helped sort all that out," Admiral Runion replied.

Cecilia saw that he, like Jim, really cared about people, about life. She warmed to him immediately.

"Jim and the team did most of the sorting," she said. "The punishment was appropriate, I thought," she added.

"He's in a nursing home in the south of France. No one knows his real identity. They'll give him good care there, for the rest of his life," Admiral Runion's voice dripped with malice. "God, how he'll hate that!"

"Now! Down to business!" Admiral Runion leaned forward and spoke for half an hour. When he was done Jim nodded in satisfaction, and Cecilia, for the first time, realized the full scope of the plan. She had played an important role in researching some of this, and in putting together the list of people Admiral Rook was working for. Admiral Runion and his intelligence people had put it all together in a neat package.

"This is a black-tie affair. I have to wear my uniform. Enjoy the show. You two have earned that privilege," he said, sitting back with a pleased sigh.

"You are expecting me to show up in a tuxedo?" Jim asked with a grin.

"Yes. Blend in, all that!" Admiral Runion grinned back.

"Why in the world can't politicians dress like everyone else, in natural clothing that's comfortable and sensible?" Jim asked, throwing up his hands.

"Good God, man! Don't wish that! They'd all appear like a pack of ravenous wolves, no offense to wolves mind you, salivating at the mouth after everyone's wallets. Some might even come looking like sharks. Ghastly scene! It may very well frighten all the children," Runion remonstrated. They all laughed at the picture.

For a time, they discussed Jim's plans to circumnavigate the world. Admiral Runion had several files piled on his desk. As Jim talked of his plans the Admiral leafed through them, picked out three, and tossed them across the desk. When Jim finished, he reached forward and poked a finger on top of the files.

"Take a look at these three and see if you think you might do something about it, will you?" he asked. He leaned back, winked at Cecilia, and waited.

Jim took the top file, and then nodded for Cecilia to pick up the second. She did so and both read through them, with much the same care. Admiral Runion liked what he saw in this young woman, noticing the looks the two shared when the files were exchanged. He smiled to himself, keeping his face still. They were in love with each other. Good! *A man like Jim shouldn't end up like me, never having tasted the joy of marriage and family.*

They read the last file together, their shoulders touching as they leaned toward each other, their eyes busy with each page.

Admiral Runion ceased his pondering as Jim stacked the folders and put them neatly on the desk. Jim leaned back and pondered everything he'd just read so carefully. For a moment the Admiral and Cecilia watched Jim. He nodded once and looked up at the two of them.

"Yes, we can handle all three of those on our way. Will you let General March know about when he can expect us to show up in his part of the world?" Jim said.

"He'll be thrilled," Admiral Runion said with a nod. "He's been putting a bug in my ear about this for the past month."

"I don't like the Chinese thing in Brazil," Jim said after a moment of silence. "It doesn't feel right. It's a cover for something else. Do you have any guesses?"

"You don't miss much, do you?" Admiral Runion said, shaking his head. "Yes. It's a cover for stealing a computer chip for a guided missile."

"Who's working it? I don't want to get killed by one of our own if I get involved," Jim asked.

"Yeah, right!" Admiral Runion scoffed. "Morrison is on it. I'll let him know you and your team will be showing up. He has a team of four down there with him. They're just gathering information right now. Two of his team are Chinese and speak about five of the dialects like natives. They're working at the consulate there."

"Okay. Morrison is good. Have him sink a yacht and need rescuing," Jim added.

"Nice!" Admiral Runion said. "My department has to pay for the yacht!"

"I'll have Ken Worthington cover the cost for you, Admiral," Jim said evenly. "I mean that. I want the yacht to be something worth salvaging. I'll recover most of the cost in salvaging it. We'll call it a loan, and afterwards my company will keep it. That should take care of any questions and explain our haste in keeping it from actually sinking!"

"I hadn't thought of that," Runion grunted. "Not bad at all. Okay, you set it up. I'll brief Morrison."

"Tell him that when it comes time for the takedown, he gets all the credit. I want him to know that up front. Our cover needs to stay intact. With him there no one will suspect we had anything to do with it. He'll take enough risks that he deserves to get the glory anyway," Jim added.

"How many times did you have to go in and save his team?" Admiral Runion asked with a chuckle.

"Twice. But the risks were worth it. I said that in both my reports," Jim replied.

"And he knows that. I made sure he knew that," Admiral Runion replied. "He'll play ball and enjoy it."

"Are you getting all the reports?" Jim asked finally.

"Yes. Sir Edward is good to his word. Ira has been keeping an eye on the international busy bodies. No one has been even the least bit curious, except Admiral Rook. After tomorrow he'll wish he'd been more curious," Runion smiled crookedly. "He'll also know what he stands to lose if he ever opens his big mouth. I can't wait to see his face."

"You'll have him on so short a leash he won't even whimper without permission," Jim said with a satisfied nod.

"You've done this country a great favor," Admiral Runion said, suddenly very serious. "And you've made me very proud. Thanks, Jim."

"Men like you inspire men like me, Admiral. The thanks are mutual. Thanks for trusting me and helping me accomplish this," Cecilia watched while Jim stood and snapped a salute. Admiral Runion actually blushed.

With a mischievous smile on her lips Cecilia stood and curtsied. Admiral Runion laughed and stood, walking around his desk he took her hand, bowed, and kissed it. When he looked up, he saw in her eyes what he expected, and wanted, and was very glad that he'd finally met this pretty young woman. Her eyes were an interesting shade of blue and green.

"You'll do, young lady. You'll do just fine," he said, meaning it. Then with a mischievous look of his own he added. "If only you were an American."

"Would you settle for dual citizenship?" she asked.

"Divided loyalties between England and America? How will that work?" he asked.

"I believe my loyalties will lie in the right place," she replied, looking at Jim with a smile. He smiled back and took her hand.

"She's something, isn't she?" he said to the Admiral.

"Indeed she is!" he answered. "Now the two of you go out and have some fun. I'll see you both tomorrow night at the Whitehouse." He ushered them out of his office and watched them drive off. With a sigh he returned to his duties, his mind on the work ahead. Placing the three files in his locking file he smiled with satisfaction.

CHAPTER 46

P arties at the Whitehouse were rare, though Jack Royce seemed to prefer having them there. During his second term he determined that he would have most of them here to simplify his life. He hated the security precautions that interrupted everyone's life when they met somewhere else. Tonight, though, he wanted the full history and atmosphere of this great house to impress itself on Admiral Rook. And, he thought with some pleasure, uncovering Rook here would remind everyone who worked for him that America came first. Too many politicians and civil servants had forgotten that.

Although it was nearing six o'clock in the evening many of the offices were bustling with activity. Jack walked through the hallways with his secret service detail and stopped in the office occupied by Admiral Runion, Secretary of the Navy. Some fought Jack on his appointment of Runion, desiring a more politically savvy officer. Prepared to fight all the way he watched his opposition melt away, one by one, until at last they grudgingly agreed.

Some of them hated Runion because he refused to play the political games they loved so much. Others had come to appreciate the Admiral, reminded again of what it was like to serve one's country for no other reason than patriotism. As time passed, they came to see those who did hate Runion as weak and petty politicians with personal agendas that were not to be trusted. But that was always the way in Washington D.C. Sad, but reality, no one even slightly intelligent missed the duality and double standards that were so common.

Royce was no fool. He knew that the political machines in Washington were entrenched, powerful, and deadly. His second term victory had been so decisive that none of them dared turn their weapons on him. Of that he was grateful. Enjoying the byplay between those who truly loved this great country and those who sought to use their office as a means to a personal end he managed to stay just shy of open animosity from the various groups that plagued his office.

He certainly loved America. Not the America of the present, but the underlying foundation, the true identity of America, found in its glorious beginnings, and at times throughout history. *Damn democracy! Mobocracy was closer to the truth. This country should have stayed a Republic.*

Now it wasn't even a democratic republic anymore. Politicians drove the statesmen out, and still work hard at keeping them at bay. But the tide is turning. My second term is proof of that. Many of the people of this country are tired of politicians who view themselves as gods, so high above the populace.

Admiral Runion stood behind his desk, in his dress blue uniform, and saluted his Commander and Chief. Jack, who had served in the Marines, returned the salute properly, though winking as he did so. He appreciated the fact that Runion's face remained passive, focused, and almost intense. Only the twinkle in those blue eyes told President Royce that Runion shared his anticipation. He stepped into the office and closed the door on everyone in the hallway.

"Sit down, Charles," he said, and the Admiral sat. "When can I expect Rook?"

"Oh, he's here already!" Charles said blandly. "He's been in here touting the fact that he was personally invited. Now he's out "cultivating" supporters for his bid at a political post."

"Ah! And everything and everyone else is in place?" Jack said quietly.

"As ordered, Sir." Charles said with a smile.

As Jack opened the door he turned back. "That was a good piece of work on the Chinese submarine contract," he said with a smile. "Keep me informed." He turned and walked down the hall. *Let them make something of that!* Whistling happily, he continued down to the hall where the festivities would take place.

Cameras flashed, lights came on and tapes rolled as he entered the hall. Already a large crowd had gathered, and he made his way through them slowly, stopping to shake hands and listen to various guests. Jim Shepherd was there; next to a very pretty woman who gave her British heritage away the moment she opened her mouth. Jack liked her pleasant accent and easy manner and warmed to her immediately. He also appreciated the very expensive tailored tuxedo that Jim wore with obvious discomfort.

"My! What an electrifying personality!" Cecilia said as the President moved away. "And he's handsome too!"

Jim grinned into her eyes but said nothing. Looking up and around he spotted Admiral Rook weaving through the crowd to put himself in the President's path, and smiled when Jack suddenly changed directions, defeating the little man's purpose. Cecilia saw it too and smiled up at him, giving his hand a little squeeze.

"That was well done!" she said softly.

Admiral Rook found himself seated at a table reserved for the Navy's finest. Four retired Admirals, two of whom held important government positions advising the President and the Navy, and the other two actually working for the Secretary of Defense in an advisory position, were seated together. Since the table was round and seated six, Admiral Rook and Admiral Runion filled the last two seats. The table was close to that occupied by the President, a good sign as far as Admiral Rook was concerned.

Important cabinet members, the speaker of the house, a chief justice of the Supreme Court, and the President occupied the table on the dais. Jim's table was near the door, and he sat quietly beside

Cecilia, watching his crew come in, mixed in with the crowd. Sturdy had agreed to be the last, because every eye would be drawn to him.

FM came in first, looking extremely uncomfortable in his rented tuxedo. He constantly pulled at his collar and worked his neck muscles as though the thing were choking him. He caught Jim grinning at him and made a face. Cecilia giggled. Master Chief Warner came in next, looking dapper in his tuxedo, and completely at home in it. FM grunted in frustration at his composure and pulled at his collar again.

Andrea came in, wearing a gray tuxedo of European cut. Anyone in the room could have pegged him as an Italian dignitary. He sat down with a smile for everyone at the table. Last to enter the room for their table was Sturdy, and as Jim surmised, every head turned as the giant strode quickly to their table. His tuxedo fit him perfectly, thanks to his credit card and a tailor who liked a challenge. He grinned down at everyone as he pulled his chair out. It was the first time Admiral Rook realized that anyone from the *Bring It Up* crew was present. He scowled, but he quickly decided not to let it spoil his evening.

Once he was entrenched in the political machine and safe, he would take care of those troublemakers. He sneered at them before turning away, not noticing that Runion was smiling at his sneer, knowing what it meant. Rook hated that they had been so successful in their first year of treasure hunting, jealous of the wealth he'd witnessed. He'd driven by the house, a mansion on acres of prime real estate. He finally dismissed his thoughts about them and concentrated on the President and his table.

Commander Cummings came in quietly, and sat down at Jim's table, the last guest to do so, timing his arrival so that Admiral Rook was looking away from the door. He shook hands with everyone around the table and kissed Cecilia's hand gallantly. Glad to be sitting with friends he too sat with anticipation, waiting for the moment Rook would be exposed.

Doc and Millie were at a table nearby, very much at ease with the medical personnel that shared that table, men and women from the Navy that had served beneath the Admiral being honored.

Sir Edward Marsh and Petros Kladas were seated at a table not far from them. With Sir Edward was the English Prime Minister, Lord John White. Jim found Lord White interesting. The man was large, round, with a red face and white hair, and eyebrows that seemed to flow out of his forehead at least four inches at the ends, tufting and giving him the look of a mad scientist. A conservative respected by everyone in Great Britain, John White was often referred to by the international press as Snow White's Prince Charming.

A Princess and her attendants, two elderly spinsters who looked competent to handle any situation, attended Petros Kladas. The Princess was beautiful, very young, and one of the girls that had been rescued from the slave trade Mercury ship. She knew who had really been behind the rescue and the looks she cast in Jim's direction were filled with curiosity.

Sturdy made satisfied comments about the dinner, enjoying the talent of the kitchen staff catering the meal. Jim found the food excellent, but the company of his crewmembers, and especially Cecilia, the best part of the meal. His attempts to let Cecilia know how he felt left her blushing and laughing until tears ran down her cheeks. It was the first time Jim had enjoyed having a woman laugh at him, at his expense.

After dinner, before the desserts were served, President Royce stood and addressed the room. His speech was short, less than twelve minutes, and complementary to the military, foreign dignitaries, and catering service. He personally introduced the men and women at his table and thanked them for attending this party. Some were pleased; some thought it their due.

He moved to Sir Edward's table and introduced the Prime Minister, and those at the table, including the two spinsters who were attending the Princess. They were very pleased that he knew their names, pronouncing them properly. Both of them rose and curtsied.

Next he moved to the table occupied by the Admirals, and introduced the four retired Admirals first, giving just a brief report on their service history and more notable accomplishments, and then Admiral Runion. As he moved away from the table the Secretary of Defense stood up and stopped him.

"My apologies, Mr. President, but you forgot one of the Admirals at the table. Admiral Lyle Rook has just returned from the Mediterranean where he has been doing important work for us," the Secretary of Defense sat down. He saw the smile on the President's face and didn't like it one little bit.

"Ah yes! Admiral Rook. I think there are some friends here who have some gifts for you, Admiral Rook," Royce said, looking at the Admiral with a beaming smile.

"Captain James Shepherd, recently retired from the Navy and Captain of his own deep-sea salvage, search and rescue ship has something for you," the President said, motioning for Jim to come over.

Jim stood, reached under the table, and produced the canister Admiral Rook had taken from his ship. He brought it over and began to unscrew the cap. Admiral Rook shot to his feet.

"Stop! That's a biohazardous chemical canister. It was stolen from my ship several months ago by international terrorists," he ordered, as Jim continued to the table.

Jim pulled the glass container out of the canister, shook it, and then unscrewing the lid poured it into an empty glass. He held it up, looked at it, and asked a waiter to bring an olive. When he added the olive, he lifted it to his lips.

"Just how I like it, shaken, not stirred!" Jim said, putting the drink down. "Relax Admiral, it's actually a Vodka martini. That's what you forcefully removed from my ship, thinking you were actually taking a dangerous virus. We had the actual virus destroyed after we learned what it was and substituted this because we knew there were two organizations trying to steel it."

Admiral Rook reacted exactly as Jim predicted. He drew himself up and launched into an attack. "You put my men at risk for a Vodka martini?" he asked dangerously.

"No, Admiral, you put your men at risk over a Vodka martini. You ignored warnings that the canister would be stolen, and your crew attacked by dangerous men. Had my crew not intercepted that attack and created an avenue of escape for your crew many of them would be in their graves today. You allowed a valuable piece of Naval equipment to be totally destroyed by explosives planted by the terrorists about whom we warned you," Jim said quietly, but loud enough for everyone in the room to hear him.

"Lies!" Admiral Rook snapped.

"No, actually that is not a lie," Commander Cummings stood up. "I'm Commander Cummings, and I was on the ship Admiral Rook commanded. He refused to heed the warnings and many of my crew would have been lost had it not been for Captain Shepherd's quick thinking. He had empty containers lined up on the dock to get us into a warehouse so that the snipers couldn't pick off our crew. At considerable risk to himself and his men he provided cover fire to get us safely inside!"

"You dare accuse a ranking officer in public?" Admiral Rook hissed at Commander Cummings. "I'll see that you never command a ship again!"

"No Admiral, I don't think you will," President Royce said. "Sir Edward Marsh of MI6 has uncovered some information that I think we all need to hear. With your permission, Mr. Prime Minister?" Jack asked. The Prime Minister nodded his head and Sir Edward stood up.

"It seems that your Admiral Rook has been cultivating relationships with some very serious money men who also support terrorists in various parts of the Middle East, especially around the Mediterranean. I have documents, offshore accounts, film and tape of some of these meetings. This man appears to be angling for a political post of some kind in your government. I can only say that he is highly unqualified to hold a position of any importance, and especially of any responsibility," Sir Edward handed President Royce a videotape, a tape recorder, and a file of documents.

"Let's all see what this evidence is, shall we?" he said, looking around.

Admiral Rook stood, his face white, and would have bolted had he not seen the four secret service operatives who suddenly stood close. He sat down without a word, not daring to look at anyone. An aide took the video and tape recorder and went back to the sound room. A moment later the projectors shot the image of his meeting on the large screens located at each corner of the room. Next the tape recording of an actual meeting with a known terrorist came over the speakers. Last, and to Admiral Rook's horror, the records from his laptop appeared on the projectors, showing his offshore accounts and much more.

"I didn't invite all of you here to witness this, but to honor a true patriot. However, Sir Edward came to me some time ago with information about Admiral Rook and his activities. I didn't want to believe him, but Admiral Runion brought further information to light. My own Secretary of Defense was ready to give this man an appointment, unaware, I'm sure of his clandestine operations.

"Let this be a lesson, Dennis," the President said directly to his Secretary of Defense. "Check every man carefully. There are no less than three lesser Admirals, and other officers involved in this attempt to seize important government offices. I know them all and will expose them all." The iron in his voice sent a chill of expectation through the room as various dignitaries suddenly felt threatened.

"Admiral Rook, if you will cooperate with us, we will allow you to stay out of prison. You will work directly with Admiral Runion for the remainder of your career, and your offshore accounts will be awarded to the department of the Navy, to be administered by Admiral Runion," President Royce said. "The alternative is prison, public disgrace, and possibly even the death sentence for treason."

"I would never betray my country!" Admiral Rook blustered, sweat pouring down his face.

"No?" President Royce asked dangerously. "Did you use taxpayer dollars to have a submarine tail a deep-sea salvage team? Did you have coastguard planes keeping track of the same ship? Did you accept money from known terrorists? Did you attempt to strike a deal with Mercury to get the canister back? Did you, for instance, sell out twenty-six Marines to General Haaman? I would call all those things a betrayal of your country. Now answer me, this instant! Will you cooperate with Admiral Runion or go to trial?"

"I'll cooperate," Admiral Rook said, his head slumped on his chest; his face now flushed red with shame. He was broken, and he knew it.

"Then let everyone hear this," President Royce announced, standing very tall in the center of the room and speaking clearly and loudly enough for everyone to hear. "From this day forward you will occupy an office in the same building as Admiral Runion. You will obey every command he gives, giving up any information he asks for. The day you fail is the day you go to prison and then to trial for treason. Is that clear?"

So powerful was his voice and personality that Admiral Rook actually stumbled to his feet and replied that it was clear and saluted the President. Royce shook his head, did not return the salute, and walked back to the podium. It was clear that the President was angry, and everyone in the room respected that fact, keeping quiet, watching cautiously to see what might come next. Some were interested spectators, others nervous staff members who wondered what indiscretions they might be called on the carpet for. But that was not Jack Royce's style.

"We came together to celebrate the retirement of one of the men who *has* served this country with honor. Let's put this nasty scene behind us now and turn to more pleasant things." The President went on to describe the life and service of Admiral John Hastings, who was finally stepping out of public service for good because of upcoming cancer treatments. By the time Jack was finished speaking every man was on his feet, applauding the Admiral, and watching with pleasure as the man was honored.

Admiral Rook was escorted out of the room by four of Admiral Runion's special security force. He was a broken man, half stumbling, his hopes and dreams smashed beyond recovery. As he went past Jim's table, he didn't look up to see the satisfied expressions on their faces.

President Royce invited them into a private room to thank them personally for their work. He grinned as he shook hands with Jim. "It took a little longer than a year, but you came through. Thank you," he said. "There is no one who will connect you with his downfall other than playing the part you did in accusing him of negligence. Your secret is still safe. And I hear you've made a reputation for yourselves in treasure hunting!" he added.

"Our cover is secure, sir. I doubt if people will be following us for a while," Jim said. "I hope we handled each situation in a manner that pleased you," he tacked on in the end.

"As far as I am concerned, our trust in you is well deserved, Jim," Jack Royce said with pride. Jim actually blushed at the compliment. His crewmembers straightened up with pride.

President Royce shook hands with all of them in turn, sharing a word or two with each. Andrea was perhaps the deepest touched, having never stood in the presence of such a man before. He bowed correctly and received the President as only an Italian could.

An aide knocked at the door, and when the President motioned his security detail to let the man in, he went directly to the president with a message. "This just came in, sir, from Saudi Arabia. I know you wanted to hear anything connected to this particular General. I'm afraid he's been beheaded by his own government, sir." The man handed the message to the President, who read it, nodded, and dismissed him.

When he had gone, and the door was once again closed he looked up at Jim. "General Haaman was just executed by his own government," he said. "Once again, I congratulate you on executing a plan to perfection! I have footage of the execution if you'd like to see it," he added.

"May we?" Jim asked.

Jack nodded and turned on one of the television sets in the room. He made a call and a moment later black and white footage of the execution came up on the screen. It was a typical scene from the Middle East, thousands in the square to witness the execution. General Haaman was led to the square, his head held high with pride, when suddenly his eyes spotted four men standing in the crowd.

Jim could see the shock on his face, his eyes almost leaping out of his head, and then the realization of who had engineered his demise hit him. He began to struggle, to curse, and to rave like a madman. The crowd jeered as he was forced to kneel. The execution was not quick, and the man still slavered at his enemies until the third stroke of the sword.

When the news cameras scanned the crowds the four men were nowhere to be seen. Jim grinned in satisfaction. President Royce turned off the set and faced them. "I wish you all Godspeed and a safe return," he said.

When he left Jim stood for a few minutes looking at the door through which the President had just walked. In a year's time he had seen a dream come true, been successful in three treasure hunts, and completed three successful missions as well. It was one of those rare moments for reflection and celebration.

"I want to thank all of you," Jim said, turning to his crew. "I've been honored by a great man, and mostly because of your efforts. I couldn't be prouder of my crew than I am right now."

"I think we're pretty much a reflection of the kind of leader we follow," Master Chief Warner said quietly.

"Hear-hear!" Everyone answered. Cecilia was beaming at him and Jim felt suddenly that life was very exciting and filled with promise. He saluted his crew, who saluted back, and they walked out of the room, and out of the Whitehouse. It was time to rest, before setting out on their next adventurous treasure hunt.

www.ingramcontent.com/pod-product-compliance
Lightning Source LLC
Chambersburg PA
CBHW061336310726
48974CB00001B/70